Programmed to Breathe

Also by Tanya Reimer

<u>Sacred Land Stories</u>
Legends on the Prairies
Ghosts on the Prairies
Cursed on the Prairies

<u>From the Dark Chronicles</u>
Can't Dream Without You

Programmed to Breathe

Tanya Reimer

Elsewhen Press

For my sister Jessica.
Thank you for pushing me to try new things.
You're my hero, my pride, my inspiration,
and above all else, my best friend. Always.

ABOVE GROUND: Cuma Village

Avery Saxton ....oldest sibling and only girl in Saxton Clan

Mother Roselle and
Father Saxton ....leaders of Saxton Clan

Hunter ....Saxton's brother, Avery's uncle

Jacob Berry ....oldest member of Berry Clan

Kanya ....Hunter's daughter and Hiltop Berry's partner

Pax of the South ....a nomad who Avery thinks looks like her

Dragon..............................the legendary god protecting the village and ensuring life

BELOW GROUND: Quma Cities

Match ....an elite, gifted with hyper-hearing and flame-hands

Yodan ....Match's best friend, prodigy gifted with hyper-vision and speed

Lins ....Yodan's oldest sister, also elite

Shandra ....Yodan's sister, dating Match

Madeline ....Yodan's love interest

Owen ....a protector with hyper-strength

Jon ....a medic with memory loss

Brisk..................................a pregnant medic, Jon's partner

Greg...................................Match's brother

Nogard...............................the Artificial-life running the cities and ensuring life

~Two Very Different Breaths~

"At our core, we will all die, that makes us the same."

—Nogard

The year is 3161 and the world has suffered a great freeze and reshaping from earthquakes. Cuma Village stands safe and warm surrounded by pipes that keep the air pure, the water drinkable, and the grounds suitable for farming. To keep the peace in this tight area, the people live in clans and follow the rules enforced by their protector, a supreme being they call Dragon.

AVERY

Above ground, Cuma Village, Saxton Clan

Avery waited until Mother Roselle's head was in the vegetable bin before she slipped the flute off the shelf and into her satchel. Then she dropped the broom in the pail softly, since the baby was finally asleep and she didn't want to wake her brother.

"I'm done cleaning everything in here," Avery said, glancing around the family hut to make sure nothing was missed in her chores. "But I promised Father Saxton I'd check the sheep." Which was true enough and the perfect excuse for her to sneak out and search the area for her missing cat.

Mother didn't respond, just kept digging in the almost empty bin. Why was she taking so long when there were hardly any vegetables left for her to dig through?

Should she leave? Tossing her bag over her shoulder, Avery was ready to take off, but Mother Roselle's body tensed. *Darn it.* Was she crying all hunched over the vegetable bin? What was wrong?

"Mother Roselle?" Avery had never seen the tough woman who'd raised her cry, and wasn't sure what to do.

Head in the bin, Mother Roselle said, "Are there more vegetables in the shed?"

"I brought everything in."

She finally stood with a couple of potatoes going to seed in her fists. Her back to Avery, she wiped her eyes on her long sleeve. "Your brothers will eat this village clean." Even though Mother still had a little extra after-pregnancy weight, she was much taller than Avery and carried it with ease and she was always warm and loving. When Mother wouldn't look at her, Avery got a sinking feeling. Something was wrong.

"Maybe you should head over to Berry Clan to negotiate for some of their older stock after you check the sheep for your father."

Avery's eye started a tic with the mere mention of the Berry name. She stared at Mother Roselle's back, her hand on the door handle. "I'll fry flour-scones, no need to negotiate for food," Avery offered, because there was no way she was going to Berry Clan to beg. She'd rather starve.

"I'm afraid the flour bin is as empty. Your uncle Hunter says Jacob Berry is done grieving and plans to start a new family after this Warming Ceremony. Perhaps he'll trade us food for a table. Something to impress his new partner. We have a lot to offer and Jacob has a soft spot for children. Rumours are that his new companion's stubborn but excellent with young ones." She still wouldn't look at her, which made Avery uneasy. "You hear who he asked?"

No, she had not. But Avery wasn't usually included in the gossip. Especially not about Berry Clan. "He's too old for anyone in the village," Avery pointed out.

"Well, he does grow bountiful crops."

"I suppose." Why was Mother talking a Berry up?

"And since Berry Clan doesn't have children to feed, they can spare a few things our way. Your father set aside that table you loved. Perhaps you could show Jacob. Just point it out politely and tell him how much you love it. Remember, he lost his last companion and son so try, please try, to be nice to him." She pulled out a pot; pointless work to avoid looking at Avery. "That means no punching him," she teased, since Avery had punched Hiltop Berry. That had been at the last Warming when he'd announced that Avery would start a family with him, though he'd never bothered to ask her first. *Stupid jerk.* Thankfully, her cousin Kanya offered to be Hiltop's partner and Avery didn't have to. "Can't one of the boys go?"

With her back to Avery, Mother Roselle froze, pot in the air. "I'd rather you go." Then she spun around and stared at Avery. Her eyes bored into Avery as if she had more to say and this was their last chance. "I suppose you can ask Stefe or Jojo to go with you, so they can see how it's done, but no one younger. Now off with you. I'll take whatever Jacob can spare. *Anything.*"

Hand on the door handle, Avery said, "You didn't happen to see Friskie, today, did you?"

Working, she ignored Avery's worry. "A smart hunter like him will turn up soon enough. We have enough to do without watching a cat's every move."

Avery hoped Mother Roselle was right and Friskie wasn't far.

"But I suppose it wouldn't hurt to play him a melody on your flute while you check the sheep, just in case," she said. Clearly, she knew that Avery had snagged the flute. "Would do you good, too. Everyone loves it when you play. Father was even thinking you could play at the Warming Celebration. I'll sing."

"I'll think about it." Avery sneaked out before she made her promise something so impossible. When everyone watched her play, it was just a reminder of how different she was from the rest of them.

A warm day greeted her as Avery stepped onto Saxton land. Then again, before a Warming, most days were nice in Cuma Village. Whatever was on the other side of the pipes was a different story, but Avery didn't have to worry about that anymore. She was one of the chosen ones, which meant her time in the Outlands was forgotten. She was safe here, chosen by Dragon their protector to survive the rugged cold.

Avery waved to the neighbouring clan and headed out to find her brothers. Father Saxton had them working. One hauled logs, another chopped and one sawed. A bunch of them rushed to her with things they worked on, all talking at once. Being the only girl and oldest sibling in a house full of boys, she was used to this demand for her attention. Seemed that today they were working on shelves.

"Where's Stefe or Jojo?" she asked her brother Hawk when things settled.

He pointed to the fire pipe. "Father Saxton's showing them how to burn designs into the wood for the cabinet doors. They use those metal rods, heat them under the flames from the fire pipe, then scorch them into the wood. Neat as heck. We have to wait here because it's dangerous, and I have to make sure these men keep working." He crossed his arms, proud of this new responsibility of looking after the younger ones. Like her, Hawk was adopted into Saxton Clan. She knew how important it was for him to feel like he fit in with the others and was pleased that Saxton had put him in charge.

Of course, with her brothers busy, she'd have to go by herself to Berry Clan. *Urgh.*

Avery jogged up the hill. With a quick glance, she could

see that the few sheep they were trying to raise were doing fine but the cat wasn't with them. Still, Avery opened the satchel, settling by a tree. Usually when she played, Friskie came over to rub up against her. She brought the flute to her lips but a movement caught her attention at the entrance of the village.

What the heck was *that*?

Avery jumped to her feet, excited when she realized that the bundle was a man. Had a nomad found them? What if it was someone from her birth family?

The stranger stood in the middle of the entrance to her village, an easy target, a fool of a man.

Squinting against the sun, Avery gaped at him in his extensive garments as if he'd survived a snowstorm from hell. She wore a skirt, a top, and layers of undergarments, but her brothers and Father Saxton didn't even have shirts on they found the weather so warm.

Seeing the nomad so bundled made her nervous. How cold was the world on the other side of these pipes?

After a quick survey of the clan huts and sacred cave, the nomad stepped closer to the warm pipe encircling the village. Where the nomad stood, the pipe allowed an entrance to the village before entering the cliffs. This sacred spot was protected by the Eye of Dragon and was the only entrance to Cuma Village. Legends said that Dragon saw all who approached through that eye and only the chosen ones could enter *his* sanctuary.

Avery's heart picked a new rhythm as she waited. If this nomad was unworthy, an earthquake would shake them in warning.

When nothing happened, even after the nomad tapped the Eye of Dragon like a curious fool, Avery prepared to greet him. He might have family, his own clan, or come with skills the clans would welcome.

Then again, this nomad might come with illness and science they would not.

After carefully wrapping her flute, Avery concealed the instrument in her satchel. Then she rushed toward the nomad to greet him. Without thinking, she called to her cat to follow. *Darn it.* Where had he gotten off to? Friskie was an excellent judge of character, and she liked to have him nearby.

"Nomad!" she shouted to Father Saxton as she dashed by, hoping he wouldn't stop her.

Saxton handed the metal rod to Jojo then rushed with her, without grabbing a weapon or even a cloak to cover himself. Stefe raced for Uncle Hunter and possibly a few other leaders which meant she'd only have a few breaths alone with the newcomer.

The nomad peered in the Eye of Dragon as she approached. He didn't turn around to meet her but said, "Hey, you know what this mechanical thing is?" He tapped the Eye of Dragon over his head, inviting her over with a fun-casual ease that took her off-guard.

"Don't touch that!"

Her snap made him face her, and she gasped as his scarf fell off, uncovering pale skin.

Oh my gosh. She forgot everything she wanted to tell him. His eyes were green like hers and over his orange whiskers were wild freckles. Like hers! He dropped his hood back and shook his long orange hair freely as he glanced up at the Eye of Dragon when the monitor moved.

On instinct, Avery stepped away from the seeing-eye so Dragon wouldn't curse her or rumble the earth to mark her as unworthy. Then, recovered from the shock at seeing someone with the same features as her, she approached for a better look. Wow. He could be her *real* brother. *He might be!* This was too much. Villagers either had dark skin or bronze skin. No one had freckled pale skin with orange hair and green eyes. Except her. She wanted to scream with joy and rush to him, but she restrained herself, grounded her bare feet in the grassy-earth.

"Are there more in the Outlands who look like you... Like us?" she demanded from this young man, who was probably a touch older than her. "Can we get them?"

"Haven't seen anyone in a long while. Was beginning to fear that I was the last man alive. Do you... Do you have a family?" His voice cracked on *family*.

"We have clans in Cuma Village; some are made up of one family and some are made up of many. I'm Avery of Saxton Clan."

He glanced over her shoulder at the village. "And which one of those bears headed this way would be Saxton of

Saxton Clan? As much as they both freak me out, I'd like to know which one is *your* family."

"The one in the lead. He'll speak with you if I feel it's safe to welcome you and if Dragon allows you to enter." She established her authority to avoid any issues. "Hunter will escort you out if I don't feel you'll fit into the clans and Dragon will rumble the earth if you have to leave this village and are not among the chosen ones. Make no mistake, nomad, this is Dragon's village and he decides who lives here."

"And Dragon would be the wild one behind Saxton with the dreadlocks and machetes?"

Avery chuckled. "No, that's my uncle Hunter. People don't usually piss him off." Uncle Hunter took protecting his people seriously because he'd lost too much family. But she didn't tell this nomad that Hunter was broken inside. She was used to men acting one way in public and being another in private. Perhaps that was her biggest frustration. She was sick of the lies and pretending. All anyone did in Cuma Village was try to fit in.

"Dragon lives underground and keeps these pipes warm. No one has ever met him."

"So you the queen or leader or chief of this oasis?"

Her face warmed because Avery was at the bottom of the status ratings until she chose someone to start a family with, and her options were poor. Then again, Avery had no idea what she wanted in a partner and since they didn't have enough land for her to offer anyone, she'd have to move clans and find someone with a hut she could make her own. And really, which other clan would she fit into? Not many were as patient as Father Saxton and Mother Roselle.

"They don't send a leader or an elder to meet a nomad," she admitted. "That would be stupid. They send someone expendable."

"That Saxton guy doesn't act like you're expendable. He clearly doesn't want you talking to me. Can I talk to him or will he pulverize me? Yikes. Your people are huge."

Avery glanced at Saxton. He was planted, arms crossed. The sun gleamed off the sweat on his chest. Hunter was right behind him. They were twins, and even though Saxton kept his hair short, and it greyed around the ears, they were identical.

Avery was excited to welcome the nomad, but Hunter said,

"Chances of us letting you in the village are small. A child we would welcome warmly, even a woman, but you're competition."

They wouldn't let him in? Avery was appalled. "But Uncle, look at him. He's harmless. He might even have skills we need." The nomad carried no weapons, just a pack and his layers of clothes. "We can't send him back into the cold if he's a chosen one. At least welcome him until the Warming. I'll teach him to fit in." Gosh, he just *had* to stay. What if he was from her first family?

"What's your name, nomad?" Saxton demanded from his protective stance.

"Pax of the South. I'm alone." He removed his heavy coverings, to reveal another layer.

Pax didn't look like he was about to cause any trouble, but still, Avery warned, "Answer their questions and keep your hands to yourself."

Pax nodded, gripping his clothing against himself as if the furry garments might bounce off their stares.

"How did you find us?" Hunter demanded.

Pax pointed to the rugged cliff that jarred up on the one side of the village, casting a shadow on them. Carved into the rocks was an image of Dragon to remind them of their place. The village was snug by the cliffs. "It was quite the trek, but I thought that sculpture was neat. Had no idea this oasis existed. What is this place? Where did the snow go?"

"That's an image of Dragon," Avery told him. She bowed her head respectfully when she mentioned Dragon. "The provider and protector of Cuma Village."

Pax frowned, his stance giving away his doubt about Dragon providing anything. "Provides how?"

"Dragon warms the pipes that encircle the village, allowing us to grow crops, to tend to our herds, to enjoy clean air and filtered water, to access fire on demand, and to grow crops in enriched soils..."

Pax gaped at the fields and huts awaiting him beyond the entrance. People gathered to watch them talk, curious. "We're settlers, rooted here. Welcome to Cuma Village."

Saxton wasn't about to let him in so easily and stepped forward to block his path. "What brings you here? Where are your people?"

Pax's shoulders sank inward as if he might run off. "Gone. The last was Penny. She died in a cave-in."

"Your partner?" Hunter stepped forward, but his machetes were at his side and he had a hand out, changing his pose from *nope-you-can't-come-in-here* to *need-a-hug?* Since Uncle Hunter lost his first family, and only Kanya and Hunter survived the massacre, he always took time for those who grieved. This weakness was something the other leaders openly made fun of, yet he never failed to soften around those who grieved.

Pax had his head down in that beaten pose that would easily win Hunter over and Avery sighed, relieved, because if Hunter vouched for him, the others would welcome him.

"Yeah, my wife," Pax said. "I'm alone." *Wife* was an unfamiliar word, but often nomads brought new things with them, including words and beliefs.

Pax's green eyes teared up and his pain stung Avery sharply. She was quick to change the subject and pretended he was welcome. "You have no status in Cuma Village until you have your own hut and are accepted into a clan as a contributor. This means you have to offer something to one of the leaders. Until then, you'll respect the rules of Saxton Clan and stay as one of my brothers. Pay attention to how we speak, the words we use, the beliefs of our clan. You have to fit in or you'll be asked to leave."

Pax glanced at Saxton for his invite, but as his mature daughter she had every right to invite a young man without a home to live with them until the Warming Ceremony.

Saxton enforced the law by saying, "The Warming Ceremony will give you the opportunity to make a deal for a hut in one of the clans, hopefully find a companion you can start a family with."

"Saxton, he's grieving." Hunter placed a brotherly hand on Pax's shoulder. "Lay off our new friend."

"I'm letting him know that we have strong women who'd love to start a family with a fine young man like him. But Avery is off limits, since she's spoken for."

"Spoken for?" Avery glanced up, shocked. "What? Since when?"

Saxton's jaw firmed but he refused to meet her eyes. "He should have talked to you by now. I have nothing more to say on the subject. But I made it clear to him he had to talk to you before the Warming and explain what he offered." More secrets. Why couldn't these men be honest with her and with each other? These games were tiresome.

"Ignore him," Hunter said to Pax. "Avery and I will show you around. You need anything, you come to us."

"Pax can stay in my clan as my guest," Saxton added. "He can eat at my table if Roselle, my partner, invites him."

Pax undid another button on his next layer of garments.

The last thing Saxton needed was another son to feed, yet he wouldn't make a scene if Pax behaved, because despite the competition Hunter had mentioned, welcoming a nomad would give him status before a Warming, especially if Pax showed interest in one of the women needing a companion or if Pax had skills that would benefit the village.

There was no doubt that Mother Roselle would care for him as a son. She had compassion for all nomads since she had been one herself when she'd met Saxton. Avery couldn't imagine Mother leaving Pax to eat alone.

"You must be hungry from your journey. Mother Roselle will have something for you to munch on." *Shoot.* Avery forgot about how she should be begging for food from Jacob Berry right about now. Well. It'd have to wait until next light. As if a reminder of how little they'd have to eat tonight, her stomach grumbled.

"Starved." Pax stepped beside Avery, seemingly excited by the prospect of food.

Saxton picked up his bag. Hunter grabbed his garments right out of Pax's hands. Then the group headed toward the village.

"Observe, learn, and try to fit in," Saxton added.

Determined to make him feel welcome, Avery sidled up to Pax. "So what was she like, this Penny you called your wife?"

"Penny was fiery." He relaxed, eager to share stories about her as they walked toward the group of villagers waiting to stare at the newcomer. "Stubborn. Brilliant. Penny could remember things and make science things work by fooling around with them for a bit. And beautiful, too. She had sharp dark eyes, and since she was hairless with snowy white skin, her eyes were never hidden and shone even brighter. I have pictures I drew of her if you want to see them?" He smiled, pleased to talk about his bald wife, but Avery was a bit taken aback by what he'd said.

She whispered, "Pax, there's one firm rule here." She met his eyes so he could see how important this rule was. "We don't talk about *science*. Ever."

The pipes that surround Cuma Village vanish underground and into the cliffs. These are warmed by Nogard, an Artificial-life. She uses them to expel wastes while she runs Quma Cities, an underground system that has existed for over a thousand years. The people there live in quadrants and study the depth of technology. These people have adapted to generations of living underground. Their skin is pure white, no hair covers their bodies, and their senses are more defined.

MATCH

Some breaths later
Underground, outside Quma Cities

Match was a part of a crew thrown together to check the pipes before the FIRE Ceremony. They were supposed to make sure there were no leaks that might cause damage when the flames purged the system, but Match was distracted by Shandra and not really caring about pipes.

"The quarry is on the other side of this wall," Shandra told the group so they could orientate themselves. She was the oldest in this crew and had made this type of safety check once before. By mentioning the quarry, she was clearly hoping to relax this bunch of newbies because the refreshing waters of the quarry were where they all liked to hang out in their downtime. "Crew, you are now officially outside of Nogard's system. Use your free-thoughts wisely." Which meant that the Artificial-life that kept Quma Cities safe could no longer communicate with them or see them. "Andret will lead a group to the right and Hilt to the left. I have to leave you, but we meet back here to return to the system as a unit."

As Shandra slipped up the side of the cliff and away from the group, they took in the quiet. No constant droning of the system weighed on them. Match's body relaxed for the first time in ages. He liked the silence, he decided, and could even get used to the dark.

The others communicated through their internal devices to get organized, but as elite, Match was device-free and got to make his own choices so he leaned by Yodan and whispered, "We'll check this side."

"Sounds good." Yodan was always eager to break from the system. "But I need another cylinder of Oxy-air. I was rationed to one, as if Nogard knew I'd take off." Yodan was flagged as a flight risk by their Artificial-life but Match didn't tell him that. He liked Yodan's rebellious energy.

Instead, Match shook his head and gently shoved his best friend toward the others. "I meant your sister and me. I don't need you chaperoning my alone time with Shandra."

"Oh. Well, don't forget to tell her about Medic Jon's

memory loss. She might have an idea about what we can do to help, since she's had a lot of memory lapses herself. Be sure to tell her that I suspect there is another system we could find. If we decide to leave this one."

He'd tell her, but they weren't gonna rebel based on a hopeful theory Yodan had. Match worked on facts, not Yodan's whims.

Besides, Shandra's memory losses were Match's fault for trying to steal time with her. Still, he didn't tell Yodan that this was their punishment for breaking the rules. "First thing I'll tell her. Just cover for her so she doesn't get in trouble. Blame me, I can take the punishment." He handed Yodan his extra Oxy-air tube. "Here, so you can do your own exploring. If I'm lucky, I'll be sharing breaths with your sister anyway."

Yodan grumbled but left. Match trusted that his friend would cover for them. He was always happy to break the rules.

Match waited for the searchlights to head down, even though he could still hear each member of the crew talk thanks to his hyper-hearing. They'd found a leak. Meant they'd be busy for a bit. It was rare that a youth like Yodan got to tag along on these types of maintenance drills, but with the numbers dwindling in Quma Cities, the team was almost all youths.

When Match was sure the crew wasn't coming back for them, he went up the face of the cliff where he'd seen Shandra vanish a few breaths ago. Her white lifesuit was visible as she dangled her legs over the edge above him, even in the dark, his vision adapted so he knew exactly where she was. He wasn't as good a climber as her, but he pushed himself, knowing she was waiting for him.

Finally, he felt a ledge where they could sit and talk and make out. Their own little hideaway where Nogard, their Artificial-life, couldn't hear them. Or send a jerk to break them apart. Or suddenly zap her memories and make her forget who he was...

Shandra lit her pen-light and set it on the rocks. "Hey. Glad you could join me. This is my favourite place. So peaceful. So quiet. No technology. Nothing but me and my thoughts."

Match let his feet dangle in the dark, next to hers. "Wouldn't dream of missing an opportunity to get in on your thoughts." He tried to catch his breath and think of something brilliant to say.

"Found this neat rock up here, thought Yodan might like it." She showed him the rock. Anything weird Yodan would love, but this had a gem sparkling in it. Match held it close to the pen-light and rubbed at the gem.

"Never seen a gem this colour before."

"I wanted to give it to my brother as a trust-gift." She gently touched Match's thigh. Having to communicate with her a lot in secret, he was used to her subtle messages. She was telling him something important.

He met her eyes, setting the rock by the light.

"Give it to him," she said. "Tell him it's from both of us. That we both trust him."

"If I do that, it'll be a message that we're on board about his new idea to leave the system and find another one."

She gently touched his jaw. "Then only give it to him if you think we should."

She wanted to leave Quma Cities? Why? Was she thinking this was the only way they could be together? He wanted to tell her that he'd find a way, but until he had a solution, he was better to just tell her about Medic Jon's most recent memory slip.

"Oh gosh, I missed you," she breathed against his neck and he forgot everything he'd wanted to say. Instead, he pulled her closer and kissed her.

"I have something for you, too," she mumbled as their lips danced, so forbidden, "but in my hurry, I forgot it in my sleeping pod."

He pulled away to stare in her eyes. "You don't have to give me anything. Your kisses are promise enough that you trust me. You taste like healing plants, though. Why?" He drank her in, gently touching the mud smeared on her cheek. "Any more memory lapses?"

"Not since I stopped connecting to the Collective." All first-term questers had Connectors installed behind their ears that enabled them to hook-up to the system and commune with the Artificial-life and the Collective. This connection allowed them to deepen their studies and many advancements were made thanks to these connections. But Match hated the idea of others messing around in Shandra's brain.

"This time my stomach was upset. Why I wanted to talk to

you in private before the FIRE Ceremony." Only she wasn't talking as her lips explored his neck. *Mmm.* She smelled like freshly turned soil and he was a melting mess.

A strange rumbling made him pause as his fingers memorized her body. "Shh. Did you hear that?" They were silent and Match heard it again. With his hyper-hearing, he was used to hearing strange things others couldn't, but this wasn't like anything he'd ever heard before. He pulled away and scanned the walls, sensing another presence around them. Eyes sparkled in the dark across from them. "There's something over there watching us."

Shandra took down her pen-light and flashed it around. Across the way was a white creature sitting on the ledge, staring at them.

"Is that a cat?" he asked her, shocked. Information about cats came to him as if seeing the animal triggered dormant facts his mind had kept buried. He retrieved this information and absorbed it, suddenly an expert on cats.

"I think so," she said, "I read about them once, something about them dying in the Big Freeze. Think it's dangerous?"

It looked harmless and very much alive. "People used to keep them as pets. Part of their family unit," Match shared.

The cat tilted its head, studying them. Then much to Match's horror it made a strange deathly sound.

"It talks." Shandra was behind him, her head against his cheek, her arms draped over him, warming him. "Yodan might be able to talk to it."

Her brother had been programmed to understand and speak over 30 languages but Match doubted *Cat* was one of them. Still, they couldn't really leave a discovery this big here on the ledge. "Think we could sneak it into the system without Nogard knowing?" Wasn't easy to slip anything past Nogard these days. She was watching Match constantly.

"Is that a dare?" Shandra asked.

Like Yodan, Shandra couldn't turn down a good challenge. "Of course. Always fun to see what we can get by her. I'd like your sister to see this thing before we show Nogard."

"Yeah, Lins will freak when she sees this." Lins was the only other elite in Quma Cities and Match's mentor as he concluded his elite studies.

"Turn the cameras off when we get back," Shandra

challenged him. "I'll walk right in with this cat and leave it in your family chamber." Shandra walked the ledge toward the creature. Match was instantly behind her. Would she really touch it?

The cat came toward them, unafraid. They were used to moles and rats running from them and he thought they'd have to trap it, but this creature liked people. It brushed up against Shandra's leg. "Seems harmless. Kinda friendly." Shandra sat to be closer to it. The cat settled beside her, making that rumbling sound again.

"It's like an internal earthquake is happening inside the cat," Match said, sitting by Shandra, studying the strange creature with her.

Shandra gently put out her hand and waited. The cat came into it, pushing its head against her hand and Shandra laughed. "Its hair tickles the skin."

Match smiled, enjoying her happiness. They rarely laughed in Quma Cities and he never wanted this moment to end. "I love it when you laugh," he admitted. "Warms me inside."

Braver than them, the cat stepped right on Shandra and stared at Match as if challenging him. Curious, Match touched the creature with a finger and pulled away. It was warm. Soft. He opened his mineral water and poured some in his hand. The cat lapped it up, its tongue tickling Match's palm.

He glanced at Shandra about to tell her that it tickled but she was staring at him, no more smile. "I'm pregnant."

The cat stopped lapping as silence dropped on them.

Their eyes were locked as Match absorbed her impossible words. *A baby?* Had he heard her right? "What? How? I mean I know *how*… I was clearly there. I just… What?" Her words took a moment to process. Dizziness hit him. He'd assumed she'd taken the mandatory sterilization ordered for first-term questers. He wasn't allowed to reproduce. He didn't even think he could. Lins had said that elites were sterilized in their youths. Of course, he had no memory of that. Maybe he should have checked his records for himself.

"I've been trying to find a way to tell you for a few cycles." *A few?*

Oh gosh. She'd been living with this alone? This wasn't about him anymore. This was about her and the life she carried.

Shandra set the pen-light and gem beside her and was stroking the cat, pretending she was fine. Match took her hand in his and placed his other hand against her cheek. Her colourful pink eyes were rimmed in tears. He couldn't even imagine what she was thinking. Illegal pregnancies never ended well. No wonder she wanted to leave the system…

"How long before Nogard finds out?" Would Artificial-life terminate her? Him? Their child? Would she take their child away? Forbid him from going near either of them?

"Medic Brisk helped me install an illegal over my internal devices. She's overriding my stats constantly using Dragon." Dragon was a ghost program that Nogard couldn't see. Elites like him used it to keep Artificial-life in line. Since they were down to only two elites in the system, they'd given a few others access to Dragon, via handhelds known as SHARPs.

"Medic Brisk said she talked to someone about it and they put in place extra security, but she wouldn't tell me who is helping us."

"Either Lins or Yodan. Maybe both. Might explain why Yodan is so bent on leaving. And why your sister is being so weird lately."

"At the FIRE Ceremony, I'll have to hard hook-up."

They didn't have much time. He had to get Shandra out of the system but where would they go?

The cat bumped his arm with its paw, then rubbed its head against Match.

"This cat… It came from somewhere. What if Yodan is right and there is another system? One where we could be together? Raise our family…"

"I'm scared. Rebels don't survive."

Match pulled her closer and rested his cheek against her bald head while the cat made that rumbling sound on her lap. Scared didn't even begin to cover how he felt. "You're safe with me, Shandra. You know I will do whatever it takes to keep you safe. Even if that means staying away from you." Gosh, that was painful to say.

"I'd rather we find a way to be together."

"It'll mean leaving the system."

"I know. Give Yodan the gem. Find out what he knows. We can leave at lights-out."

MATCH

A few breaths later
Underground, Quma Cities, study hall of Quadrant F

The study hall was considered the last natural cavern in Quma Cities. The walls were jagged from rocks that hadn't been smoothed like the other chambers. Pipes full of wires were brought in to nourish the study tables with things for them to learn, yet the roughed walls were left intact, a reminder of their history, of where they were, of who they were, a reminder that they were survivors.

It was chilly in this area, as Yodan and Match crouched in the corner of the sombre study hall. Usually the temperature was regulated in their underground system, but this slip in the study hall meant Nogard wasn't feeling so well these days. The system had suffered a lot of quakes lately.

Since Shandra told him the news, Match was seeing the world with different eyes, as if no place was good enough to raise a child with her.

Match felt the wall with his fingers. Vibrations filtered through his fingertips and to his eardrums, turning touch into sound. Something Match was used to, but this ability always troubled him, because hearing through vibrations was as unnatural as starting flames in the palms of his hands or having dormant information in his brain. As elite, he was supposed to have nothing in him that was unnatural. These were skills prodigies should receive at their Prodigy FIRE Ceremony. Yet somehow, Nogard had passed these gifts to him at his conception.

Still, the rocks carried vibrations better than the pipes in the corridor and let him know that others were coming. "We don't have long," he told Yodan. A group of youths would burst in soon for their final study session.

"What did Shandra say when you told her about Medic Jon and his memory loss?"

Match hadn't had the chance to tell her, but he lied, "She agrees with you that we should leave the system." Rebelling wasn't something Match would have agreed to earlier, but now, his entire world was in chaos.

"Really? So we're gonna leave?" Yodan looked much too excited at the idea.

Match wiggled a rock in the corner, close to the bottom, until it came free of the others and he showed Yodan the hole he'd been keeping a secret. It was one of many in this chamber hiding old codes, but if anyone could read the ancient document hidden away in it, it'd be Yodan. "I was in here making out with your sister," Match told Yodan, "and we stumbled on this. Can you read it?"

Yodan pulled out the old parchment. "I've seen such a document in the archive room. You sure the cameras are off?" Yodan didn't glance at the camera, just slowly unfolded the old paper.

Match nodded, he'd used his elite security codes to override the system. Nogard trusted that he was currently checking the cameras for bugs before the FIRE Ceremony and would let him work. Technically, he was. He'd installed a program that was scanning the contents of each camera's history, looking for anything that was out of the usual. Everything would be waiting for him in a file at an elite secured-workstation, including the video of Shandra sneaking the cat into his chamber. He'd delete it before giving the files to Nogard. "We don't have long before the others show up to study. The cameras are busy. Tell me what you see. If it's something we can use. I have more papers like this hidden away if it's useless…"

"I could shut down an entire quadrant with this and Nogard wouldn't even know what happened. It's an override code for the air system."

Air was something none of them would dream of messing with. Still, Match felt the palm of his hands warm with the possibilities. A closed quadrant would work. "Would it still have breathable air?"

"I'd fool her into thinking the air quality dropped. Then leave the grade-C air vents open. We could hang out there."

"How fast can you make that happen?" It came off a challenge.

"Before lights-out." He'd only glanced at the paper, but Yodan had hyper-vision. He folded the paper. "If I shut down your quadrant, we could have access to both the mainframe and the quarry. We could prepare, make a base, and explore on our own."

Once they rebelled, there was no coming back to the safety of this system. Match rubbed his fingers together, nervous about this idea, yet he was out of options and this was a better plan than taking off at lights-out with just Shandra. Meant he could get a team together. Maybe his brother, Lins...a Medic... The more he brought, the safer Sandra would be, and she was all he was thinking about.

Yodan handed Match the paper so he could take out his SHARP and get to work. Nogard wasn't allowed to question who had a SHARP, it was an elite privilege to use them freely and she trusted that they were for communicating with each other and not programming. Elites didn't have devices installed behind their ears like the others in the system and they needed a way to keep in touch. But just because she allowed them this privilege, didn't mean she wasn't watching those who had them.

While Match slipped the parchment back in the hole and sealed up the wall, someone snapped, "What are you two doing?"

Match jumped, busted with his hand on the rock. As he pulled back, his hands exploded in flames. *Dammit.* He hated it when he lost control like that. He tightened his hands quickly, extinguishing the fire and pulling his fists in front of his chest, close to his control-pen, in case he needed it.

Yodan stepped to the side, to let Match deal with Owen. Match might be able to make useless fire in his hands, but Owen was gifted with hyper-strength and could use his hands to crumble boulders *or break bones*. No one wanted under that grip. As a quester, he was probably here as a volunteer to watch the study group so he could annoy Match.

Owen stepped up to Match. "Heard you were on the outside. Since when does an elite volunteer for a safety mission?"

"Doing my share around here," Match lied.

"You better not be putting your mucky hands on Shandra or I will report you to Nogard."

Yodan was quick to come to his defence. "Match is elite, Protector Owen. Show respect."

Owen snorted, his black opal-like eyes glaring into Match. A crushed bone was very painful and meant intensive surgeries and possible cyborg limb replacements. So Match didn't push things too far with Owen. Instead, he stared ahead.

"He was warned," Owen said, still staring Match down. "Stay away from her. She's been selected as my family-unit companion. I won't have you getting her terminated with your out-of-control hormones."

"She hasn't agreed to that." Flames fought for air in his tight fists. Owen was the only one who Match couldn't challenge physically, and that's why Nogard had announced something so stupid.

Shut up, Match... "Besides, I can't leave her alone. All first-term questers are under my surveillance." Which was true enough. "When Yodan reported the glitch in Medic Jon's memory, as elite, I decided to supervise quester studies. Yours included," he threw in, to let Owen know he was watching him and knew that in his spare time he liked to read about weird things that used to exist above ground. "Something is wrong with the second-term questers. A program glitch I want fixed before the first-terms move up during this FIRE Ceremony." Medic Jon's memory loss was the cover for Match's freaking out. Sadly, there was nothing any of them could do to help Medic Jon. He was becoming one with Nogard. This might even be his last FIRE Ceremony. Once he merged his mind completely with the Collective, his body would die. Others would think it an honour, and some might even join him.

Not wanting to think about things out of his control, Match faced Yodan. "I better go, Yodan. That camera program won't last much longer and I should see what data was collected." He nodded to Owen. "See ya around, Protector Owen." Then low so only Owen could hear, he whispered, "I'm watching you, big guy." A cold reminder that Match might not be able to challenge him physically, but he did have the power to mess with his memories, his studies, and now, even the air in his chamber.

YODAN

A few breaths later
Underground, study hall

Yodan took his seat on a hard rock bench in the study hall. His insides shook. The code Match had shown him was perfect. Just what he'd been looking for. He opened his reader to look busy and found his assigned reading material. He clicked open the first page and smirked at the rare and exciting topic that Nogard had chosen for him. *Creatures that went extinct during the Big Freeze.* He glanced over at what his neighbour had for an assignment. He was reading about boring old cellular divisions.

Yodan fast-forwarded into the assignment a few dozen pages, scanning each one to memory and leaving it open on cats. Which looked like a fun creature. Gosh, the more he read about evolution and natural selection, the more he was sure there had to be others who'd survived the Big Freeze. Somewhere, there had to be another system of survivors like them.

He went back to work on his SHARP. If he worked fast, he might be able to read the entire interesting assignment *and* shut down the quadrant.

He was making intense links when a warm hand brushed his neck. He glanced up at Madeline as she strolled past, taking a seat so they could stare at each other from across the table. Her intense blue eyes peered into him as if she knew what he was up to.

If this program worked, would she rebel with them?

The room was getting crowded now, but it was really just him and her, as their eyes locked and they sat like that, not talking, not thinking, just enjoying the moment. What could he say? *Speak, Yodan!*

His SHARP vibrated, jolting him, reminding him that he was working on the illegal shutdown. He glanced at it, tearing his eyes off Madeline, but the codes were jumbled as he tried to pull his thoughts together.

Then, to make matters worse, Medic Jon stepped up to him and tapped his finger on the image of the orange cat on his reader. "You're supposed to be reading. Not playing on your handheld or ogling other students." His friend Jon was a second-term quester, here to help them study since this was their last session before they became questers themselves.

Yodan, slid the handheld under the table and glanced up at Jon. "Hey, Jon."

"That's Medic Jon," he snapped, which was very unlike him.

"Medic Jon, I have a question," Madeline called to him, giving Yodan a wink. Jon was walking to Madeline at the other end of the reading table, when he stopped suddenly as if lost. "Do I know you?" he glanced back at Yodan.

Yodan wanted to scream, "*Of course!*" Jon's medic studies were turning him into an idiot. He had to hook-up to the Collective to learn and this connection was making him forget certain things: like who his friends were. The idea terrified Yodan, because he didn't want to forget who he was.

Yodan recorded the slip of Jon's memory on his reader then sent the data to Nogard, to Match, to Medic Brisk, and finally to his sister Lins. *Again.* This was the third time he'd noticed such a slip. This close to a FIRE Ceremony, Jon should be fixed. Even though Yodan had no idea how to fix the glitches he saw, his studies allowed him to spot errors in their system so the errors didn't get passed to the next generation.

"I heard Brisk is pregnant," Yodan said to Jon, trying to bring his memories back. "Natural reproduction is what Shandra told me. That's amazing. First one I've heard about in a long time. Congratulations on achieving family status, Jon. You'll make a great father."

Jon didn't respond, just stood there, as if having a program failure.

"Jon, you hear me?" Yodan hated to see his friend's brain turned to mush, but reporting it was all he could do.

Resigned and head back down, Yodan read his assignment, waiting for Jon to start moving again. He used his hyper-vision to scan the page about cats and swiped to the next. This one was of a much larger creature that stood like a man and Yodan was fascinated that such things had existed, living at one with mankind. It saddened him once again that when they retreated to the safety of Quma Cities, that they didn't bring other lifeforms with them like these bears. The creature was hairy and even though Nogard said it was extinct, Yodan wanted to believe that such a solid creature might have survived the damning cold. Really, how would she know what was extinct above ground?

When Jon started pacing the room again, Yodan stole a peek at Madeline. She glanced up at the same instant and once again, their eyes locked. Did she know what he was doing on the SHARP?

Yodan's hand shook as he pushed the send button on his SHARP, firing his virus into the system.

The reaction was almost instant. Youth from Quadrant H flew out of the study hall. The supervising questers rushed out, then the others who were left gathered their things to help with the evacuation. Yodan had successfully fooled their Artificial-life into believing that Quadrant H contained unbreathable air.

He let out a long breath. It was done. The evacuation was in progress but his heart raced much too fast. If it continues, Nogard might suspect the false air quality readings were nothing more than a virus he'd installed.

A request came through Yodan's Exchanger to offer emotional support to Azala of Quadrant H. *Ugh, she was so irritating. It was just an evacuation. Why did she act like everything was the end of the system?* He ignored her pleas with a gentle tap to his Exchanger. The device was located under his skin, just above his ear. Then he thought about it and decided she might actually need help. So, from his reader, he sent the request to Protector Owen. He could help her since he liked to show off those muscles and needed a better project than annoying Match.

Madeline must have received a request from someone, too, because she did the same. Her gesture stole Yodan's focus because Madeline had a tattoo on her bald scalp above her ear, decorating where her Exchanger was installed under her skin. The image was of a cage with papers flying free from the bars and was not from the list of pre-approved tattoos. She'd told him the tattoo meant freedom of thought. To Yodan, there wasn't a bigger, *screw you* to Nogard. Yeah. Madeline was an inspiration to a rule-breaker like him.

"You up to something?" she asked, pretending she was

deep in her studies to not attract attention from the cameras, since she wasn't aware that Match had control of them.

They were suddenly alone in the big old study hall. With Nogard distracted by an unplanned evacuation, and Match in control of the cameras, they might actually get to talk or maybe even...

As if reading his mind, Madeline undid her lifesuit a bit to show off her new tattoo. The image of a dagger ran up her chest and along her silky white neck. *Yeah.* She was a rebel under that tough exterior. Skin markings always fascinated Yodan, especially those not pre-approved.

Yodan was more focused on her than he was allowed to be, but they were so similar in Quma Cities that finding someone as different as Madeline was intriguing. And despite Nogard's warnings that she was wrong for him, he was attracted to her. Heck, maybe his feelings were *inspired* by the warnings. Really, Artificial-life knew as much about their desires as Yodan did about the bear on his reader.

Should he tell Madeline that they planned to rebel and leave the system? Maybe she'd join them.

He pocketed his SHARP and asked, "What do you know about our eighteenth FIRE Ceremony coming up?" Each FIRE Ceremony held deep meaning, but this one would change their lives in a new way. They were about to make the first steps from being youths with freedom of thoughts to working adults connected to Artificial-life.

"Just that drones will install Connectors over our Exchangers." She touched the spot behind her ear where the Connector would go.

"Everyone has a blind trust that everything Nogard does is for the best. But, do you know what a Connector is for?"

"Of course, the device allows us access to the Collective."

Yodan stared at her, waiting for more. When she had nothing more to add, he asked, "And why do you want access to the Collective?"

Madeline thought about his question. "Well. At first, I guess short connections will enrich my studies. All the great minds are part of the Collective, past, present...and I suppose one day I will be. Well, I hope so. The idea of living forever at one with the Collective is the ultimate reward. Eternal life."

"So you're excited to have a Connector installed and be

allowed access to the mind of our Artificial-life?" He was almost disappointed when she nodded, but maybe it was for the best. The less they were roaming the pipes looking for another system, the easier it'd be to vanish in the labyrinths of forgotten tunnels.

"My parents said that because of this connection, their memories would live forever. I get that this might make you nervous, Yodan, but being one with the Collective is a good thing." She stared into him. "Isn't it?"

He should nod and smile but despite himself, he reminded her, "During the last FIRE Ceremony, over half died when their Connectors were inserted. Not one of those youths got to be a part of the Collective. And everyone over Forty-two FIRE Ceremonies was absorbed into the Collective. Your own parents sacrificed their lives *willingly* to nourish Artificial-life under the *pretence* of receiving eternal life. And many of the second-term questers like Medic Jon are suffering from childhood memory loss. My own sister had memory loss until she stopped connecting. She says the hum is constant, annoying, a burden, a pull…"

Madeline's eyes darted over his face as if reading him while she thought about what he was saying. "But the youths who died, they weren't prodigies like us. We should be fine, right?" Her incredible blue eyes were threaded with violet. Like him, she had red centers in her eyes, not black, which meant she could see better in the dark than most. "I don't want to die without being part of the Collective," she said.

What would happen to them, to their studies, to their memories, if they weren't a part of Artificial-life yet? He glanced at the bear on his reader. A creature like that had lived and died, but was that it? Was there more to its life? Another life after this one much like the Collective's?

"Elites like Match or my sister Lins won't ever have that connection," he reminded her that some of them got to live device-free. "Even without a Connector or Exchanger, they'll live full lives."

Madeline slid her chair closer to Yodan's rock bench, the metal grated the floor creating an echo through the chamber, reminding him that they were alone.

"We'll be fine, right?" she whispered again, too close to his cheek.

Kissing her would be seven demerits. Looking at her perfect pink lips, he held back. He was all for making his own rules but seven demerits was too high a price. Last time he received seven demerits at once he had to donate his left arm to the bio-labs for cyborg studies. They'd replaced his arm with one of their experiments that never felt natural even if it looked the same. And he really didn't need to draw attention to himself in this breath.

Madeline's finger ran up the two red prodigy stripes on Yodan's lifesuit making his skin tingle under the pink fabric.

He had so much to tell her, but even Match had been doubtful when Yodan had suggested they leave the system and Match was the most skeptical pessimistic person in Quma Cities.

"We should help with the evacuation," Yodan said coldly, turning down her advances and pulling away from her.

Frustrated, Madeline stood, too. "You're leaving, aren't you? This is what you guys are up to? Yodan. Rebels don't survive. Our ancestors suffered to offer us this perfect life. Things will be easy for us," she reminded him, but he was sick of people telling him how perfect his life was. He was trained to see flaws and there were plenty. Heck, even the temperature wasn't right in the study hall.

"At this FIRE Ceremony, we'll become questers," she promised him. "We'll discover what life means through abstinence and short hook-ups to the Collective. This peaceful time will help us grow the system. Then we'll take on the duties of adulthood like routine work and family life. We'll find purpose in keeping our system alive for the next generation. We'll raise children. Perfectly planned, flawless, healthy, and brilliant children."

Yodan did wish for this perfect life with her but that glitch in Medic Jon meant something so big it had Shandra convincing Match to run. Things were bad. Yodan just couldn't put his finger on what he was missing.

"And then, one day, we'll take the things we've studied and learned, and we'll merge our memories with the Collective, becoming one with Artificial-life who gives us our breaths from birth to eternity. This is fact." Madeline ran a hand along his cheek, but he refused to give into her seduction.

"Facts are good, Madeline," he whispered close to her lips.

"But only if you know all the facts. Medic Jon is a perfect example that things aren't right."

"I won't let you walk out of the system to die because a second-term quester lost some memories."

Frustrated him that she couldn't see the importance of this. "This isn't an engineer. A medic lost his entire memory of growing up. How the heck could he forget me? Or Match? Or even his best friend Greg? The four of us were inseparable. I introduced him to Brisk at the quarry. I saved his blasted life while we were in that cave-in in Sector 6. I inserted my first illegal memory needle thanks to him. He taught me how to kiss, for Pete's sake. Every rule that guy ever broke, I was there."

"Sounds like you should escape for a bit." From her long sleeve, she pulled out an illegal memory needle. "Let's get lost in a fun memory together." Madeline moved in closer to Yodan's lips, brushing hers against his. "Just forget about Medic Jon. Nogard will worry about his memories."

Maybe kissing her would be worth the demerits... Still, he pulled back. She didn't deserve demerits because he was weak.

He needed to focus. "Tempting, but no."

"It's nice that you're worried about your friend, but he's learning how to use the Collective to treat us of illnesses before they even occur. Azala told me that he healed her father's broken leg with his bare hands. He's tapped into parts of his brain we won't ever understand. He's actually smarter now that he's ditched those emotional memories."

Emotional memories... What? Something she said snapped in his brain and he glanced up but she had her head down, her one hand on his reader, the other still held the illegal needle. Twirling it.

Yodan memorized her features. Her bleached white skin was flawless. A sign that she was created in a lab by Nogard. Her lips were thin perfect pink slits he was dying to taste before he had to leave.

"Escape with me in a memory, Yodan." Madeline raised her head, licked her lips, then whispered by his ear, "Ever feel *unsatisfied* by all this perfection?"

"*Holy mud.*" He let out a long breath and without meaning to, his hand slid around her waist to pull her closer. *Seven demerits*, he reminded himself. *Seven*. No moment was worth losing a body part over. Especially right now. He needed to be ready to run, not in surgery…

Yodan gently raised her head so he could look in her beautiful blue eyes for what might be the last time. Much to his shock, her eyes were no longer blue. They were a dull grey like the wires leading from their readers to the mainframe. Their eyes were the only unique thing about each of them and he'd never seen eyes change colours before. Even the red had turned a solid grey. A glitch in the system?

He needed to document this, but before he could move for his reader, she dived in to kiss him, inserting the illegal behind his ear in a quick swoop that was his last coherent memory.

MATCH

Many breaths later
Underground, Yodan's family chamber

Match dipped his injured hand in the salt water while Yodan's oldest sister Lins scolded him. They were in her family chamber since he wasn't allowed in his because of the evacuation. He'd cut his hand while fake-moving his things so she was tending to his wound while she fake-yelled at him.

Fake. His entire life was suddenly one big lie.

Lins turned up the white noise and stepped closer so Nogard couldn't hear them talk if the cameras snapped on suddenly. Grabbing his hand, she pointed her medic-pen at the cut to speed up the healing.

Since neither of them were connected to the system, they only had to block Nogard's sensors and act boringly-busy if they wanted privacy. "You're putting my family at risk," Lins snapped, watching his cut heal. "This program one of you idiots installed won't last and Yodan will pay the price, then Shandra."

"Why we have to leave as soon as it's lights-out. All of us." His brother Greg was a first-term quester, too, and he'd been easy to convince to join them in rebelling once Match had pointed out how stupid Jon was these days. Medic Jon's memory loss was proving most useful to Match, serving as a great cover for them needing to get out of here, fast. Of course, Lins hadn't bought into that as a good enough reason to leave the system and so he had to tell her the truth. Which was why she was looking at him with pure disappointment right now. Even though, he had to admit, she hadn't seemed surprised.

Lins' violet eyes peered into him. "And where do you think we'll vanish to, idiot?"

He couldn't meet her eyes as she dunked his hand again even though the wound was already healed. She was the only one who talked to him like that, and he deserved to be set straight so he took it, head down. "We're gonna go above ground. Yodan thinks others might have survived, like us," he mumbled, not sounding half as convincing as he should.

Lins kept snapping at him, "You want to bring my pregnant sister and my rule-breaking brother to barren wastelands? On a whim my brother had?" She shook her head, disgusted with his stupidity. "I get it; you're scared. I am, too. Your secret means my sister could be lost to a cave-in. But you need a better plan. Crawling out of a vent tonight is stupid and frankly something I would expect from Owen."

Match growled at her inappropriate comment. Owen-the-perfect was constantly cornering Shandra. And no way did Match want to be as dumb as that loser. He pulled his hand away and dried it while glaring at her. "We're not going in a vent. Meet us in Quadrant H. I'll go over the plan with you there, in private." He had no plan and was just throwing things together, but what was one more lie to protect Shandra and their unborn illegal child?

"That entire quadrant will be purged come the FIRE Ceremony."

He had not known that, yet he pretended he had. "Why we have to leave at lights-out. Last chance."

Lins glanced at her eRobe. She'd left it by the door because the heavy garment connected her emotionally to Nogard and they needed privacy. Then she glanced at the camera that was still dead. Slowly, Lins lifted her wrist. "I found a code for cameras above ground. Don't ask me how." On her wrist was a code he could use in Dragon.

Match took the code to memory in case a camera above ground gave him some image to hold on to. Some form of hope that he could raise his child with Shandra as a family. Because right now, all he had was a cat that might have come from anywhere.

"I expect you to have one brilliant plan." Lins used the salt water to wipe the code off her skin.

Match swallowed a lump that formed in this throat. "While I go through the surface cameras, you find out what you can about Mainframe One. Logic tells me it'd be near the surface. If Mainframe One survived, we might be able to fire up the hard-drive and maintain a basic system in the wastelands."

She paused to glance at him. "You plan to ReSurface?" ReSurface was a code used among elites to signal a system evacuation. It meant killing their Artificial-life and restarting fresh above ground. No one had any idea what that would involve and no one had ever been brave enough to actually *do* it.

"If we must."

Lins unhooked the eRobe and walked out clutching it as if they were talking about their day and not something as stupid as leaving Utopia for a certain death.

The moment the door closed, Match's watch shocked him. He glanced at it. A tiny red circle lit up around the relic. His watch hadn't come with instructions but he didn't need to be a genius to know a countdown when he saw one. *Great*, as if he didn't have enough issues. Whatever had activated his watch to countdown, he'd discover soon enough. Thinking about possible worst-case scenarios, he set up every SHARP and handheld he could find as decoys so Nogard wouldn't know that he was accessing surface cameras. He fired up a bunch of bogus programs and was shooting them to the handhelds when Owen burst in.

Great. What did he want?

Without missing a beat, Match glanced up and lied, "Shandra was looking for ya, big guy. She said she was going to the quarry. Better hurry, she was flustered."

Owen nodded and rushed off like the twit he was and Match glanced at the only SHARP that mattered in his mess of decoys. He'd set it on Yodan's trunk, tilted so no cameras could see it because Nogard should be taking them over again in a few more breaths.

Then, at the secured program station that only elites were allowed to work on, he ran the code Lins had given him and waited as several above-ground cameras shot images at him. They were from an outdated system and blurry but he captured several pictures that might mean life was possible above ground. One was dark with shadows and the other was white snow, too bright.

He changed the coding a bit to access recent images the cameras would have taken, digging in the camera archives. Then he sat back, pretending to ignore the SHARP resting so innocently on the trunk while working on the other devices, but the more images he saw, the more excited he got. Maybe they could ReSurface... The idea had him so excited, he had to keep his hands down so they didn't create flames against his will.

In one image, he'd caught a footprint. In another he saw an orange cat.

His watch continued to countdown without a reason as he formed a plan. A simple plan but a good one. They would break from the system at lights-out. A group of them. Then they'd head up.

He was wondering if the ventilation pipes would be best or the old elevator shafts when Yodan waltzed in looking much too calm for a guy who'd made an illegal shutdown.

"Yodan. Congratulations. It worked."

Yodan paused and glanced at Match. "What worked?"

YODAN

A breath later
Underground, Yodan's family chamber

Relieved to be in the comfort of his family chamber, Yodan shut the door and leaned against it. Match was there, with legal and illegal devices scattered about, actively researching something. This was exactly what Match studying looked like. He didn't open a reader like a normal guy, no, he had to tear their entire perfect system apart, searching for faults.

This, of course, was his job as an elite. He took the responsibility seriously. His studies challenged Nogard and made so Artificial-life provided what was best for them and not the other way around.

"Why are you working in here?" Yodan checked the various devices. "You've accessed tracking cameras outside and inside the system? Why?"

"What do you mean why? I'm looking for life outside our system."

"Why?"

"What in all these levels is wrong with you? The cameras are still off, you don't have to pretend."

"I'm not pretending, I'm worried about you, Match. You better not do something stupid."

"Me?" Match glanced up, his left eye wincing in worry. "Did you hard hook-up before coming here?"

"Of course not. I don't like anything messing with my brain."

"Yet something clearly has. We're planning to leave the system at lights-out. I'm looking for another system, a place we can…"

"What!"

"*You* shut down Quadrant H so we could hide there. It's being evacuated as we speak. Why I'm in your chamber." Match shot to his feet and tilted Yodan's head to check his Exchanger. His *hiss* tightened Yodan's gut. "You have an illegal memory transferring needle in your Exchanger. This is Madeline's work. Why would she be copying your memories?"

Yodan didn't move. Wouldn't he remember someone

jamming a needle in his brain? "Who's Madeline?"

Match backed up, staring at him, gaping. "You don't remember your wanna-be girlfriend, man? What happened to you? She's all you yap about."

Yodan moved the SHARP sitting on his storage chest because he wanted to sit on it, but he paused, because on the screen was an image of a man with hair! His skin was discoloured which meant the D-light he'd taken in was unregulated and his eyes were a colour Yodan had never seen. "Match. Where's this camera from?"

Match didn't even glance at the device. "Not giving me much." He glided over and shut the SHARP off in his calm way as if seeing such a bundled up hairy man was normal. "Cameras are back up. Hey Nogard, nice of you to join us."

"*Elite Match. I have been busy or I would have been by sooner. Were there issues with the cameras?*"

"Actually, there was a glitch in the study hall. Some type of energy surge."

"*I will look into it.*"

They waited in case Nogard had something else to add, then Yodan stepped closer to Match. The white noise made a nice cover in the room, so he whispered through clenched teeth, "That was a hairy man on the screen."

"Just snow. Nothing but snow." Match grabbed his swimming shorts as if they were going to the quarry for a swim. Actually, the quarry might not be a bad idea. Quadrant H connected to the quarry and, if the evacuation that Match mentioned was complete, they could hide there and talk about his memory loss. Match could even pretend he forgot something in his chamber.

Match's white eyes sparkled as he glanced at his watch, nervous. His watch was a gift from a past elite at his naming ceremony. Nogard allowed elites more wealth like this watch so others recognized the status given to them at their Seventh FIRE Ceremony. Allowing this symbolized that Nogard worked with them and respected their freedom to protect themselves, even from her.

Yodan opened the door to leave.

Azala stood in the hallway leaning against the quadrant crest stamped in front of his door on the smooth rock wall. It was the same marking tattooed on Yodan's neck of a serpent tail.

Azala looked like she'd been waiting for him for hours. Golden flakes from the waters at Glisten Point Quarry clung to her pure white skin and he fought temptation to brush them off and feel her skin for himself. He wasn't sure where this new attraction to Azala came from and he backed up, bumping into Match. "My programming was altered," he whispered no idea how to explain his sudden change of desire.

"How so?" Match asked, staring over his shoulder at Azala.

Azala answered, "Nogard has chosen us as a family-unit couple. I came to invite you to the quarry."

Yodan's hand shook wildly with the need to touch her.

Match was quick to come between them. "How deep was the program change, Yodan?"

Azala brushed her lips and Yodan's hand stopped shaking to watch the motion. He shoved Match aside and snapped her in his arms, drawing her in by her waist. Before his lips locked with hers, Match's hand shot between their lips.

Yodan pulled away, Match's hand tasted like salt water and Yodan backed up, grossed out. "Back off, Match."

Match pushed him back into their chamber and shut the door on Azala. "Yodan? You hear me? Snap out of it. What in all these levels is wrong with you? You like Madeline. Remember her?" Match looked ready to shake sense into him. "Azala annoys you." Match's distaste for her was apparent, but then again, he was only ever interested in Shandra.

Yodan turned his back on Match, frustrated that Nogard was messing with him. "I don't know a Madeline and my body physically wants Azala's." Yet images of troubled grey eyes haunted him when he spoke of Madeline. Weird because grey wasn't an approved eye colour in Quma Cities.

"I told you not to hard hook-up."

"I didn't," Yodan promised, glancing at the camera. He gave Nogard the finger. A light pressure pinched behind his ear, a warning that Nogard could knock him out and reprogram him as she saw fit at any time. She allowed Yodan to live freely as a youth, and he'd better shape up to keep this privilege.

"Well, how else could she have inserted this desire? If Madeline doesn't rip out Nogard's wires, I'll be amazed.

Explain what you feel for Azala so I can evaluate how screwed we are."

"Leaves me feeling weird but Azala has no imperfections for me to fixate onto. Now that she's no longer in front of me, I'm fine."

The right side of Match's lip curled up in a smirk. "Most people seek perfection, Yodan."

"They don't. That's what Nogard requires. Think about Shandra. It's not that she looks like everyone else or acts like everyone else. You notice her because she has no prodigy stripes, because she has those strange brown lines in her pink eyes."

Match smirked, but that's about all the joy he ever showed. "Yeah, she's sexy. You forgot about the mud streak on her cheek earlier. She's actually the most brilliant person I know. No offence to you, because you're a weird kind of brilliant." He brushed his own cheek as if remembering the mud. "Oh, and that habit Shandra does when she rubs her hand where her prodigy stripe should be..."

"She refused the prodigy exam, Match. You don't know if she would have passed or not."

"Yeah, that's bold. Wish I'd done that. And where her shoulder and neck meet there's this spot—" Just thinking about her made flames explode in Match's hands. He rubbed his hands together to put the flames out, unembarrassed by his lack of control over his born-gift.

"You done? That's my sister, Mister Elite. I don't need to see how she excites you."

"Sorry. Always impresses me that she wasn't created by Nogard but illegally."

"Not illegal, just natural. My parents had permission since they were a couple suitable for reproduction." Match wouldn't know this. "Doesn't matter, anyway, you're an elite with born-gifts, Match. You won't be allowed to reproduce, you're a glitch in the system. Granted, one I appreciate, but clearly not one Nogard will. If you hadn't been named elite, you probably would have been terminated by now." Yodan imagined that like Lins, he'd undergone sterilization at a young age to prevent him from passing on whatever had gone wrong at his conception to make the flame-hands.

"What if Nogard reprograms Shandra? I don't want her

looking at Owen like you were looking at Azala. That was terrifying. I want to start a family with Shandra. Me. To heck with the rules about me not reproducing."

"I'm not a big fan of all the rules I'm given, but you were only given one. One rule that is there for our safety," Yodan reminded him, but it was like a slap. Match winced and wouldn't look at him.

Shandra was like Yodan, always breaking the rules. A rebel since her conception, she liked to use illegals to hide her thoughts and emotions, wishing she was like Lins who lived without devices inside her. This first cycle as a quester, Shandra was supposed to live in abstinence, so she refused the mandatory sterilization treatment ordered for first-term questers saying 'why would she need sterilization if she wasn't allowed to share her sleeping pod with anyone?' Which was a point Nogard couldn't argue, and given that her pod was by his, Yodan knew she kept true to her abstinence vows.

"Behave. I don't want you getting my sister in trouble."

"You siding with Artificial-life on this, Yodan?"

Were there sides?

Yodan glanced at the door where Azala waited. His sudden interest in her hadn't felt right. "About you being with Shandra? No. But you will have to visit the labs. You know you shouldn't reproduce, Match, so get that idea out of your head. There will be no natural reproduction for you. But I do feel we should have the freedom to choose who we want to start a family unit with, or even sleep with at lights-out. I don't feel that this is something that should be evaluated by Nogard. For once, Artificial-life can mind her own business."

"Yeah. That's the Yodan I know. Let's go so we can get you fixed up."

AVERY

Breaths later
Above ground, Berry Clan

Avery stepped on Berry land with a determined stomp, eager to get this deal with Jacob over with. She rubbed her stupid eye, hoping no one noticed the tic.

Storming toward the bushes she held her breath to avoid inhaling the gases filtering out of the yellow pipes. Dragon had these pipes all over the village, expelling warm gases that had different effects on them. The mist in this area always made her too aware of her body. Then again, there wasn't much good on Berry land.

Head down, Avery passed the group of Berry women splashing in the water. Most of them were much older than her.

"It's the sacred virgin," one of them taunted from the water, making her glance up. The mist made their bronze skin gleam.

Avery rubbed at her mud covered arms. Her orange hair was a mangled mess. Maybe she should have cleaned up before storming over to make a deal with Jacob. Would it matter? Avery stuck out like a thistle in a crop of wheat no matter what she did.

Ignoring these Berry women, she continued to the far end of the village where Jacob was building his hut, probably part of the deal he'd offered his new partner. As she rounded the water, her cousin Kanya strolled her way.

Since Kanya joined Berry Clan in Avery's place, Kanya had refused to speak to Avery, but clearly today they were starting anew because she said, "If it isn't my dear cousin come to visit. Rumours are that the nomad was hanging with Jacob. Maybe he'll join Berry Clan, too, since that's where the food and women are."

Rumours? Kanya probably started those rumours.

Avery planned to keep walking but Kanya grunted, clearly in distress or uncomfortable with her pregnancy so Avery helped her sit on the large rock by Berry pond. Kanya's belly was heavy with life. Sometimes, women overworked themselves in these instances. "Take it easy, Kanya. The last pregnant Berry woman died while birthing."

"Don't you think I know that? This is why *we* were chosen. Berrys need to break this curse Dragon plagues on them and our clans aren't affected. They hope... Just leave me alone."

Berrys were cursed? What did that mean? "Would you like water?" Avery offered.

"I'm fine." The bead work on Kanya's top made up colourful butterflies and flowers on the soft pink material. Compared to Avery's boring clothes, this was a masterpiece meant to show off Kanya's status as a giver-of-life and bring her luck and joy in her new journey.

"This top is simply gorgeous, you're incredibly talented, Kanya," Avery offered in an attempt to bring peace back to their relationship and seek her approval since a good word from Kanya would help her fit in with these older women whose vegetables her family needed.

When Kanya raised an eyebrow, Avery tried a bit harder. "The pink is a wonderful choice for you."

"Thank you. I have nothing but time to perfect my craft. Berrys lead a leisurely life compared to those on the other side of the village." Avery doubted this was true but got the impression Kanya was telling her something else.

"Did Pax tell you that Berry's youngest daughter paid him a visit in hopes that he'll start a family with her? She offered him land, status in the clan, his own shed, even her brothers to help them build a hut..." Yeah, Avery knew. After that Berry woman left, Pax had cried endlessly.

Kanya stood, using Avery's help. Her full belly mocked Avery's innocence.

"I should go, Mother Roselle needs me to speak with Jacob for her."

"Yeah, I'm sure she does." Kanya watched her walk off. Halfway to Jacob's Avery went back to ask Kanya what she'd meant by that last remark, but before she made it to the pond, a gentle shaker rocked the lands, making the women at the bathing pool scream.

Avery rolled her eyes. They annoyed her. Why did women from Berry Clan act so helpless? As if a little quake was a concern.

Before Avery found her footing, the elders' alarm rang from Dragon's Caves. *Great.* Meant that quake wasn't innocent. Who had upset Dragon?

Berry barged out the front door of his home, charging up the hill. Jacob also stormed from his half-built hut in the distance, even though he was much older and moved slower. Other leaders rushed toward the caves.

Avery ran up the hill to see who was to blame. "Dammit, Pax," she cursed when she saw that Uncle Hunter had Pax in a choke-hold against the rock wall by Dragon's Caves. What in all this cold had Pax done to upset Uncle Hunter?

A second shaker rattled Avery, more from worry. What was going on? Had Pax done something to upset Dragon? Something bad enough to warrant a quake-warning?

From this distance she saw the cliff break off a small piece that slid toward the forest side of the village.

When things calmed, Avery raced up the hill toward the growing crowd. Hunter still had Pax pinned to the stone wall with an arm against his neck while he whispered things in his face.

Eyes closed, Pax waited for the blows to start or maybe end. Avery couldn't be sure what was happening.

Making her way through the crowd, she planned to stop the madness but before she could step close enough, Father Saxton grabbed her. "Avery, stay out of this. Pax has devices in his bag. *Science things.*" He whispered the words to her, as if saying *'science'* aloud might upset Dragon again. She pushed past him a bit to see for herself. Sure enough, the bag was open and various forbidden gadgets had fallen out.

Shoving Saxton's hand off her shoulder, she said, "Let me talk to him. This is our fault. We should have searched his bag before we let him in the village." Still, who in their right mind would have thought Pax carried around science things?

Saxton glared at her, but she refused to back down, just as bullheaded.

With a heavy sigh, Saxton stormed toward Hunter. "Hunter, wait. Let's explain this to Pax and bury the gadgets. No harm was done."

Hunter didn't let go.

Saxton whispered to his brother, "Berry sent his daughter over last night to pay Pax a visit and after she left he spent the evening crying for this Penny. He's in no shape to fight you. Let him go."

This comment relaxed Hunter's grip a bit. "He's put us in danger."

As if in response to Hunter's words, another quake, much smaller than the last, rumbled under them, reminding them how important banishing anything science was.

Hunter stepped back as if touching Pax might get him banished, too. Pax dropped and Saxton picked him up by the back of his garments as if he were a stray cat and dropped him at Avery's feet. "You teach him and bury those gadgets in the forest." By letting the others see that he trusted Pax with his only daughter, he gave Pax a bit of status. Then Saxton glanced around at the crowd. "We can't expect a nomad to know Dragon's rules. It's up to us to educate him properly."

Everyone waited as if Dragon might disagree. When there were no more earthquakes, they looked to the elders. Fewerter and Jenica nodded and returned to their huts to signal that the issue was closed. The crowd disbanded, grouping off in their clans and heading home for lunch.

Avery helped Pax to his feet. To Avery, Saxton whispered, "You have until the Warming Ceremony. I allow this one chance to prove he's one of us because I respect the values of others and trust your judgment on this. One more quake caused by him and he's gone."

Pax was on his feet, rubbing his jaw as if wounded. He shared an *I'm-Sorry-I-Goofed* look with Avery before dropping his head in shame.

To Pax, Saxton said, "Science ruined the Outlands. There are no machines here. No gadgets. We don't ever speak of such things."

Head down, Pax said, "I didn't know they were science things. They were things Penny liked. I keep them in memory of her."

Saxton glared at Avery before leaving, reminding her that she was taking responsibility for this innocent fool.

When they were alone, Pax bent over, breathing in long hard gasps. "Wow, your people are nuts, Avery."

"They're careful. Every time a nomad shows, their ideas disrupt our way of life. The rules allow us to co-exist in this blissful harmony."

"Not feeling the bliss."

Frankly, neither did Avery. But who was she to change the

ways of the clans? On her knees, she bent to pick up his gadgets but hesitated to touch the science. Pax knelt with her and without qualms, he tossed his things in the bag. "Hunter offered to introduce me to that Fewerter elder-guy and the ground shook. I panicked and dropped my bag. Next thing I knew, I was tossed into the wall and told I was gonna destroy the village. What the heck is wrong with you people?" Frustrated, he latched his bag. "Your place confuses me. One minute I'm told that this Dragon sent me to father Berry children, then I'm told I might end up being a blasted sacrifice to this Dragon. I mean, what the hell, Avery?" His hands were shaking when he placed them on the bag. "You all right? That shaker freak you out, too?"

"We don't like the earthquakes because each one means we displeased Dragon. When we know what we did, it's easy to fix. In this case, we'll bury your science things," she reassured him. "Really, it's fine. If Hunter didn't kick you out of the village, it means he likes you. He was just scared." Or putting on a show for the others, but Avery wouldn't say that out loud until she knew Pax better. But she was onto the lies everyone was living to fit in.

They were outside Dragon's Caves, high enough to see the entire village. Or be seen by the entire village. And Avery tried to ignore those down the hill staring up at them.

"Wow," he said, "Wish I could be so unruffled about earthquakes. Every blasted time I feel as if it'll be my last breath."

"Yet here you are."

"Yup. Still here. Not so sure what my purpose in life is, but here I am."

Avery hated having eyes on her, reminding her of how different she was. She was itching to bury these things in the forest. But Pax didn't get up. Clutching his bag, he sat against the stone walls in plain sight of the entire village. Then he rested his head on his pack, creating a protective huddle with his body. Well, at least he wasn't hiding his freaking-the-hell-out.

"If you want to fit in with the other leaders, you should act braver when in public," she offered. "Pull back your shoulders."

Pax ignored her. *Great.* She'd never seen anyone so broken.

"I lost my family in an earthquake," he mumbled. "Each quake reminds me of how insignificant I am. God has given me a gift and can take these breaths away. Knowing He has this control is a comfort yet makes me feel powerless. I want to regain power, to leave a mark, to even prove that I exist for a reason."

God? Perhaps this was his name for the Creator of Dragon? The name was a comfort she liked, and she wondered if she was perhaps from Pax's clan outside the village. She knelt by him, studying his features. Wishing she could remember where she came from. Even his hands were covered in freckles like hers. Saxton told her to ignore such things but what did a man with a twin know about being different? She was about to ask Pax if he could tell her about his birth clan when Pax glanced up. The sun danced off his green eyes, making the tears glisten, and his sorrow silenced her.

"Why don't you guys like my gadgets? They're harmless, just relics." He tightened his jacket around himself as if the fur offered extra protection from the eyes on them.

She stood, prepared to drag him to the forest to bury the gadgets but someone placed a hand on her shoulder making her jump. She shoved the unwanted touch off while glaring at the intruder. "Oh," she snapped. "It's Jacob Berry." Why would Jacob think he had a right to handle her? "Berrys don't touch Saxtons," she reminded the oldest Berry, annoyed; yet remembering Mother Roselle's warning, she bit back her frustration.

Pax shot to his feet as Avery said, "Rumours are you're starting a family with someone. Mother Roselle thought you might be interested in trading vegetables for furnishings. My brothers have cabinets and tables made."

"Bring whatever you like when you move in and take what you want for vegetables, any time, my dear."

"What?"

His smile showed that someone had recently knocked out his front teeth, leaving him a gaping hole. "I'm blessing you with the honour of starting a family with me."

Avery hit him.

YODAN

During the same breaths
Underground, Glisten Point Quarry

Yodan and Match arrived at the quarry as the earthquake hit. Everyone was smashed up against the walls, but as the dust settled, Yodan saw that two stalactites had crashed by the water.

Once Yodan found his footing, he scanned the area. Azala hovered in the corner by her friends. Owen was there, which was weird, first-term questers didn't usually hang out at the quarry. He had a boulder he was supporting on his back like the freak he was. He walked it to the side, keeping the crowd safe.

Azala was gushing over him, now, *thank goodness*. Still, knowing she was safe gave Yodan a strange relief even though she was a rule-follower who wouldn't know how to do a dare if her life depended on it. *Urgh*. It was frustrating when Nogard messed with his emotions, but probably what he deserved for shutting down Quadrant H, even though he had no idea why he'd shut it down anymore. He scanned the area, making sure there were no injuries.

A moment ago, Match had pointed out Madeline to him. She'd stood out in the crowd in her powder blue lifesuit and sexy dimples, and well, she was headed his way with a SHARP in hand and had clearly recognized him, even though to Yodan she was just another face in the crowd. Granted, a face he wouldn't mind getting closer to, but still, no memories were there of having known her before.

Where was Madeline now?

The largest of the blue pipes curled behind them like a snake coiling in all directions, making waterfalls and bathing pools. Despite the tremor, life continued.

Stalactites glistened. The plants growing in this warm area were great for chewing and if a guy was lucky, while he picked a few, he might meet a gal in need of rescuing from the water bugs.

After the last of the quakes, Yodan counted to forty, as taught, before moving. When another quake didn't hit, he started the search for Madeline. She would have fled to a wall or… A girl yelled by the far wall to signal someone was injured. No one ever screamed for any other reason in Quma Cities.

Yodan rushed to check. Others gathered around the sight, but no one moved, which meant the worst.

A large boulder had broken free and had crushed someone. A shimmering image of Madeline, almost like a 3-D hologram hovered by the rocks. She raised her hand to stop Yodan or maybe reach out for him, he couldn't tell because she vanished as Owen walked through her to move the boulder.

Yodan scanned the faces around him in case others saw the hologram but they were staring at the powdered blue sleeve sticking out of the rubble.

Resurfacing memories and emotions pounded at him.

"Madeline." Not thinking properly, Yodan dived for the mess, trying to push the crashed rocks and boulders off Madeline. "Madeline is under here, help me!"

Beep Beep Beep. The warning alarm resonated and Yodan was blown back by a gust of air that knocked him on his rear.

Madeline's arm rested flat in front of him, her SHARP had tumbled from it.

Match picked up the device. Then he grabbed Yodan by the collar and escorted him to Quadrant H.

Yodan's world moved in slow motion as Match dodged the soothing gases Nogard rained on them from overhead vents. The gases were to ease the pain at losing a friend…

"Match, let me go, I have to see Madeline. Did you see the hologram? She was alive a moment ago. Triggered an image. Where is she now?"

Match kept a tight grip on him, guiding Yodan through the crowd and tossing him through the doors of the closed quadrant that should be locked up tightly but were not. Match firmly shut the glass door leading from Glisten Point Quarry to Quadrant H, disconnecting them from the perfect system.

In a mad rush, Yodan smeared himself against the glass door but knew better than to fight Match and his muscles.

"I saw nothing." Match took a deep breath before adding. "Look. Madeline had the counterpart to the illegal needle that is in your Exchanger shoved in her SHARP. Means she was transferring your memories to this needle with the SHARP I gave her. Why was she doing something so dangerous?" he demanded, as if Yodan had any idea. He would never do that. A memory transfer risked causing memory loss; he needed his memories.

Match checked the SHARP and brought up images. "Here's your last memory with her." He tilted the screen on the handheld so Yodan could see Madeline staring back at him with her sharp grey eyes.

"Why are her eyes grey?" Match demanded.

"Aren't they always?"

"She had blue eyes with violet lines in them and red centers like her mother's. No one has grey eyes like this." Match pulled the memory back a bit to watch from Yodan's point of view. They watched as Yodan's memory stared at her hand twirling the memory needle. Match was even able to bring up Yodan's interior thoughts.

"*Holy dirty water.*" Match dropped the device.

Yodan snagged the SHARP with his hyper-speed before the device hit the floor.

"You thought that Nogard had somehow infiltrated Madeline?"

"I what?" Things were clicking together and what he said made sense as if the puzzle pieces that were jumbled in his brain just needed that one missing piece. "Wait." Yodan sorted through the thoughts with his hand up. "If we merge with Nogard when we die and we become part of her thoughts and a program she can refer to, what's stopping her from reversing this and merging with us? Making us into a living resource she can tap into and use?"

"I'm what's stopping her!" Match snapped.

"Hear me out. This is what we were missing. A second-term quester like Medic Jon would be perfect for her to infiltrate as a trial. His hook-ups to the system are long while he takes in data from the Collective and turns it into information she could use to reverse the hard hook-ups. What if she's been experimenting on him so that one day, she can create the perfect host?"

"I'm gonna kill her," Match mumbled, flames warming his palms.

"Killing Nogard isn't an option or the entire system crumbles."

Match growled. "We can't run now. I have to get these people away from her. We don't need a machine getting inside our minds as she tries to figure out what a perfect host would be."

Nogard was hardly a machine. Yodan ignored his outburst as he stared at the image of Madeline on the screen he held. So many memories with her were trickling in. "Oh Madeline." Pain tore through Yodan, crippling him, forcing him to his knees as he rested his head against the glass door. From here, he could watch drones bring in a gate to block off the debris in the quarry. Owen was still out there, showing off for Azala and her friends by moving boulders that the drones could easily break with their highbeams. Already, the crowd thinned out, returning to the swimming merriment as if nothing had happened.

Match took the SHARP from Yodan and placed the device on the hook by the door. Then he took out his pen-light. "Let me remove that illegal from your Exchanger."

Yodan knelt before his friend, head tilted, feeling beaten. Match attached the pen-light to the wall. They didn't need the light, since their eyes adapted to see in the dark, but having precision light when dealing with brain programming was a comfort. When the needle moved, the pressure made Yodan wince.

Once he had it free, Match snapped the needle in half. Memory transfers were usually done by Nogard in the final stages of life, any earlier they risked interfering with brain development. Who knew how messed up Yodan would be now?

Yodan remained on his knees, waiting for the dizziness to wear off. He stared out the glass door at the quarry. Dust exploded around Madeline's body as drones broke up the rock.

Yodan touched the glass door, considering a hard hook-up at the Bench of Life across the way so he could forget that they'd be dumping Madeline's body in the recycling chamber. Once he hooked-up, he'd forget her again and this drowning ache would vanish. On his feet, he pulled on the door, but Match had his foot against the bottom and wouldn't let him out. "We go out there, we're dead. If Madeline inserted that needle in your Exchanger and stole your memories, and Nogard was in Madeline, using her like a host as you suspect, Nogard now knows we shut down this quadrant and that we are planning to leave. Worse, she had access to her SHARP and knows about Dragon and the ghost program we use to get around her. None of this is good."

"Her memories. What'll happen to Madeline's memories?" Yodan demanded of him. "Are they in her Exchanger? We need them out." Yodan glanced at Match for support but he remained an expressionless rock staring back at him.

Out at the quarry, everyone was back in the water, playing. The memory gases making them forget their grief, as if Madeline's life didn't count.

Match said between clenched teeth, "I don't believe Madeline's death was an accident."

No, probably not.

"She had no Connector. Normally, that means her memories are lost. But if Nogard found a way to infiltrate Madeline, the connection would go deeper than a hard hook-up or a Connector. She would know what Madeline knows and therefore, there would be no more Madeline. Nogard is now her."

Holy mud. Yodan stared at his friend. He wiped his tears, not used to crying, since Nogard always regulated their outbursts with gases.

Numb, he watched a drone clean up the gate where Madeline had been.

"Nogard will use us, take our memories, and destroy us, one by one," Yodan mumbled not wanting to accept that Madeline might be one with Nogard. Somehow that idea was worse than her ceasing to exist. Yodan turned away. Glisten Point was no longer a safe haven for him.

Match showed Yodan his watch. A red light circled around it. "If we compare times: this countdown started right after Madeline was infiltrated by Nogard. Also matches the energy surge from the study hall. When Nogard broke Elite Law by leaving her mainframe and entering a human, it activated some type of termination sequence. Means others thought this was possible and prepared a safety."

"In the past, Nogard moved from other mainframes and that never warranted a termination. As an elite, when Nogard over-steps, it's your job to remind her of her place. Just reset things and find a way to reprogram her."

"Elite Law is very simple: Nogard is allowed to grow into a new mainframe under an observed transfer. I didn't authorize something as stupid as her jumping into Madeline and I know Lins would never do that without talking to me about it. A human body is not a mainframe. Artificial-life is allowed to live, within our codes. She broke code. This is unacceptable."

"So… What are you saying?"

"She's truly free. She purposely broke code." Match stared at the watch. "I have no facts other than that."

"What are ways we can stop her from taking over our friends, or us?"

Match stared at the watch. "I think it might be out of our hands. My watch is counting down a termination."

Yodan stared down the long corridor of the closed quadrant. Last time he was here, this bustled with life, now shadows haunted the hall. "If an elite programmed a termination that Nogard activated, how do you think it'll happen?"

Match didn't even hesitate in his answer. Either it was part of his training or he dreamed of terminating Nogard. "Magma energy would be fast and painless and efficient." He spoke so coldly his words were frightening.

"Azala's waving," Match said. "Want me to blow her a kiss for you?" Sarcasm dripped from his voice.

"Maybe we can contain Nogard. I mean, we have one up on her. Whoever she infiltrates will have grey eyes, right?"

Match glanced at him, now, clearly seeing a plan in that genius brain of his.

"We don't have to die," Yodan said. "There is life above ground. You saw that man on your SHARP. If he exists, he has a family."

"What I was thinking. I'll show you what Shandra and I found."

Yodan followed him.

AVERY

In the same breaths
Above ground, Dragon's Caves

Avery glared at Jacob as he stumbled back, away from the caves, her punch catching him off-guard. She didn't know Jacob Berry well since he was older than Father Saxton and kept to himself, living with his lame mother after losing his last partner in childbirth. Frankly, he'd never given her a hello. When she'd turned down his nephew's offer to live with him at the last Warming, Jacob had demanded the elders sacrifice her – which put him on her 'to-avoid' list. Thankfully, Kanya had calmed things.

Now, Pax helped the elderly man to his feet. "What the heck, Avery. He's an old man. What's wrong with you? You told me to fit in yet you're hitting people."

"He assumed I would start a family with him. I will not. I'm free to choose who I want. Besides, it's fine not to fit in with a jerk who doesn't respect others."

Jacob's swollen face meant he'd survived a worse beating than she'd dished out, which was a common sight among the men before a Warming Ceremony while everyone established their place and decided what they'd be trading at the Warming. She hoped a few of those bruises were from Father Saxton or even Stefe.

Jacob snapped, "Your uncle should have left you by that wolf den where he found you, you ungrateful brat!"

"Now calm down, Elder Jacob. There's clearly been a misunderstanding." Pax addressed him as an elder. Jacob Berry wasn't named an elder but Pax's comment clearly pleased him; elder was the highest status in the village. Elder was a title reserved for the wise and experienced leaders or their partners when they could no longer lead their clan due to illness or old age. Jacob was never a leader, having left his stronger brother to take care of their clan.

Jacob stood by Pax, towering over him.

"If you're thinking about asking a fireball like Avery to live with you in that hut," Pax pointed out, "you should expect anger. Geesh. There has to be better options for you."

"Berry Clan is rooted in the ancestry of Cuma Village. Everyone is my family except her. I won't partner with family again. My actions angered Dragon and he stole my son and mate in punishment." He held his head down in shame or perhaps grief at the loss of his partner and son.

"Sorry. I lost my wife, too. We didn't have any children, though. Still, aren't you a bit old for Avery?"

Jacob leaned closer to Avery as if he wanted to whisper in her ear. She backed up.

"I have much to offer your clan, my dear. I'm building our hut now." He pointed to the far end of Berry fields. "Would you like to see it? I even found you a cat. She's orange, like your hair."

He was buying her off with a cat? "Friskie and I share a special bond. I'm not looking to replace him, thanks." Besides, her cat was white. She didn't point out his stupidity since she needed food from this jerk.

Her fists clenched. When she glanced down the hill, Saxton stood with his arms crossed, watching them. Did he know what Jacob asked? Would he be upset that she'd punched another Berry?

"Because of my status in his clan, my brother gave me permission to offer Avery's brothers enough land to each build a hut, you included, Pax of the South. Plus our food is your food. A peace offering."

"What?" Avery had no idea an offer would come with something impossible for her to refuse. Her brothers would need land soon, especially Stefe and Jojo They were old enough to build a hut and find a companion to run it with them. Plus, this deal meant Pax could stay in Saxton Clan where he'd be safe and taught how to run his own family. Then he could grieve for as long as he needed. Or he could join her in Berry Clan and find a partner among them…

She suddenly saw her fate. With this realization came a terror, because despite this being good for her family, she couldn't see herself living with Jacob and sharing his mat and raising his children. *Just no.*

"Saxton needs land for his sons to start their own families and you need status. I'm the oldest Berry, the one with the most memories and status under my brother himself. We need to break the curse killing our children and companions.

This is a safe deal for the good of the clans."

The deal also meant that Saxton's sons wouldn't take over their clans. Peace would endure in the village. Still, she said, "Others might offer—"

"I'll be the only offer you'll get." Jacob grabbed her arm, cutting her off. "You see these bruises? I fought hard for this right to bring you home." Avery stared at his hand in dismay. Why did he keep touching her?

He didn't pull his hand away but leaned in to kiss her.

She slapped him and much to her annoyance, Pax chuckled.

Jacob pulled back, staring at her, shocked.

Avery swallowed a knot. Would she have to leave her clan and make a family with Jacob?

Pax stepped between them. "Elder Jacob, best give her a breath to think about this, maybe bring Mother Roselle those vegetables she needs. And on the way, if your wounds need soothing, use those plants that grow from the side of the cliffs. Just break open the leaves and rub the gel from the inside on them. I can help..."

Jacob glared at him. "I don't take orders from a nomad."

"Just trying to help."

Avery crossed her arms, watching Jacob leave. He stopped to check the plants on his way, and she smirked when he ripped off a leaf and vanished along the side of the cave to use it. Maybe Pax would win over a few with his weird knowledge and all would be fine for him. Still, that didn't help her brothers or even their need for vegetables.

In front of Dragon's Caves, she watched the clans below. From this high, she saw the grey pipe coil around the village, protecting it. Saw each clan preparing for the Warming. From up here, everything looked perfect.

"Are you considering Elder Jacob's offer?" Pax asked.

"The deal will ensure my brothers and you a future among the clans."

"What about falling in love?"

"How do you fall into that?"

"It's an expression my dad used. You know, the way Saxton looks at Roselle. That's a guy who fell into love hard. Or how Hunter talks about his first partner. You grew up seeing that connection, you can't tell me you expect anything less from this guy you'll start a family with. And Elder Jacob… I mean, really?"

She wasn't sure if Pax was brilliant or incredibly stupid, but when he spoke of love, well, that was something she wanted. She wanted a man to look at her the way Father Saxton looked at Mother Roselle, the way he respected her ideas… But who would see her this way when she was so different? "Maybe you're right, but I could wait a long time before I find that kind of companion. This deal makes sense."

He shrugged. "It doesn't have to take long. Sometimes you fall fast, which is what happened to my parents. Mom called their connection 'love at first sight'. Things weren't so smooth for Penny and me. We fell into love differently. I called our connection hard-love. At first, we fought a lot. She was stubborn." He smirked. "Somehow, that became a quality I liked. I realized, I could no longer imagine a life without her fighting at my side."

Explained why he had such a hard time adjusting to life without this Penny.

"Sounds like something a weak, stupid fool would do," Avery snapped.

He followed her up the hill by Dragon's Caves while playing with a pin and carrying his pack. "Yup. Falling this way makes you weak, yet the bond you share somehow makes you stronger. Imagine Saxton without Roselle. He wouldn't be the same. He wouldn't have the same status. Heck, he wouldn't even have clean undergarments."

Avery chuckled, understanding what he meant. "This is true. He breathes with her. And Uncle Hunter was broken when Aunt Pattrice died. Gosh, he was crushed almost as bad as you. I mean, he's content with Aunt Mable, but not joyful like he was with Pattrice. She brought out an energy to him we miss."

"Yeah. I miss that feeling in myself. The connection a couple shares. The racing heart. The bursting inside. When love is stolen from you, you don't fall out of love. Instead your body aches as if someone reached inside you and ripped out everything you need to be you." He studied the pin he played with, no longer following her.

Avery waited.

"If she were here, Penny would enjoy your feisty ways.

She'd have struck a deal to welcome us in Hunter's clan because she'd fit right in with that crew and somehow she would have dragged me along. Instead, look at the mess I'm making. No one will call me family here. My gosh…" His face winced while he took several breaths. "I sound like a love-sick fool."

"What happened to this woman you fell into?"

"We were in ruins, scavenging for a safe place to wait out a storm and a quake caused the walls to collapse on us." He scratched the walls of Dragon's Caves. "Buried alive right in front of me. I couldn't dig her out fast enough. Rocks crumbled… And her screams… Gosh, what'd I'd give to forget. To undo it."

"Everything in your world dies." His depressing stories annoyed her.

"Everything except me. As you pointed out, I'm still here, searching for a reason to explain why I was spared. Sometimes, I think that if I found joy inside me once, some form of not-sadness should be possible again."

Avery promised herself to try and be more understanding of his moods. "I'm sorry." She truly was. "I wish to find this happiness, too. I have a spot in my gut…" she showed him where the ache rested along the pit of her stomach, "that longs for an unknown something. I thought maybe this was because I miss my first clan even if I don't remember them. And because I feel so different, even if Saxton Clan accepts me, my place with them is short lived. I have to start a family soon in my own hut, in a new clan."

"Your birth family isn't in the Outlands. I haven't seen anyone in ages." Pax stared in Dragon's Caves at the marble carving of Dragon lining the wall. "But if you need another brother, I can be that." He entered the cave cautiously, braver than she'd be if she'd lost her friend to a cave-in.

"Pax. We're only allowed in these caves to commune with the Creator. This is a sacred place. We have to bury your science in the forest. If the leaders don't see us do this, they'll ask you to leave."

Like usual, he ignored her, lost in his own world. He dropped his bag by the entrance and had his hands on the carved marble. Why did he have to touch everything?

"Wow. I've never seen anything this neat." He made his

way along the wall to the middle of the cave, his hands touching the marble the entire way. The image was symbolic, much like the one carved into the cliff protecting the village.

"This is Dragon, protector and saviour of our people."

"What is this Dragon doing to the man?"

"Some think Dragon created mankind."

Pax gaped at her, traumatized. "Why would they think a beast would do that?"

"Stories say that at the beginning of time, Dragon wandered the lands, a lonely creature. So, he created mankind. Time passed and science grew. Dragon was ashamed of the things mankind did to each other and this world. He hid underground to live alone. But then, when science brought forth the cold, men came to him with a deal. If Dragon would keep them alive, they'd never speak of science again, they'd respect each other and the land. And so, Dragon promised to keep this land warm with his fire-breath. The black pipes continue to spurt out white puffs of smoke that keep the air breathable, and the grey pipes keep the area warm. At the Warming Celebration, he ripens the crops with fire that blows out of this cave. Dragon could have left us to die in the cold since we failed him, but he offered us a second chance. We owe our existence to Dragon and must keep the promise to never bring science into the village."

Pax searched in his bag for one of his drawing tools and traced what he saw into a book while she spoke.

"Long ago, a woman with no hair, white skin like snow, and shiny violet eyes appeared from Dragon's Caves. Just walked out as if Dragon created this perfect being from clay."

He glanced over.

"See these finer carvings in the marble along the edges?" Avery pointed out the details in the frame, but stayed in the entrance. "She had markings like that along her neck. Some say the tattoo was the eye of Dragon and others say the markings were of a paw. They were burned into her skin by Dragon himself to mark her as his. A perfect example of who we need to be. For the first time, the people of Cuma Village saw what Dragon was up to underground. He had created new life since they had failed him. Some thought that perhaps she was sent to replace them, others thought that maybe she was there to teach them. As you can imagine, she was shunned by the clans and they feared her."

"You met this woman with no hair?"

"It was before my time, but the stories are that she ate rocks and drank from our healing waters. She told them of science things and how she believed we could use science to control the sun and the winds. The quakes were crazy while she was here, and soon after her arrival, the pipes stopped working. The waters stopped warming. The pipes grew colder." Avery stared down the hill at her village. "They sent her from the village to die in the Outlands." The idea always mortified Avery. "The elders won't tolerate you being different or breaking the rules."

"Wonder if she was one of Penny's relatives?" he asked. "She had really white skin, like snow-white. And no hair..."

"Might be. Some say they wanted to sacrifice her by putting her in the pit, but Dragon had sent her up so the elders didn't dare."

He gaped, forgetting about his paper.

She pointed to the hole at the back of the cave. "And maybe the elders would have eventually sacrificed her, but the moment she stepped from the village, Dragon warmed the area again. Since then, the elders are careful who they let stay. They don't want to upset Dragon again. Children are usually welcome, but a man like you will have to fit in if you plan to stay. The faster you choose a partner the better, as they'll see hope in this. And above all, you have to prove to Dragon that you're worthy of his second chance." She didn't mention the rule about not being made by Dragon because he was clearly not made of clay. He looked too much like her.

Pax grazed the letters carved into the marbled wall under Dragon. "Do your people read?"

"We don't have much need to read. You had brothers or sisters in the Outlands?"

He replaced his drawing things in his bag and latched the satchel shut. "My sister was young when she wandered off. We never found her. But my best memories are of dancing with her. I'd taught her to play this fun instrument we'd found and she'd run off with it the day she went missing. It's not like here, Avery. Things are not safe in the Outlands. If Dragon keeps you safe, I say, good, stay." Pax rubbed his jaw where Hunter had probably hit him. "I'm tired of fighting, but I don't want to go back to the Outlands." Showing her the pin, he said, "Penny told me once that a pin can fix anything, but she was wrong; I can't find a way to mend the gap she left inside me. I'm in your village, surrounded by people, yet so alone."

That she understood. "This is why we don't get attached. Our relationships better the village." Even saying it, she knew she was wrong. She couldn't see herself sharing a mat with Jacob.

"I can't help how I feel."

The seeing-eye on the wall moved, making them jump.

Avery placed her hands behind her head. "Dragon is watching us. Close your eyes and ask Dragon to send you a new woman. Maybe he'll make you one."

"I don't want a new one. I was *everything* with Penny."

She allowed him a moment of peace, to find his strength again. Suddenly, Pax blurted out, "So what does Dragon eat underground?" Leave it to Pax to think about food.

"I don't know," she admitted. "If he's immortal maybe he doesn't eat."

"Well, if he's rumbling around under the earth making heat, he's alive and needs food. Everything alive has to eat." He wandered over to peer in the hole at the far end of Dragon's Caves. "Is this where the woman came from? You ever go down this pit?" He looked ready to explore the shaft himself.

"We don't go near it."

Staring in the pit for a bit, he said, "We should. Might be answers. I see light. Doesn't that make you curious? Penny used to figure out how gadgets made those beams. Watching her work was neat."

"Get away from the pit."

He listened, but she didn't doubt that he'd ask her about the pit again. Pax strolled to the map carved into the rock and traced his fingers over it. The idiot couldn't leave anything untouched, as if he had to see things through his fingertips. Still, the map was harmless for him to touch, so she said, "It tells the tale of Dragon's world, before he hid away underground. See those numbers along the side, that's the date the map was made." While Avery talked, Pax ran his fingers over the numbers she didn't know, tracing each one.

2112. "Cuma Village is marked with an X in the middle of the long rectangle."

"Wow. This is old. This is probably one of the first maps." He nodded, right impressed. "The world lost this shape. Well, it's not how I'm seeing it." She listened closely, for elders said that nomads were skilled map readers. He traced his fingers from the X down. "I travelled this." Once again, Pax pulled out his journal and traced the image to the paper. Then he scribbled over the page with a drawing tool unknown to her people. She watched him work, fascinated with the new knowledge he'd bring to the village.

"After I lost Penny, I thought I was the last man alive but when I see your map, there's a lot of world left to explore. If I can't stay, maybe I'll travel these other areas." He pointed to the side of his paper. "Maybe there are other places like this one with clear skies and warm lands." He leaned against the grey pipe, thoughtful. The contact made a small shaker.

"Pax, never touch the pipes," Avery snapped, her fists tight.

He stepped forward to study the pipes coiling around Dragon's Caves. "You think I caused that mini-quake by touching the pipe?"

"Yes."

He bit his bottom lip and his eyes ran over the pipe. "These pipes are in incredible shape. Do you ever fix them? Replace them?"

She glanced around to make sure they were alone. "There are stories about how sometimes pipes are changed during the night. I've never seen that myself, but it'd be amazing to wake up to new pipes, don't ya think?"

His shoulders sank inward and he looked at his feet. "Avery, your stories are..." he took a deep breath, "impossible."

She clenched her fists. *He called her a liar.*

"I'm not the brightest guy, but come on, Avery. Women aren't made of clay, pipes don't fix themselves, and some beast isn't hiding away underground to create more men and women because he messed up the first batch. More than likely this hairless woman was kicked from her village because she looked different and hid out here. Penny said people were quick to judge her. Always bugged me because she was beautiful and shouldn't have had to hide this way. I know you desperately want me to fit in around here, but what I loved about Penny was that she didn't try to fit in. She was proud of who she was. It's a hard thing to live up to, but I'd like to just be me, if that's all right."

Peering over her shoulder, Avery said, "You have to fit in or you'll be asked to leave. Come with me. They're watching and want to see us head to the forest."

As Avery and Pax passed the fishing waters and the waterfalls along the side of Dragon's Caves, Avery enjoyed the warmer air coming off the blue pipes that curved through the river making waterfalls and pools. Over the years, each clan had decorated the rocks giving the area a creative allure she found peaceful.

Pax stopped to take in the scene. The artwork along the cliffs and the painted rocks, the planned flower gardens, and the colourful sculptures were made by the clans over time to document their good years. They loved to decorate their homes, their dishes and pots, and especially their clothes. Making the world colourful was exciting.

"Wow." Pax breathed the word with reverence. His reaction made her proud. "Maybe it's not so horrible here. This is full of life. The water's so sparkling blue. Is that normal? I've never seen water this blue. Green, sure. Brown, mostly. This crystal whitish-blue is... Wow."

Much to her shock, he rushed toward the water and dived in, stripping along the way. Avery shook her head. What was wrong with this guy? Marching up to him while gathering his clothes, she approached the water. He was down the river swimming and exploring. She dropped his clothes along the side, then swung his bag over her shoulder. "This blue means they're life ponds and we can eat the fish from here. We don't swim in them. Get dressed and follow me. I'll show you where you can swim. We have to make a hike through the forest." She turned her back on him and marched up the hill.

He caught up to her, his hair dripping. "Sorry, that place was awesome, I couldn't help myself."

His excitement was contagious as she rushed Pax through the woods. Pipes vented out of the ground in spots. During a Warming Ceremony, flames blew from those vents which kept the area light in vegetation. Pax was exploring like a big fool. She let him since this area was currently safe to explore and inside the protection of the warming pipes.

Once they arrived at the healing pond, Pax stared, frozen. "What the heck is that golden pipe in the middle of the water?"

The pipe bubbled over with golden liquid. The pond around the pipe was large enough for swimming and the water sparkled yellow. "That's the healing pond." Long grasses surrounded the water and a light smoke floated off the pool, dancing in the air. The denser forest was behind the pond and where they'd bury his science things.

Pax licked his lips. "The air tastes spicy." He rubbed his hand along his face again.

"The water isn't deep, go on, rush in and get healed up, maybe it'll fix that love sickness of yours."

He didn't move. "This is weird water. Why is it gold?"

The golden liquid flowed warm and soft. The gold sparkles had a spicy smell and she inhaled the scent deeply, letting the healing air cleanse her lungs. "You can drink it, bathe in it. It's for healing. When we don't feel well we come straight here and most times the waters help. Mother Roselle even keeps a bit in the hut in case illness strikes. We're not supposed to steal water, but in small containers, everyone looks the other way and Dragon hasn't grumbled about it."

Avery enjoyed swimming in these waters but she let him undress. While he was busy, she stole his bag to the wooded area and dumped the things on the grass. The cliffs loomed over them, casting a shadow on the spot. On her knees, Avery replaced the dry bread she'd stuffed in the bag for Pax this morning, his notebook, then the other things that looked harmless.

With a quick glance at Pax, she caught the back of him strutting slowly in the healing water. "You coming in?" he asked.

"Not until I get this science buried."

"I'm sorry those things upset you. They are harmless but if burying them makes you feel better; do what you must, just let me know where they are so I can collect them when I leave."

He was leaving? Avery wasn't sure why that distressed her. Many nomads passed through. Yet having someone who looked like her in the village helped her feel at home. Which was stupid, really.

He dived in and the sun made his skin gleam under the water. Then he broke through the surface and faced the sun with his eyes closed. "This pipe goes straight down. It's so warm. This is amazing. You know what I think? This is science stuff, and you're a bunch of pretenders, acting like you hate science so I move on my way, but here you are, technical geniuses. Come on, Avery, tell me how you do this." He actually scooted up the side of the pipe and stuck his hand inside it. The flowing water spurted up.

"Stop that. Enjoy the gifts Dragon provides for the chosen ones."

Pax dropped into the water. "The sun is so pleasing. I forget sometimes how my skin sucks up the warmth."

"You didn't see sun in the Outlands?" His skin was paler than hers.

"Not much. Do you get burning rains?"

She grabbed a rock to dig a hole. "We hardly get rains but when we do they're refreshing."

"Grab a pine cone to toss around when you come in."

"In a moment." One of the boxes in the pile was pink and distracting her. Finally, Avery picked the container up and shook the box, then she flipped it open, amazed at the gadgets inside. She'd never studied science objects so closely and hoped Dragon would forgive her.

"Any idea what'll happen to me at this Warm-up party? Will I get to stay?"

"The Warming is a ritual, not a party," Avery reminded him. "It's essential for keeping the peace between the clans. After the flames warm the lands and ripen the crops, we have a celebration. During this time each clan states what they plan to offer the village and what they need in return until the next celebration which will be the Moon Festival."

"Oh, I get it. This is why the deals are going on. Saxton needs land and food, but Berry needs this curse broken. So, they go to each clan and see who they'll work with for the next bit and what that'll cost them. Wow. I never settled down in one spot long enough to make long-term deals. I mean, I trade my gadgets sometimes for something I need, like a coat or boots. But not much of that going on these days. Not sure where everyone went."

His words enlightened a truth she'd ignored. *Trading.* Avery was nothing but a commodity in this Warming Celebration's deals. She had no choice but to accept Jacob's offer. This would give her brothers their own land and as much food as they needed. The union would bond rivalling clans and make them stronger. The clans would grow in peace. If she refused, the tension between the two clans would increase. The curse might get worse and steal Kanya, then Hunter would be upset with her. Or Dragon might even smite Avery with one of those falling rocks.

With a heavy sigh, she turned her attention back to the device that fit in her palm. The buttons were inscribed with numbers like the map, but the entire gadget popped apart so she could stare at the small shiny pipe that hid inside. "Where did you find this?"

"In the Outlands. Lots of gadgets in the ruins."

She glanced up, no idea how something so simple could have brought about the destruction of the world.

"The side of the pipe, by the entrance has a box like this attached to it. This isn't science." Or was Pax right and their pipes were science? She was confused as she stared at the small box.

"Let's say you're right, Avery, what if Dragon is trapped? Don't you think he's gonna be pissed when his food runs out?"

Actually, that fear ran constantly through her mind. What *would* happen if Dragon died?

LINS

During the same breaths
Underground, Mainframe Seven

Using the sleeve from her eRobe, Lins gently wiped the smudge on the monitor. That last quake had damaged the energy reservoirs and she was trying to come up with a solution so they didn't all die a slow painful death as their energy depleted.

"Thank you, Elite Lins. That smudge was bothering me."

Nogard was already working on the low-energy problem in her logical way; by using them to find answers. Protector Owen was sent to find trees, an ancient energy source that Lins was sure had died off in the Big Freeze of 2112. He wasn't chosen for this task on a whim. What did he know? What had his studies revealed? Being impulsive like he was, he was already in the pipes, searching. But before leaving, he'd removed the devices from behind his ear, disconnecting from the system. She watched him on the camera as he cut them out effortlessly. Then he healed himself with a medic-pen and broke into the pipes.

Lins was about to pull up Owen's studies but the air blowing back at her from the mainframe gave her pause. "You perfected your breathing program?" Lins stood back and watched the mainframe breathe. The action was created by a program, but Nogard had wanted to feel air rush through her mainframe and so Lins had installed the program and let Nogard work on it. Seeing her program in motion was impressive. A-life was breathing.

Lins was connected to Nogard emotionally through the eRobe and could *feel* her life but this was exciting. A-life was an entirely different species yet she could mimic certain traits they had as if desperate to fit in with the only lifeforms she had anything in common with.

The Collective was also hard at work. Lins watched the collection of great minds on the side screen as they researched, pulsating as one, flashing through possible energy sources and their benefits. So much knowledge contained in the life-drive. She touched the screen, wondering if her parents were still themselves or some type of new life.

Soothing gases entered the chamber to regulate Lins' worry and anxiety, even though she appeared calm as she stared back at herself, seeing her own violet eyes in the dark monitor where the Collective shared their findings.

"I need your help."

"Of course." As an elite, her connection to Nogard was through the eRobe. Their bond was purely emotional and ended when Lins removed the garment. Lins placed her hand on the panel, eager to help fix their energy crisis.

"I am about to die. Bring me to Mainframe One to meet my creator. Perhaps he can save me." The eRobe sizzled with the request and Lins felt a strange sensation. An overpowering urge to do exactly that.

"How do you know about…your creator?"

"Take me to Dragon." The request fired through Lins making her want to seek action but she fought the impulse because Nogard was not supposed to know about the ghost program that elites like Lins used to override her programs. And for sure, Dragon was not her creator.

"He can help."

Curious what Nogard had found out, Lins ordered, "Show me the path." A few maps flashed on-screen yet looking at them wasn't important because this information was suddenly a part of her. She had to seek out Dragon… She stared at herself in the monitor before reaching for the life-drive. Why was the light making her eyes solid grey? Weird. Yet she liked them that way and studied her reflection as if seeing herself for the first time.

A part of her worked on disconnecting the life-drive but her mind had a pulsating nagging urge to send the maps to Shandra as a safety. Finally, she fired them off to her sister without a message or a warning. Then like Owen, she broke into the pipes and scurried off.

AVERY

During the same breaths
Above ground, by the healing pond

Pax was still swimming as Avery opened another box full of forbidden science gadgets. A long rumble shook the earth, reminding her of how forbidden touching these gadgets was. She glanced up at the cliff, shocked by the intensity of the warning.

Pax scrambled to shore as if the water might gobble him up.

The entire ocean side of the cliff broke away, ripping out pipes and strange equipment she caught in a glimpse as the rocks crumbled into the waiting ocean below.

It was an endless slow rumble as she gawked.

"Yikes…" Pax stared from the bank. "What the heck was that?" In the same breath, the pipe behind him stopped spurting golden water. They both glanced at it, shocked by everything from the earth shaking to the damaged cliffs, and now by the pipe stopping its endless spouting.

"Why'd the flow stop?" Pax asked. "Does the pipe do that often?"

Avery stood, holding one of his gadgets. "The earthquake must have done something."

"Something all right. Did you see the chunk that fell to the ocean? Good thing the collapse wasn't the village side or we'd be dead." Pax took a deep breath and dove down along the pipe in the center of the water.

When he surfaced, his head was covered in golden flakes. "The pipe goes into the ground."

Avery frowned. How had they upset Dragon? Was she to blame for touching the science? She shoved one of the boxes in the hole, but the hole wasn't deep enough to fit them all so she tossed the others back in his bag, shoving them at the bottom so no one would know. "We better get back and warn the elders that the pipe stopped. This might be serious. Exit through those bushes and let them rub against your skin to shake the golden flakes off so they return to the waters with the next rains. Then dig up one of the plants at the root of the large oak tree to the left and eat it."

He did as she'd instructed while Avery gathered his garments to meet him in the bushes.

She found Pax kneeling, digging. "These are garlic roots." He showed her one as if she'd never seen them before. He swallowed it, then stood before her, naked and sure of himself. Being raised in a house full of boys, she was used to them parading around naked. They hated clothes. But her eyes locked on the mark burned into his arm. "The flame of life," she mumbled.

"You like my tattoo? Wild, eh? Penny made it."

"Did anyone see that?" She was unable to move, thinking about who might have seen him without clothes. The tic in her eye pulsed. "That's a mark from Dragon like the clay-woman had. Did Dragon send you? Is he mad at us for keeping you here? Do you know why he stopped the water? Has he sent you with these gadgets to tempt us to use them? Are you… Are you Dragon?"

"What? No." He reached for his clothes. "Penny made this. We found a device that had the emblem on it. We heated the emblem and branded the metal into my skin. Hurt like hell, but I thought the effect was neat."

"Don't show those markings to anyone." Avery flung around to grab his bag, but much to her horror, there stood Jacob Berry, arms crossed, a fire in his eyes.

YODAN

A few breaths later
Underground, Quadrant H: closed

The biggest quake they'd ever felt hit when they were in front of Match's old family chamber. Match and Yodan were slapped up against the wall waiting for the rumbling to stop. Thankfully, they'd had time to slip their Oxy-air on.

Dust inhibited their view in the closed quadrant but when the rumbling stopped, their breathing returned to normal, and Match let out a calming breath.

Since Nogard didn't release calming gases in closed quadrants, the poignant effect of grief and fear crashed on Yodan. This type of freedom created exhilarating shivers that fired over him.

Match checked his white lifesuit for supplies, a habit that always ended with his fingers grazing the extra brown and gold stripes along the side that marked him as elite. The gesture was quick, but Yodan recognized his panic tics.

With a glance over his shoulder, as if anyone would stop Match from doing anything, he opened the door to his old family chamber using a by-pass that connected from the power of his SHARP. Then he slipped in the chamber, leaving the door open for Yodan to follow. "My brother is supposed to steal us a few medic-pens from Medic Jon. I told your sisters and him to meet us here."

By flaring his pen-light, Yodan brought a warm glow to the room.

A creature was sprawled out in Match's old sleeping pod. The strange white beast stretched and jumped out of the pod, making its way toward them.

"What in all these rocks is that thing coming toward us?" Yodan backed up, ready to bolt. "Is that a...a cat?" The creature was shaped like the image from his reading assignment, only this cat was white.

"Shandra sneaked it in while the cameras were down." He petted the cat. "One of those above ground camera's captured an image of an orange one, which means if a cat lives above ground yet can find this place from the surface, then we can find its place."

He had a cat hidden in a closed quadrant? "Don't touch that thing!"

"It likes us." Match knelt to grab something off a shelf and the cat strutted in front of him. "Come pet it. The animal has velvety fur. Probably to adapt to the frigid temperatures above ground. Like you, this cat was not created in our labs yet here it is. Means we don't need Nogard to survive. Others have broken from the system and never returned."

The cat made a strange bawling sound as if reinforcing his statement.

Yodan reached for the feline. The cat arched toward him and rubbed against his fingers making Yodan pull away, shocked. "He's soft and warm, kind of frisky. He clearly enjoys the company of people." Which was weird because none of the other creatures they studied were friendly to their species. Yodan fought the urge to rub the hairiness over his face. "Does this strange beast talk more than that? Can he think? Can I communicate with him?"

"Fun sounds rumble from its belly." Match left the cat with Yodan and opened his old storage closet. Despite this quadrant being evacuated, his storage unit was fully stocked with supplies he quickly moved to several bags.

Yodan examined the cat's paw, thoughtful. Then the cat strolled onto Yodan's legs. Amazed, Yodan moved in closer and hair brushed his sensitive cheek, making him jump. In a world built with technology, simple things like this creature made him question Nogard's perfect system. The cat must have found him equally curious because he let out a bawling sound.

"What did he say?" Yodan asked.

"I don't speak Cat."

Yodan liked the plushness and pushed his face near the cat. "You find any other neat things during your explorations?"

Without a word, Match pulled a strange cut rock from his side pocket and offered it to Yodan, as if it were a gift.

"Wow." Shocked by the gem in the rock, Yodan grabbed it. The colour was the same as the eyes of the hairy man he'd seen on the SHARP from the above ground camera. Pointing his pen-light on it, he stole a better look. Maybe they were from the same system.

"It's yours, a gift Shandra and I give to you, because we trust you with not only our lives but the lives of all those we care about." Match met his eyes. "Give it to someone you trust one day." He smirked. "Hopefully, someone not from this system but our new one."

He should give it right back, since Match was the only guy he trusted. Everyone knew Match would give his life to protect them. But this was symbolic and with it a weight fell on his shoulders. All his studies about other systems, past life above ground, how they evolved... What if his theories were wrong? Doubt settled in his gut. "Maybe it'll bring me luck," he mumbled.

"Luck doesn't exist, Yodan."

"I know you like facts, Match, but with my eyes I see incredible detail at ridiculous speeds, yet I don't see everything. Which leads me to logically believe that there are probably things I can't see that do exist and luck is one of them." He slipped the rock in his side pocket over his red prodigy stripes.

Someone called weakly, "Match! Are you here?"

"Shandra?"

"I don't feel so well." Which was common these days. She'd told Yodan that she'd caught a tummy bug and Nogard didn't have a treatment for the unknown virus.

Match stumbled out the door toward her voice so fast, he tripped. Yodan had to help him up, but he pushed Yodan's hands off, rushing to her aid.

MATCH

A few breaths later
Underground, Quadrant H: closed

Running through the closed quadrant with Shandra in his arms, Match rushed toward the mainframe walkways at the other end. Those doors were always open and well-monitored by drones who'd find him someone trustworthy to help. Like Lins. Or Medic Jon or Medic Brisk... He mentally went down a list of people he could trust with Shandra's health.

"Slow down," Yodan hollered after him, rushing to keep up, even the blasted cat followed as if this were a parade and not his life falling apart.

"She needs a healing bay," Match lied. He couldn't take her to a healing bay. What in all these levels was wrong with her? What if Nogard had infiltrated her? He needed to check if the illegal blocks had fallen off the Exchanger and Connector behind her ear, but he didn't dare stop until he found her an active Bench of Life.

"Match," Shandra mumbled against his white lifesuit. Despite his training to remain calm, his insides tightened when she breathed his name. He shouldn't have even let her come back to the system. Then again, he never would have guessed that Nogard might be walking around as one of them.

Match glanced over his shoulder at Yodan who had the bags and was slowing down but still following.

Match had to keep this woman and the life she carried safe. His child. All he knew.

If Nogard scanned her, tested her urine, even monitored her heart rate, she'd be reprogrammed. She'd forget who he was and go off with Owen-the-great, this time maybe forever.

He studied her face, her lips, and the smudge of mud on her cheek. Emergency light from the mainframe walkway filtered in through the glass windows. "Why is the mainframe on emergency lighting?" he demanded, the fear making his voice too stern, because he knew. His watch had warned him that a countdown had started. Dragon would have cut Nogard off from her energy source. Explained the monster quakes.

He hated being right.

"Nogard's dead." Her whisper was so quiet, Match had to look at her for confirmation as he set her on the Bench of Life.

From the disorder in the walkway, there was obviously extensive damage to the mainframe. But A-life wouldn't be dead. No. She was in one of them looking for a way to survive. Her programming was simple: live. If Nogard lived, they lived.

"Yodan, check the monitors in the mainframe." Where in all these levels would he lead them?

Yodan dropped the bags by the Bench of Life and rushed to the panel near the door.

Match dug out a new Oxy-air mask. He helped Shandra put the mask on and she took several deep breaths while he waited on his knees beside her. His hand was automatically on her stomach. "Better?" He ran his other hand along her cheek toward the eTatt to check if the illegals were removed but when his fingers felt scar tissue, he yanked his hand away to see what she'd done.

"You disconnected?" He'd thought that disconnecting from the system would kill them. "You removed your Connector and your Exchanger? How?"

Was she dying?

"Medic Brisk helped me. She found a way using a metal device that neutralized it." She held his hand and kissed the fingers. "I went back for this. This is for you." She pushed a gold band against his palm. "Was our father's. He displayed the ring over the door to our family chamber as a symbol. The circle means never ending. The gold symbolizes strength and endurance. And if you read the engravings on the inside…"

What was she telling him? Match tilted the band to the light from the mainframe workstation so he could read the inscription for himself. "Protector, friend, father." Match met her proud eyes, terrified of failing this woman.

"I won't fail you," he promised.

Yodan returned from the panel. "There's no reading on the panel but out the window you can see that the mainframe is full of youths." Youths weren't normally allowed in the mainframe. "Those connected to the system are dying.

Bodies are collapsing everywhere." Yodan activated his emergency D-light and shone the healing rays on Shandra as he spoke. She snagged the device for herself, soaking in the rays, which was something Match should have thought of doing, but he was panicking. Frustrated with himself, he tightened his hands into a fist, needing to do something with them so the flames didn't show his distress. The ring warmed in his hand.

The cat jumped on the Bench of Life to rub against Shandra's leg. "It bothering you?" Match asked.

"It's a comfort," Shandra said. "I feel better." She brushed Match's face, staring in his eyes. "You should help the others. They'll need you."

Match gently placed the ring on her finger. "My home is where you are. Every breath we take, will be as one, which means they need *us*." Giving her the ring back was a symbolic gesture uniting them, because he would always choose her.

Shandra stared in his eyes. "One day, Rawlings, I will hear you laugh." He beamed when she called him by his birth name instead of his nickname.

"Check my SHARP," Shandra said. "Lins sent us a path to Mainframe One. It's from the FIRE pit and clearly where she wants us to go."

Yodan glanced up. "What? We're going down the FIRE pit before a FIRE Ceremony to find some old system? You can't be serious?"

"If Nogard is really disconnected, there might not be a FIRE cleansing now," Match pointed out but he didn't know enough. He couldn't risk them being incinerated but waiting too long meant they'd be terminated. He needed a *plan!*

Yodan clearly didn't like any of this. "We need Lins."

Match would like to believe she'd find them, because she always put her family first, but lately, the eRobe had her acting weird. And what if Nogard infiltrated her and knew all Lins knew?

Yodan glanced at the window to the mainframe station, his worry painful to watch. "She might be buried in that mess."

Match jumped to action. "You're sure Nogard isn't responding?" They'd have to go back into the system.

"Nothing."

"We'll split up. I'd like to know where Nogard is." He explained what had happened to update Shandra. "So we're looking for someone with grey eyes. Yodan get your digging gear out and go for Lins. I'll get my brother. We'll meet at the FIRE chamber and start our evacuation immediately." They had the bags they needed and in this chaos, leaving would be easy.

"And what if the FIRE Ceremony still happens?"

Match glanced at his watch. The light had changed from red to white. While winding it, he pushed the old watch against his skin, absorbing the pulse from the healing metals as they warmed against his wrist. According to his watch, the FIRE Ceremony wouldn't be long and matched the new countdown. "Trust me like I trust you, Yodan. I always have a plan. Meet me at the FIRE Chamber."

Then he asked Shandra, "Ready?"

She sipped minerals, trying to get up.

Someone knocked on the window from the mainframe walkway, making him jump. Match glanced over. Andret stared at him through the glass. He was their age, the best engineer in training Match had ever worked with.

"I have to talk to Andret," Match told Shandra and left her on the safety of the bench to touch the glass between Andret and him. The panel was soundproof, but he felt Andret's words as he spoke against the pane.

Hilt, Andret's best friend, training partner, and the guy he planned to start a family unit with, marched a crew by, setting people to work.

Match offered a curt nod to Hilt who nodded back. Then to Andret he stared long and hard before agreeing to what he wanted.

He wanted Match to call an evacuation. Everyone. As elite, he could make this call, but an evacuation was normally done with a detailed plan and lot of support. "Andret has teams bringing survivors to the FIRE Chambers. He's going with his crew for the life-drive and wants to meet us at 0050. He confirms that the system is down."

"We're gonna evacuate the cities?" Yodan whispered, watching them march by on their mission.

"If we find anyone with grey eyes..." He was close to Yodan, whispering. "How do we kill Nogard without harming the victim? Can Artificial-life die?"

Yodan stared at him not answering.

"Give me facts," Match said to Yodan. "I don't want your theories or ideas. Facts. I have to make a decision that will affect the survival of our people."

Yodan took a deep breath. "Nogard has evolved over the life-cycles. In a sense, each time she moved to a new mainframe, she left the old one to become something new. In her current mainframe or version of life, she's grown to experience emotions because she wants to fit in with us, be like us. She is not like us. Nogard is her own species. What is alive, will one day die. But what does it mean to die if you simply come back in an upgraded version?"

"So what is Nogard's next life-cycle? To jump from one of us to the other?"

"I have no more facts to share. The rest are theories. If Nogard can move from one mainframe to another and now into us, why can't we adapt to other systems as well? What if the Big Freeze didn't kill off life, it just changed to survive? If Nogard read my mind, she knows I plan to find out. She could have killed me to stop me. What if she wants us to find another system because this one was dying? What if she couldn't wait for a new mainframe so she broke code and made herself a temporary one?"

"Then she would have killed me, or I'd prevent her from doing so." Unless Nogard needed Match for something? What?

Match pulled out his glass cutter and cut them a hole into the mainframe station. Then he grabbed the bags and waited for Shandra.

Yodan slipped out. "I'll find Lins."

Match watched him vanish down the dark corridor. Screams haunted the area. "Emergency power is already running low," he told Shandra as she joined him, still moving slowly. Match checked his watch again since the giant life clock at the center of the mainframe was out. The countdown had him nervous. He was supposed to do something to fix this mess but he had no idea what.

The walkway should be bustling with life but only youths rushed toward Mainframe Seven. Not connected to the system, the deaths didn't haunt youths. Each had a goal in such an event and he watched them work with speed, their training reinforced by the hard hook-ups they'd received in their sleeping pods.

"What is my place in such an event? Why kill Madeline but leave me alive?" he mumbled to Shandra, the thought nagging him. He was missing something. He had trained to do everything, yet nothing. Save the youths, inventory people and supplies, evacuate to lower quadrants. He had a thousand orders ringing in his brain, yet the only one he heard was *protect his family*. He squeezed Shandra's hand, prepared to die to keep her and their child safe.

Shandra whispered, "Trust your gut, Match. You and Lins were chosen to live without devices in you for a reason."

The cat bawled at him as if shocked by the change in sounds in the mainframe. If a cat could survive the cold and find a way to their cities, surely they could figure out how to find a way to the surface and survive also.

Shandra stepped behind him, frail, but she hated when he was overprotective so Match pretended she was fine even though he was more alert than he'd ever been.

"Nogard?" he called, checking if she was there.

She didn't respond.

Youth rushed by with a nod to him. With the adults and questers down, he was among the oldest, the best trained, and even if he didn't want the responsibility, he was elite.

A woman in a digger lifesuit stumbled forward and gripped Match's arm, shaking.

"Let me remove your Connector," Match offered since that had kept Shandra alive. He pinned the woman to the wall and using his laser he disabled it. Her eyes rolled back and she collapsed in his arms.

Shandra helped him prop her up and checked the lifelines on her cuffs. "She'll be missed," Shandra said.

"I killed her?" Match was mortified. He'd wanted to help.

Shandra placed a hand on his shoulder, grounding him. Softly, she reminded him, "She was dying. You did what you could. Medic Brisk used a metal tool to remove my device. Perhaps we need that?"

He glanced around at the chaos, feeling the depth of this loss. Where was his brother? Hopefully, Jon and he had figured out how to remove their devices and were helping others. He could use solid advice from his brother right now and regretted lying to him earlier about why he wanted to leave the system.

Shandra's grip tightened around Match's arm then weakened as she collapsed against him.

YODAN

During the same breaths
Underground, Mainframe Seven

The cave-in had blocked the entrance to the mainframe and a crew was working to clear the area. Yodan had wanted freedom from Nogard's rules, but not at this cost. Not at the price of these innocent minds, this anarchy, the loss of the entire system. His gut tightened. Was Lins trapped? Lights flickered as power depleted. Soon their air quality would be noticeably worse, but air was the last to shut down.

"Whoa." Andret grabbed Yodan. "Where are you going? This area is unstable."

"My sister's in the mainframe chamber."

"Doubt that. No life is reported in the mainframe. I'll get the life-drive in case Nogard can be revived, but the crew has to stabilize the area first."

His team worked, installing beams and removing rubble. Hilt stood near Andret, staring at Yodan, clearly not about to let him pass.

Yodan explained to them, "Lins is an elite, there wouldn't be anything to monitor."

"Strap him up, he can follow me in," Hilt said, not wasting a breath to debate. Yodan had trained with this crew a few times, but he was still nervous when Hilt handed him gear.

"I'm going in first." Andret slipped into the passageway his team had prepared. Yodan followed once he wore the gear Hilt had offered.

The area was tight but reinforced and well-protected by a strong box. When they entered the mainframe, debris was minimal and Yodan studied the area using his pen-light. He'd never been in Mainframe Seven but the general lack of humming weighed heavily on his thoughts as if he couldn't think without the background noise.

The panels were unlit and Andret slid under them for the life-drive. Hilt undid a panel and pulled out a few chips.

"The life-drive is missing," Andret announced.

"Got the Exchangers and the Connector chips," Hilt said as if someone was checking things off for them.

"Where would Lins go?" Panicked, Yodan searched the room, taking in details with his hyper-vision. "There. Lins went up that silver pipe, the access door is slightly open. And she left a smudge on the rock where she pushed off to jump in."

Yodan activated the wall Exchanger that made announcements through the entire system. It was only for emergencies. "Match? Lins went in a pipe. Do I go after her?"

Nothing. He pushed the button again. Andret grabbed his hand to stop him. "We only have emergency power. I don't know for how long either. Entire system is in shutdown."

Yodan had no training for unplanned shutdowns. "What's the protocol? Do I go after her?" He wanted to go after her.

"My protocol is to ensure the life-drive gets in the hands of an elite. If your sister took the life-drive and ran, I'm good with that. Someone will have her location."

"Yeah, she sent Shandra a map to the surface through a tunnel we can access in the FIRE pit."

"Then that's how we go," Andret was firm.

"We have to gather the medics," Hilt said, as if a new mission came to him.

Yodan liked how neat and tidy their training was. Like a checklist they went down in an emergency. One focus and when that task was done, they moved onto the next. Yodan's training was nothing like this and this chaos enforced how messed up he felt, seeing too much and theorizing things he couldn't voice.

Leaving the mainframe, Yodan asked, "Why can't the medics help themselves?"

Andret answered, "The healing bay in Quadrant F has caved in. Where have you been?"

Oh no. He moved faster. "I was in a closed quadrant. Match's brother was in the healing bay getting medic-pens. Jon... I mean Medic Jon would be there..."

PAX

A few breaths later
Above ground, Cuma Village

Pax followed that elder Jacob-guy and Avery back to the village. Avery had his pack and was freaking out over nothing. Why were his tattoos such a big deal?

"I didn't do anything," Pax mumbled for the hundredth time. Finally, he grabbed his bag from Avery, frustrated that Avery and Jacob were so overdramatic.

He was leaving this village. Enough of their stupidity. This place erupted with too much tension, too many rules, and he'd never be accepted as one of them.

He planned to storm through the village and leave without a word. Yup. Leave. He was talking himself up like this, because damn, leaving the warmth would be hard.

Maybe he could camp out in the ruins down the hill where the snow was scarce. He'd already stayed there a few nights before approaching the village.

When they returned to the village, everyone was out, staring at the black pipes that extended out of the cliffs. Usually these pipes spouted white puffs of smoke, but nothing came from them now. Seeing them so barren and inactive swelled a deep panic in the group, making them even more nuts and Pax couldn't make any sense of their comments.

The elder Fewerter-guy prayed to the warming pipes, facing the science thing that Avery called the Eye of Dragon at the entrance of the Caves. "Oh Giver of Life, hear the cry of your people. We seek to appease your displeasure. Give us a sign as to what you want from us. We are truly humble as we look on all you give us. Oh Great Dragon, Warmer of the Pipes, show us mercy. We are grateful that you provide for us."

"He did this," Jacob accused, pointing to Pax like he was a monster come to devour them.

Great. Pax's father had warned him to watch encampments with too many men. He said they tended to fight each other and only the patient would survive.

"I'm leaving anyway," Pax informed them, keeping step.

Suddenly, Hunter and Saxton were in his path, blocking him from leaving. *Urgh.* "Let me pass."

Avery was at his side and whispered, "Fewerter was the elder who took Saxton and Hunter in when they arrived at Cuma Village. He's the oldest in the village. He'll listen. Don't leave until you're asked to."

Then to the crowd, she said, "Pax didn't do anything. He was with me. We saw the rocks crack and chunks fell into the water."

"He has the marking of Dragon on his arm," Jacob added which created gasps and murmurs but Saxton was quick to tell them to shut up.

Hmm. Pax was liking Saxton more and more.

"Is this true?" Fewerter asked, looking more curious than afraid. "Did you disrespect Dragon by marking your body or were you sent to check on us by Dragon?"

Others gasped, clearly they hadn't considered this possibility. Yeah. They might be nicer to him now.

Pax took his bag off, staring at the group. "Listen, I was gonna leave, but I see you're freaking out. I've seen countless ruins, a lot of pipes like this making underground mazes. I've even seen that Eye thing before. I'm good at mapping areas. How about I go in that pit and see what's wrong with Dragon? Maybe all you need is to fix something or feed him."

"He knows how to appease Dragon," Elder Jenica announced to the group and the tension dissipated, but that wasn't what Pax had said. "Without the Warming Ceremony our crops won't ripen and we'll starve. Already, the skies cloud over and the air chills. If he can talk to Dragon and restore things, he should."

Talk to Dragon? Were these people for real? What was with all the drama? The pipes just stopped. They might start again. Didn't they understand that they had science keeping them alive? Science wasn't a miracle. This technology needed to be maintained. Pax had no idea how to do that, but damn, Penny had shown him neat things. If they could calm the hell down and look at it, sometimes the answer wasn't that hard to figure out.

"Pax, what are you doing?" Avery grabbed his arm. "You

can't go in. No one ever comes out."

"Any objections to him going in the pit to investigate what has Dragon so angry?" Fewerter asked. His eyes lingered on each leader who, each in their turn, shook their heads.

"Then it shall be done." A group of strong arms came around Pax, leading him off as if he might run away. The caves loomed before him like a giant mouth wanting to gobble him up.

Avery screamed.

Pax glanced back to see Saxton and Stefe restraining her. Gosh, he hoped she didn't do something stupid. "I'm fine," he called to her, not struggling. "I can walk." Still they carried him. "I'm not afraid to go in a pit with a light." Working technology meant people. And really, travelling warm pipes was better than freezing his ass off in the Outlands.

YODAN

During the same breaths
Underground, Healing Bay F

Running down the corridor of Quadrant F to Healing Bay F, Yodan was shocked by the disorder. The entire healing bay had caved in and youths were digging for survivors. Yodan turned his Exchanger on to hear any calls for help, but the device behind his ear was dead.

No one older than their eighteenth FIRE Ceremony was active, forcing Yodan to accept that maybe everyone with a Connector had died with Nogard.

Distressed, Yodan searched for a familiar face. He found Shandra piling rocks by an entrance with the cat making rumbling sounds at her feet. They'd made a small opening at the top. Shandra handed Yodan a rock then used her laser to cut another free. "Match went in. Medic Jon was at the nursery helping Medic Brisk with an emergency when this collapse happened so he's safe and disconnected but they're the last medics. Andret and Hilt are on a mission to find more. They have a crew digging through to the surgery sector."

Yodan was relieved to hear that Jon was safe. "Last report on Match's brother?" Yodan asked.

Shandra read the reports on her SHARP. Without a power source to charge them, their time with these devices was limited. "Greg was entering sleep mode, delusional from a fever," Shandra told him.

Dread weighed on Yodan as he climbed the pile of debris to the tunnel Match had cleared, wondering why Shandra didn't follow Match and why Greg had a fever when all he came for was to ask his best friend for a medic-pen. Worry settled in as he crawled through the tunnel, seeing many possibilities, the worst being that a virus might have plagued the system. He hated his brain sometimes, but in an event, he was supposed to take these possibilities to a protector or elite.

Yodan continued to crawl in the tight area. "Match? I'm coming." The hole grew bigger and he dropped into a dark room about a metre around, cleared of rubble. How did

Match work so quickly and with such precision?

Yodan fired-up his light-pen by waving the device around, using eMove to power it. He scanned the room for anything his eyes might have missed in the dark. He was in front of the smashed cold medicine cabinet. The strong box inside contained medicine he'd have to rescue.

"Match?"

"Up here. Greg's under this rubble." He was frantically dissolving rock and hard plastic with a highbeam, which was illegal; a weapon that drones stored in their inner core.

"Where in all these rocks did you get a highbeam?"

"Where do you think?"

Match was never one to explain the obvious, but Yodan was shocked. "You smashed open a drone and stole it? What the heck, Match?"

"You have a rope? I'm going straight down."

"Be careful when you get to him, you don't want to dissolve your brother." What was he saying? No one would survive a collapse like this. They shouldn't even be in here. They risked being buried alive. As if to warn them, the earth shook.

Still, Yodan didn't bother pointing out that the area was unstable. Match wasn't stupid, he was freaking out and when Yodan had done this after Madeline's death, Match had brought him to safety. Yodan would have to do the same.

Yodan untied the rope stored over the smashed storage unit. "Here, tie this to you." He tossed one end to Match and tied the other end around himself.

"I'm at the healing pod. The safe cover dropped to protect him. Back up, I'll blast this wall so you can help lift the cover. As long as he can get air, he'll be fine in it. Just give me a sense of direction, I'm turned around."

"Aim this way." Yodan knocked on the wall.

"Back up."

Yodan glanced around, trapped. "I'll crawl back in the hole I came from. Wait." He made his way up and slid in face first, still gripping the rope that tied him to Match.

Much to his surprise Azala was there. Thankfully, his lusting wasn't wild like earlier, and he stared at her, the same annoyed as usual. Why did she always irritate him so?

"I'm safe," he told Match. Then to Azala, Yodan asked, "What are you doing?"

"I came to make sure you don't do anything stupid. Almost a relief to feel that the tension between us is gone. Gosh. To think, I almost kissed someone as gross as you."

"Urgh. Don't move, he has a highbeam."

The earth shook, dropping dust on them, but neither even flinched, waiting.

Yodan slid backwards and dropped in the room to find Match lifting the cover off the healing pod. Debris was heavy on the enclosure and the lid wouldn't budge.

"Greg? Can you hear me?" Match said.

Azala flashed her pen-light in the hole.

"Shandra, I need a medic. Now!" Match panicked.

"I'm coming," Jon's voice echoed through the overhead tunnel with a warmth Yodan had missed. Was their friend back?

Yodan snapped the highbeam from Match and handed the illegal device to Azala. "Dare ya to use it."

She turned the illegal off and set the dangerous item aside. "These are illegal. What we need is Protector Owen to lift this off."

Yodan rolled his eyes then helped clear debris, annoyed with her as usual.

When Medic Jon showed, he helped them slide the cover over—without Owen. Match climbed in the hole with Greg. He was filthy and rubbed dust on his brother's clean white skin. "Greg?"

Jon checked his vitals. "Greg will be missed."

"When?" Match demanded. "When did my brother die? Your best friend. Dammit, Jon. Remember him."

Then Medic Jon did something unlike his drone-like self this past cycle and he rested his hand on Match. "I do." His eyes brimmed with tears that were reflected in the dim light.

"You disconnected?" Match flashed his light behind Medic Jon's ear to check. "It's already scarring over. What the heck are we gonna do?" Match demanded of Jon, breaking down.

Jon stayed somber. "We have to get our people out of this system. Sir Rawlings, you have to pull it together. Look at this, Nogard was treating him for a fever even though I don't see any signs of one in his history."

Match wiped his eyes and stared at the report frozen on the screen. "Explain."

"He was treated for a fever he didn't have. Treatment involves terminal gases during a quake so survivors don't worry about the sick."

"So someone altered the programming telling Nogard he was sick when he wasn't?" Azala asked, as clueless as ever.

"More like Nogard covered a murder," Match snapped, glaring at her as he took back his highbeam.

"She would never!"

Match ignored Azala's ignorance. "Greg came to see you, Jon, for a medic-pen. Where were you? Why did he end up in a healing pod? And who removed your Connector?"

"I left to help Medic Brisk. That's my child she carries and after she removed her devices, she suffered. Once the deaths started, I couldn't focus. All the screams and demands for my skills were too much."

They were down to two disconnected medics. Bile crept up Yodan's throat. "You cut out your own devices? You're as nuts as ever."

Jon nodded. "Come, Sir Rawlings. There's nothing more we can do for Greg. He will be missed, but we must survive if we're to miss him."

'Sir' was the title given to the male protectors of Quma Cities, so why was Medic Jon calling Match that?

Holy mud.

Was that Jon's subtle way of saying Match was their protector? What had happened to the other better qualified candidates? Where the heck was Owen? Had *everyone* died?

Match didn't seem bothered by the title. With a firm jaw, he stared at his brother. The loss was clearly too much for him to process. Match had survived intense training, and seen death over the last cycles, but this was one that would clearly change him. Change them all.

"Match," Yodan nudged him. "We're leaving." Yodan placed a hand on Match's shoulder, more for his own comfort, but Match moved out of the way of the friendly gesture and headed out of the dangerous area.

Yodan glanced in the healing pod. "Medic Jon, can you remove Greg's devices? If Match can keep a copy of Greg's memories, they might help. He needs to know what happened."

Medic Jon set to work.

~A New Breath Awaits~

"I was so busy programming your every breath, I did not realize I could breathe, too."   —*Nogard*

PAX

A few breaths later
Above ground, Dragon's Caves

Pax didn't expect the villagers to toss him into the pit like a sacrifice and was shocked by their violent behaviour. He landed on a grate floor with a bruised side and a sore arm. *Jerks*.

The overhead light vanished.

"I'm fine," Pax called up. "No worries. I'm fine," he mumbled to himself. "Just in a pit."

Avery's screams sent chills over him. He sure hoped she wouldn't do something stupid on his account. "I'm fine, Avery," he called up to her, in case she could hear him. She was a feisty one. Reminded him of his sister so much that looking at her was sometimes hard. Pax was a realist, shaped by his hard life and he knew the chances of his sister surviving a wolf attack and ending up this far north were impossible. Yet he'd seen his share of impossible things. What if? What if *this* was why he was spared? It didn't matter in the end; he could pretend she was his sister. She clearly needed someone to make her feel like she fit in and for some reason, the idea that she'd survived made him feel braver; like he was invincible, too.

Sitting, he stared at the corridor of doors in front of him seeing something more symbolic than they probably were. Still, Pax couldn't help but feel like maybe he should pick a new door and let his past go.

He stood, no idea which door to pick, but the gloomy area brought the bit of light in the distance to life and he focused on it, headed that way. Maybe this was a test to see if he could figure out their technology?

They were a weird bunch, but he liked how they were so close, and he missed people. Really, he couldn't blame them for being protective. These villagers had a good thing going.

The light was over a door with a numbered panel. He pushed on the door but the panel blinked a red light. Why? Did the science gadget-panel thingy want him to do something? Pax pushed the buttons, matching them to the numbers he'd seen on the map since they were the only ones he could think of. 2-1-1-2

The metal door clicked open and he peeked inside, making sure the area was safe before he barged in. Pax had been ambushed plenty of times and wasn't about to let these villagers take him off-guard.

Overhead, along the next wall, a fine pink light pulsated. That in itself was amazing and captured his attention. He'd never seen light coming from a wall. The glow highlighted a corridor made of hard plastic. Was he inside a pipe? If he wasn't mistaken, he'd say this was the grey warming pipe that twisted and turned around the village, keeping the area warm. Or maybe a similar pipe.

He felt the wall. Above ground, every pipe he'd touched was warm. This one was cool. After a moment, his eyes adjusted to the pink glow and Pax scanned the area in case Dragon lurked in these pipes, waiting to gobble him up. Not that he believed the stories Avery had told him, but he'd seen unbelievable things, and Pax was patient enough to survive. No need to run through these pipes and get himself killed.

The door banged behind him as the lock snapped shut, making him jump.

Fists tight, ready for anything that might attack in the dark, Pax marched toward the next pink light illuminating the area. This one created eerie shadows. When his head grazed the ceiling, Pax had to stop to collect himself. Damn. He was scared.

Sitting under the light, he did what always comforted him when facing the unknown. He began to map the area. Using his notebook, Pax drew what he'd seen.

While he worked under the pink light, a quake rumbled, raising his anxiety. These types of long rumbling earthquakes were known by his people as land transformers and he'd survived more than he wanted to remember.

Once satisfied, Pax continued, but he didn't like the feel of the pipe he was in. The slight incline and tight space made him sick to his stomach. He'd had visions of what the inside of these pipes might look like: full of wires and buttons and gadgets, but this was a lot of nothing that weighed on his sanity. These passageways looked like they went nowhere. What if he walked for days and days and was lost eternally to this nothing?

All passageways led somewhere, he promised himself as he glanced back at the light then to the one up ahead. They were guides that lit the area for a reason. Did he keep going or figure out how to open one of the doors?

He stopped in front of one; there were no knobs so Pax raised a hand to push on the smooth metal but the door slid to the side when his fingers came close to the metal. Weird. Peeking in the room, Pax saw a blinking orange light overhead that shed a dirty glow on his surroundings, and a loud hum echoed around him.

Along the wall was an image of Dragon that made him step in for a closer peek. The door slid shut behind him.

Pax went straight to the Dragon-image. Was a starving beast in these pipes?

The warm area meant he needed fewer clothes so he removed a layer and shoved them in his bag. Taking a break, he also sipped from his water bottle and studied the orange light overhead, making sure this weird light wasn't dangerous. The glow was trapped in a pattern of blinking eternally. He patted the bulb to check the temperature. Thankfully, the entire science thing was cool to the touch. No wires ran to it. How the heck was this light working? Pax was tall enough to steal a closer look at the light. Around the bulb part was a white panel and in the panel was one slot with a pin-like rod he pulled on. The light dimmed, leaving him in darkness. Wow. He slid the pin back in the slot. The light returned.

Proud that he'd figured out how the light worked, Pax then dismissed the pulsating as a non-danger and made a note on his notepad in drawings. Maybe the not-working lights that he'd seen in ruins before, worked on the same principle?

He glanced around the area to see what else he could learn, as if he was a genius now. The pipes were clean and well-maintained. Empty of things to see. Still, the humming hurt his brain.

Should he head back to the corridor? Pax glanced at the map he was creating as if the image had answers. The corridor or pipe gave him no sense of direction or time, yet he'd marked each direction on the paper carefully according to how he felt, the incline, the curves. There was a possibility that he wasn't below ground but in the pipe that encircled the village and this idea tempted him to bang on the side and freak the villagers out.

Pax chuckled to himself and returned to the cylinder-type corridor.

Waiting for him was a strange flying bee-like gadget that scanned him with a bright red light. Pax tried to avoid the machine's light but the science was so quick, he had no choice but to let the machine work. Finally, the thing flew down the pipe so Pax chased after it.

The probe-thing vanished through a door leading to a room with a long panel full of buttons and a large monitor flickering overhead. White, moving, blurry lines waved through the monitor, reflecting an image of him. Pax avoided staring directly in the light but he glanced at it several times, curious as heck because he'd seen countless damaged monitors in his travels, yet he had no idea they could be lit up this way.

"Dragon, do you hear me?" he whispered, wondering if maybe somewhere in these pipes lived a beast he could tame. Funny how the story felt more possible now that he was down here.

A male voice erupted from the panel. "*I hear everything in my mainframe chamber.*"

"You speak!" Pax gaped at the panel. "Are you hungry? Are you... Who are you?"

"*I am Dragon. And you are?*"

This was Dragon? He stared at the panel, confused. This was nothing like the image Avery had shown him, or the sculpture in the cliffs, or even like he'd imagined. "I'm Pax of the South. I came to help you because you stopped making smoke and stuff." Which was true enough and about all he could say.

"*I wait for activation code ReSurface, Pax of the South. Until then, I follow my programming. Full Incineration Reprogram-access Executed right on schedule. Are you from Quma Cities?*"

"Cuma Village. You know, outside these pipes. I have a bunch of things in my bag. Want to see them? Maybe something could help you activate this code." He wasn't sure what he was talking to, but dropped the bag near the dark monitor.

No answer.

Hmm. Pax unzipped his bag and unpacked to show Dragon everything he had, thankful that Avery didn't get the gadgets all buried in the woods.

He wiped his brow. Wow. This area was warm.

When at the bottom of his bag, he pulled out bread that Avery must have packed for him and settled in to enjoy it.

AVERY

During the same breaths
Above ground, Saxton Clan

Back in their family hut, Avery fumed while she listened to Father Saxton. She kept one hand over her eye so he couldn't see the tic.

"Say nothing." He ended, letting her shoulder go. They were in their private hut and if she felt like screaming at him, she would.

Avery glanced around for support from Mother Roselle or one of her brothers but only Jacob Berry stepped forward. "I'll talk to her," he offered, as if they were friends and he could somehow undo the past and pull Pax from that pit. "She'll understand that a sacrifice was needed."

Jacob gently extended his hand, presenting her with a way out, as if she were crazy and he could take care of her or possibly force her to behave. "Let's go for a walk and I'll explain how life works."

Avery could almost hear Saxton willing her to place her hand in Jacob's, but by the frown that snapped over his bearded face, he clearly didn't like Jacob's approach either. She wasn't some child.

She refused the hand, crossing her arms, furious. "How life works? All my life you ignored me because I was different but once you realized I might be useful to give you babies to keep your clan alive you wanted me to move in with you. *Urgh.* Stay away from me." She packed a bag with water and dried jerky, determined to go after Pax. "Pax saw things and lived things we would do well to learn from. Just because he's the only one brave enough to actually do something useful doesn't mean you should leave him."

"He's not one of us..." Jacob began to say but Avery cut him off.

"You've all seen him! He could be my brother and I would go into that pit for any one of these boys, too."

Stefe handed her his knife. "I'll go with ya."

"We'll need rope," she snapped at him, and he ran off to gather some.

"You can't go in the pit." Saxton placed a hand on her shoulder to stop her from making things worse.

"A sacrifice will return the heat. We have to wait," Jacob promised. "We acted quickly, this'll be good."

"A sacrifice? Pax thinks he's exploring science. I have to rescue him before Dragon eats him!"

"Avery, reconsider," her mother said.

"Pax is my responsibility. I was to welcome him, not let him be a sacrifice. He knows nothing about our ways." Avery tossed her bag over her shoulder, not fully understanding what Pax believed but annoyed by his innocence just the same.

She glanced to her father for support. He always saw reason but this time his eyes flashed over her in panic. "No," he stated. "You're not going after him."

"I am. Pax is the first person I've ever seen who looks like me even a bit. Don't you ever wonder about your family? I do. Who was Avery before I was Avery from Saxton Clan? When I hear Pax speak about the things he saw and the way he was raised, I fit in better with him than I do with you."

"You're a Saxton," Father Saxton snapped. "I never once thought otherwise. You fit in with us just fine."

"Yet you let a Berry in here, thinking I want to be one."

"Well, I'm not joining your clan," Jacob pointed out as if that was an offer.

"Let her go," Mother Roselle said. "This is important to her. She needs to know where she's from so she can fit in, and you know that."

Saxton stared at Mother Roselle. They spoke in silence, as if able to read each other's thoughts.

"I don't agree with what they did, but I can't leave my children go after him." Saxton grabbed the rope from Stefe. "I'll go."

"Wait," Jacob said. "Give Dragon time to find our sacrifice. A sacrifice has worked before."

Father Saxton pushed Jacob out of his way, tossing the rope over his shoulder while giving Stefe and Jojo instructions as if he was never coming back. Then he stole the bag from Avery. "Stay. Jacob and I will go."

"Me?" Jacob shook his head. He looked from one to the other then stormed out.

"Great." Saxton chased after him.

Avery rushed to the door to follow, then glanced over her shoulder. "I'm going," she told Mother Roselle.

"Of course you are, it's the right thing to do, and a Saxton always fights for justice and equality. Just be safe and come home to me." She wrapped Avery in a warm hug and Avery considered not going, but when she pulled away, the pride in Mother Roselle's eyes almost pushed her out the door.

Avery hid in the shadows while she followed Father Saxton.

He met up with Hunter who asked his brother, "Where are you going?"

"To get Pax out."

"Probably a safe idea. The fool is bound to do more harm in that shaft than good. Think I was too hard on him earlier?"

"It was necessary." Then much to Avery's shock, Father said, "We can't have anyone thinking we support science."

When they arrived at Dragon's Caves, the other leaders had the entrance blocked. "Let us through," Saxton ordered.

"Nope. We wait for the pipes to warm," Berry said, calmly, as if expecting them.

Hunter swung at Berry and a fight broke out allowing Avery to slip along the side. Saxton stumbled beside her, dropping the bag. He spat out blood and met her eyes. "I told you to stay home."

"I'm a Saxton, I do what's right, not what I'm told."

He chuckled. "Now you sound like me."

"Keep fighting, distract them. I'll go in and look around. Leave the rope so we can climb out." She shoved him toward the fight and snagged his bag. Without peeking over her shoulder, Avery slipped by the brawling men and into Dragon's Caves.

The depth of the cave was shadowy and the air had a smell like burned straw. Avery shuddered knowing earth surrounded her.

Blue pipes spidered over the ceilings and travelled along the corridor to the sacrificial hole. She'd never spent too much time in these caves.

The leaders fought, oblivious of her working at the back of

the cave, in the dark, using the torches at the entrance as a guide.

The damp air tasted like metal in her mouth.

"Pax?" Avery tied a rope to the side and dropped down, landing on a grate floor. She checked the shadows for Pax in case he was hurt.

The area was lit by a faint light in the distance. Peering through slates under her bare feet, she couldn't see the bottom of the shaft. "Pax?" How deep did these caves and pipes run? There were many doors to choose from, but she limited her choices based on the lights over them. She'd never seen a light like this.

She could go through the door with the pink light overhead or the cave-like entrance with the dim light in the distance.

Avery first pushed on the door, but the metal didn't budge so she headed toward the dim light.

YODAN

During the same breaths
Underground, FIRE Chamber

Prodigies gathered in the FIRE Chamber in a strange shuffling silence. Yodan was helping Shandra settle into the last working Bench of Life when she nudged his shoulder. "What?"

"Go talk to Match. Remind him that these youths need his guidance. I just need to catch my breath."

Yodan glanced around for his friend. Match had his back to the crowd as he stared at the wall in the FIRE Chamber. The wall-art was infused with crushed gems to catch the flames. The design was intriguing but Yodan wasn't sure why Match stared so intently, holding the cat as if the beast could keep him from having a breakdown. Really, they were all at that point. Too much life had been lost and there was so little hope for the survivors.

Yodan sidled up to Match. "Shandra threw up twice but her vitals are much better now."

"She in pain?" Match's voice cracked, something Yodan never heard before. How afraid was his usually composed friend? Match let the cat run toward Shandra and leaned against the wall to watch her take the cat in her arms.

"Medic Brisk gave her a supplement and says she'll be fine. Just dehydrated, I guess." Still, throwing up wasn't normal and Yodan was worried.

Match took a deep breath. "The hardest part for me is the disassociation. I have this firm connection to everyone, which is ironic when you think about it because I'm not connected to anyone."

"Some of these children are feeling new emotions. Things like shock, fear, grieving. Our training is done and we recognize them, but they're afraid. They grew up with Nogard regulating these feelings. You were chosen to help us stand up to Nogard, to decide when we reprogram her and when we evacuate. You are elite, Match, with that comes a burden you accepted."

"I was seven when I accepted it and I sure as heck never

imagined I'd be here, leading youths to an unknown."

"Here are your brother's last memories. Take them, make him proud. Find us a system where you can listen to them."

Match took the memory needle and slid it along his sleeve. "Any idea what the casualties are since the earthquakes?"

Yodan wasn't sure if Match was asking him or about to tell him. He glanced at the group of youths gathering and told Match, "All but the youth prodigies. Medic Jon and Medic Brisk are the oldest. Lins went up a pipe with the life-drive and Protector Owen is missing."

"Did he survive?" His wince was genuine.

"The air vents in his private chamber were removed so I assume he went up them. I found blood and a Connector in his cleaning bay. He probably cut out his own devices."

"Owen abandoned our people?" Match looked horrified by this news as he faced the gem-infused rock wall once again. "Well, I won't." His jaw was firm.

"The air vents might be a better idea than the FIRE pit," Yodan pointed out.

"How will we bring these youths through vents? Plus the FIRE purges certain vents, too. As long as the FIRE doors are intact we'll travel much faster through passageways than venting pipes that might have been damaged in the quake. Besides, if Owen took to the vents, that's the last place I plan to go. The guy's an idiot."

"He does have a keen survival sense, though."

"For himself. I have to think about these youths, about Shandra."

"So we're all leaving? Together?"

Without turning to face the group working behind him, Match said, "My hyper-hearing is making it hard to focus. I hear everyone talking and can't decide who's right or what I should do."

"No one knows everything. We each know a lot of one thing. Means we can't do this alone. We need each other if we plan on surviving. Your job is to unite these voices you hear. Make us work together to find a new home."

Match ran his hand over one of the gems. "You see these gems on the wall. Each one represents a mind the Collective absorbed. These markings are a promise of eternal life, and today, that was taken from us. All these minds were lost and none of the ones here will ever find this eternity. This is as good as it gets. So what am I leading these people to? What can I promise them?" Match stared at him. "There is no more future for our children." Match closed his eyes, both hands on the wall.

"We are their future. Us." Yodan grazed a finger over a sparkling light but felt nothing except the cold rock. What they needed was a purpose. Yodan glanced at the youths gathering supplies in the dark, wondering what he could tell his friend. But without the Collective to ensure their immortality, he felt lost.

Still, he wanted to give Match a plan, a hope. "You gave me that gem because you trust me. Let that gem be the symbol of our hope. I'll go first and let you know what to expect," Yodan volunteered since he knew this was what was troubling Match. He needed someone to run the path to gather facts before he brought these children to a dead end. What good was lowering a bunch of children and being trapped? One person could run the path and make sure they'd be safe. Tell them which passages to avoid and which ones to take. "We're in this together, all of us. So let me do my part." Yodan was already checking his lifesuit for supplies, making sure he was ready to explore.

"I can't risk anyone going down until after the FIRE. Those pipes are directly linked to the FIRE pit. What if the FIRE doors don't hold?"

"We don't even know if the FIRE will come. If it does, I know how to hide. I'll be fine. Alone I can probably run the entire path before the FIRE even begins. You know I'm fast. I went over the path with Shandra and it's pretty straightforward." Of course they had no idea what had collapsed or what dangers were on that path.

Match didn't look pleased with this idea, but he clearly couldn't think up another one, so he nodded. "If the FIRE doors will hold, we'll join you. Faster we get moving, the better. If they don't look sturdy enough, come back up. Take the talker and my SHARP. Be my eyes." Match checked his watch and headed to the rope station.

Yodan followed. "You need D-light. You're shaking. The Bench of Life has active D-light. Use it." Yodan had it drilled in him that in an emergency the protectors and elites of Quma

Cities must be kept alive.

Match unloaded the heavy ropes from the hooks. "The Bench is for others who need it. I'm fine. We have work to do."

Match was going through the motions, and Yodan didn't like this. Had his intensive training programming won over? Did losing his brother break his spirits? "Then focus on your breath with me while we work. In and out. Every time you find yourself planning and panicking, or one of your tics takes over, focus on the in and out of each breath. It'll energize you and ground you so you can make clear decisions."

Following his instruction immediately, Match took a deeper breath holding his air longer than most would, letting his entire body in on each action.

"Better?"

Instead of answering, Match unclasped the talker from his lifesuit and handed Yodan the device. Well, it was actually the old two-way radios they used to play with as children. "They communicate with each other. Shandra adapted them to reach farther. Keep your mission simple. Check the doors and let me know." He glanced at the busy youths around them. "With this many of us, we need solid doors and FIRE safe areas." Match unloaded the rope and gathered it, dumping the lines by the FIRE pit, tossing around orders as he passed others as if he'd been the boss of them since forever.

Elites were always well-respected, but Match in action brought the energy levels up. Yodan followed, carrying two harnesses so he looked half as useful as a guy carrying fifty kilograms of rope. At the pit, Match peered down it. During a ceremony, flames erupted around the monstrous black pipe that ran down the middle in an explosion that signaled the life in Quma Cities was strong and ready for a new cycle. Already, heat started, reminding them that this was controlled by a working program. They weren't alone. Their ancestors had created many backups to keep them safe.

Yodan didn't look down but began to fasten the rope for his descent.

Shandra joined them, wobbly, but on her feet and she stole Match's focus. "I'm going down first."

"Yodan volunteered," Match answered. "We trust him to do his job. Here." Match handed Yodan his SHARP. "Just in case you lose track of time while exploring, the device will beep three early warnings before the FIRE Ceremony begins. Get someplace safe. Supply rooms have a fire safe you can crawl into close to the floor, behind the grates." Then he helped put the harness around Yodan as if he was taking too long. Match added, "Do I look as afraid as the others?"

His jaw was firm and his white eyes reminded Yodan of the shimmering waters at Glisten Point which relaxed him. Nothing about Match ever looked afraid.

"Wish I could look half as confident as you."

"What's your plan?" Shandra asked them, and Match filled her in, talking too close, his hands always brushing her. "We'll keep these children alive. Every one of them. Every decision we make has to be with the entire system in mind." His voice was firm.

Shandra nodded. "If Yodan's going, he'll need this." She handed him heat-proof chalk. Their system for tunnel exploration was universal and Yodan didn't need any coaching on how to mark the walls so the others could follow.

Yodan tossed the rope over the side, climbed over the railing, then studied the faces gathered in the FIRE chamber in case he never saw them again.

Match said, "Hopefully, we can follow you. I want to keep us together if possible."

Yodan's stomach grumbled, something he wasn't used to. They normally absorbed nutrients at specific times, but they were taught to ration in an event.

Yodan tested his harness and rope, ready to leap.

Shandra said, "It should be me going first."

"I got this," Yodan promised her. "Get up your strength so Match doesn't have to carry you out."

Shandra showed him how to use the talker tied to his pack. "If you have trouble with it, I stored the details in a memory pin, inserted along the side. Remember, go up. Your instinct will be to go down, but go up. If the path I showed you suffered cave-ins cut through pipes and get back on track as soon as possible."

Cut through pipes? If she was suggesting this, they weren't

planning on returning to Quma Cities.

"Lins sent me that path for a reason, she'll be there," Shandra promised him.

Yodan peered down the pit, and with a deep breath, he jumped, making them a new future.

Metre by metre Yodan dropped.

The black pipe in the middle of the hole was out of reach as Yodan descended along the rock face of the hole.

When he was about twelve metres down, Match called, "Do you see the ledge?"

First, Yodan peered without the light, his eyes making out details. He studied the center pipe carefully as he hung over the void. As far down as he could see, nothing met his view, just the pipe stretching for eternity. Match pulled on the rope and Yodan swung around. He prepared himself to hit the rock wall but swung into the void.

"Got it." Yodan propelled himself toward the entrance to a cave-like area and dropped, letting the harness go. The metal clanged against the heat resistant pipe running down the middle of the pit, too far for him to reach.

"Yodan?" Match called.

"I'm fine. Get more rope ready, another two metres. I'll see what's here." A faint pink light glowed in the distance and Yodan moved toward the beam.

"Wait for me," Match ordered, trying to change the plans.

"No worries, stick to the plan. Prepare the others. I'll radio you with what I find. If this leads somewhere I'll let you know." Yodan sucked in a deep breath. The air was heavy. His eyes were sleepy, but he didn't dare sleep in case he never woke up.

Hopefully, Lins was someplace safe because things were far too hot.

LINS

During the same breaths
Underground, Pipes of Creation

Still on her way to Mainframe One, Lins' knees were raw from crawling through pipes and tunnels. This hard physical labour deepened her appreciation for her sister. How did Shandra do this daily? No wonder she was always so filthy.

Lins crawled toward the red Pipes of Creation with trepidation. These were the pipes hiding wires that kept Nogard alive, and that ensured their survival. Was this where the Collective gathered?

The eRobe was alive around her, Nogard in it. The life-drive was in the eRobe for Artificial-life to return to, but Nogard clearly enjoyed feeling close to Lins as she hugged her through the eRobe. Their connection was bizarre since they could feel each other's emotions. Nogard was a different species and felt emotions differently than Lins. Each one was crisp and ended abruptly, jolting her.

Using her laser pipe cutter, Lins warmed the area for incision. The lasers were popular among diggers since they cut through bones, pipes, even certain types of metals and rocks. Lins clicked her laser on. With the red pipe overhead, she made the first incision into the pipe but it shook as the beam warmed it.

"Nogard," she scolded, but when the eRobe jolted her with excitement, Lins realized that this wasn't Nogard since Nogard was in the eRobe. So... "Dragon?" Her voice was a whisper. She'd never spoken to Dragon before and had assumed Dragon was a ghost program without life, but Nogard's excitement made her feel otherwise. Was Dragon A-life like Nogard? Was Yodan right? Was there another system to sustain them?

Lins touched the pipe gently since this was the Pipe of Creation. "We're dying. I have to get to Mainframe One. I'm sorry I hurt you. Can you hear me?" She had one throbbing goal: bring Nogard to Mainframe One.

"I am Dragon. I hear everything in the Pipes of Creation." A male voice vibrated off the pipes but the rumbling stopped.

Lins' specialty was words and it always amused her that Nogard was Dragon spelled backwards. All Dragon's ghost programs were unreadable for Nogard simply because they were inverted.

"Did my laser hurt?"

"*Yes.*"

The idea that these pipes contained feelings like limbs amazed her. Lins turned down the setting on her laser. All their knowledge and they knew so little about the species keeping them alive.

Lins rubbed the spot with her robe before starting the slow cut. No more quakes followed.

She slid the hard plastic she cut out of the way, expecting dust to sprinkle her face but the inside of the pipe was clean.

Lins peered inside. With the wires passing through, travelling them would be a tight fit. Before doubt won, Lins climbed in, the first human to travel through the life-veins where Artificial-life was born.

A red wire rose and danced over her, sensing her presence.

This was the most sacred place Lins had ever visited and moving was hard, but saving her people was her responsibility, her duty. Her connection to Nogard through the eRobe doubled the need to keep them alive and she needed Mainframe One to do this.

Energy slammed into her, stirring a warm turmoil in her gut. The patterns on her eRobe glowed and dimmed as data hit her, lighting the area with dancing sparks.

Dizzy from the energy, her body grew warmer. Heat radiated from her core. Much too hot. She craved touching, yet jumped when wires glided over her arms and back. She crawled faster, then slowed when the energy turned to a gentle caress.

Lins forced herself to push on. A human shouldn't be trapped inside a robe wanting to connect to wires and she considered leaving it behind, but would she need Nogard or the life-drive? The eRobe sparkled with life, blinking, chirping, creating soothing sounds as wires fondled the fabric concealing the life-drive.

Chills swept over Lins as wires restrained her, slipping inside the eRobe to search for the life-drive. Lins brushed the first few wires off, moving faster, but one snagged her ankle and yanked her back, planting her face-first into the array of wires. They enveloped her, wrapping around the fabric, removing it.

The eRobe lit up with energy, exploding wires off her, and groans filled the pipe with pleasurable sensations as things shifted around Lins.

Lins tightened her robe around her, feeling violated and used. Yet the sensations shooting at her were arousing. Her body betrayed her logic. "Nogard, Dragon, you're scaring me."

"*Desire,*" Nogard whispered, echoing her voice off the sides of the pipe surrounding them.

The tension in Lins' body tightened, searching for satisfaction. Desires escalated as the wires around her grew thicker, making passing harder, but they didn't attack again. Just grazed. Teased. Mostly the eRobe was fondled, but the connection she shared with the eRobe was emotional and each contact increased the need inside her, as if the energy in these pipes needed to be reborn, freed, *experienced.*

This was where the technology of the world was created and stored, a powerfully creative place that ignited bodily tensions. Very aware of her body, Lins passed each wire. Now, a strange knowledge came with each movement. She somehow knew which wires did what as if she'd made them. She knew how to link the eRobe to the life-drive so Nogard could continue to live and connect with Dragon. She knew that Dragon was not A-life but artificial-intelligence waiting for life. Who was giving her this knowledge? Was Lins absorbing memories? Her new self-awareness was so deep, she sensed a presence within her hovering along the surface of her body, waiting for freedom from this painful collection of cells. Waiting to explode in a satisfying release and join the others in their eternal energetic dance.

It was with great effort that Lins pushed herself forward. When she left the small pipe and entered an area large enough to stand, she sat against the wall and stretched out, aware of every muscle in her body.

Grounded, she felt strong and wise. Sexy.

The access passageway that Lins had entered was full of well-maintained supplies. They were taught to pause often, to hydrate, to breathe shallow breaths of air, and to take deeper breaths of Oxy-air. So, following her training, Lins pulled down the bottle of Oxy-air from the wall and sipped, hoping to clear her head. Her temperature regulated and her energy increased.

While she rested, wires slipped from the red pipe, creeping closer as if drawn to her. Lins stood, ignoring them. All this knowledge almost dripped from her body, mind, and energy, making her move with reverence.

A drone wheeled into the area. Most were programmed to recognize her and ignore her, since she had no Exchanger they had to memorize her features, voice, even touch, but this one was ancient and on wheels, probably maintained by Dragon. The old drone scanned her with a D-light beam. She'd never seen a drone do this. When the relic scanned the area on her eRobe that contained the life-drive, the drone backed up. "*Unknown lifeform.*" Alarms from an old system fired off, irritating her. Loud noises always rubbed her nerves and Lins was wound tight.

Frustrated, Lins swung at the drone, smashing it into the wall. Pieces broke off.

She'd never killed a machine in her life, yet she stretched, unaffected by the death. Such was life and the drone would not be missed by anyone. And that was the difference between life and machine.

She rubbed her hands over the eRobe and the fine metallic material sizzled around her.

Ignoring the mess of fragments and protruding wires, Lins searched the area. As if her sexual energy was a homing device, she stepped toward the door to her left. Someone was on the other side. She smelled his sweat, almost tasted it.

Lins shook her head to clear it, then her hands. She then shook the energy from her entire body, no idea why she could sense his presence through the wall. What was wrong with her? How was she doing that? Why did she feel in control, yet so out of control? How could she know so much? Perhaps the Pipes of Creation were not a place for humans.

The shiny metal door reflected an image of her in the dim overhead light. Her usual violet eyes were still that wicked, deep grey.

Why had her eyes changed colour?

Lins removed the emotional receptor and draped the

precious eRobe containing the even more precious life-drive over her arm. The fine garment pulsated with desire, but when she stared at herself, her eyes were once again violet.

Had she imagined the grey or had... *Oh my gosh!* No wonder she'd felt so weird. Nogard could jump from devices like the eRobe into people! This was incredible. The things they could learn and do! No wonder she'd travelled the pipes with ease.

Underneath the garment, Lins always wore a purple skin-tight lifesuit. Her breasts were restricted in this lifesuit and she considered removing her clothing and going naked, but settled on unzipping midway.

Lins felt better with the eRobe off and took a deep relaxing breath as Yodan had taught her. Sweet smelling mating gases wafted from under the door, making her hesitate. Walking through coupling gases would be challenging while sexually aroused this way.

Lins knocked by the door to activate the override switch and the door slid open. Scanning the room for danger, she barged in. A man worked on his knees by the far wall.

He glanced up, making her catch a step. Half-dressed, he gawked at her from where he lined up ancient devices on the floor. His lifesuit was in several pieces scattered about the room. Each piece was a different shade of brown made from material she didn't recognize yet her extensive memories identified them as *pelt*.

The pants he wore were made from grey hair she identified as *fur*. Strange, yet she had this weird desire in her to touch each one. As if she needed the sensation to match the facts in her brain.

He jumped to his feet with liveliness.

Seeing a perfect male before her made Lins forget what she'd planned. Her senses were more alert than ever. She smelled him from this distance, heard his breaths, tasted the minerals that sparkled on his skin.

The coupling gases pouring in from the overhead vent weren't helping her lusting.

Hair poured over him; a dishevelled orange mess she ached to stroke. He had no coverings for his chest and his freckled skin glistened in sweat. As he stood, he rubbed his arm roughly. The tattoo markings along his arm over his rippling muscles mesmerized her. No one wore the mark of Dragon anymore. Was this the programmer running Dragon? The engineer for Mainframe One?

She picked up one of the garments from the floor. This one was made from a woven material much like the blankets they stored in the archives for reference purposes. The colours were a rich purple and red mixed with more browns. Fabric and colours in Quma Cities were machine made pastels that were easy on the eyes and that reflected light so each person was their own beacon of hope. These colours absorbed light.

She watched him while she fondled his garment seductively.

He studied her back.

Licked his lips.

Get control! Lins scorned herself in case she foolishly rushed up to him. The mating gases were strong in the room and she breathed them in deeply, enjoying the sensation of desire, trying to make the want hers and not a response.

Did it matter?

It always did. The point of being elite was to always think for herself without interference of outside life. She had to be sure her programs were her own. How would she protect her people if she was a slave to another's will? To an A-life living in an eRobe?

She locked eyes with the man in front of her.

His voice echoed through her, as if he created words that brought desires to life inside her. "Mother Roselle made me that sweater. It's the first gift I received where there was no exchange." He stepped to grab the heavy garment from her, his hand out.

She struggled for a word. Any word, but her speech programming collapsed. She was a woman with no idea what to say to a creature this perfect. Placing the sweater in his hand, she whispered, "If my eyes are grey, step away."

"Your eyes are purple. I've never seen that before." He pulled away from her and held the sweater-garment against his chest. As thrilling as it was to admire this guy, a movement yanked her attention away from him and to the panel beside them. The eRobe that she'd draped over her arm gravitated toward the panel as if a magnet pulled it.

Lins stepped toward the panel, allowing the eRobe to graze

it. The contact made her gasp and she let the eRobe fall on the panel, covering the area in a heap that slowly spread out on its own.

Shocked, Lins stepped back, breaking her contact with the eRobe as the fabric expanded over the panel. The eMove that powered the eRobe would give Nogard energy to live as long as Lins wore the eRobe, but could the panel charge it?

It was possible.

These thoughts were more like a knowing than a realization and with this new knowledge came a detailed checklist she needed to do to ensure Nogard's survival.

"I'm Pax."

She ignored him and set to work to see why this panel had Nogard excited. If she focused on this Pax, nothing would get done and that might be exactly what Nogard wanted.

PAX

A breath later
Above ground, Mainframe One

Pax had no idea where this gal materialized from, but Avery's story about Dragon making a woman out of clay for him was a reality, and he had to admit, when it came to women, Dragon knew how to make them. *Wow*.

She danced her fingers over the panel with comfort, bringing a warmth with her that lit up the room. Watching her fingers play over the buttons, he stopped breathing so not to miss a movement, sure he was hallucinating. Had to be.

Knowledge bubbled off her.

"I'm Pax," he blurted out a second time as if she cared, but heck. He wanted her to care.

She didn't glance at him, just recited some perfectly planned speech. "It is an honour to be in your sector, Pax. I'm Elite Lins of Quma Cities. Are you the programmer or engineer for Mainframe One?"

"Me? No. I'm a nomad." Sweaty and needing fresh air and more water, Pax asked, "Where did you come from?" He stayed back because the energy oozing off her reminded him of a volcano erupting then forcing itself to behave.

This attraction was a new sensation, slightly out of control. He was close to Penny, but they were comfortable, familiar. This was lusty and hard to ignore. And if he was being honest with himself, this pull was scary. "Why am I so attracted to you?" he blurted out like the horny fool he suddenly was.

"Coupling gases." She pointed to the light yellow fog rolling down from the grate overhead, but she was already sliding under the control panel to check out the wiring and despite himself, he watched her, lusting over her curves, forgetting what he wanted to say.

"Just enjoy the feeling." Then she set to work. "This is amazing. This is nothing but a machine. Programmed to purge our system at specific times without fail using magma energy. Dragon has sensory programing to feel temperatures. He, and I use that pronoun lightly since this machine is nothing but an *it*—still, when dealing with artificial-intelligence we've learned to address them as lifeforms because they could develop and evolve into Artificial-life and if we don't respect that, we risk being reprogrammed."

She had to be the smartest human alive and Pax was dying to sit with her and talk about the things she knew and the things he'd seen in case she could give them life. *Talk.* That's all he thought about, he promised himself, but what a horrible lie that was. Damn. Nothing would be more comforting than taking her in his arms and unleashing his troubled emotions with her body next to his. He was watching how she moved much too closely for a guy thinking about talking. Even her breath stole his focus. Each movement compelled him to move closer.

He found comfort knowing that she'd fix whatever made these pipes stop working. Everything would be fine for Avery's people. Then what? Would Avery even believe that this magical woman appeared out of nowhere to fix wires? Would this woman stay? Be welcomed in Cuma Village? Would he even stay with those jerks? "You have a home? A family where you fit in?" he asked, ready to live with her.

"Fit in? Hmm. That's a good question. I'd have to say I'm an outsider. When I die, no one will remember me, no one will mourn me. I will pass through their lives, protecting them, ensuring Nogard respects their humanity. Sometimes, I wish I fit in, then other times, I'm glad I don't."

"Yeah. I don't want to fit in with a bunch of liars, but having a family is nice."

"That it is." She smiled. Just a quick smirk that faded, but she slid out from under the panel to look at him. "Fear and lack of education make people do foolish things. I have had to forgive many, as I imagine you did."

Pax sighed. She was right. The villagers were afraid and had pushed him in the pit out of despair. Forgiveness wouldn't be easy, but given a few more breaths, he'd find this peace in himself. "So where do you live?"

"Quma Cities, several mainframes below this one."

"Underground?" Heck, maybe he was dreaming. He was tired and starving and the air was icky hot. Well, if this was a dream, he'd enjoy his time in it.

He watched her work since not looking at her was impossible; she overpowered the room. Her eyes were vibrant purple with fiery stripes of bright pink rushing through them, and her skin was even paler than his. Her garments were shiny violet, clinging to her curves as if made for her with the purpose of highlighting her every feature. And most fascinating of all was that she was bald with tattoos decorating around her ears and down her neck. No hair at all, not even eyelashes. He wanted to slide his hands over her smooth skin and make sure she was safe from her journey, but she was the heroine and worked at his feet with an air that demanded respect.

The queen of the pipes.

What would she say if he knelt beside her?

He glanced away, the fear of losing another person he loved crashed on him and Pax even stepped back.

"Blue or red?" she asked, as if he knew. Then Pax realized she wasn't talking to him but a device she held. Reading the handheld for the answer, Lins then responded.

Pax glanced at his own machines lined up. "I have devices," he said, hoping to sound smart, but fumbling with his words like a big bumbling idiot.

Lins pulled out from under the panel and stood beside him with ease. Slim and shorter than him, Lins had an intoxicating earthy fragrance he enjoyed that made him stand much too close to her, intrigued by everything she did.

She showed him the bleeps and red lights on her device. "We save all sorts of things on our handhelds."

"I don't read." Confessing that made him feel stupid.

Lins met his eyes and a warm smile spread across her lips lighting up her eyes so they sparkled. "Would you like me to teach you?" Her seductive voice captivated him.

Was she flirting?

"Most people in Quma Cities have an Exchanger behind their ear that allows them to learn things like reading while they sleep. But I had to learn the hard way since I'm elite."

He nodded, unable to form a word as he imagined her sprawled out on the grass, spending time to teach him things.

"I enjoy teaching. Before we do that, though, I need to find a code to stop a termination program that's running on this machine."

He nodded. Of course, she had a code. "ReSurface," he said, remembering what Dragon had said earlier.

"You have it?"

"Dragon told me you would activate it. Well, not *you* exactly, just that a code needed to be activated."

She frowned, frustrated. "It has to be here." Rubbing her head, she spoke loudly to the panel. "ReSurface, Mainframe One, stop the termination clock with time itself and restart." Her gorgeous purple eyes opened wide. "Oh my gosh! Match's watch! I've been so stupid. I have to call him." She worked on her device. "Great."

"What's wrong?" He moved in closer, bending his head to whisper closer to her skin. "Can I help?"

"I'm out of range. I need to ping this location."

Pax pulled the safety-pin out of his pocket. He held the pin, debating what to do because this was his last link to Penny and giving it away to a woman he crushed on might disrespect… Yet, what good had the fastener ever done him? He handed Lins the pin. "Here, use this."

"What is this?"

"My pin. You said you'd have to pin it. Use mine."

Lins grabbed the tiny metallic pin. "You're giving me this?" She looked thrilled, as if the gift meant something more to her than he could fathom.

"Yeah, maybe it'll help. Someone brilliant told me once that a pin can fix anything."

"Someone you cared about gave it to you and you're giving this rare metal to me?"

He nodded. "Penny was my wife, mate, not sure what you call it, but yeah, I cared about her and miss her. A lot. This achy pain that never lets up and fills me full of lonely." For some reason, admitting his weakness to this stranger brought them closer and she even placed a hand on his jaw to look in his eyes. Gosh. She was so blasted sexy.

"You trust me?"

"To fix things? Yeah."

Without warning, Lins kissed his bearded cheek. "I'm sorry you lost your companion. I lost people I cared for over the years, too. The pain is enduring but when I talk to someone who understands, the memories of them return and I feel connected again. It's worse when we have no one to talk to, and in my case, quite often, Nogard would erase the memories of those we lost from the minds of everyone else, and so I was the only one suffering."

Much to Pax's surprise, Lins dropped the device on the panel and opened the pin making it longer. Then she inserted the pin into the machine. She smirked. Pax found himself smiling, too, feeling joy inside himself. How long had he been numb? Or needing to talk to someone who knew pain and suffering like him? Someone who understood how important belonging was, yet not…

"Whatever you're planning, you should do it fast. People outside this pipe are freaking out. Apparently the healing waters stopped doing whatever they do and the pipes stopped smoking. But I think that the problem is that the gases from the yellow pipes probably stopped and something in the gas keeps them relaxed. Now, everyone is feeling things that terrify them. I like emotions, bothers me that these gases made me mellow when I strolled through the village."

"I like emotions, too," she said with a wicked smirk that almost dropped him to his knees. Yeah. That was for sure flirting.

Pax couldn't help it, he grinned back, his cheeks warm. She'd think him a fool. A woman like this needed someone brilliant to talk to about wires and stuff. What did he know about anything? "Did my pin work?"

"I sent Match a message saying that his watch can end the termination sequence. He should know how to use it. I might have to go farther into the tunnel for the message to find him. With Nogard down, there's nothing for my message to bounce off. Even the drones aren't networking properly."

He had no idea what she was talking about, but he nodded, watching her lips move, wondering what they'd be like to taste.

She was distracted by the garment she'd left on the panel. The strange patterns lit up at different moments as if something communicated with them. The material was almost metallic and gleamed.

While she looked at the panel again, Pax pulled a broken device from his line up on the floor and studied the old gadget in despair. "Will something like this be useful?"

She had a wire from under the panel and stretched the long connectors out until they reached another piece. "There. Now we have a working monitor. This system was run from a remote location but now the programs are automatic. Seems to run on natural D-light for energy which isn't enough to make Oxy-air, but we could for sure make nutrients. What do you use for air?"

"Like breathing? Just my mouth." Gosh he felt stupid. She obviously meant something else.

"It is a very *interesting* mouth." More flirting? He had no idea how to respond. She grabbed the device from him and studied it. "You found this?"

"Yeah, in a cave with the device that made my tattoo." Pride swelled in him that he was smart enough to keep his relics with him.

Moving in closer to him, she brushed his skin, running her fingers over the tattoo. "This is the *breath of life*. It's what gave artificial-intelligence life. I don't know anyone brave enough to wear such a marking anymore. Well," she smirked, "other than me." She slid her sleeve over her shoulder and sure enough, she had the matching symbol on her shoulder.

Before he could touch it, she snapped the material back over her skin and placed his old device on the control panel. He was frozen to the spot, seeing that shoulder in his mind when the screen lit up.

"This old mainframe likes your device better than mine." Lins smirked with her top teeth biting into her bottom lip. "You have others?" As she spoke, she took out a fine tool and twisted the tip over parts of the device, dismantling it even more.

Her skin was so white he was sure Avery would lead her straight to the healing waters. "Your skin reminds me of snow, I mean, your robe sparkles. I..." Crap. He'd clearly been locked in this pipe for too long.

Maybe he was going insane. First, he stumbled on a village without snow and found a gal he could have sworn was his younger sister who went missing. And now, he dreamed up a woman to comfort him before he died.

She glanced at him while she worked with her fine tool, undoing parts of the device that Pax hadn't been able to remove.

"I read about snow. Have you seen it?"

"Yeah, I trudged through snow. At first, I enjoyed the way I could easily hunt and track, but then I hated the freezing because, well, the endless cold sucks. Snow is never-ending white that freezes every inch of you. Even taking a piss is a challenge. But then, I somehow found peace with the serenity snow brings. Plus, building shelters with snow is possible and leaving tracks. Overall, snow's better than fires."

She stopped working to study him while he talked. "You adapted to the low temperatures. I was raised in a stable climate at this temperature."

"This is hot."

"Will I survive snow?"

"I'll keep you warm." *Now who's flirting?* His eyes settled on her lips, the tension between them was like nothing he'd ever experienced. So physical. Raw.

She pointed to the pictures on the screen, her eyes on him. "Dragon is showing me something ancient. Do you know what that image is?"

Pax studied the image. "It's a map of the area." He traced his fingers over the monitor, imagining the land. "I can compare the map to my notebook."

"Above ground?"

He nodded. "The village has cliffs shadowing it shaped like Dragon." He ran his fingers over the screen to show her the cliffs. "But this part here broke away today and crumbled into the ocean, here." He pressed his hands over the screen amazed at how smooth the image was.

"That part you say is missing is where Nogard's energy source was." Lins slid a hand over his. The screen was high and she was on her tiptoes, close to him. Moving on instinct, he stepped closer so their bodies hugged. He considered running an arm around her, then finally did. To his delight, she moved in even closer.

"So, Dragon has no food." Pax saw the problem. "Explains the earthquakes. My stomach grumbles a lot when I'm hungry."

"What are the ways in and out of these pipes?"

"Well, I came down a shaft. I don't know much about this area but I'm good at mapping things. We could explore a bit, see what leads out of the pipes and back to the village."

"Outside these pipes is a village?"

"The pipes surround it, actually. They keep the area warm and that allows the villagers to farm and stuff."

"Will the village survive if the pipes are cold?"

"I grew up in the cold, it sucks, but we'd manage. Is this

what'll happen?"

"I'm not sure. From what I can see, this program has an override that was triggered. Shutting down is just the beginning. By the end, the entire system we live in will be brought to an end."

"End..."

"Violent explosions meant to destroy Quma Cities."

"What?" How could she look so blasted calm? Cities meant people. They needed people! "And how much time do we have before these violent explosions?"

She glanced at the device with the pin sticking out of it. "Sleeping gases have already been issued. FIRE will be next. Our evacuation window will be small. I have to get back to warn my people."

"My gosh, how many are you?"

"We're close to 700."

That was a big number. He had to help her. "I'm coming."

"You need to warn your people that this area will be unstable and dangerous." She was right, of course. Annoyed him that he even wanted to help them when they were such jerks to him, but he did. They were just acting out of fear, and really, if he was in their place, would he be any different?

"So, you'll come back?" He grazed a finger under her chin and she closed her eyes, waiting. Without hesitation, he kissed her. She tasted like the spicy healing waters and they deepened the kiss, his tongue dancing with hers while his hand slipped along her back, sliding her in closer. Damn.

"Pax..." she breathed out his name while he rubbed his whiskers against her neck. She smelled so earthy.

"Lins?" He wasn't thinking straight.

A red light interrupted them, blinding them. She pulled away and rushed to the monitor. Pax stepped right behind her, a hand on her hip.

She faced him abruptly. "We have to hurry. Seal the doors that have these symbols." She showed him the symbol of flames on the metal door. Then she took the robe off the panel and wrapped the strange fabric around a box inside one of the pockets. She shoved the combo gently in his bag. "You must protect this. Get far from this area and tell your people to seek shelter."

"What's so important about the garment?"

"It's alive, artificial-intelligence and Artificial-life. Codes in the box are for our nutrients and air. A select few among my people will know what to do with those codes. Unfortunately, I'm not one of them. I have to keep the box safe or destroy it, and until I know more I won't make that decision. Wait for us. Wait for me, Pax of the South."

He placed the bag on the floor and grabbed her hands. She was leaving him to save her people, and sending him to save his. His father once told him that even the strongest women needed comfort, and the stronger they were, the stronger he'd need to be.

She caressed his face, her fingers lost in his short beard. "You're most captivating, Pax."

"I'll keep your dress safe." He danced a gentle kiss on her lips and she deepened the connection as if they'd kissed each other this way their entire lives.

When she pulled away, he expected her to say something deep or romantic but she said, "In the next room is a smashed drone. Bring the machine here where it'll be safer. We won't have much time. Work fast and get your people far from here."

He couldn't take his eyes off her. The tint of lilac in the glimmering fabric of her outfit made her eyes sparkle.

The bag at his feet pulsated like a humming beat. Or maybe his heart beat too fast.

"Lins, what if we never see each other again?" He picked up the bag.

"Our memories have merged. If you wish to see me again, close your eyes and bring me to life in your mind." Lins was already in the next room, opening a small door that led inside a second much smaller red pipe. Pax followed her.

"Pax, thanks for the pin and the kiss."

"I'll come." Clearly Pax couldn't fit in the smaller pipe so he wasn't sure why he'd said something so ridiculous. On top of that, the idea of being in a tiny area terrified him. This large grey pipe already pushed his comfort zone to new levels. Yet he didn't want her to go without him and this need to stay with her was stronger than all that. "Life could be over in a breath. I want to take the next ones with you." Gosh. He was tired of being left behind.

She nodded. "I agree, but there is no next breath unless we make it."

YODAN

During the same breaths
Underground, FIRE Pit

Yodan explored the passageway, hopeful, yet careful. The strange taste in his mouth was as if smoke had settled on his palate. The cave reminded him of the entrance to Glisten Point and the familiarity relaxed him. A faint pink light invited him from over a heavy metallic door which would easily hold up during the FIRE Ceremony. He stood in front of the door, waiting for the panel to slide open.

When nothing happened, he pushed on the seams but the door was sealed tight, made to open from the other side. This door contained no crest markings. Yodan pulled out the radio and said, "Match?"

The device crackled. "Here."

"I have a grey door that won't open." Match had gotten Yodan out of worse predicaments.

"Anything around it?"

"A light."

"Is the illuminator lit?"

"Yeah."

"Pink or yellow light?"

"Pink."

"That's powered by Dragon. Sounds like you're on the right path, follow the pink lights."

"I can't open the door."

Shandra spoke over the talker in a calm, crisp voice. "Use the clip from the light to open the door. This is a passageway that will take us right out of the system and to Mainframe One. This is good, Yodan. You found it."

Wasn't hard.

Yodan clipped the device back to his pack and studied the light. The connections were fastened to the rock wall but under the illuminator was the clip permitting the device to communicate with an older system. When Yodan wiggled the fine needle out, the light died. He snapped his pen-light on and ran the beam over the rim of the door until he found the reader, then he slipped the needle in and the door slid open, revealing a stairwell.

Yodan clicked on the radio. "Got it, thanks." A heavy door like this was a good sign. He pulled out the needle to make sure the door would close.

It didn't budge.

"Seems the door won't close when I remove the needle."

"Try putting the needle back in the illuminator."

"Even if that works, one of us would be on the wrong side of the door." Yodan tried regardless because he'd stay back if he had to save the others. "Doesn't work. The door is stuck open. Might be from old age. I don't have tools to fix it."

"Or time. Things are warming up. Come back."

"Not yet." Yodan rushed up the steps on the other side of the door. He might find another door. The steps led to a platform with a choice. Right was a stairwell leading down and left was one going up. The way down looked newer which made sense since each new mainframe was lower. Everything inside him wanted to go down as Yodan peered up the staircase cut into the rocks.

He wished he'd brought a recording to listen to. The silence was unsettling.

His talker crackled so Yodan pulled out the device to listen but he heard nothing. Still, he said, "I found a stairwell that leads down and up. I'll run down first since there's a light below." Down made the most sense.

The radio fizzed. "Up." His sister's voice blurred in and out, reminding him of her order.

Yodan glanced up at the darkness. As much as his instinct told him to go down, he did trust his sister. "Right. I'm going up," he promised.

It was warm in the stairwell and the air was heavier. Using his pen-light, he studied the markings that lined the wall in chalk while he rushed by. '*Worship false gods*.' Yodan was taken aback. *God* was not a word they were allowed to write, think, or say. Disrespect like that was an immediate demerit. '*Death to the queen*.' '*I am free*.' '*The free shall pay*.' '*Darkness will not stop us*.' How many had passed here? Were rebels here? Would they have a way out? A system they could join? What exactly were Match's plans when they reached as high as they could go and found a cold frozen system?

Debris had broken free from the overhead and littered the stairwell, making each step treacherous, yet he rushed, leaving marks along the way for others. The pressure in his lungs felt wrong. Checking his health monitor, which worked on minimal functions, Yodan was taken aback when the readings said he was dead. He slipped on his mask and moved, trying not to think about what that might mean. He felt alive. But maybe dead people felt alive?

The stairwell curved and changed from stone to metal, signalling a new level, a new mainframe, a different era in the history of Nogard and her system. The scorch marks on the wall meant Nogard used these stairwells as passageways to divert flames during a FIRE Ceremony. Which meant the metal door wouldn't have protected them anyway.

He counted each step aloud as if keeping score was important. At 455, he landed in a chamber with a service room for an older system.

A man in an engineer suit leaned against the wall in the dark, facing away from Yodan. The blue fabric from his suit was faded and torn.

"Excuse me?" Yodan had his mask on but the man wasn't wearing one so Yodan was ready to remove his, but then figured this man might be disoriented or hostile and he might need grade-A air if chased.

The young man didn't move.

"Excuse me?" Yodan approached carefully, holding his control-pen. "Excuse me."

The man's face was rotted away and Yodan stumbled back, bumping into the empty supply cabinet. How was he standing if he was dead? Yodan stepped closer to inspect his two red prodigy stripes. This guy had studied in the same field as him. Maybe Yodan had even studied his findings and theories. The supply area was clean and dust-free, which meant drones took care of the area. So, why not clean out the dead?

The lifeless body had a smell that invaded the mask and the skin was drawn back revealing bones. Yodan was wrong, he wasn't leaning against the wall, a hook held him up by the neck. Maybe he'd fallen against it?

Yodan slid his gloves on to unhook him. Handling a lifeless body was strange and reminded him of his time in the recycling chamber, watching the bodies fall around him. He dragged the corpse to the waste portal, pulled the hatch open, and prepared to toss the body down the chute. Yodan stopped himself when the lines on the old lifesuit caught his eye. They were empty like the ones on his fake-arm yet Yodan was alive. *Wasn't he?* What if Yodan was dead and this search for a new system was all that death was? What if Madeline was currently in her own reality like this?

Alone and worried, Yodan touched the dead man's skull behind his ear to see if his eTatt held information but nothing greeted him and the spot was so wasted away he couldn't tell if he'd disconnected from the system before he died. Maybe Exchangers and Connectors stopped working when they died? Or maybe they stopped working when Nogard died?

Yodan worked his gloved fingers in the rotting skin to dig for a Connector or even the small Exchanger.

Nothing. Maybe he'd left the system before his eighteenth FIRE Ceremony.

Yodan propped the body against the wall and sat in front of the dead young man. He'd been alive. Air had filled his lungs and ideas and dreams had filled his head that weren't a part of Nogard's plans. Who was this man? Where was his life-energy now?

Yodan couldn't toss this body down the waste chute as if his life was over. Energy was more than memories. It was continuous, moving them from place to place, feeding objects surrounding them.

Hauling the body to the corner, Yodan rested him against the wall, then arranged the man's hands in front of him, across his chest as if he was being sworn into his working career. Then he piled rocks over him from the stairwell in a line across his legs. Entombing him in the rock that sheltered them, even a bit, was strangely healing. When satisfied, Yodan left messages in the stairwell to prepare the crew that would follow him that death was ahead.

Then, with his chalk, Yodan wrote, '*Here lies an engineer. He will be missed.*' He stared at the words. Had this man written the sayings in the stairwell? In case he had, Yodan added, '*He is truly free, despite the cost.*'

Exhausted from the emotional and physical strain, Yodan checked the chamber for supplies, pipe access, a place to hide during the FIRE Ceremony, and water. Each room in these types of access passageways was set up the same and drones kept them stocked. He found the water supply and drank heartily. But there was no place for him to hide which meant he had to either rush back or keep moving until he found a FIRE safe hideout.

His tank of Oxy-air was empty so he grabbed the oxygen cylinder off the wall and hung the grade-A air on his back over his lifesuit, then he fit the mask over his face. He sipped a hit of fresh air and his energy returned almost instantly.

The red Pipe of Creation caught his eye overhead, peeking out from the corner. The pipe travelled through each mainframe and would eventually lead him to Mainframe One. Meant he was on the right path. Excited, Yodan followed. The red pipe didn't reappear but several flights of stairs later, Yodan ended up in another chamber. Here he checked the shelves for minerals and filled his pack with more supplies: an energy blanket and, of course, he added water. He might be able to tolerate poor air for long periods, but his body needed water every hour. The latch on the FIRE safety was broken so after sealing up the storage units, he took the next flight of stairs.

The scorch marks on the wall meant FIRE passed through this passageway. He checked his SHARP, which also only had minimal readings on it, but the area was getting warmer. Maybe he should go back? Yodan glanced down the stairwell. Would he have enough time?

The stairs were along a silver pipe with several doors for drone entrances. Any of these pipes could lead him to a safer area. But these stairs could also lead him to Mainframe One. How far was the first mainframe?

He left a mark on the wall announcing that he'd kept going. A strange putrid smell greeted him, but the area was empty. Seeing a drone would ease the worry.

He continued, counting each step. The chalk warnings on the wall ended, but he added his own marks so he knew which way he'd travelled and others could follow. The air had a dead tension. More scorch marks on the walls confirmed his suspicion that Nogard was using these old run-off passageways to filter flames. These chambers would burst with flames when the FIRE started.

Yodan glanced at his health monitor again, worried because the lines still read that he was dead.

After the next flight of stairs counting 455 steps, Yodan arrived at a metal heat-proof black door with a red doorknob. Doors in the chambers slid and Nogard opened them as they approached. This one didn't. The light overhead was pink.

Excited, Yodan gripped the handle and pushed. He wasn't sure what to expect, but the creature trapped under a landslide of rocks was not it. He reacted, turning his pen-light to full beam and attaching his light to the wall. Then he studied the structure of the area since the area had suffered from an explosion-type of cave-in.

The area was safe enough for him to approach the creature, and so he did, trying frantically to remember everything he'd read about this hairy beast.

AVERY

A few breaths later
Underground, lost in the stairwell

Moving slower, Avery searched the dark, following the pink lights, lost in endless passageways with no sense of direction. Where was Pax? She had no idea it'd be so endless underground. Calling his name was useless. She was lost.

The tiny glowing pink mini-suns that hung over each door were her only comfort. When she opened a heavy grey door, a strange light blinded her and a growl made her jump to action. Avery whipped out her blade, ready to fight, even blind. What growled like a bear underground?

"It's hurt," a guy said, his face coming into focus as she moved out of the intense beam, arms up to block out the assaulting light.

She stumbled back when she realized the stranger was bald and his skin was white like snow, his garments were a metallic shiny light pink. Was this guy made by Dragon? On his knees he helped a bear trapped in an avalanche of rock, not looking at her, his attention on the bear. She didn't dare take another step in case the bear attacked.

"What are you doing?" she demanded, ready to run, but he was the first person she'd met and might be the only one.

"He's alive and hurt. I can't leave this creature to suffer alone."

The growling was more like a rumbling now.

"That's a hurt wild animal. It'll kill you." She had her blade out to protect herself. "Not to mention the avalanche might squash you."

"The area's secure. That pipe dropped this debris as backlash from an explosion."

The bear groaned and swatted the air with its free arm. Long claws caught the guy's suit and tore right through the shiny fabric making a strange crumpling sound. She had no idea what his clothes were made of but Avery stepped back, afraid.

She was never this close to a bear before, let alone a young man created from clay by Dragon. Behind his ear and along his neck were markings that looked like Dragon's tail.

The guy worked, clearing away rubble. Blood dripped from his wounded left arm where he was scratched, but he didn't pay the wound attention as he pulled rubble off the bear.

His solid white skin hadn't seen the sun in...ever. His pink one-piece uniform had pockets, two red stripes along the legs, and straps holding gadgets. The most curious thing about him were his eyes. They were pink with red centers. In any other setting, he might have terrified her because he looked so different, but on his knees, saving a bear cub, well, he was clearly harmless. Stupid, but harmless.

She gripped her blade, ready for an attack from the bear that was almost free.

This strange young man dug frantically, shoving rocks aside. The bear attempted to sit but fell back and the guy pulled the strange mask off his face and tossed the breathing device over his shoulder as if in his way.

"Help me," he pleaded, his focus on the dying bear.

Having suffered an injury to its head, the bear moved with a groan. Blood pooled around it. Its leg was clearly broken and when she slid her hand over the fur, the bear was cold under her fingers. "We're too late," she told this guy. "I should kill this beast to end the suffering. Compassion is all I can offer."

He cleared the last of the rubble and pulled the bear's head in his hands. "Breathe," he commanded the creature as if the bear understood. Pushing against the markings behind his ear, the young man said, "Nogard, I need healing gases. A medic. I have a creature in a stairwell headed to Mainframe One."

Avery glanced over her shoulder. Who was he talking to?

The bear grumbled and in a huff let out its last breath. It rested a paw on the guy's arm while Avery sat in silence, watching them stare each other down.

When the cub fell limp, the guy crumpled on the animal in a heap of tears.

His pain was so deep and moving that the sorrow rolled off him and onto her lap. Acting on instinct, Avery placed her hands over his and decided a prayer might help him cope with the loss. Perhaps this was his pet, and well, she'd lost Friskie and knew the depth of that grief.

Hunter had said prayers had helped him while he grieved and so she tried. "Dragon, Bear was strong and fought death. Now recycle this body while guiding the surviving spirit on a peaceful journey."

The guy moved the bear's arms over its chest. "This life will be missed," he said solemnly and for the first time, he glanced at Avery. His eyes grew bigger and he stared, his mouth rolling in tight. Having no hair over his eyes made the lines more prominent as he frowned. "Who are you?"

"Avery of Saxton's Clan." She bowed as was their custom. "And you?"

"Yodan of Quadrant F, Section 33, Mainframe Seven, Quma Cities." He placed his fingers by her ear without touching her, the bear between them. Was this a form of greeting? She didn't move. He waited, still. Finally, she did the same thing to him. She couldn't see enough in the dim light so she rubbed behind his ear. When her fingers grazed his skin, he pushed behind her ear, feeling her hair.

"You're not connected to the system," he said.

"Is that what this bump behind your ear does?" She sensed something strange on his skin and gave the bulge a light tap. Skin bounced back, like something alive pulsated underneath.

"Youth connect by tapping each other's eTatts when we meet to identify each other and share stories since we aren't fully connected to the system. The sensors in our fingers read the Exchanger and share information."

"Well, I guess we'll share stories my way since I don't have sensors or an Exchanger."

"And how do you share memories?" He moved rocks into a straight line across the bear's belly.

"We talk. What are you doing?" she asked.

"Trapping his body to the earth we come from."

What a terrible waste of energy. Still, Yodan was so upset over this death, she helped him bury the bear in rocks, making a neat line like him. She was used to grief making people do weird things.

"The mama might be kicking around. Must be a den that caved in. Regardless, the bear hurt you and you should've left the creature alone."

"I don't wish to die alone. I won't allow that for others." He ran his hand over the bear's fur. His tears made the pink in his eyes sparkle. "We respect life. All life."

"In my clan, we believe that when we die, our spirit goes on a journey to find a place we can call home for eternity. For each of us that home is different." She explained Saxton's beliefs to this guy who stared at her like she was the most amazing thing in the world. Why was he studying her?

His pink eyes almost ate into her life-essence.

"You believe in a transfer of energy? How do I see this spirit that moves on?"

"You don't. You just know it's there. You trust this."

He nodded. "I can do that, but others in my system need facts. When my friend Madeline was crushed by a rock, I saw a hologram of her glimmering beside it. I thought maybe her memories struggled to exist. But... Could she be energy somewhere?" he asked Avery as if she knew such things.

Her first instinct was to snap at him, but when she saw how serious he was and how important this Madeline clearly was to him, she offered the most comforting idea she could. "Yeah. Perhaps the image you saw was her saying good-bye."

"She was dead, that's impossible."

"How do you know what's impossible when you die? Have you died before?"

"Well, no."

"How did you get down here?"

"Downhere?" He peered around as if this was the name of where they were. "I travelled up steps. This is my first time in this section." He worked so fast, his movements were precise, well-planned, and efficient. Once satisfied with the job he'd done of trapping the dead bear to the earth, he removed his gloves.

She told him, "I came down a shaft that flames usually shoot out from."

He glanced at his device. "Is it far?"

"I'm lost," she admitted.

"We'll need to find shelter." The wound on his arm was healed. He glanced at his arm when he saw her staring and pulled down his sleeve to cover it, as if embarrassed.

Then, calmly, he used chalk to write things on the wall over the tomb.

"What does your writing say?" she asked.

"Here lies a beast known as bear. I was with him when he left this system for another. He will be missed but is free."

"That's powerful."

"Thanks. I like making people think with my words. We're told a lot how to think in my system and it feels right when we think for ourselves and push our ideas."

He handed her a cylinder but she looked at it not sure what he wanted from her. "The air is poor so use this. We'll feel better if we bring our energy levels up." He showed her how to breathe from the hand-size cylinder but she backed up.

"I can't use that, it's science." Her eye immediately started to tic. He tilted his head to watch it.

Embarrassed she covered her eye. "Science destroyed the world. I'm not allowed to use that."

He held the small pipe out anyway. "Dare ya to try."

Was he calling her a coward? Defiant, she snapped the cylinder from him. The material was cool in her grip. "How does this work?" she demanded.

With a full smile, Yodan placed the mask in front of her nose. "Feel the air?" Despite the tickling sensation, she found this air gave her a strange energy. This was the air from the healing waters and she enjoyed the spicy scent. Nothing was scary or weird about that. "Take a deeper breath and hold it in." He lightly grazed her gut. "Focus on the breath whenever those tics bug you. Doesn't always stop them, but it reminds you that you control something: your breathing. In and out. Deep as you want, as often as you want."

She watched him breathe, copying how deep and long he pulled air in from the cylinder.

The tic stopped.

She wasn't sure if this was science. It was more like contained air. "Did Dragon create you?" Her voice was a whisper.

He removed a panel from the pipe, glancing inside. "Not me," he answered with this head in the pipe. "But I was programmed to identify the differences in each of us, then to sort these traits as attractive, desired, or disposable so the Collective can use my studies in the creation of the next generation."

The pipe was dark but he had a faint light in front of him. She followed him in the pipe, not wanting to be left behind.

"And what do you think about how different I am from you?" she asked.

"Your eyes are the strangest colour," he said. "I've seen the colour once before on a gem."

"Green? You don't have green eyes in your village?"

He shook his head. "Green. Nope. We don't have anything green. The word even sounds fun."

"No plants or nothing?" They crawled and Avery was thankful that his light-thing made seeing easier. Was it science, too?

"Sure we have plants," he said. "We grow them everywhere, but they're grey and white, growing low to the ground or along the walls under the D-light. How was this green achieved?"

"I..." She had no idea what he meant. Green was everywhere. "I've never seen red centers in eyes before." She sounded too sharp and cursed herself for not using a softer tone. She didn't want this guy to abandon her in these pipes because she'd insulted him.

Much to her relief, he chuckled. "In another few cycles, everyone created in the system will have red centers in our eyes since I see better in the dark. I need less D-light and sleeping gases so I take less energy to maintain. That was part of my studies."

"I like your eyes."

"I like yours, too. Madeline had grey eyes. Well, I remember them being grey, yet my friend Match says they were usually blue." His entire posture changed when he mentioned her and sadness oozed off him once again.

"I'm sorry. This friend obviously meant a lot to you."

"I was made to forget her. Using scientific data, Nogard chose a more appropriate life-companion for me and erased her from my memories. Bugs me. I always thought I was free to choose my companion."

Avery followed as they continued to crawl through the pipe. "I'm supposed to be able to pick, too, but it doesn't feel that way since if I choose this old guy, my brothers get land to raise their families. If I don't, where will they go?"

"Hard to do what's best for the system sometimes. I mean, I know Nogard would choose properly for me, based on evaluations, but this choice doesn't *feel* best for me. There are things that facts can't explain."

"Exactly. This is someone I'll get naked with, shouldn't my feelings matter?"

He stopped crawling as if the word *naked* added tension to the area. Then, without a word, he took out a device that cut into the pipe.

"More science?" she asked.

"It's a laser. We use them to cut into rocks, pipes, even cut off a limb if you're trapped under rock. It's saved my life quite a few times." He climbed out of this new hole he'd made and she followed.

"So science is good?"

"I wouldn't use it to hurt anyone." His promise was solid.

The walls in this new room were made of rock. Well, not simply rock, they were alive with colours. Blues, reds, even shiny gold gleamed when he scanned the area with his light-tube-science-thing.

Then, much to her horror, Yodan climbed in a new pipe at the other end of the small room, leaving her. What was he doing?

She went in after him. "Do you know where you're going?" she asked, feeling foolish that she was trusting him blindly. He could be leading her to Dragon as a sacrifice.

"There's a safe room on the other side of this tunnel."

"You were there before?"

"I studied a map my sister was given."

"So you looked at a map and are going by memory?" Oh my gosh! They were so gonna get lost!

"I can recall the memory and review the image from different angles like a file. No worries, it's like having the copy in front of me."

They entered a new pipe big enough to walk in and he helped her to her feet and removed his mask so she did the same. He had that lighting device in his hand. His smile showed off perfect teeth, so white, she reached out, and without thinking, she touched one, her fingers lingering by his lips.

"Sorry." She pulled away, embarrassed.

He licked his lips. Silently watching her.

"Yodan? Say something."

"I...I...you..." he let out a long breath, then cleared his

throat. "Wow, this rush of *wanting* is hard to filter. No wonder Nogard controlled how we feel. I mean, earlier she'd made me lust after someone, and the connection felt forced, weird, unnatural, and extremely physical. This connection between us is grounded. Like I was me before I met you, but now, wow, now I'm *really* me."

She smiled, amused. "I meant say something about me touching you. Was that wrong?" How foolish did she sound? Of course she shouldn't shove her finger in someone's mouth and touch their teeth.

"Wrong? I..." He took something out of his pocket. She looked at the sparkling rock. "This was given to me by someone I care for and has brought me luck. I give it to you. When you get luck, you give this rare gem to another person you care for."

"It's beautiful."

He stared at her. "Yeah. It is."

Avery understood what Pax had meant about falling. Her smarts slipped, making her act foolish in a dangerous situation, but she took the rock from him and kissed his cheek lightly. "Thank you."

Yodan offered her water and a golden liquid. She smelled it. "This is the water from the healing pool."

"It's our nutrients. Drink," Yodan insisted. "We heal faster if we stay hydrated."

"You do heal fast." She looked at his arm where the bear had clawed, amazed that the wound was healed.

Yodan rubbed his left arm. "My arm...it's..." He sighed. "My arm is artificial. Nogard used my own skin to cover the device, and my arm looks real, but it sucks."

Clearly something had happened he didn't want to talk about so Avery let the issue go and took jerky from her bag. "I eat this."

Yodan smelled the dried meat then handed the meat back. "The stink reminds me of the recycling chamber." He sipped his gold water. "I had to spend one hundred breaths once in the recycling chamber because I received five demerits for breaking a rule. Each death haunts me."

"Your place sounds horrible. No wonder you want to leave."

"It was perfect, as long as we followed the rules. I have a

hard time with rules."

A soft misty fog gathered around them. "I need to sit." Stumbling, Yodan rested against the pipe. Avery joined him. He was warm and Avery snuggled beside him, feeling safe with this stranger. Why was she so relaxed?

She glanced over at Yodan, who was already fast asleep. *Sleeping...*

Avery stifled a yawn, then put Yodan's mask on him, since he had needed the breathing device earlier and she didn't want him to struggle with this air. Why was she so tired?

YODAN

A few breaths later
Underground, lost in the pipes

Yodan woke to the beep of the SHARP. He glanced at the device, shocked to see that time had slipped away. Had he fallen asleep in this chamber? That couldn't be right. He would never...

Strange panic smashed into him. *Be calm*, he ordered himself. The first rule of survival in any event was to remain calm. This single beep was just a warning to get to safety. He had time. But how much time?

Avery slept against him in her vivid colourful clothing. How plain he must seem to her in his one-colour lifesuit. He glanced at himself, too aware of how he must look, which wasn't something he'd ever thought about before. In a system where everyone looked close to the same, it didn't matter.

The poor air must have knocked them both out, but he was wearing his Oxy-air mask and didn't remember putting it on. A mist of sleeping gas filled the chamber. He stole a clean breath then put Avery's mask on, too.

Running his tongue around his mouth, he tried to remove the taste of sleeping gas from his palate as he woke the young woman gently, leaving the mask in place. "Avery of Saxton's Clan, we have to keep moving." He was in her face, watching for signs of life. Her wild orange hair covered her face and he gently pushed the orange strands aside, curious about the hair on her eyelids. Didn't that bother her sight?

When she woke, he had a strand of coarse orange hair between his fingers, wondering what the hair would feel like against his face.

"What are you doing?" she demanded, removing the mask.

He dropped the strand of hair and replaced the mask for her. "Your hair-garment distracted me." His grin felt ridiculously innocent as she glared, clearly infuriated with him. Why was he acting like a curious child?

"My hair is not for you to fondle." She pushed him back and pulled the mask off. Fists clenched.

Gosh. For some reason, her temper was another plus.

Seeing a woman react with such intense fury was not something he was used to. This was a gal who thought for herself; who wouldn't tolerate Nogard reprogramming her. "You have me curious, Avery of Saxton's Clan. I didn't realize touching your head garment was unacceptable and this won't happen again." He reached out to invite her to follow. "Come, we need to get to safety. The air will make you sleepy so keep the mask on."

She stared at his hand without taking it, then she replaced the mask around her face while asking, "What do you mean by safety?"

"Flames will purge this area." The SHARP let out two beeps. "Anything coated in heat-resistant alloy will protect us from the fire."

She stared at him, lost. How much technology was in her system? She was clearly intelligent and a lot like him, despite their physical appearances, but he needed to use words they both knew. Their usage of language had evolved.

He opened the access to the silver pipe. She followed.

"I'll mark the wall with chalk," he explained, "so we won't get lost. We won't be in these pipes for long."

She climbed in the next pipe behind him. "What happens in a quake if we're in this pipe?"

"We don't worry about things we can't change like quakes. The speed we move at is something we can change, so hustle. If a sleeping gas came through this area, it means the place will be full of flames shortly. The gases promise a painless death." His emergency training kept him calm. "Stay close and use your smarts."

PAX

A few breaths later
Above ground, Mainframe One

Pax watched Lins vanish into the red pipe. Knots formed in his stomach, making him want to puke up his earlier snack. What if he never saw her again? He glanced at his bag. It contained something so valuable she couldn't bring the gadgets with her.

When Lins vanished, so did the warmth. As Pax stood, a deep chill settled on him, growing from his shoulder where he'd flung the bag.

Determined to be useful, he did as Lins had asked and raced through the doors, opening them as she'd instructed. With his keen sense of direction he mapped the area, sometimes stopping under the pink lights to draw out the map in his notebook. His hand moved over the images quicker than usual and with more details.

The last door he opened sent shockingly cool air at him as he stumbled into the outdoors. Before him was the entrance to Cuma Village, where he'd first met Avery. And suddenly, the course he'd travelled, the pipes he'd entered, fit with what he knew of the outside of the pipes. He was right; those corridors were nothing but the inside of the pipes protecting the village.

The moon shone bright, leaving him in an eerie darkness, but the fresh air cooled his skin and he extended his arms to enjoy the sensation. Being alive felt great and that was his purpose—to just breathe it all in. He rushed out of the village to the forest. In the ruins, he found an old cellar and swung the trapdoor open. He'd spent a few nights sheltering down there and knew the cement staircase well, even in the dark.

He descended carefully and found a lantern along the wall. Once lit, it danced shadows around him.

The cellar was cozy and leaving Lins' precious cargo here was safe. Pax tucked the package nicely in the corner and tossed a fur blanket over it from the makeshift bed he'd used. Parting with the bag made him uneasy, but the notebook on the bed distracted him, as if he didn't know what the book contained. He did. Of course he did. But the information was blurry in his mind.

He'd left most of his belongings, not wanting to bring them to the village until he knew the place was safe. The notebook was what had pushed him out the door and to the village to find people. *And they'd pushed him in a pit.* Well. A pit that had led him to Lins…

Penny used to say that everything happened for a reason. Maybe there was sense to that.

A part of him chortled at the innocence behind such an idea. Was he so cold that he didn't even believe in fate?

He snagged the notebook and flipped open the pages. They were mostly drawings he'd made of Penny that didn't even come close to capturing her radiating energy, the feisty fire that was *her*. Her dark eyes brought images of her back to him. Like Lins, she had no hair, born that way from a mother who was also hairless. In his travels, he'd seen many without hair and ivory skin. Had they come from Lins' city and integrated above ground, generations ago? Penny had never mentioned anyone she knew living underground. Then again, she'd always felt safest underground and liked to explore ruins with him.

Taking out his pencil, he added in details to make the images come even more alive, not sure how he'd missed these strokes before. His hand worked so fast, he couldn't even reflect on the movement. And when he was satisfied, he sat back to look at the image of her.

She was beautiful.

The longing didn't assault him like usual and a warm peace settled on him that maybe his time with Penny was for a reason. Strange that it took meeting someone like Lins to realize that.

Well, he didn't have time to feel sorry for himself or reflect on this new person in his life. A different mission pushed him to his feet. If Lins was right and things were going to explode, his new family, as weird as they were, would be crushed.

Determined to save them and impress Lins, he hurried back to the village, rushing directly to Avery's hut, needing to talk to her because really, she was the only one in this village he trusted with something so big.

When Pax stormed in, he found Mother Roselle tossing things in a bag, working by candlelight. She was a plump woman full of vigour, and he'd grown fond of her ways. "Pax! Avery found you?"

His heart sank. "Tell me she didn't go in the shaft." *Of course she did.*

"Saxton went with her but got in a fight with the others. He's with the healers getting his nose and shoulder reset but he's determined to follow her in once they bandage him up." *Of course he was.* "He says that Avery sneaked in and the others removed the rope. She'll be trapped. I won't let that happen so I'm going after her." *Of course she was.*

Pax took the bag from Mother Roselle. She was a nursing mother with a baby in a sling in front of her. He wasn't letting her go down a shaft. "No worries. I'll hang a new rope and watch over it."

"We tried. They're guarding the pit and locked the boys up for trying."

He respected Avery's mother; Roselle had a fire to her.

"They'll be shocked to learn what I found while exploring." He smirked. "Just stay. There are other ways out of the shaft and she might find one like I did. I met a woman while in the pipes who says she has family and friends and she plans to bring them to live with us." He had this urge to reach out to this motherly woman and cry on her bosom as a troubled son would. Instead, he stepped back, resisting this weird longing as if parts of him were debating.

"What? A woman was in the pipes?"

"A beautiful one with purple eyes, who saw right into my fears and made them vanish."

"Oh my."

"Tell Saxton. She also said that there might be an explosion so to get everyone to safety, away from the cliffs."

"You trust this woman?"

"She was brilliant, and really, even if she's wrong, what would staying safe hurt? I trust my instinct, it got me this far and something isn't right about these quakes. They are building up to something nasty."

Roselle nodded. Picking up the candle, she gathered her younger sons, leaving Pax to rescue Avery. Well, rescue was a bit much. She was probably fine, wandering inside the pipe like he'd done.

When Pax marched up to Dragon's Caves, the leaders stepped away from him as if he was diseased. He didn't let their distrust bother him, being a nomad he'd lived with that type of reaction his entire life. Besides, he felt incredibly bold today.

"Pax," Elder Jacob whispered. "How? Whatever happened to your eyes? Why are they grey? Weren't they green?" Elder Jacob moved in closer with his torch.

"Must be the lighting." Pax faced them, a torch in his hands. "I saw a woman in the pipes. She says this area might explode and we need to get to safety. I sent Mother Roselle to gather the others, but she'll need help. The woman I met said others are in those pipes and will need a new home. Get your families to safety until they arrive."

"Dragon is to punish us?" Elder Fewerter asked. "How did you get out?" He stood over the shaft with a torch. Spiders scurried in a strange cluster toward the back of the cave, catching Pax's attention. *Great.* That was never a good sign.

"I walked out the door by the front entrance. Actually, the woman I met says that Dragon will help us, but she needs these others to do it. Why she has to go for them."

Elder Fewerter looked doubtful. "Dragon's people are coming?" He didn't seem surprised to learn about a woman in the pipes. Not as amazed as Mother Roselle had been.

"You knew people lived in these pipes?"

Elder Fewerter glanced around. Leaders stepped closer to listen to his answer. "Go home to your clans and stay safe in your huts."

"If the cliffs blow or crumble, everyone needs to be further down the hill out of harm's way," Pax insisted but no one cared to listen to him when the elder had spoken. He would have to convince the elder so he followed him to the back of the cave as the others left.

"We keep rope in that back area," he told Pax. "My grand-father was young when the clay-woman came from Dragon's Caves. She told him about her city underneath us."

"And he didn't tell others about this?"

"Didn't want them to think him crazy."

All this time, this old man suspected others lived underground. Yet he'd told no one? Pax was shocked. "Why didn't you find them?"

"Some people don't want to be found. I even set up camp in a room I found. Brought things like seeds and aloe plants. I never saw anyone. There's a labyrinth underneath us. The air is hard to breathe and it's much too hot. If people live there, they've adapted to things we won't understand."

"We can." They were at the back of the cave, facing well-stocked shelves with all sorts of items, but a rat was dead in front of them and the spiders scurried to the back crevices of the cave. Pax glanced around, paranoid. He knew from experience to be careful when he saw dead animals in a cave or building and what was with the spiders? Before taking another step, he placed a handkerchief over his mouth. The cave was warm, so warm he could almost see the heat emerging out of the glowing hole in the distance.

"Breathe through your garments," he ordered Fewerter, then he bent over the rat, curious. The air grew hotter and that was his last thought before something hit him on the back of the head.

YODAN

During the same breath
Underground, in the pipes

The heat in the pipes increased. Even Yodan was uncomfortable. Avery was slowing down at a time when they needed to speed up. To encourage her, Yodan offered her his pen-light. "Take it."

She did but said, "I'm not allowed to hold science things. You don't need it?" They continued to crawl.

Her fear of technology was perplexing for him. "It's a light. If you move the pen around it'll stay lit."

Activating the light with a swoosh motion, she chuckled. "This is amazing. Are you sure it's not science? Can I keep this?"

"It's yours," he offered, calculating where they were. He'd taken a wrong turn someplace and was lost. They needed out of this heat, but if he cut into the wrong pipe he could actually incinerate them.

"I'm hot," Avery complained as they crawled.

So was he.

A chirp echoed from the SHARP, making him crawl faster. Before he entered the adjoining silver pipe, Yodan touched the sides to make sure they wouldn't be cooked. Things were warm under his fingers but tolerable.

"Why is your machine making those noises?"

"Purging the system means flames travel the pipes to clean out any debris, any unwanted viruses, anything that might affect our life in Quma Cities. This cleansing happens automatically so that if Nogard has a virus or an intruder, these fires kill it. All we can do is get to safety. These old passageways will redirect the flames." He glanced back. Avery wasn't there. "Avery?" Where in all these rocks did she get off to?

He backed up and found her around the corner, passed out. Probably from the heat. Working fast, he took off his lifesuit, rolled it under her shoulders and pulled her. He'd practised this enough in their emergency scenarios but he felt the pressure. He didn't have time for hydrating her or air. He pulled, realizing too late that he'd left his pack around the corner when he'd snagged her.

Didn't matter. The heat had him dizzy.

At a drone exit, he kicked open the door, letting the cool air assault his almost-naked body. Tumbling out of the pipe with Avery, they landed on a cold marble floor. Yodan caught Avery to stop her head from smacking the hard floor. Then he rolled with her against the wall and jumped to snap the door closed but flames exploded out the door as he pushed against it to lock the fire in the pipes.

They were safe but his chest had suffered serious burns. His pack had remained in the pipe and his lifesuit had gotten caught in the door and was half burned. He was wearing his mask, but his Oxy-air tank was missing. What he needed was the medic-pen in his bag…

In pain, Yodan collapsed against the wall. Avery shifted beside him, promising him that she was alive. He focused on her while he breathed through the pain. Moving carefully to avoid aggravating his burn, Yodan undid her restricting garments so she could breathe and cool off.

"Where are we?" Avery whispered, shining the pen-light around and bringing the room to colourful life for him.

"Looks like a living chamber dating back from Mainframe Two. Do you need air? We won't be in here for long."

"I'm dizzy. Why are you naked?"

"Lost everything getting us out of there. We'll gather what we can in this room."

"You're burned?" She dropped beside him for a better look.

Her spicy scent reminded him of the quarry and Yodan opened his eyes to stare at her, the pain too much to move. Pain like this meant death was close and if she was the last person he would see, he planned to take in her beauty.

Cool fingers grazed his shoulder. "It looks like a sunburn. This will heal."

Yodan had no idea what a sunburn was but he doubted he'd survive this, the pain was too intense.

Avery tore the room apart and returned with something soothing she gently smeared on his irritated and red skin. Each stroke brought magical relief. The goop came from a plant she'd found and broken open. Such simple technology.

"I would have never used a plant for this pain." She had to be the most brilliant thinker he'd ever met.

"How does that feel?" she asked, in his face.

"Nice. Your touch is magic. What's the cool goop you're rubbing on me?" He relaxed. Maybe he wouldn't die.

"Aloe gel. My new brother Pax showed me how to use the gel inside the aloe plant for all sorts of things. See that plant growing along the side of the wall? It's green above ground, but you break the leaves open and use the gel inside for things like burns. This one smells sweeter than what we use, but if this plant helps, good."

"We use medic-pens to heal. Mine was in my bag." He rested with his back against the cool marble wall afraid to move. She knelt beside him, carefully working on his burn, meeting his eyes every once in a while.

He placed a hand on her arm to stop her so they could stare at each other. "If I die, follow my chalk marks."

"Just don't die," she ordered, then continued to rub the goop on him. Now that the pain was easing off, the attention was rousing and his adrenaline kicked in so he got up to explore the area. A breathing station along the far wall had several tubes of Oxy-air. Yodan gathered supplies, but without his lifesuit, he had nothing to clip the cylinders to.

Avery searched the other end of the room and called to him, "Hey, look at this. These are pants from Berry Clan," Avery said. "What are pants from above ground doing here?"

"Your people were here?" He took the garments from her and slipped his legs in them but had no idea how to connect them.

"Let me help." She pulled the strings, tying the pants shut as if they were ropes.

Standing close to her, Yodan watched her agile hands work the pieces of garments together, mesmerized by her movements. His body reacted on its own whenever she touched him this way and the heavy garments weren't doing much to conceal his physical attraction to her.

When she glanced up, he smiled. "Thanks."

"There's a shirt, but with that burn, maybe it's best to tie the fabric around your waist." She went to help but he stopped her and gently took the garment from her.

"Probably best if I do that myself. I'd like to decide with

my mind if I like you, before I let my hormones distract me."

She blushed. "Never met anyone so bluntly honest."

"Try it. Just say what you're thinking. It's freeing. Only thing that helped me stay sane in our perfect Utopia."

Her face flashed even deeper red. "Gee, you're the first guy I thought looked *good* in pants from Berry Clan."

He smirked, pleased that she saw him that way. "Thanks. They feel nice. But we need to keep moving. The FIRE Ceremony is over now; feel how the pipes are cooling?"

As she climbed in the silver pipe after Yodan, Avery said, "I can almost hear Mother Roselle freaking out. These pipes are sacred and we're climbing around in them." She didn't sound impressed. "How's your burn feeling?"

"Better. Thanks."

"Never seen anyone heal so quickly."

"I'm not much of a liar but I can pretend my burn hurts if you want to rub more of that goop on me. Never had anyone take care of me, was nice."

Her chuckles echoed down the pipe making him joyful inside. The sound warmed him, and he tried to remember the last time he'd heard laughter.

They crawled for a bit. Yodan needed water, but had none. He talked to distract himself from the intense warning signs his body screamed. "So this deal you mentioned that you need to make for your brothers to get land… Can I ask you a question about it?"

"Sure."

"Is this land actual dirt?"

"Not really, more like a place my brothers can build huts."

"Weird thing to trade when we have all this land to dig into." He wondered how a person could own land or even a person. "Sometimes, we trade illegals, like needles filled with memories or knowledge we shouldn't have access to, but I never heard of trading people or land. I mean, land belongs to anyone and everyone. People belong to no one."

"Above ground isn't all habitable. We fight for territory and areas where we can build our clans, and well, people are useful and serve a purpose so we add ourselves into the deals to make them worthwhile. Think about it, if you grow crops but don't have enough help for the work required, you could trade a family with hard workers for food they need since you'll have lots."

The idea was hard to wrap his mind around. Nogard was so good at assigning them jobs and ensuring everyone had what they needed. This sounded like an unbalance. "You're trading your skills?"

"Sure."

"That makes sense. In our system, everyone has a skill and everyone knows their place. Nutrients are readily available so aren't a commodity. What is rare to us is free thoughts, time away from the system, knowledge the Collective doesn't know. These are the things we trade." Yodan's hand shook as he placed it in front of himself, focusing on each movement. "I need water and minerals. I'm used to having these things at certain times and my body hates me." Dizzy, he rested against the cold wall.

MATCH

During the same breaths
Underground, FIRE Chamber

Waiting sucked. But Match trusted Yodan and used this time to prepare their people for their trek through the old passageways, because every breath was one less they'd have next cycle.

The medics had removed the Exchangers in everyone to disable the system completely. A few questers with disabled Connectors had survived but everyone else would be missed.

His people were free, like him, and looking to him for guidance.

Shandra called for Yodan again with no response which made Match want to puke. Why wasn't Yodan responding? After a moment, Shandra threw the device, smashing the machine against the wall. Silence fell in the FIRE chamber.

"Shandra, let's walk this off. Everyone back to work." Match led her to the corner, pressing against her warm body so their faces brushed. "What is it?"

"Yodan's SHARP was incinerated."

Match gently wiped her tears. "We're going down this pit to find him. He would have left us a trail."

She nodded. "I'd like to know that he survived the FIRE. This unknown annoys me."

"I can try things." Since Match normally used drones to stay in contact with others, he called one over. "I'm Match, an elite. Yodan of Quadrant F has taken a passageway from the FIRE pit to Mainframe One. He could be in any pipes, any safety hideout, even in a stairwell. He might be alive, hurt, or dead. Report his status immediately."

The drone attached itself to Match's SHARP to give him a quick report of the collective mind of the drones and their system. Waiting, Match stared at the blank screen. What was taking so long?

"Why is the screen blank?" Shandra stared with him. "What does that mean?"

"The mother drone must be down."

She grabbed the SHARP from him and opened the coding

connecting the device to the drone. With a few program changes she had the drone communicating with another, by-passing their mother drone. Every drone that met with a new drone would add to the report.

"We'll keep that one and send this one exploring," Shandra said.

He glanced at his watch. Now the relic turned blue circles as it counted down as if pleading him to change the termination program somehow, but there was no way to reprogram Nogard. The Artificial-life as he knew her was dead.

Medic Jon approached as they watched the drone float down the FIRE pit to trace the path Yodan had taken. "Let's do this, Sir Rawlings."

With a deep breath, Match pushed down the panic. He wasn't ready for any of this but when he met the medic's eyes, Jon didn't look any calmer. If one of them needed to be calm it was the medic, so Match gave him a reassuring smile as he snapped the last hook in place on Jon's lifesuit and led him to the ledge.

"We do this for Greg. I'll be right behind ya." Match guided the ropes down.

The air had Match dizzy, but he kept his eyes locked on the pipe in the middle of the FIRE pit so no one would notice his fatigue. His training pulsated in his mind. *Calm. Precise. In control. Stand tall. Shoulders back. Short breaths.*

When the line reached the end, he called down, "All I got." He waited, gripping the rope too tight.

"I see the passageway," Jon answered. The rope fell limp under his fingers but he didn't haul the line up just yet. He stared down the hole as if he might see Jon. "We'll need someone older to guide the first crew, there isn't enough room for all of us. If we send them in groups of ten or so that'll work. The red prodigy left notes that say the next section is a stairwell and that the door is jammed."

Fighting the flames wanting to erupt in his hands, Match snapped his medic-pen in half, not sure when he'd grabbed it. The popping sound grounded him, reminding him of when the D-light clicked off in the comfort of his sleeping pod.

"Sir Rawlings, how should we help?" The youth addressing him was about Twelve FIRE Ceremonies. Pink eyes with black centers studied him. Behind her were five youths about the same age. Clearly, a new training team; at their age they'd be focused on taking orders. Match checked their eyes, making sure none were grey.

The youth glanced at the leaking pen in Match's hand so he tossed the broken medic-pen in the FIRE pit and forced a grin while relaxing his shoulders.

He gave these youths tasks so they'd make themselves useful and forget the fear. "While we get these young ones over the ledge, you stronger ones get supplies. Each of you will lead a pack younger than you. We need Oxy-air, medic-pens, laser-pens, a few control-pens, water, and nutrients. Line everything up that you can't strap to yourselves. I'll lower kits and you'll carry them."

"May I bring this tool I made?" One of the youths asked, as if such details were his decision.

His training was clear, if they asked, the answer was no.

"Ask yourself if this device will save your life or not?"

She opened her hand. In it was a fine filament. "This connected devices to my Exchanger so I could map out how they work. With a few tweaks I could connect to something else, like a SHARP."

Nice. "It's small enough, wrap the filament around a memory needle and slide the combo along the sleeve of your lifesuit." He showed her that he wore several program-scramblers, memory needles, identification pins, and programming needles on his sleeve, which was standard for an elite. He couldn't use them on himself or even the others now, but he could insert them in a SHARP or even in a drone. "Never know when you might need something so brilliant."

She nodded and rushed after the others but she had him curious. All these children... Were they spared by Nogard because they could bring her back to life?

So why spare him? What could he possibly contribute to any new system?

The team knew the drill and what to pack. Evacuations and relocations happened regularly. Only this was the first time Match gave the orders. They usually had experienced engineers organizing the relocation based on carefully planned orders. Protector Owen wasn't among the group and Lins was hopefully successfully activating the system in Mainframe One to welcome them. So really, Match was all they had.

The huge fear screaming at him was 'where will this hole lead'? They hadn't heard from Yodan in a long while, but Match refused to believe he was lost. He checked the drone then connected it to his SHARP so he could have detailed reports instantly. "Shandra!" he called to her. "The drones have reports."

She glanced up. "Any sign of Yodan?"

Jon called up to him, "The red prodigy left a trail. Looks hopeful at this end."

A trail to where? Match glanced at the SHARP again. A drone sent him an image of writing on a wall that was clearly Yodan's scrawl. Yodan had found a bear. A wild hope hit Match. He spoke to Shandra who was on her knees, putting harnesses on the children, "Yodan was right. The Big Freeze didn't kill everything. He found more evidence of another system."

Her smile lit the darkening chamber.

Medic Jon called up to them, "Lower the first batch. Let's do this."

Match heaved the harness up and glanced around the room. Prodigies lined up tanks like soldiers ready for their orders. Without Nogard active, they couldn't refill them once the refill stations were empty, but their lifesuits were equipped to strap on several, plus other gear. They could empty the refill stations along the way since Match didn't plan on leading these people back. They were going up, despite the training he had to always travel down.

Shandra hooked each of the younger ones up with four cylinders and four water. The older ones would carry the rest of the supplies.

"Anyone know how to program a machine to make air?" Match double checked his fastens.

"Breathable air?" Andret asked. "Filtered or natural? What grade?"

Match spun around. Andret was loading a bag with the heavier bottles of water and nutrients. Hilt dropped off more for him. Both their eyes were normal.

"I enjoy a challenge. I'll make you air. Whatever you want, but not with a machine," Andret said.

"Bring the programs you need. Get rope and lower these packs you're filling. Make them light enough so Medic Jon can haul them in or get your ass down there to do it yourself."

"Don't need a program to make air. Just need this." He flashed a pack of seeds at him. "Few grow-anywhere seeds, a little D-light, splash of water, and we're breathing."

They could do this. "Pack what you need. Include speed growth, I believe there were two bottles under the Bench of Life."

Hilt took off for them.

Shandra spoke to the children calmly. Several were ready for him to lower. She was good with the young ones despite her worry for Yodan.

Match approached the nearest child and checked her harness and eyes before lifting her over the ledge. "You all right?" He asked the child as he fastened her to the rope.

"I fear." She refused to look at him.

He bent so they were eye to eye with the railing between them. Her eyes were violet with black centers. This terror was crippling and hard to filter so he knew what she meant. "Fear means you'll fight to survive. You've never needed the emotion before so Nogard suppressed it. Now you need it. Use it."

"So Nogard's fine? Shouldn't she be helping us?"

He brushed the tear on her cheek. "We're fine. Programmers can fix Nogard. Until then, I keep you safe so you can help us survive. What are you studying?"

"A code to help with Nogard's new emotional regulator." She smiled, proud, the fear washing off her.

In all his training, Match never expected this bond with the people. He never considered these moments more than in an event, he'd do this or that. But here he was, in an event, bending to peer in the eyes of a child and seeing her future, feeling a connection as if she were part of his existence.

"We can do this," he promised her, or maybe himself.

The youth started her descent with a determined look, and that was the look he wanted to give each of them.

"Keep your eyes on me. It's a short drop and you'll be hauled to the side by Medic Jon. He's strong and waiting for you. Keep your hands out and ready to grab him."

A strange taste festered in his mouth and Match assumed the bitterness was from the air quality, but he didn't have time to find a mask.

"Once you make it to the ledge with Medic Jon, you'll help the younger ones. Eyes up. On me, all the way down." He lowered her slowly.

When the harness loosened, he pulled the rope up. "All good?" he checked, suppressing the urge to cough. If he coughed, Shandra would think something was wrong with him and he didn't want to distract her.

The answer took longer than he liked but a strong, "Yup," from down below relaxed him.

Match glanced over at Andret and Hilt as they sent down their first load. They'd created a shelf and had several bags and three youths on it. Match approached them. "This crew you're lowering, did you notice their eyes? I'm checking everyone for a virus that turns the eyes solid grey."

"Would have noticed that. Is it contagious?"

"Programmed virus. Don't want to create a panic, so you're the only ones who know but anyone with grey eyes reports to me. Don't touch them, don't let them touch any devices. I don't know where it's hiding but I have to find it."

Hilt gave him a full report anyhow. "That was Grit, Bella, and Neige. Fifteen FIRE Ceremonies and all passed their endurance training at the top of their classes. We'll use them to lead the first few crews down. Eyes were blue with red, pink with red, and violet with black, in that order."

Andret continued the thought, "They're climbers, swimmers, and survivors." The rope jolted. "You heroes safe?"

"Yup."

Match let them do their thing, glad he had two strong leaders he could rely on.

Shandra approached him, to say, "Including us, Yodan, and Lins there are ninety-nine survivors total. I sent Quip to check every room so we can lower the sick or sleeping." She bowed her head. "Owen's missing. Those not joining us will be missed."

Match clenched a fist, making smoke, but the motion was his only external reaction. Inside, he threw things, yelling at Nogard, at himself, at everyone for not noticing their A-life was killing them. They were ninety-nine survivors. Not long ago the cities boasted life at seven thousand and forty-four. Then they were seven hundred. And now not even one hundred.

"And," Shandra added. "The drone is sending images of Yodan's messages."

"And Yodan?"

"Nothing yet."

This news didn't comfort him. Match wished he could rip Nogard's wires out with his bare hands. All these lives lost. And for what? Even worse, their last protector took off.

Well, Match wasn't about to leave anyone behind like some coward.

"Thanks, for the update." His tone was flat. He hated these emotions he couldn't express. Yet he understood that doing so would freak these children out. They looked to him for strength, to show them hope to fight.

They were the outsiders rejected from the system. He was ready for this challenge, but to bring these children with him, to be responsible for finding them a safe place to grow and work and play and learn...

The child in front of him was about seven. "What's wrong with my father?"

"He'd want you to listen to me until we get you someplace with better air. Focus on the drop. I'll strap your sister to you. She's too young to do this alone." The girl glanced over her shoulder at her younger sister and nodded. She was a toddler but stood, holding Shandra's hand. Each group he sent needed to be of mixed training and ages.

Match harnessed them together and dropped them over the ledge. Quicker the better.

He didn't know the first thing about looking after babies. Worried, he rubbed his heavy eyes on his sleeve.

"You with me?" Shandra checked.

"Wondering who in all these levels will raise a toddler. How many are there?" He watched them dangling until they vanished from sight. Then the harness was free and Match held it, numbly waiting for an answer from below.

"We'll be fine, Match. Medic Brisk will show us how to raise children."

Match wiped his brow on the sleeve of his white lifesuit.

He needed air, water, and minerals, but time slipped by. Everyone blurred together yet each one filed away neatly in his extensive memory.

These people needed him.

Spinning around for the next one, he bumped into Shandra holding a bottle of minerals. "Drink."

He was about to dismiss her, but obeying was faster so he drank the minerals and waited for his energy to increase. The change was almost instant. "Everything is crashing on me at once."

"Now breathe." She placed a mask in front of him. The air was so pure he was instantly revived. "A drone found Yodan's burned lifesuit. There is no indication that he survived."

"He did," he promised her, no idea why he was lying to her now, or maybe he was lying to himself because he couldn't deal with the thought of Yodan being incinerated.

"Medic Brisk will keep the line going for me, I'll do the final check for survivors myself and see where that cat got off to." She stormed off, clearly needing a moment by herself to process that Yodan might be dead. He wanted to chase after her, but youths crowded around him.

MATCH

A few breaths later
Underground, FIRE Chamber

Andret was the last survivor Match lowered over the ledge into the FIRE pit. Shandra wasn't back yet so Match was getting ready to search for her. She might be sick or passed out somewhere.

Before leaving, exhausted, Match called over the ledge, "Get moving. I'll catch up. I'll do one final sweep."

Leaning on the railing, he watched the lights dim as the crew moved on.

CRACK!

His weight dislodged the railing and Match stumbled forward, propelled into the hole. Frantically, he reached for anything to grab onto. Fumbling with the railing. The light metal bent from his weight as he dangled in the void over the pit.

Focus, he ordered himself, hanging, not even breathing. If he moved, he risked breaking the railing and falling to his death, but for how long could he hold on? He stared at the wall at the far end of the room with the gems gleaming, a haunting reminder of his mortality. He'd always accepted that he wasn't like the others and that, one day, his life would end and there would be no more Match. No memories, no one studying his work. But letting go was hard.

"What in all these minerals was that?" Andret called to him from the pit, reminding Match that he had a job to do.

Match's arms burned as he dangled over the pit. His grip slipped, but he had to hold on long enough to make sure the last crew left and knew where to go. Keeping his voice calm, Match said, "Just me fighting with the cat. Don't wait. Go." His voice echoed down the hole. "I'll be right behind," he lied. "Reach the surface. I'll meet you at Mainframe One. We're going to reactivate it."

"We won't leave anyone behind, Sir Rawlings."

His grip slipped as Shandra whispered, "You are getting way too good at lying. Hold still. This'll sting a bit." She zapped the bar he gripped and the shock jolted him. Match flew against the black pipe in the middle of the hole. His body was stuck to the side of the pipe with nothing holding him. How? Much to his shock the broken railing followed, smashing against him, knocking the air out of him.

Pinned against the pipe by the railing, he struggled for freedom. Match worked the railing off and the metal snapped tight against the pipe beside him. His head hurt where the railing had smacked. "What was that?" Match grumbled, but he had to admit that whatever she'd zapped him with was neat. The shot had turned him into a magnet, making him stick to the pipe.

Shandra tied a rope while she explained, "It's something my father made in Cell Manipulation Class. The pipetizer isn't approved because using the rays might have long-term effects. Ultimately, the minerals in your body become attracted to the pipes and you stick to them, like a magnet. The effect won't last long so grab the rope." She tossed him the rope but he missed it. Slowly, he slid down the pipe as she vanished from his view. His last sight of her was with the cat at her heels and the drone waiting beside her for orders.

"Rawlings is against the pipe. Break a hole in it, he's sliding down," Shandra called down, as if someone from the ledge below could help them.

The invisible hold loosened as he slid down the side of the pipe. Match dropped down and down, connected to the pipe. The railing also began to slide. It knocked against him as it fell, almost ripping him from the pipe but he pushed himself against the pipe as if he could magically make it hold him tighter.

The railing kept falling as Match rubbed his head, breathing through the pain of the injuries the railing had given him.

A pen-light shone from the ledge where he'd dropped his people across from him. Andret was still there working with Hilt directly across from him. They were pointing a laser cutter at the pipe below Match. Would it reach that far?

"You two are supposed to be gone," he grumbled as he slid down the pipe, injured.

The railing hit the bottom of the pit with a violent clang.

The large black pipe let him go as the effect of the pipetizer wore off. Match reached wildly for anything to hold onto.

Much to his surprise, a warm blast of air pushed against him, smashing him against the pipe. He went right through it and landed on a grate stairwell inside. Match scrambled to his feet, activating his pen-light. He looked out from the pipe up at Hilt and Andret on the ledge across from him. "What was that?"

Hilt chuckled. "Can't believe that worked. That, my friend, was a hot air pulse. Neat, eh? Andret made it and Nogard told him it was useless. Nice to prove her wrong sometimes. I blew a hole in the pipe with my laser and he timed the pulse perfectly. Really, we impress me sometimes. You hurt?"

Instead of telling them he was bleeding, he said, "There's a stairwell here. You two know that?"

"Nope. Figured you could hold onto the pipe, but that works, too."

"We have to get Shandra down, then I'll swing over your way. Shandra? Andret and Hilt are waiting for you."

Before she could answer a quake shook the area.

Match leaned up against the side of the black pipe to wait it out. He counted to forty then shone his light around. Hilt and Andret were blocked in. The ledge where they'd been had caved in. "Hilt? Andret?"

No one answered. Dammit.

"Shandra?"

"I'll join you."

He waited, looking up, unable to see anything but debris and dust...then a fine light came from the ledge and vanished. And again. "Andret and Hilt are signalling us. Maybe as you pass, signal for them to move on. Tell them we're going down this pipe to see where it leads."

"Will do." Shandra was already there, knocking gently on the fragile rocks in code.

Match waited, holding his breath. "They answer?"

"Yup. Moving on."

"Perfect. Swing this way."

Shandra pushed herself off the side toward the pipe where Match waited with open arms. His head was swimmy but he shook off the pain and prepared to catch her.

Time was spotty and one moment she was swinging, the next she was in his arms. "You should've taken a hit of the pipetizer; sliding down would've been easier."

"I can't. I have to watch what I use." Probably a good idea.

He pulled her to safety with him. His pen-light was fastened to the wall, even though he didn't remember doing that. "I feel like I'm missing moments," he mumbled.

"You hit your head pretty hard." She took the cat out of her bag and set the feline at her feet. Match brushed a kiss on Shandra's lips while he held her. Mmm, she tasted like mint. His favourite.

The drone floated in as Shandra pulled away.

"You feeling better?" he asked her.

"I'll be better once I know my family is safe."

Him, too.

Match nuzzled Shandra's neck, slowly undoing the rope and harness around her. The cat purred warmly, relaxing him as Shandra melted against Match, fitting perfectly in his arms. Protecting her was his duty yet this task crashed inside him with his other responsibilities.

"Let's get you and our child to safety." Match caught her lip and tasted her, slowly. When he pulled away he said, "How much Oxy-air do you have left?"

She glanced at the cylinder on her shoulder. "Two cycles. For both of us. Let's get moving. We go down until we find an exit. Each mainframe has an emergency breathing vent that leads to someplace with breathable air. Plus, this pipe feeds the FIRE, there has to be air vents."

Shandra was a digger and understood how the mazes underground worked so he trusted her, despite knowing that he'd sent everyone in the opposite direction.

"I checked every single person who went over that ledge. Not one of them had grey eyes," he told her. "What if Lins...?" He couldn't even say it.

"We'll find her and contain Nogard. There is a chance that Nogard was in the mainframe when the energy was cut. There is a chance that A-life went dormant."

Match nodded, squinting to get her in focus. He hated everything about this situation. "What bothers me, is that my entire purpose, like Lins', is to protect our people from Nogard breaking code. Yet she did, and didn't terminate us. So many elites died this last cycle, yet we survived. Why? I get that Lins and Nogard share a connection through the eRobe that might have saved Lins, but why does Nogard think I'll let her live?"

"Probably lost energy too fast and just jumped ship. That's all."

Match rubbed his throbbing head. Something was wrong but he couldn't put his finger on what. "But the energy loss happened after, as part of the termination another elite had put in place..."

"Stop rubbing your head. You're bleeding." She checked the wound on his head.

"Giving me a dizzy headache I can't think around."

"You need a medic. A medic-pen would be nice."

His was in two pieces at the bottom of the FIRE pit and he'd forgotten to grab another. "I'll be fine. Let's go."

AVERY

During the same breaths
Underground, in the pipes

Air weighed heavily in Avery's lungs, making her sluggish as she crawled in front of Yodan through the pipe. They had to backtrack and travel a side vein so she led. In his haste to crawl through earlier, Yodan had missed marking a turn and they were possibly lost in the pipes and the idea of dying down here was making her eye tic.

"See the exit to the right? Push on the door," Yodan said from behind her. "Just a gentle nudge."

His hand grazed her bare foot, close behind her. Knowing a bigger space was close created a desperation in her and Avery whacked the door somewhat harder than she should have.

"Oh no," Yodan said.

"What?" She breathed in from the opening but the air wasn't any cooler. Avery rolled out of the tight pipe into the stairwell. The air had a burned taste and she prayed the flames didn't restart.

"My eTatt snapped. Three snaps I usually pass out." Yodan entered the stairwell, full of energy. Avery glanced up at the light radiating on them from a mini-sun in the ceiling.

He said, "Another snap."

She glanced around. "Snapping where?"

"My head." He showed her the skin markings behind his ear that led to the serpent tail on his neck. "It must be a fail-safe to kill off any youths who didn't die with the system or the purge. Means an over-ride program like Dragon will terminate the system. *He shall give life and he shall take it away*."

Avery's hands flew to her mouth. Dragon put a machine in his head that could kill him?

Yodan rested his head against the wall. "That was the third." He curled up on the ground, sheltering his head.

She had no idea what to do when he passed out in front of her.

"Yodan? Yodan!" Avery pushed the spot behind his ear, but a zap sent her flying.

A surge of panicky terror slapped at her, overwhelming her to take action. She pulled out her small blade and prepared to cut out the device behind Yodan's ear, but first she searched for his life-pulse. The life inside him pumped strong along his neck and he was breathing. She placed the mask on him.

Maybe cutting this device out while he was unconscious would be easier. Tapping her knife to the strange tattoo behind his ear, she waited for a reaction. When nothing happened, Avery sucked in a breath and pierced the knife into Yodan's skin, making a fine red line as she sliced. The cut spread open revealing a throbbing device.

Blood trickled from the wound onto her skirt. Using the tip of the blade, Avery dug around the device and like a splinter, she flicked it out, sending the small item flying across the stairwell.

When the disconnect happened, the overhead pink light flickered and went out, leaving her in darkness. She had no idea if the two were connected, but she searched her garments for the science-light Yodan had given her and moved the light over his ear to see the damage. Blood flowed behind his ear. Quickly, she removed her over-shirt to apply pressure on the wound that was no bigger than the tip of both thumbs.

Her undergarments clung to her from the sweat, but in the dark, no one could see her anyway. Avery kept pressure behind Yodan's ear, sitting with him, about to pray for Dragon to keep him alive when she realized that Dragon was the one killing him. Why?

Panicked, Avery flashed the light around the area in case something could help her. Much to her shock, a child stared at her with huge purple eyes.

Avery fumbled with the light device. The cylinder slipped from her grip and hit the ground with a dry thud.

PAX

A few breaths later
Above ground, Dragon's Caves

Pax came to with his face smooched in the dirt. His head felt like lead. He moved body parts and was sore pretty much everywhere but got to his feet, dusting himself off. He was still at the back of Dragon's Caves, but something had happened. Debris littered the area and by the size of some of the fallen rock around him, he was lucky to be alive.

A quake shook the caves, but he planted himself and began counting. It was harmless, he calmed himself, nothing to worry about. With a deep breath he rated the air quality and stopped his count when the rumbling stopped. Each emotion was so crisp and clean, despite the aches, he felt great about being alive and stood taller.

His vision blurred as he took his first step, making him pause and reassess. He seemed intact but his head had an injury that would require treatment. And he felt like himself, yet *not*. Something was off. Almost like his soul was fighting for space inside his body and losing.

From the back of the cave, he could see the rising sun light the skies, but nothing in the cave looked familiar anymore. Debris littered the area from quakes.

The ground rumbled again. This time, he dismissed it and marched unafraid to the dragon carved in the marble cave walls. The script under the image was ancient but he could make out the words clearly. He could read! Why could he read? He ran his fingers over the script.

Welcome to Quma City, experimental city controlled by Dragon, artificial-intelligence—2112

The rest of the script had flaked off and had become illegible. Still, he held his hand over the date before making his way to the entrance of the cave. Morning broke, giving him the perfect view of the mess. He let the sun warm his skin, thinking about Lins. She'd like this sunrise. He had no idea why he knew so much about her suddenly, but he even knew that she liked to dance when her brother played the flute.

He was liking how neat and tidy his emotions had become.

Debris meant he had to climb his way out of the cave but he arrived at the entrance easily and surveyed the village. The quake had destroyed a few of the unstable huts. Rocks and chunks of broken black pipe pieces stabbed the earth. Pax didn't know if they'd rained down on the village or had erupted from the ground. Maybe both. Studying the mess, he evaluated the cleanup strategies, seeing the world with such clarity.

Despite his head aching, he was in control of each breath and they felt good filling his lungs.

Elder Jacob's new hut was flat. No people were in the village. Looking out, he saw them outside the village, huddled on the other side of the warming pipes. Together. Relieved that Saxton and Roselle took his warning seriously, Pax returned inside Dragon's Caves. He needed a *shutdown* to heal this wound on his head.

He headed back to the hole when someone cried out to him. Glancing around, he spotted Elder Fewerter pinned under a large rock by the entrance. His instinct was to keep the elder alive and this need overpowered all other thoughts.

Pax used a branch to prop the rock. The elder passed out in his struggle and Pax dragged him out of harm's way, bringing him inside the cave where debris couldn't harm him. He scanned the area. This was the safest place to be when the next quake would hit and it wouldn't be long now. Parts of him could feel it coming.

He checked the life-pulse on the elder and was working hard to make the elder comfortable when a wave of dizziness hit him. Everything blurred. A shutdown was imminent. Pax felt the back of his head. It was covered in sticky blood. His head was so heavy he had to fight to stay with it. He shook his head and stumbled.

A quake knocked him off his feet…or was he falling?

YODAN

A few breaths later
Underground, in the stairwell

Yodan opened his eyes, trying to focus but his sight was blurry.

"Just keep your eyes closed and relax," Medic Jon whispered.

Where was he? Yodan trusted Jon and closed his eyes. He heard children whispering. Avery breathing beside him. Felt her squeeze his hand.

He opened his eyes again. Shadows moved around him in the dark. A pen-light moved over a group of children, highlighting each face to check them.

"They found us," Yodan mumbled, moving his arm to see if he could. He touched his chest. The fire-pain was gone and he was healed. Only his head felt heavy and he couldn't move it. "What are you doing to my head?"

"Trying to fix you. You're crazy." Medic Jon's familiar relaxing voice calmed him. "Always were, but this takes the mud pie."

"Jon. You remember me?"

"My memories were hard to access but they're back." Jon pulled away and the pressure ended.

Yodan closed his eyes, breathing through the dizziness.

"What ya doing in these weird garments?" Jon asked.

"Better than being naked in these frigid passageways."

Avery squeezed his hand, again.

"I suppose. So how you feeling now that your Exchanger was removed?"

The pressure was gone but his head throbbed. Yodan grazed his eTatt with his fingers, not sure what Jon was mumbling about. He froze with his fingers on the scar behind his ear.

His Exchanger was missing. Yodan shot up. "What did you do?" he snapped at Avery while studying his surroundings. A bunch of children had joined them. They were taught not to panic or yell in front of children, ever, so Yodan restrained himself from further outbursts.

"You cut off my eTatt and took out my Exchanger?" he demanded of Avery. "Where is it?"

She stood. "That thing in your head was killing you. I squashed it."

"What will happen to my memories now?" he demanded, as if she knew.

"Whoa." Medic Jon sat him back down. "Since I've disconnected, my memories have returned. She saved your life. This young woman is a hero."

Yodan talked a lot about breaking free with Match, but here he was, no longer part of the system. Panic swelled in him. "I meant when I die. My memories were in that Exchanger. Where will they go when I die?"

Avery was in his face. "I'll always remember that you existed. Just like you remember your friend."

Yodan forgot his fears and studied her. Even in the dim light, studying her features relaxed him. Did she know where his memories would go?

"I don't remember my family from the Outlands, but I know they must have existed because here I am. Memories aren't something you need to be alive: they're something you share with others through stories to get closer to people and learn about them."

Well. He liked that idea and found her views a comfort. "How did you know removing my Exchanger wouldn't kill me?"

"I don't have one."

He tightened his hand around Avery's, needing her reassurance that he'd survive this.

They sat like this, staring at each other. Him realizing that he had no idea what his future held. "Sorry I freaked out. I'm a little terrified," he admitted.

Avery got up and Yodan was quick to follow her, not wanting her to leave him behind, but the medic snagged his arm to keep him back and checked behind Yodan's ear. "You had me worried but the bleeding's stopped."

"We ready to keep moving?"

"We move as a group from here." Medic Jon showed Yodan his pressure reader, another device not connected to the system. "This pressure is unrecorded so stay in a tight group in case someone passes out."

"So Medic Jon, are Match and Shandra with you?"

"They were the last to come down. Hilt and Andret said they were going down the black pipe in the FIRE pit. They want to go after them once we get this crew to a safer area."

With a heavy sigh, Avery added, "There are so many children."

Now that the pressure from behind Yodan's ear was missing, he felt lighter, happier.

The group travelled in silence, moving with their pen-lights to guide them. The odd pink light overhead promised that they were on the right path.

The flow of faces spanned endlessly down the corridor. Yodan scanned them in the dark, searching for anyone needing attention.

A toddler cried, which was a strange sound Yodan wasn't used to, but Avery went for the child and brought her back. She held the toddler making soft cooing sounds that even relaxed Yodan.

"You like children?" Yodan asked Avery, since babies were raised in the nursery he hadn't spent much time around them.

"Of course, they're our future. I have a bunch of brothers I helped raise."

A lump formed in his throat as he watched her handle the child with such expertise. He had no idea mother-like qualities were a factor he'd find appealing, but seeing Avery this way made him burst with pride. Which was confusing. Why was he proud that she could hold a toddler?

"Can I try?"

She handed him the child who looked at him and slapped her hands around his face. "She's cute."

The child wriggled in his arms and he set her down, letting her run back to Avery who swung her up naturally and plopped her on her hip.

"You don't have siblings?"

"My sisters are older than me. We don't allow infants or toddlers in our family chamber. They stay in the nursery and come home after they survive their fifth FIRE Ceremony."

"Well, we don't leave little ones out of our sight."

Yodan liked that idea. Maybe things wouldn't be so bad in their new system.

It didn't take them long to stumble into an elevator shaft.

Avery said, "Hey, this is where I came down."

A rope dangled, ready for them to use, which was probably the easiest. By the time Yodan and Avery made it to the shaft, Hilt and Andret were already up the rope, exploring the chamber above while everyone waited in silence for their verdict. "Caved in," Hilt told them. "Surface dweller are you sure you came in here?"

"Yeah," Avery told them. "Large cave that overlooks my village."

"Then we can dig through this. Plenty of grade-C air filtering in. Lots of working room. Area is secured by a strong box. Safe place to be if the system is about to terminate."

Andret looked over the ledge. "First, I need a medic. There are two unconscious heroes here. One has wild orange hair like the surface dweller you're hanging with."

Jon joined Andret and Hilt on the ledge above them.

"Might be your family," Yodan said to Avery.

"My brother Pax is the only one with hair like mine. Is he hurt?"

Medic Jon answered, "I see this injury a lot, they'll both be fine. Just need some healing. You guys can start coming up. We'll be fine here."

Everyone was going up now and Yodan was helping where he could. He passed the rope to the next child while he prepared the toddler to fasten her to another's chest. "Want me to help you up so you can check on your brother?" he asked Avery.

"You coming?"

Yodan glanced at the top of the hole seeing another level of life that looked the same as the one he stood in. "Actually, the pink lights continue. Might lead us to another way out. I can run ahead and check."

Everyone was almost up. Many of the older youths weren't even using the rope but each other or leaping from the railing.

She glanced up, worried. "Will Pax be okay?"

"Oh yeah," Medic Jon promised her.

When the children were on the next level, Yodan offered to help Avery up, again. She didn't grab the rope. "Someone has to go with you," she said. "Your healer is skilled and tending to Pax. Doing something feels better than not." Avery glanced up, then let the rope go to follow Yodan.

"If you're coming, let's go." His own words surprised him but things were better with Avery around. Plus, she was brave as heck and her courage motivated him.

Avery headed back where they'd come, but Yodan stopped her. "See the pink glow? That's the way we go."

"What if we get lost?" Avery asked as they climbed into an access pipe large enough for them to stand in.

She worried a lot about being lost so he reassured her, "Hilt gave me more chalk. I'll keep marking things and we'll come back. You don't have to come," he reminded her.

"I know, but I like that you let me make my own decisions without making me feel like a child."

They entered a room with silver pipes and Yodan opened the access panel and peeked in. A flying drone stopped abruptly and backed up to wait in front of Yodan. "I'm Yodan."

The drone gave him a green follow-me light then cut a hole in a silver pipe and headed down.

"Where is that metallic bee going?"

Yodan glanced at the pink light in the distance. They could head that way or follow the drone. "The drone is taking us away from Mainframe One but wants us to follow. Maybe one of my sisters are hurt or Match…" He climbed in the silver pipe.

"How is that thing working?" Avery asked, following him.

"Drones create their own energy through eMove and keep their programming until they hard hook-up."

"Is it science?"

"Artificial-intelligence like drones make decisions we pre-set but can jump to conclusions."

She still looked leery. "Is it alive?"

"We have different classes of life like plants and mammals and viruses and Artificial-life and so on. The criteria for artificial-intelligence like this drone to become A-life is that it knows it is alive and tells us this. The drone is not alive, but it could be at any moment. We don't know what sparks that life in artificial-intelligence, so we always show great respect for the machines that serve us."

They were headed straight down.

LINS

During the same breaths
Underground, in the pipes

When the earthquake made the pipe collapse around her, Lins must have passed out. She woke to a drone clearing debris off her. When she moaned, the drone offered her an Oxy-mask.

Sipping the air, she was amazed to see she was in a grade-C air zone without a vent to offer her better air quality. Still, if a drone found a way to her, meant she could get out. Meant the collapse wasn't final. "I'm Elite Lins. Take me to Elite Match," she ordered the drone. All of her ached. She should be dead and had no idea how this drone had found her.

In pain, Lins crawled after the bot and was annoyed when the drone vanished upward in front of her. She wasn't one to rush in after a drone; instead Lins examined the area where a hole was cut in the silver pipe big enough for her to fit through.

After deciding she had no other options, Lins took the exit, leading to another silver pipe. From there, the drone travelled down again. And again. The final silver pipe exited into a corridor cut in rock.

She checked for markings on the wall but found none. Shining her pen-light at the walls, Lins tried not to miss anything. A small engraving along the connections told her she was near Mainframe Six. Many of the mainframes were no longer accessible due to earthquakes collapsing them centuries ago, but as far as she knew, Mainframe Six was uninhabitable but intact.

The drone waited in front of an orange overhead pipe. Before attempting to heave herself into this new orange pipe, she sipped Oxy-air and drank a shot of minerals. When her strength and energy were at their peak, Lins wrapped her fingers around the hole in the orange pipe and pulled herself up. She was never much of a climber, and each pull was a struggle.

The new pipe was much larger and the drone was already missing. "Hey, wait up."

The drone popped up.

The pipe went down now, an adaptation made to the system to allow Nogard to reach the newest mainframe: Mainframe Eight. Would Lins finally see it? Why would Match be there?

Lins climbed in after the drone and slid down the pipe, landing in a white pipe. She'd never seen a white pipe. Her bare feet itched. Feeling naked without her robe for extra protection, she moved through the white pipe to a silver pipe. Unfortunately, the air had a musty smell.

Resting against the wall were three dead bodies. Not being used to dead bodies, Lins had no idea what to do. She rushed to them even though they were lifeless. The drone had brought her to dead people. Why?

The woman held an empty Oxy-tank which Lins picked out of her hands to study.

"Lins?"

She jumped at Yodan's voice and flung around to see him in the doorway with a young woman who looked a great deal like Pax. How did she get here? And what was Yodan wearing? Her drone met with one that Yodan must have followed. They communicated and one remained.

"I found Avery and these garments in a higher level." He filled her in on what had happened, leaving Lins distressed. So much life was lost.

"This is Avery, she's from a village above ground."

Lins faced them, concealing her emotions. "Avery, I'm Elite Lins, Yodan's sister." Lins smiled to ease the tension from her shoulders.

"Nice to meet you."

"Shandra and Match weren't with the survivors. The drone brought us to you and these dead bodies. What's going on?"

"I just found them. These were outsiders, rebels, and they will be missed. We can't stay, termination is imminent."

Yodan tilted his head. "Maybe we could put these bodies in the recycling chamber?"

Death was always hard on him so Lins blocked his path. "Keep moving."

"It's not right to leave them. They were alive with thoughts and purpose."

She didn't look back, leading them from the room. "And

we shall remember."

"We're almost out of Oxy-air. Do they have any?"

"No." Lins spoke to the drone. "I'm Elite Lins. I require a refill station for our Oxy-air. Find one on the way to Elite Match."

The silence was eerie and wrong as the drone communicated with its system. This was normally done in an instant and the delay weighed on them. Finally, the drone lit the way and led them down a large corridor.

"Remember," she told her brother and the stranger with him, "look for blue air vents blowing cool air. They lead to above ground."

"Did you find Mainframe One?" Yodan glanced at her, hopeful, as they hiked through the passageways.

"I did. It's controlled by Dragon an artificial-intelligence. Dragon is programmed to terminate Nogard and her system. I don't have the codes to override the termination."

"So who has this code?"

"I was hoping Match."

AVERY

A few breaths later
Underground, lost

Avery was exhausted from their excursion in the pipes. She had no idea how much time had passed. Starving and achy, her only comfort was knowing that Yodan had found one of his sisters. They were close which made Avery a bit homesick for her own family.

As they followed the drone, Avery noted how different Lins was from women in her village. Actually, Lins reminded Avery more of a clan leader, commanding and demanding. Her violet eyes were always checking around Yodan. The idea of a woman being a leader and a protector intrigued Avery. Her garments glistened. Almost like flowing lilac metal.

They waited for the mechanical bee to cut a hole in the door to the next room. Then they walked through and the bee led them to a violet chute-pipe they slid down. Darkness surrounded Avery as she flew blindly down this steep pipe. Yodan hollered excited in front of her so Avery closed her eyes at the pipe's mercy. She popped out the bottom and Yodan steadied her. "You all right? That didn't freak you out too much?"

She stuck her jaw out bravely and watched Lins land gracefully. "It was fine," Avery lied.

"You're one brave woman. The first time I went down a sliding pipe, I screamed."

The drone continued to shine light on them while leading them to a yellow pipe next, then vanished about midway through a door.

"Where did the bee-drone go?" Avery asked, activating her light-tube thingy which she was keeping handy.

"In the yellow pipe. The drone closed the door because that's a gas pipe. Means there'll be several levels of doors to keep the gas in."

"Good thing we never cut into one," Avery said.

"I would never cut into a yellow pipe."

"No breathing when we're in here," Lins ordered. "We don't know what type of gas this'll be."

"Breathe?" Avery needed to breathe. Could they go without breathing? The tic started in her eye, and like a trigger, Yodan stepped closer with a calming smile.

He showed her the cylinder she wore on her back. Avery had forgotten about it, but he pulled the mask over her face gently. "We use this to breathe like I showed you." He studied the monitor. "Yours is empty." He had another clipped to his baggy pants and pulled the cylinder off. "We'll share mine. This one has a bit left. There should be a refill station soon, they're usually around these gas pipes. Breathe in from it, then slowly breathe out as we crawl. It'll be hard to see at times. We don't know how far or how long this pipe is so we'll save as much air as we can. Practise with me."

She inhaled deeply, then slowly let air out, mimicking Yodan. Their eyes locked while they held their breath and released it.

"We'll be fine, but we'll share this air with Lins, too. She has no pack."

Lins looked indifferent, ready for anything. "We hold our breath for a long time, but we've had practice so don't feel like you have to do like us."

Avery enjoyed how Lins didn't let things bother her, yet how she absorbed details all the time. She reminded Avery of a cloth taking in water. She could suck in so much before she had to share those thoughts with the world, overflowing with knowledge.

"Why are you staring at me?" Lins asked, without glancing up.

"Are all the women of your clan like you?"

Yodan snickered. "No one is like Lins." His voice quaked a bit and Lins glanced up to meet his eyes.

Then Lins removed the shirt tied around Yodan's waist and helped him put the top on properly. His chest was already healed. While she helped him dress, Lins said, "No one is like me, because I have you as a brother. Even at a young age you tested Nogard's claim at life by telling her that she would never know the comforts of a kiss or the warm embrace of a mother." She backed up to see him in the garments and Avery shone the light on him, giving her a better view. "You remind me of who I am, of why I exist." Standing her full height she headed to the yellow pipe, fearless and determined.

Yodan dug around in a box fixed to the wall and pulled out mitts that fit over their feet. He whispered, "Everyone in our system serves a purpose. Lins is a backup for when the system fails. She's trained hard to hopefully never need her skills. She needs to ground herself so she remembers what she's fighting for: Nogard's survival or ours? How linked are the two?"

Yodan glanced Avery over, making her feel like she belonged. "Ready?"

Avery nodded, terrified, then Yodan helped her into the yellow pipe. The first one was a holding tank where Lins waited.

"The drone wouldn't put us in danger, their ultimate program is to keep us safe," Yodan promised Avery, then he opened the door and Lins scurried in first. Avery followed behind Yodan. Inside the pipe was a white fog that burned Avery's eyes so she couldn't see Yodan.

When the pipe shook, Avery panicked but Yodan was there with his light and a smile on his lips as if this was nothing. He was right against her face, then he turned around and vanished in the fog again.

How could he be so foolishly calm? Still, his relaxed way was a strange comfort so Avery focused on him. She pulled a breath from the mask and offered the device to him. He returned the mask and Avery arranged it while they kept moving.

Not seeing was almost as bad as not breathing.

She took a deep breath, holding it until her eye relaxed, amazed that such a neat trick worked on a tic that had troubled her for so long.

Release the breath.

Another... Avery drew in nothing. The air tank was empty. Panicked, she gripped Yodan's bare foot as he crawled in front of her.

He kept moving.

Her eyes grew heavy. Her body weakened. Finally, Avery slumped against him, feeling herself melt into Yodan.

YODAN

Not one breath later
Underground, in a gas pipe

Yodan had Avery in his arms. Lins was too far ahead of him in the gas pipe for him to signal. He had no idea what type of gas this was. Was Avery dead? Poisoned? Dying?

He pulled her, moving them quickly but not fast enough. His lungs burned for air as he fought the urge to breathe. Forcing more air out.

Hold it.

Hold it.

His eyes burned and Yodan stole a quick shallow breath, tasting the sweet air of sleeping gases.

Relaxed, he fought sleep. *Keep moving.*

A clink made him glance over his shoulder even though he was blind in this fog. Lins was out. She slammed the door. He was close but his muscles gave up and Yodan fell against Avery.

Fight it.

LINS

A breath later
Underground, near the gas pipe

Lins filled her lungs with air from the next room. What she'd wanted was fresh air, but this stale poor quality air made her cough.

Grabbing the tank of Oxy-air from the wall in the holding tank, Lins pulled a breath while fitting on the mask. Then she opened the yellow pipe and pulled on Yodan's legs which were inches from the door. Either he was dead or sleeping.

Sleeping meant he'd wake refreshed. Anything else she refused to think about.

Lins rested him against the wall outside the holding tank and returned for Avery.

Once they were both propped up safely against the wall, Lins scanned Yodan with her personal SHARP. The reports were usually thorough, going into detail about heart rhythm and emotions, but all this one said was that Yodan was in sleep mode.

A drone buzzed over them and Lins sent the bot for more Oxy-air as she fixed the mask in front of their faces, blasting them with Oxy-air so they'd wake.

She waited, but neither of them responded. These gases always had a potent effect on Yodan.

Her only option was to leave them to sleep the gases off while she explored the area. Hopefully, they were close to Mainframe Eight and could stop the termination from here by overriding the system.

With a quick survey of the area, Lins placed their location by the large black pipe from the FIRE pit.

A powerful motor blasted from the room to her left, and Lins could have sworn she'd heard a woman cry over the droning echo.

A quick glance over her shoulder let her know that Yodan and Avery were asleep so she went through the door to see who was here.

The new room contained a giant life-cycle clock ticking backwards over a motor. Lins studied the energy panel with the cooling equipment. There was no place to hook-up a device. Meant Dragon was directly in control of this panel and only the ReSurface code entered at Mainframe One would allow them access.

This mainframe harnessed magma energy and nothing else. Mainframe Eight wasn't a mainframe, it was a termination station and how Dragon controlled the flames for the FIRE purges.

"Dragon do you hear me?"

No response.

Lins rushed back to Yodan and the young woman. "Yodan?"

They were gone.

"Yodan?"

The drone had vanished, too. They couldn't be far. Yet really, they could be in any direction. Where would they go? "Drone?"

Panic set in as the heat increased. They didn't have time to get lost.

AVERY

During the same breaths
Underground

"I'm fine." Avery stumbled again as she followed the drone. Her legs dragged, but Yodan was on a mission and she didn't want to be left behind. He was sure this flying thing would lead him to his sister. Frankly, Avery was annoyed that she'd left them.

Avery liked this new area better since she could stand and the ceiling was higher, but the bottom of Yodan's eyes were rimmed in grey marks as if he'd been fighting which had her worried.

"My head hurts." Yodan held himself up using the wall. "Lins!" he shouted. "Where did she get off to?"

"You all right?" Avery asked. The humming from the wall vibrated her thoughts.

"I'll be fine. I never handle sleeping gases well. Nogard stopped using them on me. How about you?"

"I'm wobbly, as if I was jolted from a deep sleep."

The drone cut them a way through a door. "It'll be loud in here. These are energy chambers. A supply room should be close. I've never been here, few have, but we're given the basic layout of how the system works in survival class," Yodan yelled over the sound as he climbed through the hole in the door.

"Is it safe?"

"These rooms need air, means there will be air vents we can travel."

Every room or pipe they entered was an assault to her senses. This one was too loud. The mechanical bee hovered in the corner so she investigated while Yodan headed for the control panel.

A woman crouched behind a metal crate-thing, and at first, Avery thought this was Lins in different clothes. She leaned over a guy about Avery's age and when she stood with her hands out in front of her, she turned, letting Avery see the blood covering her white garments. The red was the only colour to the couple. They were each dressed in a white one-piece suit that matched their white skin perfectly.

To add to the shock, her cat was with them.

The drone flashed the light on them and when Avery called to her cat, the young man glanced at her. His eyes were like sparkling white crystals with a small red dot in the middle that faded in and out in light. Avery stepped back, terrified. Was this a machine or a guy?

The cat rubbed against him, and she'd always trusted Friskie's judgment. But... Torn between fear and trust, Avery remained frozen, staring at them.

YODAN

A breath later
Underground

This mainframe wasn't like the others. It was too loud and broken into work sections. But right now, all that mattered to Yodan was that they'd found Shandra and Match.

"Whoa." Yodan grabbed Shandra's arm as she tried valiantly to protect herself with a screwdriver, as if Avery was a threat.

Keeping his free hand up, Yodan signalled for Avery to remain calm. She stood with her fists clenched but he had no idea what her reaction might be to any of this.

"What are you doing here?" Yodan demanded from Shandra, noticing the blood smeared on her clothes. Match was semi-conscious, the top of his head covered in blood. His red pupils were slits as he lost focus.

Once things calmed, Yodan checked on Match, shooing the cat aside.

"Friskie," Avery stammered. "Where were you? I thought you were dead." She petted the cat while scolding the feline this way and the cat responded with a pacing action.

Their drone flew off as if someone called it, leaving them in the dark, but Avery moved the pen-light so Yodan could get a detailed look at Match's injuries. "What in these levels happened to him?" Yodan demanded.

"A railing hit him. This one actually." Shandra pointed to the railing jammed in the marble floor beside them from a solid impact. "The wound wasn't bleeding much at first, but now it's worse." The desperation in her voice spoke for him, too.

"Change of pressure will do that," Yodan said as he fished through the bag Shandra had dropped to search for a medic-pen. He found a medic-scanner and wrapped the fine filament around Match's finger and waited for the report. *He was breathing.* Yodan stared at the simplicity of the report. Usually a scan went into detail about how to heal injuries. "What's wrong with him?" he asked the device as if the machine had another way of knowing.

No one had an answer.

"I'm hot." Avery knelt beside Match and touched his neck. Match pulled away from her, glaring. She didn't back down, though. "He needs the clean air you guys carry around plus water and food. He's dehydrated, exhausted, and lost too much blood." She used her slipper to wipe around Match's injury. Then she placed the fabric on the cut like a cover, holding it over the open wound. "We have to stop the bleeding."

"You're a medic?" Yodan was impressed with Avery and her abilities. In Quma Cities they had one or two medics per quadrant and the training took many cycles, beginning in their youth. He glanced around for a supply station but this was clearly not an area people usually travelled.

The cat pawed at a broken medic-pen on the floor. Yodan snagged it from the creature. "Where are we?" he asked Shandra, checking to see if there was any fluid in the medic-pen that they might be able to use.

"This is the bottom of the FIRE pit. We came down the black FIRE pipe from the middle. Flames need air, figured there'd be pipes leading to air from here or some type of exit, but Match collapsed and he's too heavy for me to move. These diverters are so loud it's making me light-headed."

The juices from the cracked pen were dried but Yodan used a bit of water he found on Match to activate them, then rubbed them on his fingers. Avery lifted the garment and Yodan spread the healing ointment on Match's wound, hoping that'd help.

"Never thought I'd see the day when science actually helped someone." Avery splashed water to Match's lips. She gently cleaned the blood from his face.

Shandra paced. "We have to get out of here. These air vents drop into the body of water we use for salt-healing. Surface dweller, do you know if this water has a beach?"

"Ah..." Avery glanced at Yodan, lost.

He explained, "If we jump into the water, will we be able to swim to shore?"

"Don't know where we are. Probably."

"Is there ice? Snow?"

"Not around here."

"We're not leaving without Lins. She's around here

someplace," Yodan told his sister.

"I'll call for her." Shandra headed to the door they'd come from.

Yodan filled Match in on what had happened while staring at his watch. The countdown circles were black.

Match listened with his eyes closed, then asked, "Why are you dressed like an ancient?"

"Found these garments on a higher level. We can get you some if you like them."

"Sure, that'd be great."

"To your feet soldier."

Match tried to hop up, in his usual pretend-I'm-fine way, but his legs gave in and he stumbled against Yodan.

"Wow. You're tired. Drink these minerals." Yodan handed him a bottle from the bag.

Avery glanced at the black pipe in the middle of the room. "A black pipe like this comes out the top of the cliffs. We could take this up. Those stairs look sturdy."

"We came down them. It's unbearably hot in it," Match told them, rubbing at the tattoo on his neck. His Quadrant H tattoo was dark swirls united by a wall. Yodan always thought the markings looked powerful even if no one could explain where the symbol originated.

Lins stumbled through the door with the bot and headed straight for Shandra. The cat jumped to action, too, following Shandra to greet Lins. Before they spoke, a quake shook the entire room.

Debris crashed between them, dividing Match, Yodan, and Avery from Lins and Shandra.

Yodan pulled Match against the reinforced wall as Match screamed for Shandra, trying to push past Yodan to reach her.

YODAN

A breath later
Underground

The cave-in had them separated.

"Shandra! Lins!" Yodan shouted, reaching for the talker device on Shandra's bag. Did Shandra have one on her so they could communicate? He was used to knowing where everyone was in an instant and this wedge between them sucked.

He surveyed the scene. Their drone was crushed. Match was freaking out and too weak to focus. Avery was smashed against Yodan.

His ears rang so loud they made him disoriented and he hollered in the talker but heard nothing in return so he clipped the device to his weird leg coverings. Match searched for a break in the dusty debris so they could get to Shandra. The rocks were mostly around the pipe but had them trapped. If they had time, they could easily clear the rubble, but by the shake to the ground and the increased pressure in his head, Yodan didn't think they had time.

A blue pipe near the bottom of the largest motor caught his eye and became his focus as Yodan pushed his friends toward it. "We have to get out of here."

"Shandra!" Match screamed, fighting him off.

Yodan unclipped Match's control-pen and zapped him, making Match collapsed against him.

"Avery, pull the grate off that vent, get in, and head toward the air flow. Go." He pulled Match. Between his wound, his poor hydration, and the zap, Match remained unconscious. A loud grumble from the ground turned into a long shake as Yodan rolled into the vent, he slipped an arm around Match's shoulders and slid Match in the vent with him. The sounds, the smells, the vibrations meant they'd escaped in time. The pipes were durable and holding. Cool air with a salty taste meant this was the way Shandra had suggested they go.

Lying down, he shimmied backwards, pulling Match. "Let me know what's ahead, Avery. I'm going in backwards." He was about to remove his top to use it to pull him when Match grumbled.

"What in all these levels did you do to me?"

"Control-pen. You're in rough shape. Can you crawl, we have to move fast."

"Where's Shandra?"

"She was headed this way, let's go," he lied.

The heat and the shaking meant business.

Match flipped over and crawled. "She's pregnant," he whispered in Yodan's face as they moved.

"Who?"

"Shandra. I need to see her."

Explained why Shandra gave Match their family ring and why Match was so determined to keep her safe. "She said something about the salty water. Smell it? We're headed there. She won't be far."

The air vent was small compared to the other pipes they'd travelled. Between the salty air and the blood loss, Match moved slowly. Too slow for comfort. Yodan didn't know where the vent led, but he pushed forward regardless.

Match leaned back, feet against the pipe. "I can't go on. My ears are ringing. Do you hear that?"

Actually, Yodan did hear it but Match was unconscious again.

"Hold up, Avery. I'll have to pull him, again." He slid his hands under Match's armpits and tugged.

Space was too tight and awkward.

"The pipe drops off so get a grip and pull him into the next area," she offered.

Yodan brought them into the dip. Match was much bigger than him, but he wouldn't stop until they were out.

Avery went ahead. "I see light. Something is blocking the exit. It looks like science."

Yodan peeked. "Just a cooling fan. Here." He slid her the screwdriver he'd taken from his sister. "There'll be small screws keeping the fan in place along the side, use this tool to turn them out, then kick the fan out of place."

Yodan continued to pull his friend. They needed minerals but the ringing grew louder, forcing him to move faster.

He bumped into Avery working on the fan. "I see light, a way out." The excitement in her voice was hope but the light in front of her was dim compared to the light rumbling behind them.

Avery kicked at the fan and an assault of cold air hit them. Avery said, "The pipe is tore up and this drops into the ocean. Quite the fall."

The ringing turned to rumbles as the light behind Match grew brighter and warmer.

Flames headed their way. Yodan pushed Avery. "Jump, jump! Go!"

LINS

During the same breaths
Underground

Lins and Shanda were alone after the cave-in. They huddled against the wall with the cat. Debris had them trapped in tight quarters.

"You hurt?" Lins asked her sister.

"My leg was scraped, but I'll live."

"To your feet then."

"Match?" Shandra said, knowing better than to scream in an unsafe zone.

"Debris is thick through to the other side. Best option is to get in that pipe at the end and see where it takes us." If only she could access Nogard's memory and find them a quick way out.

Lins stepped aside as Shandra almost assaulted the dead drone sticking out of the debris. "Find me Match," Shandra ordered the lifeless drone.

"Perhaps relying on this technology is useless," Lins said, more to remind herself than her troubled sister. "The cat has found a pipe he likes."

"But Match is…" Shandra stared at the rubble.

"The chances of them surviving that are the same as ours. They'll be headed out an air pipe. Feel the pressure change? We're out of time. Termination has started." Her voice remained calm and factual, but Lins had her control-pen out. She showed the device to Shandra with her light-pen, a warning that she'd knock her out and drag her out if she had to. "You're carrying life, Shandra, you have to think about your child first. Match wouldn't want you to risk your life or his child's."

"You know?"

"Of course I know. You think you survived this long without my help? You think Owen just happened to always be right there to save you from all those accidents Nogard sent your way? I was controlling him via his hard hook-up. I guess Nogard didn't approve because she made him cut out his devices and leave. I watched it on the monitor. Move."

They scrambled in the pipe, the cat in the lead as if the feline knew where to go.

"That was wrong, Lins," Shandra mumbled. "We owe Owen an apology."

Ignoring her, Lins tried placing them on the map she'd seen with Pax in Mainframe One. If this was the shoreline, this area had ways out. This knowledge wasn't something she would normally have but merging with Nogard must have integrated certain facts with her own understanding of things.

The air grew heavy in the pipe. And hot. Rumbling and crashing happened on the other side of the pipe, but they were safe inside it. For now.

Shandra had a light, as they followed the cat leading them right, left, down, and up. "Someone's swearing."

Lins followed the voice, crawling through the next black pipe that shook under their fingers, cold to the touch. Too cold. Lins was used to the regulated system, but this change in temperature meant they approached an exit. She prepared herself for what might be on the other side.

The cat led them to Protector Owen.

"That way is collapsed," he said, as if meeting him in these pipes was perfectly normal.

"Our way has no exit," Lins informed him.

"There was a turn off about 100 metres back." Owen crawled backwards.

When they reached the opening, Shandra followed Owen in. The ground shook severely, making them pause. Lins had no idea where they were since these pipes were arranged at the dawn of Nogard's existence and weren't used anymore.

"I see light. Strange light." Owen raced on, not checking how close the others were. Shandra slowed when Lins trailed behind. Lins wasn't used to travelling these tight areas and her knees hurt. Her back ached and the pressure in her head was intense.

When they reached the light, Owen was already out in the open. Shandra peeked out of the pipe into the system, then offered Lins a spot to look.

They were on the face of a cliff. Hard ground below and so much open air she hesitated to join their protector. Owen climbed the face, toward trees. Which made sense since Nogard had sent him orders to find trees as a new energy source. The cat didn't seem to have issues climbing the cliff either.

"Up or down?" Shandra asked, watching the feline.

"We follow them."

Shandra climbed the face of the rock but when the earth shook, she lost her grip. Lins snagged her, grabbing her foot and leg as she passed. Owen must have lost his grip, too, because he slammed against the pipe opening, snapping his massive hands along the ledge, staring at Lins with the calm demeanour a protector always kept. He held himself up with one hand; using his hyper-strength, he helped Lins bring Shandra to safety inside the pipe. Then he climbed up the face of the rock with ease. Lins was shaking when a rope dangled in front of the pipe.

"Tie her to this rope and I'll pull her up, then you."

Her sister was unconscious. The scrape on Shandra's leg bled and her face had smashed against the rock, but air filled her lungs. Lins fastened her to the rope and helped Owen get her to the ledge he was on. He hauled Shandra up. Then the rope was before Lins again. She tied the rope around herself and scurried up the face of the rock. Not agile, but she scrambled on the ledge before the next quake and dropped by her sister to collect herself.

The cat greeted her, then took off.

Owen picked Shandra up and tossed her over his shoulder, following the cat.

"Where are we going?"

Owen didn't answer, just stormed through abundant trees as if he knew where to go.

~Where Breathing Begins~

"Either you do things their way or you become the enemy."
                                                    —Nogard

YODAN

During the same breaths
Above ground, ocean side

Yodan pulled Match out of the pipe with him as flames exploded behind them and into an endless blue overhead. The fall was quick, probably the distance they usually jumped at Glisten Point, so Yodan didn't have time to orient himself as they tumbled freely.

Avery splashed in the water moments before him with a scream that made Yodan's gut lurch.

The impact knocked the air out of him and the cold jabbed him. Yodan surfaced, taking in gulps of air. These garments offered little protection against this frigid temperature. Wild waves pushed him down but his concern was for Match and Avery. Thankfully, the cold jolted Match awake and Avery swam toward the shore with strong strokes.

Yodan enjoyed swimming but the assault to his senses ranged from the cold invading him to the salty taste raiding his mouth.

"*Mud on a rock*!" Match cursed as they fought waves and followed Avery. "What in all these levels is going on? I've never been so blasted cold in my life. Nogard! Control these waves," he demanded. In his training, Match had simulated various temperature changes so Yodan was surprised by such an outburst.

"We fell out of that ledge." Yodan pointed to it. "Didn't have much choice. See the flames coming out the side? We were in that tunnel. I don't know if Nogard can help us anymore, Match. I'm not even sure Dragon can."

Avery was almost at the shore. Match was full of vigorous energy, following her. Still, Yodan didn't like the trail of blood Match left behind. Why was it taking him so long to heal? "Match? How dehydrated are you?" Yodan spat out the salty water. "Have you taken D-light? Minerals?"

"Urgh. As if I had time. We have to go back and find Shandra."

Yodan glanced up, hoping to see her somewhere, but this system was too large to see it all.

Flames spouted from the top of the cliff and rocks shot high. And the overhead was high. Yodan couldn't see the end of it. This was the biggest system he'd ever encountered. White and grey gases polluted the overhead making cloudy images. All this open space was hard to take. Too much rushed at him, even the water was hard to handle and it was the calmest of the assaults. The air had too much flow and not enough shadowed areas. The energy from the rocks crumbling grew louder creating a pressure in his ears and head. Hot mixed with cold, making Yodan shiver yet burn.

Yodan closed his eyes as he curled up on the beach, hiding from nature attacking him. *One breath, Yodan. You can do this.* The sand under him was warm and he smeared himself into it, composing his thoughts.

Match mumbled something and Yodan had to look up to see what he was saying. "Over there."

Yodan looked. Long cylinders stood like pillars along a cliff. The D-light gleamed off something. "That's Lins," Match said. Yodan trusted Match's eyes, since his own were taking in far too many details.

"Then we'll go toward those cylinder pillars," Yodan offered, to keep him moving.

"Trees. Those are trees, just giant plants," Match said, but already he looked less tense having a sliver of hope that the reflection might be Lins or Shandra. "I studied their purpose. Trees produce oxygen and nutrients, which means energy. People used them to make shelter, to eat, to heal, to feed other food sources, and for warmth. This is a self-sustaining system."

"I can't think straight," Yodan confessed. "Too many things are happening to me. Why am I cold yet so hot? How is this possible?"

By his ear, Avery whispered, "Just breathe. Block the scary stuff out."

"My wet clothes are gross," Yodan complained.

Match added, "It's weird that this strong D-light doesn't offer enough heat or that the moving air doesn't warm enough to help. How do we access the system to demand for warmth that'd be effective? What type of system has no control units?" Match stormed up the hillside so Yodan and Avery followed.

Yodan considered getting out of his clothes yet having a protective layer between him and the assaulting environment was crucial. The garments were protection from the unfamiliar.

"Where are we?" Yodan asked Avery in case she knew everything or even anything about where they were. The D-light shining on them was impossibly bright yet this light was so far away, Yodan remained wet.

Match stared at the flames blowing out the side of the cliff as they paraded along the beach. "We're above ground," he mumbled. "This is what above ground means."

A terrifying rumble and explosion shook the area. That was not a quake. "What the—?"

Yodan glanced over his shoulder when Avery screamed, "We have to move. Now!" She pulled Yodan's hand.

Out of the trees, creatures charged toward them.

"What are those?" Match tumbled into Yodan.

"Stampede!" Avery screamed, diving out of the way.

AVERY

A breath later
Above ground, along the cliffs

The explosions were terrifying as Avery led Yodan and Match toward the hillside. She didn't have time to show them around or explain things. The blasts had caused a stampede that headed their way.

Yodan dived for cover against the rock, shielding his eyes, hiding from the sun as if the light hurt him. Maybe bright light bothered him. Someone who could see in the dark might be vulnerable to such things. With his snowy-white skin, Avery wouldn't expect him to spend much time in the sunlight anyway.

Avery pointed out the various dangers as they ran: the debris falling, the landslides, the herd stampeding...

Match's frown made deep ridges along his forehead. "We'll be safe up there." He grabbed Yodan's hand and guided him away from Avery.

"Where are you going?" she hollered at him.

"Debris is falling, but in that crevice, we'll be safe." Match stopped in a divot where the cliff created a natural shelter from the sun, winds, and now, the stampede.

"Avery, we can't run like this," Match snapped as she joined them, squeezing into the tight spot.

The guys were panting.

Boulders fell, some crushed the herd.

"The air is too weird," Yodan complained. "It hurts to breathe so fast."

Avery glanced over her shoulder at the stampede closing in, relieved that she'd followed them into this safe area. She had to hand it to Match, he had a real eye for saving his ass. "Fine. We'll wait while the herd runs by. Yodan, are you hurt?"

Match had his hands on the rock, as if feeling for a life pulse.

"The pressure is making me dizzy. My head hurts. We're too high, yet when I glance up and see how high the overhead is, I feel small."

"Warmth," Match demanded from the walls. "Heat," he tried again. "Not so much blasted D-light!"

"Who are you yelling at?" Avery demanded.

"Your A-life."

The cliff exploded repeatedly.

"I feel the insides collapsing," Match said.

"Inside the cliff?" Avery was shocked. How could he feel that by touching the rock? She tried but pulled away when she felt nothing. He was creepy-weird, yet fascinating.

"Surface dweller, how do we activate your system? We need warmth to dry off but your light is too far away." Match spoke over the sound of the approaching stampede. He had a twig in hand and snapped the stick in several smaller pieces in a musical pattern. Then he tossed them and started over with another twig he grabbed from a pile of nearby debris.

"I'm frozen and blind." Yodan looked as eager to learn the answer.

She wasn't sure what they wanted from her. "Unfortunately, we don't get to control our sun."

"Who controls it?"

"The Creator."

"Take us to meet this creator." Match looked about ready to wrestle a beast.

Were they for real? "The Creator provided us with Dragon who keeps the pipes warm and that allows us to grow our crops and keep herds. But we can't question it or bring in science or Dragon gets upset and well…" She pointed at the exploding rocks. "This is my fault. I let a nomad in the village with gadgets and ideas about science. I called him my brother because I liked the idea of having someone else in the village who looks like me."

"This isn't anyone's fault. Our A-life died," Yodan reassured her.

"What are those animals?" Match pointed to the stampede as they huddled around her. Match snapped his twigs every few breaths, making an irritating sound.

"We call them biscows. They group to stay safe from our hunters. We use their fur for clothes and the meat is wonderful, but they are protective and hard to hunt."

"You eat those things?" Match's eyes were huge as he snapped a twig once… twice.

"Yeah, but they aren't stampeding when we hunt them, and they're harmless while they stand around and eat grass."

Snap. "Still. That's wow." Match was mighty impressed and by the gleam in his crystal white eyes, she was sure he'd hunt them first chance he got. "You guys ever ride them?"

The herd rounded the hill and vanished. "No." That was a lie, because Hunter rode them but she didn't want these idiots trying that.

She watched Match. The red in the center of his eyes slinked bigger and smaller as he surveyed the horizon. "What are your eyes doing?" she blurted out.

"Focusing. I'm not used to seeing at this distance or in this light, but I can self-program the coding that runs my eyesight and essentially tell my eyes how I want them to see. I'm searching the area for Shandra."

A few elders had gone blind. Being able to make their eyes see was impossible. She glanced at Yodan. "Can you do that with your eyes?"

"I have hyper-vision. I see details at great speeds and record them to memory to reanalyze. Nogard gifted prodigies with a mutation. These traits sometimes get passed to others or evolved, like our ability to see in the dark. If we go back four generations, shadow-vision was a gift and this was passed on. Now, over half of us see in the dark since the trait is useful."

Oh boy. The clans wouldn't like this. "Maybe we should get away from this cliff," Avery offered when the herd passed. "I'm impressed that each one of you is so different even though you look alike. Well, except for the eyes. But when you get to my village, don't go into details. Just say your eyes adjust to things. Keep your science simple. My people aren't comfortable with technology."

"Gotcha," Match nodded, walking in the open fearlessly.

"The cliff sounds as if it might blow right off," she said. "Be careful." The chilly air entered her lungs smoothly as Avery scrambled to her feet. Being out of the tight tunnels and pipes was a relief, but she kept a close eye on these young men, curious what they were thinking. She couldn't imagine being above ground for the first time. Seeing the world in its hugeness. She was thankful that they weren't far from her village, but the climb was mostly uphill.

Match kept them moving up the sandy hill. "We have to get closer to those trees in case of avalanches."

"Good idea," Avery agreed.

When they left the beach area, both guys knelt to brush their palms over the grass before they stepped on it.

"It's grass," Avery said.

"It resembles a blanket covering the earth in the same colour as your eyes," Match said so-matter-of-fact as he snagged another small twig from the grass and snapped it. This close to the forest, the twigs were blown everywhere from the blasts. "There's less debris around the trees. We'll have a shaded path closer to them."

He was obviously a planner so Avery respected that because as long as they went up, she didn't care where they walked. She'd never travelled the deeper parts of the woods but Hunter said they ended abruptly and opened onto a world of snow.

Yodan rubbed the wound behind his ear, feeling the mild scar. "The air tastes different. I... I have to adjust to the idea of not having Nogard around me or doing things for us. And everything's moving around me which is hard to follow."

The top of the cliff erupted in a deafening explosion that knocked them off their feet. A grey cloud blocked out the sun.

Match helped his friends up then hurried them toward the trees and Yodan flung an arm around Avery.

"It's loud," Yodan said, an echo lost in the rumbling.

"And how is the air doing that?" Match glanced around, searching for something.

Avery wondered, "I guess the open is hard to take?"

"Where is the end of the overhead?" Yodan asked. His eyes watered as he watched the explosion. "Less light," he requested, probably out of force of habit.

"It wouldn't take much to overdose on that light, eh Yodan?" Match teased, snapping another twig.

Avery removed her stained over-shirt and handed it to Yodan. "Use this to shield out the sun and winds while we walk. We have hats that might help when we get to my village." Gosh. Would they even be welcomed?

He draped the cloth over his head.

"You'll be fine," she promised him. "Focus on me and stop

asking the world for things. We never ask. We trust that Dragon provides."

She pointed to the grey warming pipes up the hill. "Look. I'm almost home." She missed her clan, her brothers, Saxton, and especially her mother who'd taught her so many important things. "My people will give you shelter." She might be lying but she'd worry about that when they arrived at the village. If there was even a village left after all these explosions and quakes.

They strolled carefully but she was eager to get to her family. Still, Avery understood their trepidation. They were used to moving in tunnels without the world crashing around them in violent explosions.

"My feet are cold," Match mumbled. "This protective suit is not warm enough for this environment. I don't see how the surface dweller stands it."

"My name is Avery and this is a beautiful warm day."

The tall black pipes extending out the cliffs ripped another bomb on them but this one was less intense as flames shot through the sky for several breaths. They stood by the grass to watch.

Then silence fell on them. And Avery wondered if she'd gone deaf.

Match glanced at his watch. "The countdown is over. The system has terminated."

"The world is peaceful again," Yodan said, testing the silence for echoes.

Sounds returned, heavy on Avery's ears. "My village isn't far. Just up there."

An eagle flew by and the young men gawked, amazed.

A rustle from the bushes made Avery tense and she stepped in front of them, with her knife drawn.

Shimmering creatures stepped from the bushes just ahead of them.

MATCH

A few breaths later
Above ground, forest

Match rushed toward Shandra the moment he spotted her slung over Owen's shoulder but Owen didn't even acknowledge him as he stepped from the cluster of trees in front of them.

He continued his march under the shelter of the trees.

Lins caught up to Match and rushed beside him.

"She's safe." Lins blocked her violet eyes from the extreme D-Light. She wasn't wearing her robe and seeing her in a glistening purple lifesuit was weird for Match. "How did you guys get out?"

"No idea. Owen wait!" Match called to Owen. But the big brute didn't even glance his way.

"Stop. If Shandra's hurt we have to help her." The air tasted smoky and wasn't grade-A, but the air was moving too violently; it almost felt like grade-B. He wanted to get them somewhere else. But where?

Lins looked over her shoulder at Avery and Yodan who trailed behind. "Calm down. You look ill, he's strong and determined to help, let him. Fill me in. What do you know?"

Match checked Lins' eyes before trusting her. Staying on Owen's heels, he said, "Nogard is dead." She'd better dang well be.

"No. I got her out."

"Dormant?"

"Not really, she was using the eRobe to stay alert. I left the eRobe and life-drive at Mainframe One with Pax of the South, a surface dweller. He said he'd protect my devices during the blast. I stored the drive in a pack he carried. Nogard was in it."

He felt the weight of her words on his shoulders. "You left active Artificial-life with a surface dweller?"

"I wasn't thinking clearly."

Great. Her subtle way of saying she'd been infected by Nogard. "You thinking clearly now?"

"Dragon's controlled by a hard-drive," Lins informed him.

"The programs are impossible to override. We needed an access code called ReSurface to stop the destruction."

"Not what ReSurface is for." Match instinctively covered his watch while he ducked to avoid a branch. Everything about this system was too much. "Nogard was supposed to be terminated in the destruction and then we could use the codes to make a new A-life when and if we need one."

"Make a new A-life?"

"Yeah. I have the *breath of life* on me. But now I'm worried. Who knows how many others Nogard infiltrated? If she gets that code, she could reproduce. What if she's in this Pax of the South? What harm will she do to him?"

"Why wasn't I made aware that A-life was merging with us?" she demanded.

"I found out too late."

The cat had found Avery and she carried him as if he were a lifeline to her sanity in this quick moving system.

"What's wrong with Shandra? Why is she unconscious?" Match demanded since it was obvious Owen wasn't about to stop for him to check on her and what could he do but follow the brute?

Lins explained, "Shandra's leg was hurt. Her face suffered from scrapes. He won't let me look at her, on some mission to find a medic as if he can sense where one is."

Maybe he could? He wasn't that bright, but there had to be something useful in that big bulky head of his. Owen looked like a walking statue as he stormed up the hill in his grey glimmering lifesuit.

Yodan and Avery caught up to them. "Owen," Yodan was panting as he stepped beside him. "My friend Avery is a medic in-training. She can help us heal Shandra until we get her to a healing bay."

Owen stopped instantly and set Shandra against a tree and Match was thankful for Yodan. He always knew how to talk to idiots.

Match watched how gentle Owen was with her.

"Heal her," Owen ordered Avery, taking charge like he wasn't some coward who'd left them to die.

Avery set the cat down and knelt by Shandra. Match went to join him but Owen pulled him back by the shoulder and there was no shaking his iron-fist grip so he watched Avery check Shandra's injuries. Was she a medic?

A few breaths ago, Match had lied to Yodan to convince him to shut down a quadrant so he could hide Shandra and stay closer to her. He'd even lied to his brother so he'd find enough supplies so he could keep Shandra safe. And now, he might lose her.

The cat pushed between them, jolting him back to reality. Yodan petted it, and Match found the motion soothing.

"Shandra is too warm," Yodan whispered while at the Surface Dweller's side. Lins stood on the other side, studying the horizon, keeping watch for them.

"She's also suffered a great deal of damage to her face we need to clean."

Match felt his palms warm as his panic threatened to create flames in them. He snapped the small stick in his hand, the sound was a grounding comfort that stopped the panic. "I got our people out," he told Owen, glancing at him to make sure his eyes weren't grey. Like usual they were black.

"I can sense them," Owen said. "I knew you would."

"So you planned to sit back and let me risk my neck so you could take the credit?"

"A protector doesn't need credit. He knows his people and trusts them to do their jobs. You are elite. I trust you with the lives of every other breathing life in Quma Cities, but I will never trust you with my life. Ever since Nogard announced Shandra as my life-companion, every time I hard hook-up to update my knowledge I'm terrified you'll terminate me. I finally couldn't take it anymore and cut out my devices and left."

This brute was afraid of him? "She's pregnant with my child. I'm protecting my family."

"But she's a quester."

"Yeah. We screwed up. Why Nogard got you involved. You're the only one I won't challenge because physically I can't win against you."

His grip eased off a bit.

"This ain't so bad," Avery announced. "She's a bit banged up. Nothing a cold cloth won't help. It's just a fever and a few scratches." Then the cold survivor ordered Yodan to remove his weird damp top and she used the fabric to clean Shandra properly.

Owen let Match go to open his pack. Match instantly fell beside Shandra, brushing his fingers along her jaw, wishing she'd wake up.

Owen brought over his mineral water and handed the liquid to Avery.

"Fevers kill," Yodan told Avery.

"Fevers heal," Avery argued. "Her nose looks broken but she's sucking in air so it's not as bad as my brother's was. Father Saxton had to actually crack the nose back in place."

The cat stayed with Shandra, lying on her feet.

Match watched how Avery checked Shandra's life-pulse. She was in control. Bossy. Clearly having studied as a medic and seen this type of injury before. He needed her help and used compassion to keep her focused. "You have a brother?"

"I have many brothers."

"My brother didn't make it out of Quma Cities."

"I lost a brother once, too," Avery said.

Match studied her bright clothing. So many colours and patterns mixed in her garments that they gave him a headache. Why was everything overdone in this system? Didn't they know moderation?

"Mine was climbing the sacred rocks," she pointed to the rock formation shadowing them. "He fell. He knew better, but I should have been there to remind him not to be so foolish. Eats you up to live with that guilt."

"Mine was running an errand for me because I'd lied to him, tricked him into doing it because I didn't want to see the disappointment in his eyes if I would have told him the truth."

"I'm sorry."

Yodan placed a hand on Match's shoulder, even though he didn't deserve the comfort.

"Father Saxton took his death hard. Do you have parents?" she asked Match.

"The parents in my family unit were both female and were each allowed one pregnancy with in-lab fertilization as long as one of my mothers agreed to let Nogard run an experiment on them. My father was science, one of Nogard's experiments. Why my eyes are white. Means I have no father. Nogard created human life without male sperm, but in exchange, I have cyborg abilities, like being able to program my own sight or make fire with my bare hands, and sometimes, information I didn't know just comes to me when I need it." Match ripped the fabric around Shandra's leg so Avery could work on it. "Because I'm made of half science, I'm forbidden to reproduce. Because of the fire-hands, I'm considered a failed experiment. But because I was chosen as elite by our people, Nogard couldn't terminate me without going against their wishes and she liked to show that she respected elites."

Yodan sighed beside them, clearly understanding how serious this pregnancy was now. They had to keep Shandra safe, make sure their child was healthy. The unknown possibilities were too much.

"That's not a story you should tell the people of my village. They don't do so well with things made of science."

"Why would he tell your people anything?" Owen asked. "I'm the protector. I'll decide who does the talking."

Match didn't expect his people to be welcomed in a new system and he was getting good at lying so he nodded. "Perhaps a medic of your people could help us, show us how to use non-science to heal, then we can be on our way."

"Well, with so many brothers, I've seen my share of broken noses and bones. We'll get Shandra fixed up, promise. No need to involve any of our healers. If you ask me, they're over-dramatic with their rituals and singing and praying. And that stuff doesn't work as well as actual hands-on treatments."

Match could see that they'd need Avery to help them adjust to this strange world. If she taught Yodan what she knew he could show the others in a way that would work. Yeah, she'd come in handy. Even if she was unusual looking with her wild head full of hair.

Yodan brushed that hair from her eyes to peer in them. Had he ever seen Yodan smile so warmly? Sure he'd crushed hard on Madeline because she challenged his theories versus facts, pushing him to be brilliant. But this was…*happy*.

Avery cut pieces of Yodan's leg garments that were too long with her knife and tied them around Shandra's leg. Easily distracted, she glanced at Yodan and blushed.

Well, this was interesting. They were crushing on each other?

"What are you doing?" Match asked, trying to get her focus back on helping Shandra and not Yodan sitting there petting her cat with no shirt on. "Did you lose your..." he wasn't sure what her word was for a medic-pen, "your healing tools?"

"When cuts bleed, stop the blood loss with pressure. Or you get weak like you were and pass out. Prayers help, but only after you stop the bleeding. That's always first."

He touched the wound on his head, finally the area scarred over thanks to the extra minerals in his watch but he had a bump forming. "In Quma Cities, you healed or you died."

"Well, in my village, we show compassion for our sick. They're able to contribute, or they did contribute and deserve our respect. Life is precious."

"I agree," Yodan said. Of course he did. That was his motto.

Match put his watch on Shandra hoping the healing properties might help her. "Offer Shandra minerals so she gets her energy up and I'll carry her to your medic," Match said, determined as he scrambled to his feet.

Yodan shook his head. "I'll carry her, you're weak. I don't need you passing out again. Avery's right, you lost a lot of blood and haven't had proper healing. That wound should be healed, look at mine. You're dehydrated and should have taken D-light."

Match growled. "You're not touching her. I'll carry her." He wiped his head, dizzy. If he let Yodan carry her, Owen would think he could help.

"Fine, whatever. Be stupid." Yodan let the issue go, but offered him minerals with a glare that implied he'd better take them. Match drank. It'd take a few breaths before his energy returned, then they'd go. He offered the last two sips to Shandra but she was unconscious so he wet the minerals to her lips and splashed a bit on her wounds.

Yodan nudged Avery then pointed to the overhead. "Your A-life is far away. How do you maintain it?"

"The sun's not science. It's a gift, like the grass, like the wind and waters."

Yodan looked lost in the possibility of the world so Match added, "This unknown looming before us is scary and factual guidance would be welcome. What you say contradicts with what we know. For example, it is a fact that this grass is a plant. Plants are not a gift from an unknown being, it's a lifeform we make or destroy. We classify life into different categories and plants are one of them. Another fact is that since we arrived above ground your D-Light has shifted spots in the overhead indicating it's part of a patterned programmed system. Who installed this system?"

"The Creator," she said to him.

Determined to find and meet this Creator, Match scooped Shandra in his arms, gripping her as he marched with his crew. Owen led, then him with Shandra in his arms with Lins at their side. Yodan and Avery trailed behind, Yodan taking off in different directions to smell different flowers or touch this or that, which was typical Yodan and nothing to be concerned about.

The cat took charge when they filed off this way by venturing in front of Owen to lead them up the hillside.

Once they were free from the crowded shelter the trees offered and passed the burned section of land, Match spotted a grey service pipe. Interesting. If service pipes were outside that meant Mainframe One might be accessible.

The pipe didn't look far, but after a long walk Match had to rest and he knelt by Shandra. Distance was hard to judge in this system.

"I can carry her," Owen offered.

"I'll ask if I need your help. Your job is simple: lead us to safety, find us a medic, find the children I sent up, and act like a blasted protector. Just leave me to tend to my family." Without him wanting it, flames erupted in his palms.

"We are your family, even Nogard," Owen reminded Match before he backed off.

It took Match a breath to collect himself and get the flames under control. *Dammit.* He couldn't do that when meeting these new people or they'd terminate him as a threat.

Shandra's fever was already easing off and she woke enough to take a sip of nutrients someone handed her. "You made it," Match promised her. "Sleep. You need rest. I won't let anything hurt you."

Much to Match's annoyance, she mumbled in her delusional state; "Owen." What if her programming was screwy when she woke and she left him for that idiot?

Owen kept them going, ignoring her now that Match had

her in his arms.

When they arrived closer to the pipes, boulders littered the area. Even though they were higher from where they'd started, this area was flat and extended far, offering a safe place for a village. The village was like a scene from a mystical story. Huts were erected above ground inside the protected shelter of the pipes instead of making their homes in the service pipes or in the rocks.

Match stared at the huts as they marched. From this vantage point he saw up to the top of the mount where a giant carving of the beast of Quadrant F decorated the top and weaved along until meeting the pipes. The bottom half looked like the tattoo Yodan wore on his neck of a serpent tail. Yet when Match looked back from where they'd come, he had a perfect view down the cliff to the water and the trees. This cliff division between the trees and water reminded Match of his own tattoo and symbol of strength. Someone must have brought these images with them to Quma Cities and used them as symbolic images. Meant at one time, their ancestors had stood here and looked on this village, not for the first time, but the last.

His home was in that rock. Well. Not anymore. Still, Match knew the entire layout of the piping system and the tunnels, and standing here, he saw how they weaved through the cliffs from the outside. A large chunk was missing. Mainframe Three and Four should be where the water was, in the actual spot where they'd jumped. Meant they'd lost vital parts of the older systems, including Nogard's energy source and that explained why the energy loss was so unexpected, and so severe.

"This will take getting used to," Lins said, catching her breath in gulps. "They live in huts like our fabled stories. Their technology will have evolved differently than ours. Prepare yourselves."

Match had altitude simulations as part of his training, but this environment made him much dizzier. He glanced at the tall foliage to the south. Old shelters were visible.

"We'll adapt," Owen promised them.

Match didn't agree with him. Some of them would struggle. This was too much change.

Shandra opened her eyes. The pink in them was a touch

deeper when she smiled.

"We made it," Match whispered to Shandra, letting his guard down, ready to confess his fears. "Yodan, Lins, Owen, and us." Having his brother missing was a tough loss. "Now we need to find the prodigies. They'll know what to do with the life-drive Lins saved."

She wrapped an arm around Match so carrying her was easier. "Owen," she mumbled.

"He got you out of the pipes safely."

Owen was suddenly in their space, annoying him, but he couldn't tell him to back off. "Can I help you?" Match could hardly see. The overhead light was much too bright, even with the fogs that grouped in strange clouds, but he did better than Yodan who had Avery's extra clothing over his head as if the light blinded him. He was never good in bright lights.

"Are those people by the service pipes?" Yodan asked which distracted Owen and got him out of their space. Shandra was already unconscious again.

"Those are the clans of Cuma Village," Avery informed them with a hint of excitement in her step, as if she might rush to the crowd. They were dressed in even more colours than Avery. Shades of browns, blacks, blues, reds, yellows. Each one vibrant and bright. These colours were more an assault to his senses than anything. But the shock was their skin colour. It was enough seeing Avery with her peachy freckled skin, but this group was a variety of colours. The scene was so impressive, Match had to force his eyes off the group.

Yodan gave Avery back her garment and she dressed, adding another layer.

"The village was hit by a landslide," Avery shared, waving to the men who broke free from the group and headed toward them. "The warming pipes run around the village, protecting it. This is the only way in. They must be waiting for the area to be safe."

Owen glanced up at the cliff with the reassurance of a protector. "It's fine now. The worst is over."

Match kept his stride. *Keep moving. Even when afraid. Especially when afraid.* He remembered Nogard's training as if the words were implanted in him. He purposely relaxed his shoulders, grounded his steps, and held a serious smile. The image was one of an elite and he'd trained hard to master this serene, in-control look, despite the wild raging panic ripping him apart inside. *More lies.*

Did he look and act as annoying as Owen? Maybe he should stop lying and be himself.

"When adapting, remember that even though things feel different they are essentially the same," Owen said.

Match added, "He's right, we stop bleeding with a medic-pen, Avery uses pressure. I see homes grouped in sections like our quadrants, and somewhere in that mess are our prodigies."

"They're called clans and each one has a leader. A clan can have several huts. In each one is a family with a father, a mother, and their children. These huts form the clan and they share beliefs with the clan leader. He speaks for them and earns them status." Much like their protector did. "How he earns his spot in his clan is up to the clan. Some vote him in, others do games to earn their spot, and some inherit it. The leaders form the council with the elders. The elders bring the wisdom to the group since they lived the longest in the clans. They settle the debates and disputes and sometimes suggest challenges between leaders to keep things peaceful."

"Gotcha." Match nodded, focusing his energy on the system instead of the fear gripping him. "Same as us. We have protectors of quadrants and they band together to form a diverse and complete council. Protectors get the most memories but need the Collective to understand them. See? Same thing," he told them, needing to see them relax.

Owen stood with his shoulders back, making sure he came off the protector. Match let it go. As long as Owen helped, he didn't care what muscle-man did.

"If new people had come to our system, we would have been curious and leery of them. They'll be the same. We must find our youths and our medics before we integrate in their system. I want Medic Brisk to check Shandra. Finding them is priority." Match marched toward them on a mission, his arms numb, but he refused to give Shandra up.

"I don't see the children. Saxton's coming to meet us." Avery pointed to the man headed their way. "He's my father and welcomes nomads to the village."

"*Or he asks them to leave,*" Owen mumbled.

"So your people are used to strangers?" Lins wondered.

This Saxton was the biggest man Match had ever seen. He towered over them. His hair was black, darker than his skin. But his clothing threw Match off. Did these colours and symbols mean something?

"Not many outsiders show up anymore."

Match didn't believe that. Not many were brought into the village, but if some showed, there were plenty more.

"People think my green eyes are weird so you might get strange looks since your eyes are so different than ours."

Green. So that was the name of this abundant colour covering everything.

"Does anyone have grey eyes?" he inquired.

"Ah… Not that I noticed. Why?"

"Tell me if any of you see someone with grey eyes."

The green covering on the ground was slippery so Match marched with determination. Falling might hurt Shandra and the life she carried. Pregnant women in Quma Cities were normally confined to the maternity ward for training. The life they carried was important and her being in explosions and grade-B air didn't sit well with him. This was supposed to be a time of relaxation and preparation.

They were almost at the pipe entrance and he had to come off looking as tough as these taller, wider, and rippling-with-muscles men. Even Owen was clearly not measuring up as he took several deep breaths. "You got this, Protector Owen," Match promised him. "Just like you trusted me to get your people out, trust whoever you have to, but get us in there to find our medics." *They're just men*, he reminded himself, *probably more afraid of you than you are of them.*

"There are no women in the group," Owen pointed out. "I had hoped Avery would be our way in."

So had Match but seeing these marching men form an imaginary vibrant and colourful line they wouldn't be allowed to pass, he was having doubts.

Saxton approached, their chosen one. The others crossed their arms, giants guarding their kingdom. The cat ran to them and strutted around their feet. Most ignored it, but when it went to Saxton, he bent to pet and speak with the feline like Avery had.

Would this Saxton listen to one of them? Who would Owen send in to speak for the group?

AVERY

A breath later
Above ground, the entrance to Cuma Village

Avery worried when she saw the shape Father Saxton was in and rushed to him. "Father Saxton, what happened?" They were outside the safe area, and no one looked too eager to get back to the village.

"Nothing." He frowned, unhappy about the nothing.

"Are the others hurt?" She gripped his hand.

"Pax gave us a warning. When things rumbled, we got out in time. Could have gone either way, luckily the evacuation increased our status as a protector. I see you found Friskie and…Dragon's people? Did they kill Dragon?" He glared at them over her shoulder. "Are you hurt? Are they dangerous?"

"They've come to help. They've kept Friskie safe. These are good people, Father Saxton. They look and speak differently than us, and they won't fit in, but maybe we can be welcoming." She didn't dare tell him about the science things she'd held or that had saved them; or that Match was *made* of science.

Both groups stayed back, leery. Avery glanced at Yodan's clan. Owen remained in the front with his fists clenched, but he looked like any other guy. Match with Shandra in his arms was the real threat. He stood like Hunter and met their eyes. Shandra was limp once again, resting against him. Lins remained inches behind him. As for Yodan, well, he was checking the seeing-eye hanging from the side of the warming pipes. Yodan studied the lens, not bothered by the group of men watching.

"Come, Father Saxton, I want you to meet Yodan." She pulled his hand, guiding him to Yodan. When Yodan noticed her coming toward him, he bounded in their direction, shielding his eyes.

"Sorry," Yodan said, with his winning smile. "I thought I saw the camera move. Hopeful, I guess."

The silence had Avery nervous. Even Saxton glanced at the seeing-eye as if the guard might have moved.

When they met, Avery reached for Yodan's hand, too, and

joined it with her father's. "Father Saxton, this is Yodan," she announced proudly. The symbol of united hands meant she presented him to her father for his approval as a potential she might want to move in with. Which was crazy when she probably still had to agree to Jacob's offer for her brothers. Yet this introduction was instinct and fit with her better than Jacob.

Saxton raised an eyebrow, surprised, but ran his rough hands around their linked hands, accepting her presentation without more pushing from her. "Yodan? That's an interesting name."

"Thank you, Father Saxton. Yodan means seeing beyond the facts, and wasn't easy to earn in a system where facts rule." He smirked while they held hands like long lost brothers who couldn't be more different.

"I earned mine, too. Saxton is the name given to the guard. Why my clan is the first at the entrance." Father Saxton tilted his head to study Yodan's pink eyes and clay white skin. "I would kill to protect my family."

If Yodan caught his subtle warning, there was no indication. He beamed. Tilting his head, too, Yodan showed off the markings he wore on his neck. Saxton stepped back as if Yodan had given his own warning. But Yodan said, "Your skin is almost black like the soil we grow our plants in."

"Yours is white like the snow we freeze our asses off in."

"And your eyes are so brown you must see through the dirt."

Saxton chuckled. "I have to admit, your pink eyes threw me off, but welcome to Cuma Village. Your clan is invited to join mine tonight for a meal." Avery was amazed at how relaxed Father Saxton was with Yodan. "Place is a mess, but children are always welcome." He slapped him on the back before heading toward the others. The rare symbolic touch he'd given Yodan on his back was one Saxton offered to his sons and Avery. She'd never seen Saxton greet a stranger this way and was amused when he called Yodan a child. Then again, his words might be a strategic way of making the clans accept them because they wouldn't turn away children, no matter how different they were.

Still, this acceptance pleased Avery, but really, Yodan didn't come off intimidating. Match might be a different story, even Lins might face doubts. Owen was too weird. Avery couldn't see her people interacting with them and their gadgets, even though they'd proved most useful.

Jacob stepped forward, rushing to Saxton. "Avery!" Much to her annoyance, Jacob got in her face. "You survived." Then as was the ways of Berry Clan, he wrapped his arms around her in a claiming hug she weaseled out of. Yodan was at her side, instantly, blocking him from touching her again with an arm out. *Oh my gosh.* What was he doing? Jacob towered over him and would crush him.

"Jacob Berry!" she scolded him but Jacob went to shove Yodan, but he stepped back so fast, Jacob missed and pushed air.

Stumbling, Jacob said, "Get your white freakish paws off the mother of my children." Jacob dived for Yodan again, but he was already out of the way and on the other side of Saxton.

The only way to end this was to assure Jacob that she would take his deal. "Jacob, enough. I will not be seen with a man who acts this way."

He put up his hands. "I won't tolerate you presenting others to your father as long as my offer is unanswered. This white freak has no business interfering in our deal."

"In this moment, we have no deal. I'm considering your offer for my brothers' sake. But your attitude dissuades me."

"Is this common in your system to fight and manhandle each other?" Yodan asked Saxton.

"We do this a fair bit."

"Why?"

Saxton smirked, holding out a hand as a warning to keep Jacob back. "See who the boss is."

"Boss of what?" Yodan wanted to know.

"Whatever. Everything. Nothing. The situation. The moment. I don't know. If I'm the boss I have control and respect. Right now, I'm the boss because Jacob wants something from me more than I want something from him. He wants me to order Avery to accept an offer he made her that we can live without."

Could they? Was he saying that to ease her guilt?

"But he forgets that in my clan, she is allowed to make this decision freely, without fear of reprimand. Regardless of her decision, we'll still be family because I taught her well and trust her to know what is right for her."

Jacob glared but respected the warning. Really, even beaten and exhausted, Saxton could knock him out.

Yodan stepped away from Avery instantly. Her heart sank with the motion. She was no better off. She had to accept Jacob's offer, only now, she risked hurting Yodan whom she wanted to know better.

"I require an answer," Jacob demanded.

Yodan took another step back but Father Saxton was there and he bumped into him. "Go on, tell Jacob what you want, Yodan-who-had-to-earn-his-name."

Oh no. Yodan was so blunt, he'd make things worse.

"Sometimes in Quma Cities, we fancied someone but Nogard would evaluate our compatibility and couple us with another. I not only studied this aspect, but was victim to it. Statistics show that those who couple by choice were happier, lived to the end of their life term, and raised prodigies every time. Those who were matched by Artificial-life had a ten percent suicide rate, a ten percent early mortality, and over fifty percent had a longing factor that was never resolved."

"What?" Jacob stepped closer, fists clenched he swung.

Yodan backed up and snagged the fist coming at him. He shoved it back and Jacob stared at him stunned. "What I learned in my studies is that when people form connections between each other, others shouldn't mess with that."

Much to her surprise, Saxton chuckled. "I like that. This seems like affairs worth settling later with words, not fists. This young man moves at alarming speeds. We have children to welcome, Jacob. Dragon's people are here and we need to know what they want and what they offer. Our village is in shambles from the quakes and the debris. Let me talk to my daughter."

"She is no longer your daughter but my partner."

"My patience with you is dwindling."

"Would you like to meet the others, Father Saxton?" Yodan said smoothly and despite herself, Avery giggled when he called him Father.

"I would," Saxton said. Much to Avery's surprise, his voice wavered when Match met his eyes, even at this distance. She understood his unease. With the sun gleaming off him, Match looked like a white glimmering mirage. And her cat sat by him, waiting.

Walking by Saxton, they met Match who hadn't moved, not even to shift Shandra in his arms. He remained planted like a machine made of science and not a man with emotions... This thought terrified her. What if he was a machine? She for sure didn't know anyone who could control how their eyes saw. What would a walking human-machine look like? She stared at him and decided that it'd probably look like Match.

Hunter stepped forward to keep Jacob back with a hand on his shoulder. Saxton stopped a hut distance from Match and Owen. "Welcome to Cuma Village. I'm Saxton, leader of Saxton Clan and the one chosen to meet nomads who visit our village."

"I'm Protector of Quma Cities. You may address me as Sir Owen."

"I'm Elite Match of Quma Cities, only the cities were destroyed and we're the last of the survivors. We're not here to visit. I'm searching for the children. Are they safe?"

Saxton glanced to the others and back to Match. "Children? You're children."

Avery jumped in to say, "Younger than us. My new friends are smaller built but they're grownups. The children he's looking for went up the shaft in Dragon's Caves. Pax was hurt but was with them and their healer."

Saxton took a deep breath. "I'm afraid the caves collapsed."

Avery glanced at them. "We have to get Pax out."

Suddenly, Lins was at Match's side and moved around Yodan. Avery turned to see why.

Jacob dived for Yodan.

Match, who carried Shandra, kicked out his foot and struck Jacob before he reached his friend. At the same moment, Lins reached toward Jacob. Just a brush of a cylinder she then whipped away. Was that the same type of device Yodan had used to knock Match out earlier?

Jacob dropped as if dead, sprawled out in front of them.

Saxton stared down at him. "What did you do to Jacob?"

With his eyes on Saxton, Owen said rather coldly, "I'm

done with his attacks on my people. If this gentle caring woman can take down one of your toughest men with one finger, imagine what I can do." He picked up one of the boulders that littered the ground. The rock was about the size of Avery's basket for gathering berries, and he crushed the stone between his hands as if it was made of soft dust.

"Holy hell." Avery had never seen Saxton look so terrified as he swore. "Is Jacob alive?" Saxton asked but he didn't dare touch Jacob to check for life. Of course, her cat wasn't so fearless and he marched right over Jacob and sat on him as if he was the one to take him down.

Match said, "We don't believe in taking lives, we simply reprogram."

"We don't believe in taking lives either," Saxton shared. "We simply hit."

"Problem with that," Match pointed out, "is that you must also be fast enough to make contact and strong enough to take a hit back."

Saxton nodded. "Yeah."

"He'll wake up shortly," Match said. "When he does, I want him out of my face. Next time I reprogram him."

Saxton faced Hunter. "You deal with him."

"I got him," Owen said, clearly eager to show off. He picked Jacob up like a doll and tossed him over his shoulder even though Jacob was much bigger than him.

Hunter rushed over, regardless, but when Lins stepped up to him, he instinctively backed up from her.

"We want the children I sent up and a medic for Shandra." Match kept his eyes on Hunter as if he could get him those things.

"We're not hiding your children," Saxton promised, his eyes bloodshot and his clothes a mess, yet when children were involved, the clans would step up. Children were their future and adapted much easier to the ways of the clans. But these guys were coming off scary.

"Maybe we could go to the caves and see if there are survivors," Yodan offered and his voice was like a breeze easing the tension between the two groups.

Saxton was quick to point out, "You can't bring science in the village."

The sun gleamed off Match's white head and the red

centers of his eyes pulsated bigger and smaller as he studied their village from this distance.

"Your entire village is surrounded by our science," Lins whispered in her skin-tight glimmering purple suit.

Owen ordered, "Remove what makes them nervous and pile them near those ruins. No one touches our things. After we find our people we'll collect them and leave. But I'm keeping this guy until I feel safe in your village."

Everyone stepped back, letting them enter the village and they walked in like they were about to take it over.

MATCH

A few breaths later
Above ground, Cuma Village

Match marched by Saxton to the village. They approached the men guarding their home. Yodan had a good way with them but Match had no idea how he did it, so he kept him close.

Match was sure to lock eyes with each of the leaders to check if they were grey and infiltrated by Nogard. But they were clear and so he nodded to them.

Saxton introduced each one. "The leaders are Berry, Mel, Kraigon, and Fulton." Fulton and Mel nodded. Kraigon crossed his arms. But they each met his eyes, as if they were used to confrontation, to defending their own, to living with this lie of strength. He was suddenly happy to have Owen with them. He was proving most useful. Seems even the brute had his place in this new world. Was it still Match's place to protect his people from Nogard? If she didn't surface and was dead, what would he do? Or were these villagers the new threat to his people?

"Where are the women?" Yodan blurted out. "Are you the only one?" he asked Avery, making her chuckle.

"Women have too much status to meet newcomers," Avery said. "We always send those who are expendable."

Made sense to Match, since the women were the ones who would carry life and ensure the future of this village.

Once Shandra felt better, they'd leave these worried leaders alone. *Show no fear. Establish yourself as elite.* He was anything but, yet Nogard's training was such a part of him that her programs endured. *You were chosen, Match, to defend your people from threats, even me.*

His senses were more alert than ever. Match was even picking up the shifting Hunter did to his right.

Saxton opened his hands, displaying the chaos like a proud father. "Our little haven is a bit of a mess."

The cat left to explore.

Avery gasped when she saw her village up close. Hands to her mouth, she surveyed the damage. Match was used to tunnels and doors. This open space was hard to take and the homes looked like scattered huts bombarded with rocks. What worried him was the damage to the service pipe along one side. Would they have the ability to repair that loss?

Match kept his shoulders even with Saxton's so they remained equal, then he glanced at Yodan. Avery was on the wrong side, but Yodan held her hand so she stayed with him, her bright colours distracting. Leave it to Yodan to boldly hold her hand in a village full of giants who wanted to kick his ass for even talking to her. Yodan never took it well when others told him no. Still, the tension she created between Saxton and the other leaders meant she was of no help to them so Match's hope of her easing this transition was lost.

Shandra was unconscious again and in serious need of a medic.

They paraded along the huge service pipe. A door was up ahead. Match headed straight to it.

The sign overhead read, *'Mainframe One'*.

Lins pounced on the door, yanking on it, but the entrance wouldn't open. "I need a code," Lins demanded as if Match had it. "We have to check if the equipment survived the blasts. Do you have the code?"

Did he? Match closed his eyes, processing numbers. Codes. Service pipes. Dragon. Nogard. Mainframe One. Nothing triggered a number. It would be simple. Easy to pass down from generation to generation.

"ReSurface," Lins said.

Well. That he did have. He handed Shandra to Yodan and removed the watch from her wrist. While putting the relic on his wrist, he glanced at the *breath of life* stamped on the back. Under the stamp was an inscription *'ReSurface 2112'*. He put the watch on. "Maybe it's the date Artificial-life took over, making us a home underground. What cycle was that?" he demanded in case someone else could produce the number they needed.

Yodan did. "2112 was the date A-life announced her self-awareness."

Lins punched that number in and the door clicked open, allowing her to vanish inside to prepare and evaluate the system, their first priority because they needed nutrients and D-light. And to find Nogard before she brought harm to these people above ground.

Match gathered Shandra in his arms again.

"You want me to follow her?" Yodan asked.

"Lock the door and let Lins study the system," Match said, "Working with mainframes are her specialty, stick to yours."

Saxton interrupted them to ask, "So Dragon exploded out the side of the cliff. Will he return?"

Match glanced up at where the explosions left a hole in the face of the rock. Unsure what their understanding of advanced technology was, he kept the answer simple. "That was the scheduled termination of our system." He explained how the backup worked and didn't allow them to suffer a slow death. "Trouble was, the backup forgot to take into account that above ground might once again be habitable."

"Always was," Saxton stated. "We just had to adapt."

Match explained, "Our A-life made a hard attempt to keep us from discovering that because then she would have been useless to us and possibly terminated."

"Yet here you are."

He was right, they were still survivors. Despite her not making the cameras above ground easy to access, Lins somehow did. Despite them being told to explore certain areas, Shandra and he had managed to venture off and find the cat that promised another system somewhere... Match stared at the door where Lins had vanished. Lins had given Shandra the easiest path to the surface. She had brought the life-drive to the surface. Her eyes were fine, but that meant nothing. Her eRobe was always connected to Nogard and might have been influencing her. And the bottom line was that Lins and Match had been left alive for a reason... *What? Dammit!*

What if Nogard had led them here on purpose? But why?

"I was coming with just my family, plans changed when I discovered the entire system was in danger." His grip tightened around Shandra, as every face he'd sent down that FIRE pit haunted him. "Our adults are dead. We're among the oldest. I couldn't leave those children behind to die."

Saxton let out a long breath in agreement.

Yodan said, "You did well, Match. Not once did we feel like you were unable to make these decisions or that you were putting your family's safety above anyone else's."

But he had and still was. If he was doing his job, he would

have followed Lins into that mainframe to see how bad this was. He might even have to terminate Lins. The idea sickened him, but he could not allow Nogard to play them like this. *Ugh*. Maybe he was just being paranoid.

"We need to find the youth." All Match answered, because with the youths were two medics he needed. Shandra grew heavy in his tired arms yet he held her firmly while marching by Saxton and studying the area. The mountain of rocks, the black pipes coming out of it; everything found a home in his detailed mind. "Are you sure you didn't see our prodigies?" Match asked Saxton again, almost annoying himself, but the order throbbed in his brain. "Most of them are younger than us. Our medic is pregnant."

"Pregnant women?" Berry asked, listening closely as he marched behind them.

Match was uneasy with Berry's interest.

"We won't be a burden on your village. We'll find our own system, I mean village." Match forced himself to look confident, despite the panic throbbing in his head. Shandra in his arms grounded him. He had one chance to make a first impression. He couldn't mess this up or he'd be at war with Avery's people in a system they didn't understand.

"The cave-in is thick," Saxton said. "Do you think they might have survived? Pax is in there, and one of our elders."

"They know how to survive. And if they didn't, we dig them out regardless. We'll need diggers. Then we can help you rebuild using the rocks to make homes that are sturdier and more durable. I'll show you how to do this. Owen's strength will be a great benefit."

"The caves are sacred ground. We can't dig there. The rocks are not for us to displace. They either survived and a path was left to rescue them or they're lost. I trust Dragon to provide."

He didn't plan to help? Match looked to Yodan for an explanation. Yodan explained, "They believe a superior lifeform exists that's hostile. They're careful about where they venture and stick to tried and true things. It's more like a belief in theories they can't prove right or wrong."

That made sense to Match, since they lived on edge with Nogard, but without exploration they wouldn't advance to find the answer to those theories. "We have no choice but to break the rules sometimes. Our prodigies have memories we need to produce better air and warmer temperatures. Everyone will have a place in this new system. They were chosen and spared for a reason."

"Need someone to examine the woman in your arms? We have healers."

"Yes," Match said, almost too eager. "Where do I bring her?"

"No," Owen snapped from behind the parade they were making. "We only trust our medics with our people." His order was firm and Match nodded, showing others that he respected the brute's rules. Besides, that was smart; he was clearly not thinking straight.

Saxton glanced at a couple of men. "By the caves is a place to rest her. Want me to carry her? You look injured."

"No one touches her without my permission."

"Fair enough. Goes the same for our women." He pointed to Yodan's hand holding Avery's. Saxton's voice was soft, but his words were a threat. As if Match had any control of whose hands Yodan held. Yodan's response was typical Yodan. He stepped closer to her, a hand going around her waist instead of holding her hand.

"There's a difference between a woman who can't make her own choices because she's fevered and unconscious and one willingly holding hands with a theologist like Yodan."

"I could knock her out, then I could decide for her."

"Yodan will see you coming before you even finish making your decision."

Yodan didn't respond, just held his head higher, holding her tighter. His actions speaking for him.

"He does move fast." Saxton glanced at him.

Yodan leaned over and whispered something to Avery. She giggled.

Saxton chuckled, bouncing the hair over his eyes around. "Look at that, my daughter smiled. Ah, maybe I'll let this one go. Don't think I've seen her smile in ages. She needs friends her age."

After Saxton said this, Yodan went back to holding her hand.

While Avery and Yodan went for water, Match rested Shandra in the soft dirt near the cave-in at Dragon's Caves. Saxton knelt by him and grabbed Match's hand. He studied it. "Can tell a lot by looking at someone's hands. You worked hard, young man."

Saxton was right. Nogard was hard on him. Incredibly hard. After taking away his mothers when he challenged her, she never once offered him comfort gases to deal with the loss. She cut off pieces of his skin, burned him, let him go without nutrients or D-light. Match never complained. As elite, everyone thought his life was one of blessings and that Nogard let him do as he pleased. No one knew that Nogard pushed him to the brink of death several times and forced him to connect with her emotionally. No one knew the draining games she played with him to better learn compassion and understanding. No one even knew that he changed his name because he was determined to match her in skill and endurance. Match knew how far Nogard would go to experience living like them. She didn't like her species and wanted to be more human. Things like breaths, kisses, even desire were important for her to learn. Nogard was no longer content watching them; she wanted to be them. And she'd pushed their studies until she found a way. And yet. Through all that, she'd let him live, knowing full well that he'd do anything to protect his family.

"Without Shandra to ground me, I wouldn't have survived my intense training. Or accepted how different I am. I wouldn't have even pushed to get us here."

"A good woman keeps me focused, too," Saxton agreed.

Match relaxed.

"These are the hands of a young man who knows work. A climber. A digger. A survivor. Like I said, a man's hands tell a lot about him, but more so how he uses them, how he grips his property."

"Me holding Shandra is not a question of property, but safety." Match ran a hand along her face, wishing Shandra would wake up. "She's carrying life and this has taken a toll on her. I was told to stay away from her and refused a direct order. I should have been stronger."

Saxton checked Shandra's temperature with the back of his hand. "Your first?"

"Illegal." Despite himself, Match smiled, full of unexplainable pride.

"You mean unplanned? I remember the first time Roselle carried life. I was a wreck the entire time."

Shandra's eyes opened and without moving she took in the area.

Match was quick to update her. "We're in Cuma Village. The prodigies were in a cave-in." He glanced around. The other leaders weren't far, ready to help Saxton, but they stayed back to let him do whatever his job was.

Match offered Shandra nutrients and she drank the entire cylinder.

Saxton glanced over his shoulder at the others. "He speaks like my brother," he lied, or perhaps joked.

"I don't talk that smart," Hunter snapped, making everyone chuckle at such a strange moment. Why did they laugh this way?

Still, his words reassured Match that they'd be welcome for now, but he watched every action these men made, paranoid.

Jacob was awake and standing in front of Owen, but Owen had that iron fist on his shoulder. Still, Jacob said to Berry, "I will not give up my claim on Avery Saxton."

Match processed this and filed his bizarre comment in his programs, searching for an explanation while he knelt by Shandra and Saxton. The answer was unnerving. *It's a game to these leaders of who owns the most people and things.* A woman like Avery would make this Jacob character a strong confidante in his family unit, but surely he didn't mean he meant to mate with her? He was past the end of his life cycle…

Match continued to listen, but said to Saxton, "Are we welcome or do I collect the children and leave?"

"We welcome new clans like yours but you have to respect the rules."

"And what are your rules for us?"

"Same for everyone. You offer something to the village, you make something for the village, and in return you are allowed to ask for something from the village. Make sense?"

"Yes," Shandra said since Match was too busy listening to the leaders behind Saxton talk and registering their conversations with his hyper-hearing. Match unclipped his D-light pen and shone the healing beam in her eyes to give

Shandra a direct dose while he listened. She instantly perked up. Maybe she was drained physically. She'd pushed herself too hard. He checked her leg, but the wound wasn't healing over. The wounds on her face were, though.

"Match? What are you thinking?" Saxton asked.

"There are no cats in our system and records say they died in the Big Freeze. Yet Shandra and I found Avery's cat. At first the hairy creature frightened us, but then we learned the feline was harmless and liked people. Even though I'd never seen one, I knew what a cat was. The knowledge was real but this knowing hadn't existed until I actually saw the cat and needed the information."

Saxton swallowed a hard lump. "How did you know a cat if you've never seen one?"

"I was born with memories that stay hidden until I need them. With them," he pointed to the leaders, "talking about me like I'm the enemy, my thoughts are darker than they should be, and I have countless memories surfacing explaining to me how to defend myself and my family."

"Tell me what you're thinking and I'll help you voice your concerns properly to these men." Saxton sounded fair and calm. "No need for violence."

"Is there a divide between men and women I should know? Is Jacob's claim on Avery one of a companion or a father? And why are they classing me as a leader they need to control and Shandra as someone I've claimed?"

"Aren't you the leader?"

"I'm elite. I make the rules that keep us safe. I speak for my people when they're being mistreated, endangered, or repressed. When I can't fix things, the protector eliminates anything that threatens the existence of my people."

"Oh. Well, for us, when it comes to the women, it's not a claim but more like an offer on the table. She can refuse to be his partner. I'm her father, well, her adopted one. As for them classing you, it's how we know where we stand. They have to protect their clans."

Match stared at Saxton to make his threat clear. "I tolerate a lot, but end the disrespect they're saying about Shandra or I will." He extended his hand and thought up a fire ball. It appeared, burning like a blazing ball in the palm of his hand.

"Holy hell." Saxton stumbled back and Match extinguished

the flames before others could see.

Despite how unnatural creating fire with his anger felt, the action always got the point across, even to Nogard.

Saxton jumped to his feet. "Hey. Listen, guys. Do you remember being a young leader and having a woman you cared about pregnant? Do you remember standing among us as an equal leader for the first time? Or how afraid you were to fail, to mess up and change the fate of your entire clan? Whatever you're mumbling about, he hears you, and he'll defend his people and the mother of his child. It's his job and this young man will not fail at it. His hands promise that he clawed himself a path through hell to get them here." He glanced at Match. "And that he's capable of things we are not. We have legends about Dragon breathing flames on us to protect us and warm the area. Here sits a man he made, capable of mastering those flames. A child of Dragon. Let us show respect."

They remained silent after that and Match was able to focus on Shandra. "How did you do that with your hands?" she whispered.

"You clearly hit your head and damaged your memory. I could always do that. Usually you yell at me and remind me to use words not flames," he teased.

"So I should know you?"

Ah great.

"Yeah. I'm Match. You're carrying my child."

She rubbed her head as if that information should be there, and the gold band she wore caught her attention as she pulled away. She stared at it, clearly confused. "Rawlings? Do you know the name?"

"That's me. You said you prefer my birth name over Match." He smirked to show he wasn't worried about her memory loss. "It's fine. Forget about it for now. It'll be fun for me to win you over again. How about we work? There are almost a hundred children who were in a cave-in. I need your brilliant insight." They were about two metres deep inside and the rubble increased so much that they couldn't walk farther. "Where do we start?" he asked her, pretending she was fine. Pretending this was nothing big.

"Do you hear anything?"

He touched the rock to feel for vibrations. A fine energy

whispered to him, or maybe it was hope. "There's life behind this wall." His voice quaked because he couldn't hear words or even sobs. "A scratching or digging is all I hear. Centered, at the top."

Shandra tilted her head, evaluating things. "Then we go in as if they're alive. Clear the rock along the right side. We pile the boulders to extend the entrance out which will add shelter. I need two cutters. Any tools you guys have I want to know about. Supports as we dig will help." Hearing her give orders so naturally was a good sign. Maybe she'd be fine. Her memories were messed with a lot over the last few cycles so she might need a moment to replace them, he promised himself.

Shandra glanced at Avery's people; these strong men stayed back which was weird; most jumped to action when Shandra glared at them that way. She was a digger and had led many expeditions, cleared many cave-ins. "All can help. We form a line and pass rocks from hands to hands to speed things up and use less energy. And Owen! Let that man go and get crushing rocks. What good are you standing there?"

"Yes, Shandra." He dropped the older man and set right to work where she'd pointed.

"Him you remember?" Match mumbled, but tried to act like it was fine. A powerful medic like Jon might be able to bring her memories to order again. Clearly things got knocked around in there.

Shandra checked the lifelines on her suit then remembered they were useless. "We don't have time to waste, we dig until I decide it's over. They have a chance because over this is the blue pipes for the venting system."

None of the villagers helped, but Yodan and Avery came in, handed them water and set to work where Shandra pointed.

Wanting to help, Shandra stepped closer to the debris but her leg crumpled under her and Match caught her.

Yodan was already at the top, freeing debris with Owen. Avery helped. They worked well together.

"We need your best trained to follow Shandra's orders carefully," Match said to Saxton but Saxton stared at Yodan and Avery clearing rubble as if them working was horrifying.

"I told you, we can't dig on sacred ground. Avery get out of there."

Match thought about what sacred ground would mean, but he couldn't even pretend to know. The area was stable enough to dig. The children were on the other side. He saw no reason to not find them. "Explain."

"There are rules to follow. Dragon doesn't like us touching his pipes, his caves. They aren't ours. When we break the rules, we suffer earthquakes," Saxton whispered. "It's a sacred place. The reason this happened is because Dragon was angry with us for allowing Pax in the village. Now, he's buried. It saddens me, but digging will just make it worse. The best we can do is leave it alone." Saxton glanced at Shandra. "Plus, these men are currently equal in status, but if one digs on sacred land at the request of a guest…"

Match was used to people putting rules first. Probably why he liked hanging out with Yodan, he would never do that. People came first. He dismissed Saxton and set to work.

Sitting against the side of the cave-in, Shandra gave more orders. "Keep the lasers to a minimum. Make an even tunnel straight in that middle part. Bring in supports if anything shifts." Even hurt, she lifted rocks. Match worked by her, picking the bigger ones so she wouldn't have to.

"I'll help her," Saxton offered, which was a sudden change of heart Match didn't comment on. "You go up and keep my daughter safe." Owen was already doing that, but Match squeezed Saxton's shoulder as he climbed the debris toward Yodan and Avery. Owen was studying the area so they didn't make things worse.

Match caught Yodan and Avery lying with their heads in the opening they were clearing, staring at each other. "Get to work," he ordered and they jumped as if caught making-out.

"I'll get those minerals you like," Avery whispered and left him alone with Yodan.

"Just kiss her already, this tension between you two is annoying. Put this energy to work and dig."

Yodan dug without a comment, but his face burned red.

"Hey, I was just joking around. It's fine." Perhaps he should have been more considerate of Yodan's feelings, since he was never allowed to express them. "You can kiss whoever you want, no demerits, promise."

"A demerit would be welcome right about now. This ache I feel when I think that she might be moving into that Jacob guy's family chamber is hard to breathe through, which is stupid. I hardly know her." He worked, passing Match a rock. "But I want to know everything about her. Everything."

"I need to toss things around, move over."

"Why you so frustrated?"

"Your sister's memories were tampered with again. She doesn't remember me, yet she remembers Owen."

"Not the first time she forgot about you. You used to find winning her over a challenge."

"I'm tired of these games. Feels like Nogard is trying to break me." Match was sick of challenges and had to work out his anger.

"Nogard is dead," Yodan reminded him.

"Maybe. But I feel like she led us here for some reason, I just can't put my finger on what."

"Probably to meet Dragon in case he could make more Artificial-life. It has to bother her a bit that he's a ghost program to her. Would annoy me to find out I was secretly being manipulated for someone else's good."

Match glanced out of the hole they worked in, worried now what Lins might be doing in Mainframe One. The bright sun had poured into the cave when they'd started but the skies grew dusky. No one panicked about the change in lighting, but they brought fire on branches to light the entrance to the cave.

It didn't take many breaths before Match and Yodan had a path cleared that Yodan worked in, passing rocks to Match which he then handed to Saxton who passed them to Hunter, since Shandra was passed out and Hunter had made her a make-shift bed of one of his garments. She looked safe enough, so Match kept working.

How far should they dig before calling a break?

They worked in silence with the leaders lined up watching. Some called insults at Saxton and Hunter. Match suspected they'd be paying for their betrayal later. Still, he was glad they were helping; more people saved time.

"You need a break," Owen told Yodan. His own body ached but Match let Yodan out. He stumbled toward Avery and drank from the cup she held for him.

Match slipped deeper in the hole to take his place, determined to do what he could. The rock in front of him was unstable and he didn't even know which one to pull so the entire thing didn't crash on him, but two voices from the other side fired him up. He grabbed the top left rock but before he could pull the stone, it slipped back. "Hello!"

"Sir Rawlings?" Andret answered filling Match with relief.

"Good to hear you, Andret. Hilt all right?"

"Yes, sir, we're eager to get these children to better air. Azala, crawl back, give me room."

Match pulled out a few rocks and stared at Andret. He was covered in black dust. "Count?" Match demanded. "How many survived?"

"We're all here, sir. No worries. It was shaky and all, but we built supports out of the elevator shaft." Of course they had. Andret and Hilt were the most brilliant engineers of their time. "We found two injured from another system. One is the oldest man I've ever seen. Both are healing nicely thanks to Medic Jon. We didn't have a protocol in place on what to do, so Medic Jon helped them because he wanted to."

"That's fine. Let's get our people out. There's an entire system here."

"With air?"

"Yeah. Moving air but it's breathable."

While Andret backed up, Match heard a deep voice with a rolling accent. "I like your magic wand, Jon. Can I try that?" Many spoke and each conversation sorted itself in his mind as Match listened, relieved.

MATCH

A breath later
Above ground, Dragon's Caves

Crawling out backwards from the cave-in, Match then waited to help the younger children, nervous how they'd be greeted.

He glanced at the leaders, surprised to see them pushed aside by dozens of women led by Avery, but much to his fear, Owen and Shandra were missing.

Avery was talking to Match and he had to focus on her in the rumbling chaos. "When they heard you were digging out children, the women came to see if they could help." These women didn't seem worried about status or the sacred ground rule.

"They're alive and coming through," Match told them. "We'll need them cleaned up." Match glanced at his dirty hands and the mess he'd made of his lifesuit. He hated being dirty. "Did you see Shandra?"

"Owen brought her to Hunter's. She'll be safe there."

Still, Match didn't like her leaving without telling him why. He was ready to go after her when the first youth came through, guiding a crying and exhausted toddler.

Hunter stepped from the pack. "They're babies!" He rushed to help Match and so did several others.

The stream of youths coming out was long and Match greeted each one, answering their questions. He was nervous about leaving his people with these power hungry men, but they had a soft spot for children that was almost amusing, and now that the women were here, they did as the women ordered as if status with their companion was more important than between them.

The man from the image taken on the surface camera came through before Hilt, helping a very old and frail man. Match had to agree with Andret. This was for sure the oldest man Match had ever seen and Match helped him, wanting to put his hands on the ancient body. He was cold and wrinkled. Hunter helped bring him to safety.

Hilt came out last. "Area is clean." Code for a safe evacuation. Meant the protector had to go in and shut it down. But of course, Owen was missing. Which meant an elite would have to. Match waited for them to leave.

Hunter remained in the entrance. "You can leave," Match told him.

"If Dragon comes back to bury you, I want to see how you kill him." He grinned. "You're a bit of a crazy one, aren't ya? You like hunting?"

Match slipped against the rocks, exhausted. He took off the watch and looked at it. This was nothing compared to the decision he'd have to make soon if Nogard survived, or even compared to the thought of losing Shandra because of a memory shuffle.

"I don't know what I like. I was told what to like for so long, I'm fearful," Match admitted, giving up the lies to say what was on his mind. "I wanted to break from my system so I could be with Shandra, and here we are, and she doesn't even remember who I am. On top of all that, I let you crazies walk off with our prodigies."

"Relax. If there's one thing we're good at, it's protecting children. They're our future. Gosh, when I saw that stream of little ones pouring out, I understood why you were so worried. Come, Shandra is at my place. My partner will be watching her closely. You did good, young leader."

Match stood. "Actually, I have to go in this hole and make sure we have everything and everyone. One missing Exchanger or filament could be the death of us."

"I'll wait," Hunter promised. "Holes make me kinda itchy, but if you're in trouble, holler. I won't hesitate to get my brother." He chuckled as if that were a joke.

Match slipped the watch back on and did his final sweep. While in the dark on the other side, he breathed by himself. In the silence, little details came together. Hunter might know this Pax of the South! He was the last one Match had to check in case Nogard had infiltrated him. Determined, he climbed out.

When he arrived on the other side, Owen was there. Hunter was trying to talk to him, but Owen stood, arms crossed, waiting.

"Where's Shandra?" Match demanded.

Owen just stared ahead.

"You don't touch her."

"I keep my people safe. Only order I have, Elite."

Match had flames in his palms, ready to incinerate the brute, but Hunter came between them. "A lot of tension between us leaders sometimes, too. We settle the strain by knowing our place. Why we assign status ratings and jobs. Everyone feels important and can work for the good of our village. At your core, you both have the same goal, focus on that."

"You still think Shandra belongs with you?"

Owen chuckled, which was an odd sound. Like static crackling. "I never once thought that. I have my eye on Azala."

"Then why you always cornering Shandra?"

"Protecting her. Since you are an idiot, you put her life on the line. Earthquakes, cave-ins, pipe collapses. Nogard had her on the termination list but she survived because I shadowed her and agreed to be her companion." He crossed his arms. "I don't need a reward, I need you to lay off and let me do my job."

"Oh. Thanks." And just like that, the tension between them was over.

"Hunter, do you know a Pax of the South?" Match asked, turning his focus to the next danger awaiting them.

"Yeah. He came out with the elder."

Shoot. Match had been so amazed by the aged man, he hadn't checked the redhead's eyes. "I need to see him immediately."

"We can hunt him down, I'm sure he's not far."

LINS

During the same breaths
Above ground, Mainframe One

Lins was under the panel studying the wires and the veins of life that kept Mainframe One active, when the door slid open. She glanced up and was to her feet in an instant when she saw Pax. He was covered in dust, had the backpack with the eRobe over his shoulder and it was all Lins could do *not* to rush to him and throw herself in his arms.

Pax didn't move. Just stared. He was at the other end of the room. Without thinking, she bumbled, "I studied Dragon's basic system. Everything's working great. This system runs on the powerful D-light outside, sucking it up with panels and storing the energy. It's primitive but the program has a structure that allows Dragon to respond to certain things based on evaluations. This is essentially the before-Nogard. Probably one of the first artificial-intelligences. Nogard basically upgraded this system to create our drones."

Pax took a deep breath.

"You all right?" Lins asked, approaching to kiss his cheek but their eyes met and she froze. His eyes were grey.

"Desire," he whispered. "Unlike you, I feel one emotion at a time and experience them with my entire body. I know so much about you, it's impossible that someone so perfect for me exists. I *desire* to create life with you."

Nogard was merged with Pax. He looked healthy, just dirty. He clearly wasn't in any distress so she pushed the knot of fear in her stomach down and focused on what was important. Nogard wanted to reproduce, to find a way to make more artificial lives. There was no rule against that, however, she was not allowed to use people for this purpose.

Of course, Lins' first priority was Pax. Lins herself had hardly felt Nogard infiltrate her. The connection had played with her emotions but left her with knowledge and confidence. But how would Pax handle it? Lins brushed Pax's cheek. "Pax, tell me how you feel?"

"I feel great," Pax assured her. "I can read." He smirked. "I understand what you're saying when you talk science stuff.

It's like I'm smarter. Why do I feel so brilliant?"

"Our Artificial-life has evolved and developed the ability to move her self-awareness from devices. Apparently, the human body is such a device. She is currently in you, feeding you memories and toying with your emotions."

"So this awesome life is making me smarter and more in control of my feelings?" Pax asked.

"We studied this possibility for generations. Trying to find the proper way to blend A-life with the human species to create a new species we call cyborg. People like me see many advantages of such a union. Like you said, we could be smarter, faster, more balanced. We could even tap into parts of our intellect we leave untouched. Others don't like the idea."

"Why not?" Pax grazed her face. Lins enjoyed the fondling, but she wouldn't kiss him until Nogard was out of his body.

"Elite Match, for example lives with these adaptations and has trouble controlling them. He worries that Artificial-life will take over our free will and make us do things we wouldn't normally do."

"Feels more like enhances things and gives me detailed data when I need it, and wow, I feel your heart pulsating." He held her shoulders. "Gosh, Elite Lins, make life with me."

"You see, you called me Elite Lins, that's not how you should be talking, Pax. Besides, I can't create life. I'm elite and had to undergo sterilization that Nogard requested so she's not even sharing the facts with you. What I propose is that we get this system running, then we find Nogard a proper device where she can live as she chooses. I don't like you acting differently, Pax. This isn't you. I won't kiss you again until you get Nogard out of you." She was firm with her statement.

"So you believe this Artificial-life could reproduce? You believe she could live as one of you and feel kisses and desires?"

"Why shouldn't she reproduce? Artificial-life can do anything she wants." The scientist in Lins snapped to work and she took out the eRobe from his pack and hung the device by the door. Then she studied the monitor. Flashing on the screen was, *'ENTER RESURFACE CODE**'*

She didn't have the stupid code. Frustrated, she punched in *2112* in case it was that simple.

Pax stood beside her, the eRobe in his hands as they waited for some type of reaction from the system. When nothing happened, she glanced at him. "Why did you take the robe off the hook?" His eyes were no longer grey. The patterns on the eRobe sparkled as Nogard travelled it.

"It needs to go here." He dropped the robe on the panel and the fabric spread out on its own.

"Why does she do that?" Lins wondered aloud.

"Dragon is her father and she's hugging him, searching for codes to reproduce. It's lonely being the only one in her species. I know how she feels. I was alone for so long, it sometimes feels nice to be around others, even if I have nothing in common with them. And you can reproduce, she didn't sterilize elites in your generation."

"It was standard procedure. When did this change? Why?"

He shrugged. "Because if she chose an elite, who was chosen by the people, they would think it an honour."

"Chose an elite for what?" Only one reason to change protocol; Nogard wanted them to reproduce for a reason. What?

"I don't know. All the sharp things I knew, they're all cloudy now." Pax looked so ridiculously crushed that she dusted his skin and met his lips with a soft kiss. His large hands gripped around her waist, digging deeper into the kiss as he backed her against the panel, shooting thrilling desires through her. How did this guy do this to her?

"It's a relief to see you safe. Is the life-drive in your bag?" she asked, distracting herself from his sexy muscles tensing under her fingers. "I'll need it."

"Work, eh?" He pulled away, slowly. "Thing is, I know that you distract yourself with work when you're afraid. Don't be afraid of me." Pax rested against her cheek.

Maybe she didn't like that Nogard had shared so much with him. She felt vulnerable.

"Let me show you what you desire." His whisper jolted her as his lips slowly tasted her neck. What was he doing?

Oh my.

YODAN

A breath later
Above ground, Cuma Village

As Avery strolled with Yodan to her family chamber, or hut as she called it, gloomy overhead sheltered them and was much easier on Yodan's senses than the bright light from earlier. He was able to glance up and study the overhead. Smaller lights sparkled in the darkness. He could also see Sir Owen crouched on a ledge on the cliff, watching them.

Avery glanced up. "What is he doing up there?"

"Protecting."

"He gonna sleep up there?"

"He doesn't sleep. His black eyes mean his body heals while awake. Sometimes he gets into these semi-alert states that mean he's walk-healing. He's still taking in details to process later. I studied the traits and didn't recommend Nogard use the no-sleep healing gene in future lives."

"So he'll sit up there all night and protect your people?"

"Yeah. He told me he senses those he protects, not sure how and he's frankly too stupid to explain it to me, but I trust he'll always be there when I need protecting. Like an extra sense, he knows when he's needed."

"I must be exhausted, because your weird world is making sense to me. You coming to my place to sleep?"

Yodan wasn't sure if she was inviting him to her sleeping pod or just to her place as a friend and he wasn't ready to be turned down by her. "I'd like to see how Lins is doing." Yodan's vision was blurry.

Avery helped him steady himself. "Yodan, what's wrong?"

"I need to rest." He collapsed in the soft grass. A bug landed on his arm, emitting a strange hum. He blew on the insect and the bug flew off and hummed closer to his ear. Annoyed, Yodan swatted at it.

Avery chuckled, sitting beside him. "Bugs are abundant in this area. Pax says that's a good thing but it's why we sleep in the huts. Here, I have the water you like. The nutrients might help. You were working hard for a long time."

He took the minerals from her.

The darkness from earlier became a slow dance of pinks, oranges, and yellows.

"What's happening to the overhead?" Yodan wondered.

"Sunrise. The sun will light the skies until after supper, then the sky will be dark again. This cycle happens over and over," Avery explained.

"That's predictable. I see why Match thinks you have an A-life controlling things." Yodan's energy was already returning. He had to remember to hydrate often, since there were no reminders here. With light at certain times, he'd feel the strain on his body. Hopefully, Lins found a way to get Mainframe One working and they'd have a D-light station there.

"I should help Lins. Or Match." He glanced at the huts and the mainframe where Lins had vanished earlier. "Not sure who needs help or even what I should do. Feels weird not having a place or a role. Maybe you could show me where you keep your minerals?" He swallowed the last drops from the cup. "I can see what the supply looks like. Might make everyone feel better if I had minerals waiting for them when they wake up."

"Sure. Rest and I'll grab a few bottles to fill."

He slept in the grass while she was gone, dreaming of cats.

When she woke him, Friskie was rumbling against his face. Avery waited for him to follow her. Yodan was stiff, feeling muscle pain he'd never experienced before as he tried to stand. "I feel creaky. Not used to aches. Nogard usually heals me while I sleep."

"You get used to it. I can give you a massage."

"You flirting with me?" He smirked but that faded. "Or are you considering the offer from that guy with the land?"

"We need land and the food he'll provide but..." She sighed. "But he's not you."

"So if everyone owns land, who owns the land on the other side of the pipe where we left our things?"

"No one. That land has no value. We need land that'll produce crops. Land we can live on."

"Or, maybe your brothers could build there. Not huts like this, but homes made of rock. I can show you how, and we can even heat them. Then we can use where you live to grow your crops."

"Really?"

"Of course."

"We could talk to Saxton, see what he thinks."

"Good. Then maybe you can flirt with me a little more and forget that aged man."

She chuckled. "You didn't have older men in your cities?"

"Not anymore. At about Saxton's age everyone merges with the Collective, giving their lives to advance the system. So, what do you do to contribute to the survival of your system?" he asked as they walked up the hill with several bottles. Light filled the overhead much quicker than he thought it would, yet the new light was ridiculously slow compared to flicking a switch.

Sir Owen was still on his perch, watching the entire village.

"I tend the sheep for now. Play my flute. Teach my brothers things. Help Mother Roselle plan meals and make us clothing. My brothers grow at ridiculous rates."

"I play the flute, too. Maybe we can play together?"

Her smile faded. "Soon I'll have my own hut with children. I won't have time for playing."

She clearly didn't feel ready for this type of commitment so he kept the moment light. "There's always time for fun. Besides aren't you young to start a family? We normally wait until after our Twenty-first FIRE Ceremony. There are exceptions, sure, but how many life-cycles are you?"

"Father Saxton says everyone grows differently and I can take the time I need, but lately, I feel like maybe he was saving me for a trade for land. Then when Pax showed, I realized that no one wants me, just the fact that I'm different."

After they passed Dragon's Caves, they walked along a hill by blue waters with pipes around them that reminded Yodan of Glisten Point. The paintings and the colours were an assault to his senses, and dizziness crashed into Yodan. His energy was so low he wasn't sure if he'd make this hike she had planned so he slowed his steps. "Avery." The pressure in his head increased. The system seeped in with new light and too many colours.

Yodan collapsed.

When Yodan woke, Avery had a cup of water against his lips. Dehydrated, he downed the bland water. "Yodan, you petrified me. I thought you'd died." She helped him sit, in view of the gentle waterfalls. "I forgot you need to rest and drink often."

"The pressure makes me dizzy." He rubbed his head, amazed to see the skies so bright. "This strange light is exhausting. I want to turn your sun off and curl up in my sleeping pod. I prefer the darker overhead, yet no light exhausts me, too. I need light but not this light. This is confusing for my body."

"The healing waters are ahead if you can get to your feet. They always help me."

He forced himself up.

She led him to a pond with minerals and dropped the bottles beside it. A gold pipe came out the middle identifying it as a food source.

"Water usually boils over from that pipe."

Seeing the water triggered Yodan's appetite. He scooped up a handful of liquid and drank the mineral waters. Then he rested on the grass and let the nutrients return his energy.

As he stared at the waving trees overhead, he wondered why their nutrients were in a swimming hole. The pool itself was large and would do, but they'd need a tap and pipes to bring the nutrients closer to their quadrants…

Avery rested beside him, on her tummy, watching him. "We usually bathe in it, not drink it."

"This is our nutrients, Avery. Don't bathe in it. Without Nogard to make more, we'll see how this could connect to Mainframe One so Dragon can maintain it." He checked along the sides for exit valves and found two facing the cliffs.

"Will you be able to make more healing water with your science stuff?"

"Not me, but someone will have this knowledge. Help me gather some to take back to the others." He unclasped his bottles and filled them, sitting by the pond.

"Yodan…"

He stopped working to study her, at ease and comfortable in this strange system because of her. "Come here." He invited her to sit with him and pulled her closer. "Funny how happy you make this place for me."

"I was thinking the same thing." She leaned against him.

Her hair was neatly pulled back, but her clothes were dirty and dust covered her face. Mud streaked her cheek. Gosh, this feeling of safeness had him hooked. He rested his face against hers.

She held his hand, relaxed against him. "Everyone will make Match offers to help with the children. They'll trade him people for goods. I overheard Mother Roselle ask if Father Saxton would consider putting me in that trade for a few young women closer in age to my older brothers, since Mother Roselle will need help once I leave and she thinks I'll agree to living in Match Clan over Berry Clan. Will Match make the deal?"

He tried to hide a smirk; Match Clan? Match would hate that. Owen might even flip out. "Um… I can't speak for him. Feels like we were torn from everything we know. The comfort I feel is knowing that I'm safe with you."

"Planning our next breath is all we do."

Made sense since they didn't have an A-life to consult and give them the best options. But he had no idea what the next breath would be like and trusting himself to make the right choices was weird yet freeing.

"I'm enjoying not knowing what the future holds. Kind of liberating."

She nodded but didn't look any happier about things. "I guess, maybe Father Saxton should have a chat with Match so he understands before we insult him with trades."

Her depressed demeanour shook him and Yodan leaned in to kiss her cheek, his own programming willed the moment forward, but when she met his lips, he deepened the connection, his hand around her waist, pulling her hips against his. Slowly, he guided them to the long grass, their lips dancing. When he tore himself away from her lips, he stared in her eyes.

"Gosh. I like kissing you." He felt so dreamy.

The hair over her eyes danced with her smile. "Feeling better?" she asked, as if her kiss was a nutrient he needed.

"Gross! You're kissing them?" Someone snickered from the bushes.

Yodan sat when Avery pushed him away to see who was there.

A tall woman stepped from the trees. She carried life, her belly round. Her skin was dark like Saxton's and her eyes shiny brown. Her wild hair-garment was knotted on her head. She glanced him over and made a bitter face.

Avery was quick to her feet, a rose blush washing out her freckles. She rushed to the woman without glancing at Yodan. "Don't be silly, we were just talking."

What? He jumped to his feet, distressed. Why was she lying?

"I'm telling Saxton." The woman stormed off.

"Kanya, no." Avery chased after her, leaving Yodan alone.

Was she embarrassed to be with him? Would she get in trouble for kissing him? Yodan was confused as Avery ran off, leaving him by the mineral pond to fill the bottles alone and rejected. He'd left the strict rules of Nogard to find himself in a system with the same rules, only these ones sucked, because he liked kissing her.

He was working to fill the bottles, feeling rather achy and lonely, when the bushes moved again. Thinking Avery came back, he glanced toward her, unsure what to say. But Jacob stumbled into the clearing with his fists clenched. "Let's settle this," his speech was slurred.

Yodan got up to help. Was he sick? Jacob's eyes were bloodshot. He breathed too fast. Had he taken an illegal?

Jacob swung without a word and Yodan saw his fist coming and pulled back, stepping closer to the water. Then he stepped to avoid the second punch coming at his gut and his foot slipped on a bottle. The bottles flew as Yodan fell to the grass, knocking the wind out of him. His head dipped in the frigid healing waters. Jacob dived for him, pinning him.

Yodan had never trained to fight and didn't know what to do, but Jacob had many wounds and so Yodan squeezed his arm where one festered, causing him enough pain he hoped he'd let him go, but Jacob dunked him in the water.

Drawing in air before he went under, Yodan had breathed the same air as Jacob, tasting his sweet pungent breath.

Not struggling, Yodan remained relaxed in the tight grip, letting out air slowly.

Jacob yanked him up and shoved him under the water again. A wild fury heightened his actions, making them the actions of a program fail. What had happened to Jacob's wiring? With no A-life to reprogram Jacob, Yodan had no idea what to do.

Yodan fell limp. Waiting. He held his breath. Jacob pulled him up again. "Had enough, snow boy?" he demanded, in Yodan's face.

"I didn't need any to start with," Yodan reminded him, hoping to help.

He dunked Yodan again.

Jacob pulled him out of the water and shook him. "Leave her alone."

This was about Avery? How forbidden was she? Was this why she'd taken off?

Yodan wiped the minerals from his face and opened his eyes. The powerful D-light Avery called sun filtered through the trees finding them along the edge of the mineral water and Yodan was temporarily blind.

"Freak!" Jacob dunked him again. This time Yodan wasn't ready and water entered his lungs. He struggled, coughing under the mineral nutrients. Jacob held him firmly as he thrashed out.

He pushed against Jacob needing another breath. *Just one more...*

But there were no more to have.

A calm settled on Yodan. A warmth he hadn't felt since his youth when his mother wrapped him in an energy blanket and sang to him.

Yodan pulled away from himself, disconnecting from his heavy body until he was no longer struggling but lightly floating like a hologram, watching the scene unfold as if an on-screen memory. He was himself, yet he was watching his lifeless body without panic or fear.

The cat strolled into the area and looked up at Yodan's energy. They made eye contact and the feline stared, seemingly amazed, but not afraid, as if seeing Yodan out of his body was normal. Yodan felt peaceful, no longer part of the scene but at one with the energy surrounding it, connecting to everything, not just his body. He tickled the cat's life-essence. Friskie was calm. Content.

Avery rushed through the bushes, running like a madwoman, but her actions were a part of him and he watched her rush, much like adjusting the speed on his reading screen. With his new eyes, he saw things about her that he hadn't before. Sure, she was lovely in her wild way, but he saw a light around her that reached out to him and connected to him. Which made sense, really. Explained why he was so comfortable with her.

The light slowly turned a sizzling green, to match her eyes. Vibrant. Alive. Why couldn't he see this dynamism to her before? Her hair slipped from the tie and flew around her, like flames exploding energy into the world. His entire being beamed at her liveliness, eager to connect.

Was it possible that even without the Collective, this continuous movement of energy that he was would find a new way to survive? Meant they were more than memories trapped in a body. They were a spiritual being using a body as a host, much like Nogard used the mainframes. If he could do this, then all life could. So… Where was Nogard?

Disrupting the peace, Avery kicked Jacob, making him fly off Yodan and creating a wild fire that erupted in her life-essence.

Yodan watched her pull his own body out of the water. Felt her graze his cold skin, and the touch jolted through him as he watched the scene unfold from outside of that body. He tasted her salty tears as she blew life into him with her own breath. And another.

As he hovered over the scene, the warmth coming off Avery was luring. *Tempting.*

Avery had an amazing glow to her, but why was she so sad? How could he show her this freedom?

AVERY

Not even a breath later
Above ground, by the healing pond

Avery pumped the water out of Yodan's lungs and breathed into them. She'd seen Saxton save Jojo this way when he fell in the water, knocked his head, and just about drowned. "Breathe, Yodan!" she screamed, terrified.

Why had she left? Why would she even care what the others thought of her? Tears flowed. Yodan was more different than anyone she'd ever met. Different was good. Different would save them.

"Yodan. Stay with me. Yodan!"

Owen was suddenly at her side. He placed a hand on Yodan's chest and pushed gently. Yodan coughed and rolled over, shooting water out.

Relief overwhelmed Avery and she collapsed on him in a heap of tears.

Yodan pulled her against his chest and held her. "I saw you," he whispered. Eyes closed, he rested. "Life after death is more alive."

Avery had no idea what he rambled about. She never wanted to let him go, but Jacob sat in the grass and she planned to punch the drunk idiot again.

Owen shot to his feet before she could and pulled Jacob up, ready to tear the old fool to pieces.

"I just meant to scare him." Jacob looked terrified.

"Wait," Yodan ordered his protector. "We must first evaluate."

"He hurts you, I hurt him. Evaluation complete."

"Life is precious," Yodan reminded him. "This is my rule. Respect it."

Avery agreed. "No one has ever taken a life in Cuma Village, just the idea that he might have killed Yodan is enough for the elders to banish him. He's drunk."

Saxton walked onto the scene. He had bottles to gather the healing waters Yodan called minerals. Yodan was still in Avery's arms. Owen had Jacob's neck under his arm, ready to break it.

Saxton dropped the bottles and rushed to Jacob's aid. "Stupid fool, what did you do? If these people don't want to help with their science, how will we survive?"

Avery was shocked by his words. Did Father Saxton believe that the village needed science to survive?

She was quick to explain what had happened, but Owen refused to let Jacob go.

Saxton faced him. "How do I fix this, Sir Owen?"

"Yodan is who he harmed. Yodan must determine his fate. There's no other way. I'm waiting for his evaluation."

"Me?" Yodan stood, somewhat wobbly but he planted himself. "I slipped and he took advantage of my weakened state. This decision needs proper evaluation. Nogard will—" He glanced down. "I need more nutrients and rest. This environment is taking a toll on me." Then with a sigh, he said, "I want to hear his side. Why attack me? Why is Avery forbidden to me? I need facts."

Jacob mumbled from under Owen's arm. "I need a woman to help me care for my mother, all I was thinking about."

"I can understand your compassion for your mother. Mine died in a cave-in," Yodan told him.

"Well, mine is a burden to Berry Clan and I was asked to take care of her and leave the clan because I bring them bad luck."

Yodan sipped his nutrient water and rubbed his neck. "What are your studies?"

"I..." Jacob struggled, but Owen held firm. "I work the vegetable fields."

"He's drunk," Avery snapped.

Yodan relaxed against her. "Owen, give Jacob to Saxton to bring to his sleeping hut-thing. I need to evaluate this further. I'll give my judgement later."

Owen dropped him and Jacob scurried to Saxton who hauled Jacob off with Owen in tow.

"I was terrified you were dead," Avery mumbled to Yodan when they were alone.

"I was." He sighed dreamily. "I was a part of everything. An energy that felt incredible. Dying is living more. If Nogard was alive, then she found this state in her death and will be back."

"I'm sorry I ran off." She kissed him.

"Why did you?"

"I wanted to avoid that scene." She bowed her head, and when he raised it with a gentle finger under her chin, she admitted, "I wanted to fit in."

"Why when you're so perfect as you are? But I'm out of element here. Was kissing you wrong?" His frown was so painful she ached to see him smile again.

She leaned in to kiss him again. "I choose you, Yodan."

MATCH

Many breaths later
Above ground, Mainframe One

On his back, Match stared at the panel from a new angle as if seeing Dragon's hardware from a different view might make his decision easier. Should he enter ReSurface code or not? What would happen?

A recording played of his brother's last thoughts, making Match feel closer to him and braver about the decision he had to make. "*Not once, not ever did I doubt you. Always trust your gut, it's better than facts.*"

Match removed the cover and stared at the wires. These were new, updated with their best quality. Meant Nogard was keeping this mainframe maintained and in top condition.

Match shut the recording off.

His gut was telling him not to do it. Nogard had set him up to come here and do exactly this and until he knew why, he couldn't give Dragon the code to create new life.

"Nogard knew she was dying," he told Shandra while she worked on a code one of the prodigies had produced to bring the nutrient pond to working order. "I mean, something happened that changed her plans a bit, but Nogard set this up so we'd bring her here. Why? Why us? I feel like we were all chosen and spared. Nogard could have terminated any of us at any moment. I watched her do it to Madeline."

Match replaced the cover and slid over to Nogard's old life-drive. Such a small box with so much promise. It was connected to the computer system and Dragon had access to the codes so the system could continue. Nogard was no longer in the life-drive to make these decisions for them, she was in the eRobe charging on the panel.

"These people survived without A-life," Match continued the debate with himself. "So we can, too. It'll take some adjusting but it should be possible."

"They survived thanks to Nogard's wastes." Shandra shoved the eRobe aside.

"Actually," he told Shandra, "a lot of what happened above ground was thanks to Dragon. With minor tweaks we'll keep things going, maybe even better because we'll be in control. This feels better. I didn't like the idea of being at the mercy of A-life." He was pleased with the way their people were integrating with the villagers who proved to want to learn, they were just afraid, but learning from children wasn't hard.

Slowly, he ran his fingers in the indentation on the hard-drive box that awaited his watch. Tiny sensors reached out to him like veins of life. In the center of the depression was a stamp of flames that symbolized the *breath of life*.

"Dragon," he said, "do you want to be alive?"

"*I wait for activation code ReSurface.*" Of course, a machine didn't want. It waited. Match flipped the watch over. He stared at the inscription wondering if the relic was as old as this system. *ReSurface 2112.*

"We need this area warmer," Shandra said, her back to him. "We need a better governing system than the clans. Their religious beliefs are primitive."

"What?" He slid out from under the panel. Just how hard had she hit her head? "Shandra, we're not here to change the villagers or the climate. Think about the basic elements we need to survive: water, fire, air, warmth, and nutrients. That's all we really need."

"Then at least allow for artificial-intelligence. For instance, the air filtration was damaged in the explosion. Engineer Leader Andret is climbing up there to see what he can do with his crew. But this is dangerous and unneeded. Enter the code and Dragon can create drones to do this."

Leader Andret? What was wrong with Shandra? Why would she call Andret this?

She stopped typing and her hand lingered on the eRobe. The violet fabric sparkled under her fingertips, communicating with her. "There, now Nogard's interfacing with Dragon's programming. She's searching for the ReSurface code." She stared at the monitor and Match glanced over at it. He ripped the eRobe off the panel and tossed the garment across the room. Still, the codes continued.

"Dragon's a ghost program that Nogard can't see. How is Nogard doing this to Dragon's coding?"

Shandra placed both hands on the panel. "She's a ghost now, too. A leech. Evolution has changed Nogard into a new type of entity. Besides, the coding was just reversed, it wasn't hard to figure out once she realized this." Really, they knew so little about A-life and the stages of her evolution, he didn't know if this was good or bad.

Match slowly tried to remove the SHARP he'd set on the panel but Shandra's hand rested on it. "Leave it. She infiltrated our SHARPs." The lights flickered and Shandra glanced at him. To his horror, her multi-coloured pink eyes were solid grey.

Nogard was *inside* Shandra, using her to find the codes in Dragon. How would he get Nogard out of Shandra without hurting her or their baby? Bad enough she'd forgot about their time together, what kind of damage would Nogard do to her other memories?

"She's learning how to jump from devices that come in contact with the panel."

People were not devices. "I did not approve this." He pulled his watch behind his back and stepped away from the panel, nervous. It was as he'd feared, Nogard could do anything, be anyone. He couldn't trust anyone anymore. The freedom from a moment ago vanished because... What if she liked living as Shandra? How much control did Shandra have right now? He couldn't even touch her, which was all he ever did.

What if Nogard infiltrated the watch? She could then create as many A-lives as she wanted, infecting the entire village.

"Do you remember me?"

"It's better if I don't."

"If you do..." A shiver passed over him as Match let his selfish desires win. "If Nogard restores your memories of me, I'll tell you where the code is to create A-life."

Shandra blinked then tilted her head awkwardly. "I remember you wiping the mud from my cheek." She touched her cheek. "So gentle."

"And the ring you wear. What do you remember about that?"

She twirled it, thinking. Slowly a smile lit her lips. "Rawlings on his knees whispering to me that his home is with me."

"I'm Rawlings. That was me. I changed my name to remind Nogard that I match her in wit."

"Oh my." Shandra placed a hand on her belly. "Match?"

Her eyes flashed to pink and back to grey. She was in there, struggling for freedom.

True to his word, he whispered, "The code is the watch." Then he stepped closer to the exit door which opened as he approached.

"*Insert it.*" Shandra pounced on him, tackling him to the floor, removing the watch. He let her, then held her wrists while her eyes returned to pink. Nogard had transferred from her to the watch, accessing the codes he didn't want her to have. "Throw the watch out the door," he whispered.

Shandra did and they gasped on the floor until, finally, Shandra collapsed against him in a fit of tears unlike her. "Oh my, that felt weird. Like I was me with more confidence…"

"Nogard was inside you. Give yourself a moment." He held her.

"Our baby?" Shandra panicked which made Match fake-relax, acting at ease with the situation, but so incredibly relieved to have Shandra back and safe.

"Think about good things. She was in you for a flash, nothing happened. Remember the youths rolling down the hill? They were laughing. Our people were laughing. Just visualize that joy and stay with me until you feel like you again." Still, he worried. With him being made of science, their child was already at high risk, he didn't need Nogard getting involved.

Lins stepped into view. "What are you two doing?" She had a bag with her. "At least lock the door if you plan to fool around." She moved to pick up the watch.

"Don't touch that," Match ordered, leaping to his feet. "We need to contain the watch in a device-free environment."

Lins froze, her hand above it, no contact was made.

"I collected the gadgets these people had to see if we could repair them. Pax had a strong box." Lins dropped the bag on the floor and dug in it, pulling out a pink plastic box. "Would this work?"

"Sure, set it there and walk away."

"You're acting strange." Lins had a somber look to her. "And why is my eRobe on the floor? You two weren't messing around in it, were you?"

She picked the robe up and wrapped the garment around herself. Match stood by Shandra, waiting. "Why isn't Nogard responding to my emotions?" She stared at them, then the watch. "What did you two do?"

"Nogard jumped into Shandra," Match told her, worried that Lins might be addicted to having Nogard wrapped around her.

"She's harmless. Shares her knowledge with us and we share emotions."

Match shook his head. "Shandra wasn't herself. Lins, you might be able to keep more control, but anyone who was a part of the system could be controlled by her. We can't allow this, especially now. In the watch was the code she needs to recreate A-life. We have to keep her away from Dragon and away from us."

Shandra gasped and grabbed her stomach.

"What is it?" Match pulled her closer, forgetting about the watch.

"The baby moved. Feel. This is life, Lins. Nogard should not exist. She was inside me, directing my thoughts and emotions with ease. It was eerie."

Lins winced. "Am I different when I wear the robe?"

Match had no idea. She'd been wearing the eRobe for as long as he'd known her, so he ignored her question and ran his hand over Shandra's belly, waiting, nervous. "You are the one who got us here, Lins. The one who introduced me to Shandra, who made the devices to block her from the system so we could be together. You're always the one... What if Nogard was controlling you through the eRobe to get us here so she could merge with Dragon and make another A-life and they could reproduce and infect us—" Shandra's belly moved under his fingers.

A strange bliss came over Match that exploded from his lips in laughter that brought him closer to Shandra as he held her, so full of warmth and thankfulness. "Our baby moved! I felt the life we created." Happiness. So, this was how *happy* felt. "Lins, feel this."

YODAN

A few breaths later
Above ground, ruins near Cuma Village

Yodan was dancing a kiss on Avery's neck when a bright light interrupted them. *Seriously, a couple couldn't even hide away in peace?*

He was about to tell whoever interrupted them to scram when the cat jumped up hissing with his back against the wall. "What the heck?" Yodan spun around to see who'd found them in the ruins. Would Avery run off again? Someone try to kill him again? He let her go, but she slid behind him, peeking over his shoulder as if he were a shield.

Match stood at the bottom of the steps to the underground cellar they'd found, holding a plastic pink case and a penlight. Shandra was behind him. "Well. I thought Owen sent you to find a place where we could set up a new quadrant?"

At first, panic settled on Yodan that he might get demerits or face punishment for his actions, but then he realized Match was teasing. He pushed past this fear and reached for his shirt. The garment was one of Avery's brother's but he said Yodan could have it. He slipped the clothing on, waiting for Avery to take off again, but she actually stood closer to him which made him proud. "So we're busted not working, get over it. I happen to like kissing her. What are you two up to?"

The cat hissed again, pawing at the air. All its fur was on end and poor Friskie looked shaken.

Match showed them the pink case. "I need your advice on how to kill Nogard."

"If she is truly alive like she claims, it can't be done. Like us, she'd become a new form of energy and start a new life. She's safe in the eRobe, I vote we leave her in it."

"Nogard jumped from the eRobe into Shandra and since we left Quma Cities, I suspect she did this to Lins, and possibly others. Pax can read codes."

"What?" Avery looked mortified.

"Where is Nogard now?" Yodan demanded.

"In this box, in my watch."

No wonder the cat went crazy. Maybe it could sense the

presence of A-life or even see it. "You're sure?" Yodan demanded. "You saw her go in the watch?"

"Where else would she go? The watch was the only device she came in contact with?"

"What about living things?"

"Nothing except me."

Yodan examined his friend's eyes. "Your eyes are still white. You feel normal?"

"Yeah."

Yodan checked Shandra's eyes, not used to her being so quiet. She was fine. "At least we know where she is."

"I don't trust anyone with this."

"And you shouldn't. You were chosen to decide if A-life crosses a line. I trust that. But, you should respect life and each stage of life. Artificial-intelligence was created by our ancestors to keep us alive and enhance our lives. That intelligence created A-life. Is it fair that we use her when we don't want her to use us? If Pax can read codes without training, really, there isn't much danger to us using Artificial-life for advancements, but we must accept the balance. She will use us for advancements."

"With our rules, maybe."

"We don't get to be the boss of another life-form. Not anymore."

"I could supervise such experiments but I refuse to let another lifeform change our inner programming without our consent. It feels unnatural."

"You changed her programming without her consent all the time. She knows no different."

"Please limit the science," Avery whispered. "The others are already upset with the gadgets you bring and the things you do in the pipes."

"This isn't science, Avery," Yodan promised her. "We're talking about life. One with the ability to live on her own or with us by infiltrating our bodies. It was bad enough when she allowed us to merge with her when we died. In Quma Cities, we were the leeches, forming a Collective in her mainframe to keep our memories alive for future generations. Now, above ground, she wants to reverse the roles and join with us to keep her alive. As an elite, Match gets to decide if this is safe for us. It'll mean testing and finding her a better alternative if he decides that it shouldn't be done."

The cat was still hissing.

Shandra said, "When I was compromised I changed my entire view on the clans, saying they needed to adapt to our technology. And for a moment, I believed this."

Yodan frowned. That wasn't like Shandra at all. She was never a fan of technology. "I see why you're upset. Artificial-life should enhance our views not change them."

"And the way Pax can write codes and works with Lins as if he grew up working with programs… It's unnatural." Match stared at his hands, probably thinking about the things he could do with them that he hated. "Everything alive must die," Match mumbled. "Tell me how to terminate A-life and I will. I don't want Artificial-life to be a part of our new life. These villagers have the right idea."

"You're talking about destroying an entire lifeform. She is the only one in her species. What does Lins think?"

"She's compromised. The eRobe had her doing things for Nogard. And Nogard was inside her. It bothers her that she's no longer in the eRobe. Which supports my case. We shouldn't be reliant on Artificial-life to boost our emotions. I'm deeming merging with Artificial-life illegal."

"Which is your right as elite, but you found me to ask my advice on this. And this isn't even a theory. I witnessed it, I *lived* it. There is no death, Match, just a new form of life. We might not remember the details of past lives, but A-life might which means if you try to kill her she might feel threatened and retaliate. Bury the box and let us dig it up when we're ready. More like a timeout while we regroup and settle in."

"Ready for what? In my watch is a code for her to reproduce. Multiply. Now that I see what free people look like, I will not allow her to make more of herself and live inside us like some leech. No. Yodan, you were kissing a woman you chose, without permission, without even a worry about demerits. You can't tell me that doesn't feel better."

Yodan smirked at Avery. "Yeah, being with Avery does feel special."

"Nogard wouldn't hesitate to destroy us if we were a threat to her."

"And she might do exactly that if you try to kill her. It's better to help her find her own existence. Perhaps we could alter a drone or create a robot that resembles us so she feels like part of…"

"Yodan, that's not possible. Look at that cat freaking out. That's how I feel inside. This is wrong. Dragon was created to terminate Nogard's system with fire if she crossed a line. I'll do the same. For the safety of my family, of our people, if there is a price to pay, I will be the one to pay it." He stormed out and Shandra followed.

Great. Now what?

AVERY

Warming Celebration
Above ground, near Dragon's Caves

Avery rushed to Dragon's Caves, excited for the celebration. This was the biggest Warming they'd ever had.

She hadn't seen Yodan all day since he was working in the pipes. Apparently, his clan figured out how to make the panels outside the village turn sunlight into energy and this warmed the pipes. Match reassured the elders that this was not science but a smart way to capture energy and they let them work, but Avery suspected he was lying. Regardless, there were no more earthquakes and the area was once again safe and prosperous thanks to them.

Some were saying that since Dragon exploded out the side of the cliffs, they could use science again, but only approved science and the guy who could make flames in his hands was the one who approved that, which made sense to everyone.

Yodan's people were accepted as their own clan, but no one wanted to join with them. Already, rumours started about her kissing Yodan, but really, she didn't care anymore what they thought or said about her. He was a good kisser. *Darn good.*

As Avery approached the ceremonial area, her steps slowed. Dragon's people sat in front of Dragon's Caves, lined up like soldiers with Owen in the far back, standing over them, arms crossed like a statue. The children had their legs under them, their faces held no expression as they watched her people join the group.

The air had a sweet smell of pork roast since several clan leaders had butchered their fattest pigs to share.

Yodan sat, cross-legged between Lins and Shandra and she was tempted to sit with him, but she'd promised Father Saxton to play the flute and didn't want to disappoint him since he'd talked to Jacob for her and kept the peace.

Match was by Shandra. Medic Brisk and Medic Jon were shoulder to shoulder. The others sat quietly behind them as if waiting for something. Even the smallest of children sat alone, serious and alert.

She'd never seen such disciplined, clean children before.

They wore heavy garments draped over their lifesuits, each held a bottle of minerals and one of bland water. Most eerie was that they took a sip at the same time from the one, then the other, in perfect unity.

Pax stood by himself, facing the setting sun. His hair was a wild mess, and really, if comparing the two groups, he was the opposite of Match Clan in every way, yet he was always hanging out with them, well, with Lins. He laughed a lot more lately, which was a warm sound Avery loved.

The Celebration was a coming together of the clans in a peaceful harmony. Each would be allowed to speak, share their culture, and trade with the others. Each group was told what to expect so they understood. People would switch clans, deals would be made, all before another cycle of life began.

Avery waved to Yodan. He smirked but remained sitting. Her people were a mess compared to his neatly stacked group.

They were pouring in, sitting with their clans, visiting with family, and she had to pull one of her younger brothers back when he tried to run off. She didn't need him stumbling into the giant flames in the center of the circle they'd formed.

Avery had brought her flute, despite it meaning she was different than the others. Or maybe inspired by the idea... She smirked, feeling good about tonight.

Berry women paraded in their newest dresses, showing off the designs.

Jacob stood by his younger brother Berry, arms crossed, staring in the fire. Their mother was Jacob's responsibility as the oldest and she stayed by him, using crutches since she had club feet that got worse with age.

When Fewerter joined them, he sat on a stump. The woman-elder, Jenica, stepped forward to speak. "This was a time of trials for our peoples. We welcomed a nomad and now an entire clan." She nodded to both Pax and Match, even though that was a lie and they sure hadn't made Pax feel welcome. Pax crossed his arms but didn't correct her.

"We gather at peace. And to show this peace, each clan who wishes to live in harmony and in trade will present their offerings to the group and smoke from the pipe of peace."

Berry Clan was the oldest of the groups, having lived by the pipes the longest. And so, Berry stood first. "I'm Berry. This is Berry Clan and as I look at the faces around this fire, many of them are my family." This was important to mention because family meant at one time he'd already shared a hut with them and they couldn't make a new family together. He needed to trade more people because they were related to almost everyone. Cursed to lose their linage.

His clan gathered around him. Only Jacob didn't join them. Berry let his clan show off their garments and Kanya made a big show of her belly which was painted and decorated to display their excitement, their promise of a future. "We grow crops, we make clothes. As you see, we have no children in the clan. The life this Berry Clan woman carries is precious and we'll do anything to keep her safe, offer anything." He closed his eyes as if praying and Avery sensed his desperation. Last Warming, there were others who were pregnant in his clan, but the babies didn't survive; some of the women didn't either.

Finally, Berry said, "We believe in freedom." He smoked from a long thin pipe and blew the smoke toward the fire. Then he passed the pipe to Saxton because he was at the other end of the village and currently held the most status, since Mother Roselle had insisted they leave the village when the explosions started and she'd saved lives.

"My brother," Berry said, "I offer you the pipe as a gesture of peace. Our clans are often at odds these days, but let us restart in peace."

With the pipe, Saxton stood. "I'm Saxton. My clan is my family."

Avery helped her brothers gather around him. Then he invited Avery to play her flute. She played for Yodan since he liked the flute. Taking her time, she started a slow melody that Mother Roselle joined with her soft voice. When the pace escalated, her brothers started a beat that got Pax dancing. He sure liked to dance.

When they finished, Avery glanced at Yodan. He clapped for her, pleased, which warmed her insides.

Saxton added, "We raise sheep. We make wood objects. We need to expand. As you see, I have many sons who will need huts to start families and grow Saxton Clan." Like Berry had, he paused in prayer and she reflected on what they needed. Perhaps if they expanded, she could stay? "We believe in equality." He smoked from the pipe and carried the cylinder to Pax. "My brother, you joined us at our table. I offer you this gesture of peace since you are our guest. You're new to the clans and welcome to remain with us, but I invite you to state your own beliefs before the others and encourage you to share what you need and what you offer so that as a village, we can welcome you properly and help you achieve your goals. You showed great bravery in going in the pipes and taught us that all is not what it seems. You brought new members to our village and your warning saved our people even if some of us were too stubborn to act on it and I had to drag them out. We will be more tolerant and open-minded and respectful of new ideas."

Pax took the long cylinder. "Well, I guess I'm Pax. I'm new to the village and wasn't sure I'd stay. I don't have people or a clan or even a family." He looked mighty uncomfortable as everyone watched him. "As for talent, well. I guess I read maps and know how to survive when the weather gets cold. What I need is a family. As you see, I'm alone and it sucks." He closed his eyes in prayer then added, "I believe in God and that He brought me here for a reason. Everyone I love has died, but I survived. Why? There has to be a reason and I plan to discover what." He smoked the pipe and brought the relic to Lins.

She rose with Match as if they were one unit. "My dearest Lins, when I first saw you, I thought you were the queen of the pipes sent to me by Dragon. I present this to you because I see hope in your eyes and a future I want. Will you start a family with me as my wife and partner?"

What! Avery jumped up, shocked because he hardly knew Lins and he'd been so upset...

Saxton pulled her back. "Shh. Have respect. He's a grown man and does as he pleases." Still, Saxton looked mighty pleased by this offer.

After handing the pipe to Match, Lins placed a hand around Pax's chin and much to Avery's shock she kissed him right on the lips and pulled away, speaking to him. "Yes!" She lost her composure and tossed herself in his arms. Pax twirled her around in his excited dance.

"You must speak and continue the ceremony," Jenica reminded Lins.

"Oh yes." She looked flustered, leaning against Pax.

Match brought the pipe to Owen. "This is for Sir Owen to smoke. He's our protector."

Owen remained standing, arms crossed. "You saved these people. This is your clan to speak for." Coarsely, he ordered, "Clan, stand for your elite."

The children jumped to their feet in a powerful union that made Saxton tighten his fists, ready for battle. Even Avery's wild brothers stopped moving to watch them. Seeing them work as one unit when Avery knew how different each one was, made Avery proud of her new friends, yet a little afraid of them. Working together this way while developing their individual strengths made them stronger than the other clans who couldn't even bathe in the same waters.

On his knees, Match gathered dust from the ground and made a bit of a show before he tossed his dust on the roaring fire in the middle of the circle. Everyone gasped when the fire grew much bigger and pure white flames danced among the fire. "I wish to give these survivors all that you have; from the tears to the laughter. You see children, but I see warriors, survivors, and family. I see possibility and freedom."

Lins tilted her head and gathered her own dust. She tossed hers on the fire and this time flames danced purple, sparkling like the robe she wore.

How? "Magic crystals," Avery whispered, causing a gasp from the group.

The fire expanded and burned hotter. Match picked up the pink case. "We agree with you that science can go too far, and so, as a gesture of peace, we burn what our ancestors created. In this case is Artificial-life and we are destroying her because she is a threat to our freedom."

Match tossed the pink case on the fire. The flames were high and hot, but Match watched, unmoving.

The collective of people inhaled at the same time and let their breaths out loudly as Match said, "I give my people freedom, this will come with struggles and a price I willingly pay. My people will need your teachings."

Lins added, "In exchange, we offer heat. The pipes will

warm and will require maintenance. We can show anyone who wants to learn how. We'll maintain the system since this is what keeps the waters clean, the air breathable, and even the area warm."

"You'll be Dragon?" Fewerter asked.

"In a sense, we always were," Match offered, casually turning his palms up and letting flames burn in their palms. Avery watched the crowd for a reaction, but already it wasn't a secret what they were capable of and when Elder Fewerter bowed, so did the other leaders and their families.

Brisk stepped forward when they returned to their feet. "We bring knowledge and understanding of your issues. Our technology is so advanced that with a glance, I see your genetic readings. Berry speaks of needing new blood. Generations of no new bloodlines created a mutated gene that is causing a high mortality rate among your clan. We can better match genes and even remove the mutated gene causing the problem and help your people survive. I need a working lab that'll take time to create."

Andret spoke next, "Saxton spoke of expansion. We can create quadrants above and below ground, using tunnel systems as passageways and building homes with rocks."

Hilt nodded in agreement. "We have children who study to be engineers, producers, ecologists, and so on. Their skills will come in handy."

Yodan spoke, head down, "All this is fine to offer and take, but what we need, what we *really* need, is the faith Pax spoke of, the trust you have in a blind deity." He closed his eyes. "We've lost a huge part of us. We've relied on technology to keep us alive, but now we face cold and strangers who fear science. We see visible signs of illnesses and mistreatment and so many unknowns we can't control. We fear and we have no Almighty as Pax speaks of. We know not who hears our pleas. We believe in science yet we are self-aware and wish to learn more about our inner energy that we can't see but feel. Of all the gifts you could teach us, faith and hope will be what builds our resilience."

When no quake answered their science blasphemy, the clan leaders nodded as if they knew this would be the case and had to accept it.

Match Clan sat and the celebration continued with leaders

making their statements and clans showing off their talents. When Fewerter asked for new leaders, Jacob didn't stand to announce his claim. But he called Jacob forward regardless. "We understand that Jacob Berry has almost ended the life of someone in the village. Sir Owen has requested that the victim stand and cast his verdict."

Typical Yodan remained sitting because he was asked to stand. "I've evaluated this by speaking to many of you, including Pax who is new to the village like us. I thought about what you ask me to decide at great length since Sir Owen insists I cast this judgment to keep peace. He promises me that my verdict will be respected." He stood. "Jacob offers knowledge, like a memory. I ask that he be recognized as an elder, respected as such. He's the oldest of Berry Clan and has knowledge others can benefit from. The best I can offer is this new task, a reprogram for him, a new life for him to focus this energy on in a positive way. I trust his purpose in this system is one yet to be discovered."

Silence met his verdict as if the others couldn't understand.

Jacob glanced at Yodan. "I'm not worthy of this honour, but I will do my best to teach and guide the clans as an elder."

"I believe Yodan has shown compassion," Sir Owen mumbled.

Elder Jenica nodded. "And so we expect you to return that compassion now that your status is raised. Let us learn from his just insight and forgiveness."

When other trades were done, Fewerter asked Match, "What are your plans for Match Clan?"

"Please call us Liberty Clan, a name chosen to represent the family and friends we lost for this new found freedom we feel. We'll build in the rocks around Mainframe One for now, calling our home Quadrants. We'll stay out of your way, yet be close so you can meet Dragon and understand why these pipes warm. We'd like to openly share knowledge since, despite our studies, we're unprepared for this environment, for your stares, for even the quality of shifting air."

"You cannot dig on sacred ground," Jenica said.

"We can. We will." Match's statement was that simple and created a buzz among the leaders but in the end, his calm attitude left them no choice but to accept.

One of the women from Hunter's clan stepped forward. "You have children who need care. So many. We can help. You know our beliefs. You know our needs. And children are welcome in all clans." She stepped back.

Avery jumped up. "That's not a good offer, Match. They want your children without trade."

Match glanced at Shandra, she nodded. Match said, "Our youths are welcome to travel and stay where they feel comfortable. I see a future here, and we'll adapt, but your clans will also need to realize that we'll remain free, family, respected, equal..." He looked to each clan leader and repeated their beliefs this way, taking their beliefs as his own.

Hunter said, "Digging in the sacred earth will take time..."

Match stood and removed a small cylinder from one of the hooks on his suit. He marched toward the rock face and aimed his device at the rock. With a flash, he blew a hole into the rock large enough to walk into. He faced the group. "We found a power source. The sun creates energy in those panels on top of the pipes. We can use that to charge our equipment. We'll have shelter soon."

Hunter frowned. "You sure that's not science?"

"It's common sense."

Hunter smirked. "Well then, you have my blessing. Hell, it's warm around the pipes, we might join you."

Pax asked, "And when will the next gathering be? Can Lins and I have a union celebration then?"

Jenica said, "Our next celebration will be with the next moon cycle. It sounds like a perfect time for you to willingly enter into a deal. Give everyone time to adjust and come back with new needs and requests. In the meantime, we'll work together to keep peace between clans. If an argument arises, it'll be settled as a family."

Fewerter added, "All leaders will leave with equal status as we begin a new moon cycle."

Jacob asked, "But who does the new clan appoint as leader?"

All eyes were on Match, since he was the obvious leader. He said, "There's no leader among us, we all have our own knowledge and responsibility."

"This'll create conflict," Jenica said. "How will we know

who to speak with?"

"We'll know," Lins promised them.

"I don't like this," Hunter said.

"Me neither." A few of the others agreed.

Match stepped forward, calming the outbursts. "We each have skills. We're trained to work together."

"You said you wanted to learn about the Creator. So if I come by, who will I talk to?" Mother Roselle asked in her warm voice.

"You'd speak with Yodan. Any of us would point you in his direction."

"And if I wanted to speak about healing?" one of the healers asked.

"Medic Jon will handle these discussions," Medic Brisk answered. "I handle things about gene and cellular reproduction." Avery had no idea what that meant so she doubted anyone would go to her.

"And do you know how to fix my mother?" Jacob asked Medic Jon.

He smirked. "Of course, that's a Medic Brisk question."

"Well. As long as you know who to refer us to, but we should pick one of you as a reference for our meetings."

Owen spoke, creating a silence in the village as if his words would be wisdom. "Elite Match handles meetings with the men, his companion Shandra with the women. You need to know where to go to, ask me."

"But the women don't have meetings," Mother Roselle pointed out.

Shandra jumped to attention. "They will now."

Roselle chuckled, looking delighted by this news.

"We want you to appoint a leader," Fewerter insisted.

Owen answered, "Andret and Hilt will make fine leaders."

That ended the discussion, mostly because it surprised everyone, yet Liberty Clan remained emotionless with this news. Even Andret and Hilt kept staring ahead without a response.

~The Cost of That First Breath~

"The price of freedom is mortality."   —*Nogard*

AVERY

Finding a new breath
Above ground, Yodan and Avery's new home

Avery was listening to Yodan play her flute. His music sounded nothing like hers and watching him play always mesmerized her. He owned the instrument and dug into it as if the music were a part of him. He told her that it was much different than the flute he'd played in Quma Cities, yet he never needed her to show him how the instrument worked.

Even Friskie found the melody relaxing and purred peacefully at her side.

Avery was stretched out, the sun warming her pregnant belly when something caught her eyes on the horizon. Yodan stopped playing. "What's that?" His eyes struggled in this light but he wore shades to protect them and help him see in the daylight.

Avery jumped to her feet. "A nomad." Their stone house was visible from far and the first one that would greet nomads, and they were many. The explosion had invited a lot of nomads to make the journey to their village.

Yodan jumped up. "He's carrying a child. And is that a wolf on his heels?" Yodan flipped open the device that he called a talker and spoke to Saxton, since Match was busy with Shandra. "Nomad with child and wolf coming our way."

The device worked smoothly and Saxton's voice echoed back, "I'll be right there."

The nomad wasn't approaching even though Yodan waved a friendly greeting toward him. Saxton joined them and the three of them stared at the nomad. What a sight they must be, on the hill by their rock hut with an array of pipes warming the area. Avery smirked, proud of her family, sure that no matter how different this nomad and his family were, they'd find a home in Cuma Village, a new chance at life, one more breath. Their home was now a place where everyone was welcome, no matter how different.

Saxton nudged Yodan. "I'll handle this, Match needs you. He says the baby's here and he wants to talk to you."

"The baby's here?"

"A girl."

Avery held her own growing belly. "Is everything all right?"

"Roselle says so, but Match can't stop throwing up. He needs to talk to you and looks worried. I thought his strange behaviour was first-time father jitters, but I can't get him to calm down. He's mumbling things about how the price was too high and he keeps doing that thing with his hands where fire erupts. I gave him a stack of sticks to snap until you can talk him down."

Yodan didn't waste time. He headed straight to Match and Shandra's stone house. Avery followed, the cat in tow. They found Match leaning against the house and Yodan slapped him on the back. "What you looking so sick for? You're a father."

Match whispered, "I understand now why Nogard spared me. She needed me to protect Shandra. To find her a safe home."

"And you did," Yodan reassured him.

Match took in a long breath as if his lungs needed air before he could answer. "Nogard found a new life, one I can't destroy. She no longer needs a program to breathe."

Avery had no idea what that meant. They often spoke of things from their past system, so she let them be and rushed in to see what she could do to help, letting Yodan deal with his friend.

Mother Roselle held the infant and handed her to Avery. "Hold her while I get Shandra comfortable."

Lins stared on, not moving, with a traumatized look to her which made Avery chuckle. She remembered seeing Mother Roselle give birth for the first time and had probably looked much more distressed than Lins.

Friskie was in the doorway, hissing. Which was unlike him. He usually liked babies, but lately he refused to go around Shandra.

Avery cradled the child in her arms. Yodan had warned her that Match and Shandra's baby might be different since Match was made of science and they had no idea what him reproducing with Shandra who was made naturally would do. They were expecting birth defects or strange abilities.

"Her name is Spark," Lins whispered, still staring at

Shandra, numb.

The child's skin was white but darker veins moved around like long grey worms. Avery remained welcoming despite their differences. She ran a finger against the dimple on the infant's chin and got a shock. The child didn't seem to mind the jolt and smiled at her, much more alert than her brothers had been at birth.

The cat let out a terrified yowl and scrammed as if someone had kicked him.

"She's so quiet," Shandra said. "Is Spark all right? I'd like to hold her." She put out her arms for her child.

And Avery brought the baby closer. "Oh Shandra, she's perfect. Breaths fill her lungs and like her father, she has a gift blessed on her by Dragon: a spark of life. And she has the deepest grey eyes." Avery knew that red centers meant they could see in the dark and black meant they didn't sleep. "What does the grey centers in her eyes mean?"

"It means Nogard walks as one of us," Lins whispered.

Elsewhen Press

delivering outstanding new talents in speculative fiction

Visit the Elsewhen Press website at elsewhen.press for the latest information on all of our titles, authors and events; to read our blog; find out where to buy our books and ebooks; or to place an order.

Sign up for the Elsewhen Press InFlight Newsletter at elsewhen.press/newsletter

THE BLUEPRINT TRILOGY
KATRINA MOUNTFORT

The *Blueprint* trilogy takes us to a future in which men and women are almost identical, and personal relationships are forbidden. Following a bio-terrorist attack, the population now lives within comfortable Citidomes. MindValues advocate acceptance and non-attachment. The BodyPerfect cult encourages a tall thin androgynous appearance, and looks are everything.

In *Future Perfect* we are introduced to Caia, an intelligent and highly educated young woman. In spite of severe governmental and societal strictures, Caia finds herself attracted to her co-worker, Mac, a rebel whose questioning of their so-called utopian society both adds to his allure and encourages her own questioning of the status quo. As Mac introduces her to illegal and subversive information she is drawn into a forbidden, dangerous world, alienated from her other co-workers and the companions with whom she shares her residence. In a society where every thought and action is controlled, informers are everywhere; whom can she trust? Katrina's story examines the enforcement of conformity through fear, the fostering of distorted and damaging attitudes towards forbidden love, manipulation of appearance and even the definition of beauty.

In *Forbidden Alliance* we return to Caia and Mac some sixteen years later in a story that poses questions of leadership, family loyalties and whether it is possible to justify the sacrifice of human lives for the greater good.

In *Freedom's Prisoners* tensions have escalated. The rebels may have won the first battle in their fight against the Citidome authorities, but can they win a war? The Citidomes are fighting back and no-one is safe any more as RotorFighters rain down fire on defenceless villages destroying them and their inhabitants. Katrina explores betrayal, guilt, hope and endurance in an explosive conclusion to the *Blueprint* trilogy.

The *Blueprint* trilogy is a thought-provoking series with a dark undercurrent that will appeal to both an adult and young adult audience.

Katrina Mountfort was born in Leeds. After a degree in Biochemistry and a PhD in Food Science, she started work as a scientist. Since then, she's had a varied career having been a homeopath and forensic science researcher, and currently works as a freelance medical writer. When she hit forty, she decided it was time to fulfil her childhood dream of writing a novel! She now lives in York with her husband and dogs.

Book 1: *Future Perfect*
ISBN: 9781908168559 (epub, kindle) / 9781908168450 (288pp paperback)

Book 2: *Forbidden Alliance*
ISBN: 9781908168900 (epub, kindle) / 9781908168801 (288pp paperback)

Book 3: *Freedom's Prisoners*
ISBN: 9781911409120 (epub, kindle) / 9781911409021 (304pp paperback)

Visit bit.ly/BlueprintTrilogy

The Lost Men
An Allegory
David Colón

In a world where the human population has been decimated, self-reliance is the order of the day. Of necessity, the few remaining people must adapt residual technology as far as possible, with knowledge gleaned from books that were rescued and have been treasured for generations. After a childhood of such training, each person is abandoned by their parents when they reach adulthood, to pursue an essentially solitary existence. For most, the only human contact is their counsel, a mentor who guides them to find 'the one', their life mate as decreed by Fate. Lack of society brings with it a lack of taboo, ensuring that the Fate envisioned by a counsel is enacted unquestioningly. The only threats to this stable, if sparse, existence are the 'lost men', mindless murderers who are also self-sufficient but with no regard for the well-being of others, living outside the confines of counsel and Fate.

Is Fate a real force, or is it totally imagined, an arbitrary convention, a product of mankind's self-destructive tendency? In this allegorical tale, David Colón uses an alternate near-future to explore the boundaries of the human condition and the extent to which we are prepared to surrender our capacity for decisions and self-determination in the face of a very personally directed and apparently benevolent, authoritarianism. Is it our responsibility to rebuke inherited 'wisdom' for the sake of envisioning and manifesting our own will?

David Colón is an Associate Professor of English at TCU in Fort Worth, Texas, USA. Born and raised in Brooklyn, New York, he received his Ph.D. in English from Stanford University and was a Chancellor's Postdoctoral Fellow in English at the University of California, Berkeley. His writing has appeared in numerous journals, including *Cultural Critique*, *Studies in American Culture*, *DIAGRAM*, *How2*, and *MELUS*. *The Lost Men* is his first book.

ISBN: 9781908168146 (epub, kindle) / 9781908168047 (192pp paperback)

Visit lost-men.com

TANYA REIMER

Born and raised in Saskatchewan, Tanya enjoys using the tranquil prairies as a setting to her not-so-peaceful speculative fiction.

She is married with two children which means among her accomplishments are the necessary magical abilities to find a lost tooth in a park of sand and whisper away monsters from under the bed.

As director of a non-profit Francophone community center, Tanya offers programming and services in French for all ages to ensure the lasting imprint and growth of the Francophone community in which she was raised. What she enjoys the most about her job is teaching social media safety for teens and offering one-on-one technology classes for seniors.

Tanya was fifteen when she wrote her first column. She has a diploma in Journalism/Short Story Writing. Today, she actively submits to various newspapers, writes and publishes the local Francophone newsletter for her community, and maintains a blog at *Life's Like That*.

Programmed to Breathe is her fifth title published by Elsewhen Press.

www.ingramcontent.com/pod-product-compliance
Lightning Source LLC
Chambersburg PA
CBHW030615170726
48283CB00002B/615